THE ADVENTURES OF PERI AND MAWG

By: Jen Xant

COPYRIGHT

ISBN 979-8-9928609-4-8
Book cover created by Jen Xant
Editor: Jen Xant
Guest Editor/Formatting: G.M. Parrillo
www.authorjenxant.com
G.M. Parrillo Publishing, a subsidiary of The Inkbound Publishing
Roselle Park, NJ

Reviews are the key to an Independent Authors success. Please feel free to post your review on both Amazon and Goodreads. Thank you for your consideration.

Dedications

To every middle-aged woman whose hormones are wildly out of control, whose chin is now sprouting a beard, and who pees just a little bit every time you laugh…this story is for you. Never forget how fucking glorious you are.

To my swan, who lived with a feral raccoon for the past six months, who brought me snacks as I grunted unintelligibly from the office, who never once complained as we survived on chicken strips and frozen pizza night after night, who never got upset over all the missed date nights, who told me every single day how proud you are of me…I will forever love you to the moon and back times infinity.

To Gina and Phin, I will never be able to express my gratitude for all that you've done, including giving me the confidence to see this through. You are angels, and I love your faces.

To my Alphas and Betas, thank you for picking this story apart with lovingly critical eyes. You made this so much better than what it started out to be, and I am forever grateful. Also, shoutout for teaching me how to spell flaccid.

To Pedigo, for keeping me sane with ridiculous arguments as we each trudged through the editing process, for your unending support of my writing, and for being an awesome friend. Your palate is trash, but you are amazing.

To Ashe Grayson, thank you for being the ultimate cheerleader. You lift me up with your support and your laughter. Also, huge shoutout for Toe Pesci and Danny DeVi-Toe!

To the Indie Authortok Community, thank you for being my inspiration, my cheerleader, and my friend. You are a rare breed of creative souls and I am honored to know you.

To Masktok, I thank you ever so humbly for the dopamine hits that kept me going throughout this process. You know what you did, and I thank you for it. ☺

To my real life Gina, Tori, and Nikki, you ladies are goals. Your bright spirits lift me up and make me want to be fearless. You are absolute goddesses.

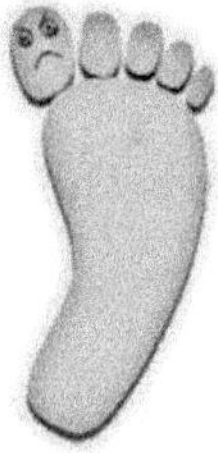

CHAPTER ONE

"Adult birthdays are garbage," thought Mawg. Each year, she marked the passage of time by counting the wrinkles around her eyes (five now) and patches of cellulite on her ass (volume too high, calculation unavailable). She was prepared for the typical societal rituals; texts and calls from loved ones, tepid "Happy Birthday" posts on Facebook from almost-forgotten high school acquaintances, and a card from her seventy-two year-old aunt, whose penmanship got shakier every year. She was NOT prepared to be inhabited by a demon on her forty-fifth trip around the sun.

The three hundred and sixty-fifth day of her forty-fourth year was no different than any other. A creature of habit, Mawg religiously stuck to a nightly routine. "Good habits lead to good results," was her motto…or at least, that's what she hoped. After washing and moisturizing her face with some fancy cream found online for a discount, she brushed her teeth and put on a matching two-piece pajama set. The final step? Ingest ibuprofen so there would be no morning back ache. That started three months ago, when she added "having pain for no reason" to the litany of changes occurring within her body. She was in bed binging her favorite show about vampires for the hundredth time by ten o'clock.

At four-thirty a.m., she woke up to pee. Trudging her sleep-deprived body across the carpet, she wondered if a day would come when she could sleep through the night again. Mawg couldn't recall the last time that happened. Sitting on the cold toilet seat, one bright note did occur; the ibuprofen ingested last night worked, and there was no back ache. So, there was that.

Turning off the bathroom light, she stumbled back toward the bed in the dark, stubbing her left toe on the foot of the bed frame.

"Ow, watch where you're goin'!"

Mawg's heart slammed into her chest, her eyes flying open at the sound of the slightly high-pitched male voice with the New Yorker accent.

"And seriously, could you be ANY more depressing?"

Freezing momentarily in panic, her fight or flight kicked in at the thought of someone in the room. Groping under the mattress, she found one of the knives hidden on each side of the bed for protection. She'd learned that little safety tip from a true crime documentary where a woman saved her own life by surprising an ill-prepared intruder.

With a white-knuckled death grip on the knife, she backed up against the wall. Mawg had no idea how to actually wield the weapon, but primal fear can be a quick teacher. Having watched enough of her favorite vampire show to know the basics, she knew one thing: stab them with the pointy end. Hopefully her predilection toward clumsiness wouldn't cause accidental self-stabbing in the process.

She waited in silence, forcing her breath to stay shallow while her pulse raced off the charts. Mawg loved cheesy horror movies, and they taught her the louder you are, the faster you die.

The voice sighed, sounding exasperated.

"Oh for fuck's sake, no one's tryin' to murder ya, Mawg."

Her brain screamed an alert that the enemy was nearing, like a lookout stationed at the top turret of a castle. With eyes wide as saucers and knife in hand, she lost her shit. Pivoting her body left and right like a cornered animal, she swung the knife wildly, yelling, "That's what every serial killer says right before he chops up your body!"

"Put that down! Your form is terrible and you're gonna hurt yourself!"

The adrenaline rushing through her veins was pumping hard, as if her heart was attempting to break through the wall of her chest.

"My form? You broke into my house and you want to…what? Give me lessons on how to wield a weapon?! I don't know who you are or how the fuck you know my name, but get out of my house!"

"Mawg, put down the knife. I'm not here to hurt ya."

While the calm voice was attempting to reason with her, Mawg was frantically scanning the darkened room, eyes searching for a shadow or movement. In forty-four years of life, she had never experienced a life or death situation first-hand.

Mawg's parents were quiet, unassuming people, and her small town experience growing up left her sheltered from the harsh realities of the world. She'd never been taught to protect herself.

"No, uninvited creeper in my bedroom, I will not put the knife down," Mawg retorted, the terror reflecting in her tone. The voice sighed in exasperation.

"Ok, ok, ok...clearly we got off on the wrong foot. I'm not gonna touch ya, and I'm not gonna hurt ya, Mawg."

Mawg continued to swing the knife, barely listening. Nothing he could say would matter at this point when her nerves were so frayed. Her shields were up, prepared to defend.

"You're a middle-aged woman, correct?"

Her eyes widened in surprise that the voice knew what stage of life she was in. Who the fuck was this guy? Did she know him? He was waiting for an answer, but received none.

"Ok, I'm gonna assume that answer is yes. Would it help you to know that every middle-aged woman experiences exactly what you're going through right now?"

Her brow furrowed in confusion. "Abject terror from a random man being in her house in the middle of the night?" The snark in Mawg's tone was heavy, but it only made the voice chuckle.

"What if I told you I'm not random…nor a man?"

Silence encapsulated the room as the voice waited for a response. The knife stopped swinging, but her grip remained tight as her eyes continued to dart around her surroundings. She remained silent, the confusion and terror warring inside her.

"Mawg…. I understand this might be overwhelming. Can we just talk? I'm not here to hurt you. In fact, turn on the light so you can see there's no intruder. I just wanna talk. Can ya please turn on the light, put the knife down, sit, and let me explain?"

Taking a moment to consider the request, Mawg slowly and deliberately inched her way over to the bedroom light switch and turned it on while still holding the knife out, ready to stab if necessary.

Light flooded the room.

As her eyes adjusted, and she realized the voice spoke truth. There was no one there. Her eyes narrowed, still not trusting this person. "I'll sit, but there's no way in hell I'm letting go of this knife." She sat on the edge of the bed, white-knuckling the knife handle in case this asshole was hiding somewhere.

"Ok, deal. Now take two breaths, and slowly inhale and exhale."

Grumbling and rolling her eyes, she couldn't believe the nerve of this guy. "Oh, now you provide yoga training, too? What a thoughtful intruder." But, she complied, her body relaxing slightly as she imagined the inhaled air filling her from head to toe.

The voice waited patiently for her to finish, then began.

"Let's try this again and I'll attempt a proper human introduction. My name is Peri. I am not human. I am what you humans consider a demon, although I don't appreciate the negative connotation you associate with that word."

Mawg sat on that information for a few seconds, her head tilting to the side. "A demon…like an actual demon?"

"Yeah, a real demon."

Her face scrunched in confusion. "I've never heard of an invisible demon. Don't you normally have horns and pointy goatees?" The voice sighed in frustration.

"I really wish humanity would evolve more creatively. No, no horns or pointy goatees."

"So you're a real, actual demon?"

"Yes! For fuck's sake, I'm a real demon! When every human woman reaches middle age, she's inhabited by what's known as a Change Demon. Except you humans don't address us properly anymore, and that's unintentionally my fault. In the 1990's, my cohabitant accidentally alerted a scientist friend of my existence. At that time, she addressed me as "Peri, a Man of Pause." She was goofy, and would say weird shit like that. The stupid scientist misunderstood and called me "perimenopause", and that's what humanity has called my demon clan ever since."

Frozen in silence, all Mawg could do was sit there wide-eyed as Peri continued.

"The specific age for cohabitation varies from woman to woman, but the universe decided your Change birthday is today. So…Happy Change birthday, Mawg."

Mawg stared at the wall for ten seconds while Peri waited, then walked into the bathroom to survey herself in the mirror. "I mean…you don't look crazy." She began to feel her head, looking for any bumps she may have acquired in the night. "No concussions, so that can't be it."

Muttering to herself as she walked back into the bedroom, she stopped short, coming to a halt in the middle of the floor, looking confused. "Why did I make him sound like Joe Pesci?"

She closed her eyes, massaging her temples with her fingertips. "You could have at least created a James Earl Jones voice, but nooooooo…you watched too many mobster movies." Her nervous system fraught, she laughed uncontrollably at the absurdity. Peri waited for the laughter to subside, speaking only when it was absolutely silent.

"First of all, rude. Second, Joe Pesci is a national treasure so watch your fucking tone. Third, bold of you to assume your brain has the creativity to concoct me. Your wardrobe is fifteen shades of brown just like your hair and

your aura. And...are those loafers I see in your closet? Who wears loafers, Mawg?!"

"Hey!" With no physical person to receive her frustration, Mawg yelled toward the ceiling, annoyed the imaginary brain demon insulted her wardrobe. But Peri was on a demon-sized rant now, his voice raising.

"No seriously, do you have ANY idea how arrogant you humans are? Do you really think your brain synapses and meatsuits are that advanced? You got a lot to learn, Mawg."

Dumbfounded, Mawg walked back to the bed and sat, mouth agape. Was she losing her mind? And if so, why did her brain create such a jerk?

"Ya got somethin' to say, Mawg? Let's go! Say it with your whole chest."

The frustration of the past twenty minutes grew to rage, and Mawg unloaded. "FUCK. YOU. I don't know if you're a demon or a brain tumor, but you're definitely an asshole! If you are a demon, then you're a cowardly one...showing up to scare a woman in the dead of night?! That's so cliche." Not caring if it looked ridiculous, she threw up her fists and continued, "If you want me to believe this bullshit, then you'll show yourself. Now!" Peri began to laugh maniacally.

"Oh Mawg…silly, silly Mawg. Just remember you asked for this. Take a look at the big toe on your left foot."

Mawg looked down. In the middle of the taupe-polished nail on her big toe was a small, smirking face.

"Hi Mawg."

Mawg fainted.

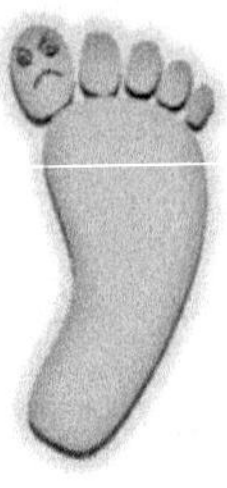

CHAPTER TWO

"Now ya see why I wanted you to put the knife down."

Feeling fuzzy, not quite sure where she was or what happened, her eyes came into focus. She was crumpled on the bed, and the memory of the past hour came flooding back. She straightened into a sitting position, a little dizzy from rising up so fast. Eyes closed and breathing deep, she prayed this was just a vivid, odd nightmare.

"You're not the first woman to wish I wasn't real, but no such luck, Buttercup."

Scrunching her eyes together, she looked back down and sighed. In the middle of the toenail on her big left toe was a cartoonish face with a snarky expression and comically-raised eyebrows.

"Avoiding me only makes it worse, just FYI."

Mawg threw her hands in the air, exasperated. "Can you please just give me a minute to digest this? My fucking talking toe just turned my life upside down. Forgive me if my…what did you call it? Oh yeah, forgive me if my brain synapses need a moment to process." She pinched the bridge of her nose and let her eyes close. Peri rolled his eyes impatiently.

"Ok well, can you make the wheels turn a little faster? Ya burned a lot of calories freakin' out, and now we're hungry. I promise I'll tell you everything in detail, but I'm starvin' and we need snackies."

"What are you, twelve? Who says 'snackies'?" Peri's little eyebrow raised.

"Said the judgmental woman who's currently talkin' to her toe."

With an eyebrow raised back at him, Mawg's eyes lit up with an idea. Hopping off the bed, she ran to the bathroom and grabbed her toenail clippers. A sadistic smile spread across her face, and Peri's little eyes got wide.

"Whatever you're thinkin' of doing with those, think twice. Every attempt to harm me will earn you one chin hair."

Slowly lifting her foot on the edge of the tub, Mawg dangled the clippers directly above Peri's face. "Answer my questions. I'll put down the clippers if I'm satisfied you're telling me the truth. Then, and only then, will we go get…snackies."

It was clear Peri wanted to rage at her, and she waited to see what his next move would be. He was mad…but he wanted snackies.

"Fine, ask your questions."

With clippers dangling precariously above her toe, Mawg asked, "Why me?"

"Because your human body no longer wants to produce tiny humans, and the universe decided it's your time."

Face scrunched in confusion, Mawg asked, "But time for what? I don't understand exactly what's happening."

"Oh Mawg, did your mother never explain this to you?"

Hearing his little voice drip with fake sympathy pissed her off. "Did my mother tell me that I was going to magically sprout a demon when I turned forty-five? No Peri, she neglected to mention that. All she told me was there would be night sweats and mood swings. There was no mention of a fucking demon." Her sarcasm caused one of Peri's little cartoon-like eyebrows to raise comically.

"Ya know, my cousin Eddie inhabited your mother. He said she was a stubborn broad. I see she passed that gene down."

Mawg froze. "What did you just say?!" Peri closed his little eyes, took a deep breath, and exhaled with exasperation.

"What part of 'every middle-age woman goes through this' don't you understand? Yes, your mother was inhabited. Mawg, there's almost a BILLION women in the world right now that are inhabited."

Her jaw dropped. "A billion women have toes talking to them right now?"

"Yup."

She flailed her hands wildly in the air. "And no one thought to share this information?!"

"They tried. The first time in the 1600's they got burned at the stake. In the 1950's they tried again. That time
15

they just got committed to mental institutions. I mean, think about it…what would you say if someone told you their toe was speakin' to 'em?"

Mawg plunked her ass down on the edge of the tub, stunned. She stared off in the distance with a glazed expression, trying to comprehend what she was hearing. "So, how long will you be here?"

"It varies a little dependin' on the woman, but I'd say…about ten years."

She jumped up, holding the clippers in her right hand and pointing them like a weapon at Peri's face. "TEN FUCKING YEARS?! Are you kidding me right now?" She grabbed her left toe in a vice grip, attempting to strangle him.

"That does nothing, you know."

Enjoying the rage that radiated from Mawg's aura, Peri's little toe face basked in its glow as she released the toe from her grip.

Mawg was getting pissed. "Why are you smiling?"

"That anger you're feeling right now? That's just one of the many gifts I bestowed upon you."

Bringing her knee up, she drew her face down closer to Peri. Which, considering her age and lack of physical activity on a daily basis, was quite impressive. "Look at me you little freak. YOU did not gift me anger. I had plenty of that before you came along." Peri's little eyes lit up.

"You've had NORMAL anger up to this point. Reasonable, justifiable anger. But you're about to experience an elevated version, and it will be a work of beauty comparable to some of the world's most sought-after art pieces. I'm gonna gift you rage, and it will spring up in the most unusual circumstances."

Mawg's shoulders dropped in defeat. "That doesn't sound pleasant at all. And you do this by clinging onto a middle-aged human woman for a decade?"

"You make me sound so dirty."

The idea of listening to his snarky little voice for the next decade made her head hurt. "No, I'm making you sound like a broke ex who is an ex for a reason. Do I get anything out of this relationship, or are you just here to toe suck the happiness out of me?"

"EWWW, not with that athlete's foot you've got going on. A break from the never-ending loafers might help that, just FYI."

Waving the clippers, she glared. "Leave my shoes out of this and get on with it, Peri."

"Ahhhhhh, I can see our time together is gonna be an absolute treat. You asked what you get out of our relationship. You get the joy of communicatin' your most twisted inner thoughts to me and no one will ever know. You get to experience pure rage, which IS A GIFT. And you get to experience metamorphosis, like a caterpillar becoming a butterfly. That's what ya' get."

With a sigh of existential dread, Mawg said, "Then why do I have a feeling I'm not going to enjoy our time together?"

"Oh I won't sugarcoat it, this is gonna be a difficult time for you. Your meatsuit and your mind will go through changes you could never imagine. Metamorphosis isn't easy, Mawg. But think of it like that old expression you humans have: Iron sharpens iron. You and I will grow together and we'll refine each other in the process."

Mawg was fuming, but also exhausted. "Fine. One more question and then we'll get…snackies. Why the toe?" That made Peri smile a devilish little grin.

"Because it's the only part of your body that ain't gonna be in pain for the next ten years."

She stared down at Peri, a horrified expression plastered on her face.

"While you're processing that, can we PLEASE get food? You don't understand what happens when I don't get snackies."

Hanging her head, Mawg sighed in resignation and padded her way over to the bed to pick up her phone. The day was off to an eventful start, and she had to admit she was starving. "There's nothing in the house so I'll have to order delivery." Peri's expression looked like a child about to throw a tantrum.

"But that's gonna take almost an hour!"

Opening the food delivery app, she gawked down at him. "There's nothing to eat in the house! My deepest apologies for not planning for an unexpected and unwanted house guest. It's your own damn fault for not giving me any notice this was happening! I'm doing my best, so back off and let me order!"

Peri was fuming and his little cartoon face was all scrunched up like a Pug. His expression, combined with the events of the morning, was too much for Mawg. Laughing so hard she had to wrap her arms around her belly, she wheezed out "I'm sorry, I can't help it. You look...you look ridiculous."

She had no way of knowing what would happen next. The sound that erupted from a mouth the size of a pushpin exploded in Mawg's ears, causing her to put her hands over them. Unfortunately, the sound was inside her head and there was no blocking it out. Her fight or flight response, finally calmed, went from zero to a thousand in half a second. She blacked out.

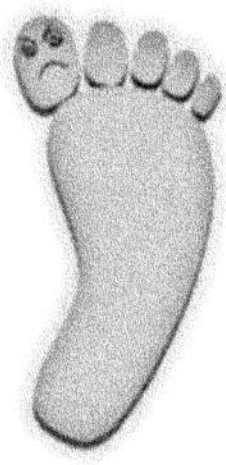

CHAPTER THREE

When she came to fifteen minutes later, Peri was humming and her phone was laying next to her on the bed. "That little fucker!" Mawg thought.

"I can hear your thoughts…you remember that, right?"

Grabbing the phone to open the app and order, she said, "Oh my God, do you know what a diva you are? First, you DID look ridiculous and pathetic. Second, now it's going to take even longer for your food to arrive, so you only hurt yourself."

"The food's on its way."

Mawg stood up, staring down at her big toe in defiance with her phone in hand. "And how exactly is THAT possible?!"

"Because I ordered it."

She opened the app and there, to her disbelief, was a placed order. She bent over to get closer to Peri's little face. Quietly and sternly, she held out the phone and asked, "How does a toe order food from an app, Peri?" His expression was smug.

"I don't think you fully grasp the nature of our relationship. You're focused on the toe situation, and you're forgetting that I'm a full-fledged, larger than life demon. If ya' let the hanger get too bad, I can take control of ya'."

Staring down at her toe for ten seconds, her eyes never blinked, and she wore the same expression her mother had made whenever she was cross with Mawg as a child. "What did you do, Peri?" He smirked.

"That little blackout incident you just experienced wasn't a blackout. That was me, takin' the reins. It still looks and sounds like you to the outside world, but I'm drivin' your meatsuit. While you were enjoyin' your little brain nap, I ordered us a breakfast pizza...and three lava cakes. And if you're gonna bitch at me about the desserts, don't. I know we're both cravin' chocolate, so be thankful."

Mawg's cell lit up in her hand and the old 16 Tons song began to play. It was her supervisor, Julie. Rolling her eyes to the back of her head, and Mawg not surprised to get the call on her PTO day. Julie had no respect for work/life balance boundaries. For the past three years, Mawg worked as a marketing specialist for one of those massive corporations where backstabbing and ladder-climbing were the name of the game. Mawg had no desire to climb the corporate ladder. She refused to play the game, instead keeping her head down and contributing no more or less than her weekly workload required. Julie, on the other hand, loved the game. She took every opportunity to throw Mawg under the bus to make herself look better. But Mawg's practical nature, and her love of holding onto email conversations as receipts, had kept her ass covered whenever Julie tried to abuse her power.

"Ooooooh, I wouldn't answer that if I were you."

Mawg shushed him and answered. "Hey Julie, wha—"

"Where do you get the audacity?" Mawg held the phone away from her ear as Julie screeched at her. "I've bent over backward trying to cover for your mistakes for the past three years! Three years, Mawg! And you thank me by calling me the worst human on the face of the planet?! You are soooooo easily replaceable, Mawg. You're done. Don't bother coming in to get your things. I'll ship them to you and your final check will be mailed. I don't ever want to see your face again. Happy freaking birthday." SLAM!

If it weren't for the confusing situation at hand, Mawg would have appreciated Julie using the office landline to physically slam the phone down. Cell phones ruined that little pleasure for everyone.

Closing her eyes and counting to ten, she took deep breaths and threw the cell phone on her bed. Calm enough to form words again, she looked down at Peri with hands on her hips and frown lines deeply etched into her forehead. "I'm going to ask you one more time. WHAT. DID. YOU. DO?"

Peri had the good sense to at least look sheepish.

A tiny vibration came from the spot on her bed where she had tossed her phone, alerting her to a text from her co-worker, Shannon. Mawg and Shannon had become casual work friends over the years, enjoying the occasional happy hour where they had margaritas and complained about what a bitch Julie was. Mawg checked the text.

What the hell happened? Julie's ranting and raving like a lunatic. Did you really get fired?

She bent down and glared at her toe. "Peri…If you don't answer me, I will gladly accept a chin hair for the pleasure of torturing you. Why did my boss just fire me at eight o'clock in the morning on a day when I'm out on PTO?" Peri's little eyes darted back and forth, avoiding Mawg's gaze.

"Hypothetically, she might have called you with a work question…while you're out on PTO. Which is totally rude, by the way."

"Ok, and then?"

"Hypothetically, you may have told her she could figure it out herself. You may have also alluded that since she takes credit for all your work, she could start doing some of it. And that's when you, hypothetically, called her the worst human on the face of the planet."

Mawg's jaw dropped. She stood back up, stunned and speechless.

"Hypothetically, our hanger might have made us a teensy bit irrational."

Her vision blurred to red. Her eyes darted around the room, searching for some way to throttle Peri without hurting her own toe.

"Mawg...what are you doing, Mawg?"

Would he drown if she submersed her foot in the bathtub?

"I can hear your thoughts, Mawg. And no, I won't drown."

The idea came to her like a shining beacon of light from above.

"I can hear your thoughts!! Don't you dare, Mawg!"

She ran to the kitchen, opening the fridge. There it was. Her beautiful piece of revenge, sitting in the corner of the vegetable drawer. She opened the crisper and pulled out the onion. In this moment, it was the most beautiful onion she'd ever seen.

"If you do what I think you're about to do, I'll make that chin hair curly like a pube!"

Taking the onion to the counter, she grabbed a knife and began to violently slice rings.

"Demon dammit, Mawg! I'm sorry, it wasn't my fault! I forewarned you! I told you things happen when we're hangry!"

Mawg grabbed the sliced rings of raw onion that were making her eyes water and stormed back to the bedroom. She reached in her dresser and grabbed a pair of old socks.

"MAAAAAAWWWWWWG!!!"

Cramming the onions down into the sock, she took one last look at Peri before she put it on. "If you're so hangry, you can chew on these!"

With one last look at Peri's horrified face, Mawg slid her foot into the raw onion-filled sock.

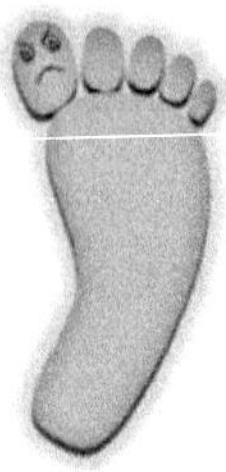

CHAPTER FOUR

The doorbell rang. While Mawg was slightly horrified to meet the delivery driver reeking of raw onion, she refused to release Peri from his sock chamber of torture. Opening the door, she internally chuckled watching the exact moment the onion fumes hit the delivery driver's nose. His expression went from shock to disgust before he could put his customer service face back in place.

"Hey. Breakfast pizza and…" he looked down at the receipt, "three desserts?"

"Yep, here you go." Mawg handed him a twenty dollar tip for giving it his best effort to mask the disgust as the stench from her onion foot violated his nose.

"DEMON DAMMIT, MAWG!! LET ME OUT YOU HATEFUL HAG!!"

"Hey thanks, enjoy." The delivery driver turned and booked it back to his car.

Hauling the food back into the house was fun, especially when she stopped every few steps to torment Peri.

"You wrecked my life!" She picked her foot up and smashed it on the kitchen floor, the raw onion sliding between her toes.

"You took over my body without consent!" She twisted her foot like someone stamping out a cigarette.

"YOU GOT ME FIRED!" Mawg now screamed. All rationale lost, she jumped up and down, over and over as the pizza and bag of desserts bounced in her hands.

Hearing Peri make little gagging noises gave her a bit of satisfaction. Not even bothering to get a plate, she instead threw the bag of desserts on the counter and brought the pizza box into the bedroom. She sat down, opened the pizza box on her lap, and turned up her nose. "Why is there pineapple on this? You really are an evil demon."

"Oh for fuck's sake, are you one of those humans? You'll put pineapple on a ham, but if the ham is on pizza, now

it's disgusting? For the love of all that's unholy, don't ever travel. Your palate will offend everybody. Now let me out of this torture chamber or I'll conjure that chin hair!"

He wasn't wrong about the pizza, it was pretty damn good. But there was no way she was going to tell him. That made Peri sigh.

"When is it going to click in your brain that you don't have to TELL me. I can hear your internal voice, remember?"

"Yeah, about that…Peri, we're about to have what's known as a 'come to Jesus' discussion." Mawg paused to savor her bite.

"Um…I might not be the target audience for that."

Mawg rolled her eyes. "It's just an expression. What you did today is not acceptable. I'm willing to admit that you have power I can't quite understand. But just because you can do something, doesn't mean you should." She paused for another bite. "You threw my entire existence into upheaval! Without discussing it with me first! Do you have any idea what you've done?"

"I honestly had no idea you'd be this upset about three desserts."

Throwing her hands up in frustration, Mawg yelled, "It's not the fucking desserts, Peri! You got me fired and I have a mortgage and bills! I get that rage pleases you, but we don't do shit that gets us fired in this economy. Do you have any idea how many people are looking for work right now?"

Peri stayed quiet. He wasn't openly admitting to making a mistake, but he knew he was in the wrong about getting Mawg fired.

"And guess what else, Peri…The 'snackies' that you adore so much? Yeah, those cost money, too. No job, no money. No money, no snackies."

Out of nowhere, Mawg's eyes filled up with tears and she began to sob, which felt surprisingly odd. She wasn't sad about losing the job itself, just the loss of income. Julie really was the worst human on the face of the planet, and there was a touch of relief at the idea of never dealing with her again. That job was nothing more than a paycheck with benefits.

Peri began to plead woefully, and that's when Mawg realized it wasn't her crying, but Peri crying through her.

"I'm sorry. I promise, I tried to warn you about my hanger! It makes me do crazy things…illogical things. But see, you ate, and now I feel bad about what I did because the hanger's gone! Please just keep me fed and I promise I'll find you another job."

Peri and Mawg sobbed collectively momentarily, releasing the weight of the day's events. Mawg was having a difficult time processing the emotional rollercoaster of the morning. Then she began to laugh uncontrollably.

"What's so funny?"

"I've had forty-four birthdays prior to today." She paused for a bite, the pineapple juice running down her chin. "In all of those years combined, I've never had as much excitement as we've experienced in the past two hours. Guess you shacked up with a pretty lame human, Peri." She wiped away the pineapple juice as Peri's muffled reply came through her sock.

"I don't think you're lame. I think you've just lost yourself. Tell me about your experience as a human up to this point. Start from the beginning. I want to know everything there is to know about Mawg, pre-45th birthday."

She held up a finger, telling him to hold while she finished the last bite of pizza. "I thought you already knew everything about me?"

"I wanna hear it from you."

"We're gonna need dessert for that." Mawg started to hop off the bed, remembering Peri was stuck in onion sock jail. In an appeal for truce, she removed the onion sock and looked down into his little eyes. "Are we good?"

Gasping in a deep breath of fresh air, he squeezed his eyes shut like he was praying for a miracle, then opened them.

"Now we are. I owed you that one."

She walked into the bathroom and looked in the mirror to find a rough and wiry hair growing out of her chin. "Dick!"

"Hag! Ok we're even now. So what is there to know about you?"

Mawg grabbed the tweezers on the counter and plucked the hair, then headed to the kitchen to grab a lava cake. "There's not much of a story, except for my name. That one's kinda funny."

"Yeah, I was wondering about that."

Grabbing a plate from the cupboard, she pulled one of the lava cakes from the plastic bag. "My parents never intended for my name to be Mawg. My mom always loved the name Marguerite. Unbeknownst to the hospital staff, she couldn't spell to save her life. On my birth certificate, my legal government name is Mawgerite.....hence the nickname Mawg." Peri's eyes were huge and his tiny mouth was wide open in horror.

"Oh. My. Demon."

She plated the lava cake and grabbed a fork. "Yeaaaah…my parents loved me a lot. They just accidentally set me up to sound like a swamp creature." Peri's little eyebrows were raised so high they almost reached the top of her toe.

"When you went to school, were the other little humans mean to ya' because of your name? Young humans are awful creatures. I'll take a mid-life crisis over puberty any day."

She chuckled, heading to the bedroom with the lava cake in hand. "Yeah, when I was in elementary and junior high, they were pretty rotten. But, to be fair, everybody was fair game for torment. It was part of the rite of passage when I was growing up. I have no idea if that's changed at all in the last thirty-ish years."

"Trust me, it hasn't."

Peri let out a disturbing little moan as Mawg ate the first forkful of lava cake. Attempting to ignore it, she said, "But then a weird thing happened. When I hit high school, they realized I was kinda book smart. I got good grades, and tests and writing were pretty easy for me. That's when they realized I could help them, and started being nicer once I assisted with their homework…for a small fee."

"You did it for them?"

She leaned back against the headboard, a cheeky grin on her face and the paper plate balancing on her thick thighs. "I cannot confirm nor deny that I built a thriving small business at the ripe age of sixteen, and it may or may not have provided essays and test answers to struggling athletes."

"Daaaaaaaaaaamn, Mawg! You were a hustler!"

Peri looked impressed, his little eyebrows raising in surprise, making Mawg chuckle. "Not a hustler. More like a start-up entrepreneur. I was able to cover my first two years of college with the money from that."

"Ok, you just got a whole lot more interesting to me."

Mawg rolled her eyes. "Gee, thanks so much."

"Ok so you graduate, then did you go to college?"

Wiping the lava cake crumbs from her lips, she nodded. "I got a very generic degree in business administration. I figured that was broad enough to be applicable to a lot of jobs, giving me more options."

"Mawg the Practical."

She shrugged. "I am a Capricorn, so that tracks. Once I had the degree, I started applying for a bunch of random office jobs with bigger corporations so I could get good benefits. I had a few different gigs…customer service, administration, human resources. The job you just got me fired from was a marketing specialist. I mainly chased people around and reminded them of deadlines."

"Nothing personal, but your career seems like an absolute snooze. Is that really what ya' wanted?"

Mawg laughed. "Of course not, Peri. Nobody wants to be in those jobs. We do them because life is expensive and the benefits are like handcuffs. If money was no object, I'd do something fun where every day was different. I hate the corporate world. It stifles the humanity out of me."

"Maybe you're not as much of a drag as I initially thought."

She rolled her eyes, taking the dessert plate to the sink.

"Listen, I got an idea. It's your birthday and I know I screwed it up. Why don't we go out tonight and have some fun? Have an adult beverage and let your hair down, Mawg."

She leaned against the sink, pondering. "It's been a long time since I've been out on the town…maybe that's not a bad idea."

"Clearly it's been a while, because nobody says 'on the town' anymore. BUT, you need an outfit. Your entire wardrobe is sad, Mawg. Simply atrocious."

The hurt reflected in Mawg's eyes, and she got pissed. "Why are you so hateful about my clothes? I'm thick, Peri. Fashion options for bigger girls have historically been limited because no one wants to see our fat." Peri's eyes got wide…well, as wide as tiny toe eyes could get.

"Wait…are you telling me you dress like this to hide your meatsuit?"

Sighing in exasperation, her eyes narrowed on her demon toe. "Peri, do you have any idea how cruel people can be to bigger girls? In the sixth grade, a boy saw me in a swimsuit at the pool and called me fat in front of everyone. In junior high, someone posted a photo of a whale on my locker. I can't even count how many times I heard, "She has such a pretty face," when I was in college. So yes, I hide my body because the world has confirmed to me over and over again that no one wants to see it!"

"Oh Mawg…Listen, I know someone who can help change your mind. Want to go on a little shopping adventure?"

The pity in his voice and the sad expression in his eyes were too much for her. She sighed, turning on the faucet to wash the dessert plate. "If I do, will you stop making me feel like a bag of potatoes?" Peri's little face lit up.

"Deal. Now go wash your onion feet and throw on your 'going outdoors' potato sack. We got a lot of work to do and little time to do it."

39

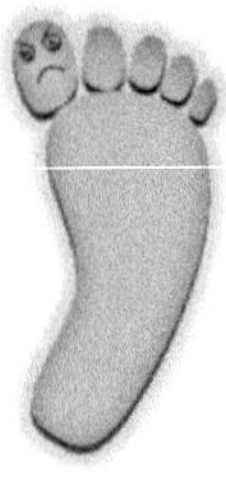

CHAPTER FIVE

Onions, may have been a terrible idea. She scrubbed and she scrubbed, but no amount of body wash could compete with the powerful stench of Mawg's onion feet. The lingering odor refused to dissipate and Peri couldn't contain his sarcasm.

"Bet you'll think twice before doing that again."

"It was worth it," she said, turning off the shower and grabbing her towel. "So who is this person we're going to see?"

"Her name is Tori, and she was my most recent human cohabitant. Just name-drop me and tell her you need coverings for your meatsuit. She'll know what to do."

"You know we don't have an unlimited budget. Fired…remember?" Mawg said as she dried off her hair.

"Don't worry, Tori will give us the hook-up."

Drying off, she took extra time to smother Peri's face with the towel. Then she got changed and threw her wet hair in a bun. She was getting ready to put on her loafers when Peri stopped her.

"No. Absofuckinglutely not! In fact, let's burn those with some sage to cleanse the loafer aura from your life. Just put on flip flops or sneakers like a normal person."

Mawg sighed dramatically. "Diva." She put on the sneakers, grabbed her purse and keys and headed out the door. Peri gave her the address, and they began the drive in Mawg's silver Toyota Corolla.

"Do you ever buy anything that's not a neutral color?"

She peeked down at her toe while signaling to change lanes. "Neutrals are practical. Plus, I read that neutral colors on cars are associated with higher visibility and lower accident rates. So yeah…practical. And safe." She heard her toe make an exasperated noise as she merged into the lane.

"Not everything has to be practical, Mawg. Why do you want your aura to be so beige? It can't possibly be much fun."

Mawg sighed in frustration, tired of this topic. "Because neutrals blend in, Peri. When you blend in, people don't see you. And if they don't see you, they can't judge you." Peri's little face scrunched up in confusion.

"So, wait…just to clarify, you've made decisions your entire life that are based on the possibility of another human judging you?"

As they pulled up to a stoplight, the driver next to Mawg watched with wide eyes as she yelled angrily down at her foot. "I don't know why you're going all psychiatrist on me ON MY BIRTHDAY, but yes I would say that's a reasonable assumption!" Peri's little face contorted with confusion.

"But why?"

The light turned green and the other driver waited as Mawg took off, giving the crazy lady a wide berth. She sighed. "I don't know, Peri, I guess because I've been judged a lot. And it feels like shit. I told you what it was like growing up. The only reason the kids were nice to me in high school was because I learned that if I helped them, they wouldn't be mean."

With her eyes never straying from the road, the painful memories welled up in her chest. "Then in college and after graduation, I dated an awful man…a man child, if we're being specific. That relationship was toxic from the beginning. He was sweet early on, but after a few months he started saying these little digs about my weight and my looks. My self-esteem was so low that I tried to lose weight and become someone else to please him. That may sound ridiculous, but I was starved for someone outside of my parents to show me affection. So yeah…These days I prefer to blend in and be boring rather than to chance another asshole coming into my life."

"Oh Mawg…"

Coming to a stop sign, she looked down at her toe defensively. "Please don't pity me. I learned a valuable lesson from that pathetic excuse of a relationship. The next one was less toxic, but comically boring. I stayed with him for four years because he seemed safe. That safety was comfortable, but there was no spark to the relationship. We mutually ended it on good terms. I heard he has a wife and two kids now. Good for him."

"So are those the only two men who have seen your meatsuit?"

The GPS alerted her to turn right. "No, there were a few more, but I wasn't dating them. A couple of friends-with-benefits situationships, and one regrettable one-night stand." One of Peri's little eyebrows raised in surprise.

"Look at Mawg with the hook-up! Was it good, at least?"

The thought of giving details of her sex life to a virtual stranger, demon or not, felt intrusive. "I…I don't know if we've reached the point in our relationship where we have girl talk, Peri. This is a weird discussion to have with you." That made Peri laugh as they continued down the block.

"Mawg…hypothetically, whaddaya think happens to me if you're having a night of fuckery?"

As she pulled into the parking lot for their destination and parked, she sat considering the question. "I guess I haven't thought about that."

"I don't go anywhere. I'm right there the entire time, watching your meatsuit get poked. Since I'm a part of you, technically I'm getting poked, too."

Mawg froze, her fingers gripping the door handle and face stuck in a horrified expression.

"We can talk about that later. Let's head in. Remember to ask for Tori and tell her I sent you."

Still shook, Mawg got out of the car and locked the door. Looking up, she saw the brightly colored sign for Torific, an inclusive-sizes women's clothing store. "Wait, Tori owns the shop?"

"Yep, thanks to me."

His unbridled arrogance forced yet another eye roll from Mawg. "So humble and gracious you are." Taking a deep breath, she headed into the shop. The bell dinged when she opened the door, and a stunning woman popped her head out of the back room.

"Be with you in just a minute!"

Mawg gave an acknowledging wave and thought, "Is that her?"

"It is. Isn't she a knockout?"

"She's absolutely gorgeous."

The store had a warmth about it. Clothing was lined on hanging racks along the rose-colored walls, with shoes and accessories being toward the back. The three mannequins spread throughout the store were all different sizes. There were plush, white velvet-covered chairs scattered near the dressing rooms for those who were waiting, and a huge low-lighted three-way mirror and pedestal to get a complete view of the outfit.

"The mirror was my idea."

"Of course it was," Mawg muttered, as Tori came out of the back room, and she found herself blown away by the woman. Her skin was smooth as silk, the braids in her hair perfection. She was wearing a crocheted tankini with intertwined oranges, reds, and yellows. It looked like a sunset, and her beautiful dark skin made the colors absolutely glow. She was spectacular.

"Hi, can I help you?" And she was cheerful? How did this woman survive Peri for ten years?

"She didn't just survive, sweetheart. Clearly, she thrived."

Ignoring Peri's massive ego, Mawg said, "Hi, I was recommended by a friend to come and see you. I'm looking for an outfit to go out tonight, and he thought my current wardrobe is too depressing."

Tori frowned. "I mean, I can absolutely help, but…FYI, your friend sounds like an ass."

"He definitely is." Mawg chuckled.

"Hey!"

"But he's also a mutual friend to both of us, or so he says. I was recommended to come here by Peri."Mawg paused and waited. Tori's eyes flew open wide in surprise, then the laughter came as she clapped her hands together. It was lilting and sounded so free.

"I should've known when you said he was an ass. I absolutely do know Peri." Tori smiled, and Mawg couldn't tell if it was in sympathy or not. "If you don't mind me asking, is he on your left or right toe?"

It was Mawg's turn to be surprised. "He's on the left."

Tori looked down at Mawg's left foot. "Peri, are you tormenting this poor lady? Be nice to her or I'll share my secrets about keeping you in line."

"This is unacceptable, ignore that."

Mawg's eyes lit up in laughter. "Oh we absolutely need to talk!"

"I'm regretting this already."

Still looking at Mawg's foot, Tori said, "I know you're running your mouth. Pipe down and let me do what I do best."

Silence from Peri.

Mawg's jaw dropped. "How did you get him to do that?"

Tori laughed hard. "Peri and I have a mutual love and respect based on a decade of verbally throwing hands at each other. The two of you will get there as well, it just takes time. Now, tell me where we're going and what kind of outfit we need."

"Well, it's my 45th birthday, and since Peri got me fired today, he—"

"He got you what?!" Tori hunched down until her face was near Mawg's knee. She looked at the toe, pointed at it and said, "Did you not learn the last time? If I EVER catch wind of you doing that again, it's back to the gelatin bath for you, Danny DeViToe!"

Mawg chortled at the name then her eyebrow raised. "Gelatin bath?"

"LA LA LA LA LA….DO NOT LISTEN TO ANYTHING SHE'S SAYING, SHE'S A FILTHY LIAR!!"

The beautiful woman's gaze held a tiny bit of mischief in them, never waivering from Mawg's toes. "He's got sensory issues. He hates things that feel squishy."

"Lies!! Filthy lies!"

Mawg's grin lit up her face. "Tori, I think you and I are about to become very good friends."

As Tori stood up, she gave Peri one last glaring look as she turned back to Mawg. "Agreed! Hey just out of curiosity, does he sound like Danny DeVi-Toe to you?"

"My initial thought was Toe Pesci, but I could see DeVi-Toe as well." That sent Tori into a fit of laughter.

"I'm a thousand years old, you hags. I sound like ME."

"I was always curious if he changed the voice from person to person." She shrugged. "Good to know. Ok back to the question at hand…what is tonight's event?"

Mawg looked down at her toe. "Peri thinks I should go out and have a night on the town. I haven't been on the scene lately, so I'm not really sure where we're going."

"Tell her it's 'The Church'."

She peered up at Tori. "He said to tell you it's 'The Church'."

The kind shop owner's eyebrow raised in a way that had Mawg about to ask more questions when she said, "Ok, I need to know a couple of things before we pull the outfit together."

"Fire away."

"Do you wear heels?"

Peri began to laugh hysterically. Mawg glared down at her toe and said, "Gelatin bath."

Peri shut up.

"No, I prefer flats."

Tori was studying Mawg's form, and Mawg could tell she was mentally pulling an outfit together. "Ok, dress or pants?"

"Hmm, good question. Can the dress be flowing?"

A sweet understanding smile grew on Tori's face. "Of course. Any particular colors?"

"Beige, taupe, off-white, eggshell, light brown, dark brown, coffee…"

Tori saw Mawg's face sag and glared down at Peri. "Whatever you're saying, knock it off." Then she looked back at Mawg and said, "Ignore him. With your beautiful green eyes, I think jewel tones would look phenomenal on you. How do you feel about purple?"

Mawg shrugged. "I haven't worn it much, so I'll trust your judgement."

Tori's eyes lit up. "Excellent! Hang on one second and I'll be right back." She ran off to the back room and Peri cleared his throat.

"Hey listen, I'm sorry. I'm just giving you shit."

Arching her eyebrow down to him, Mawg just glared. "That doesn't sound like much of an apology."

"No, I'm getting there, I promise. Listen, Mawg...I'm kind of a powerful demon in my clan. I'm a big deal."

Something so tiny having such a massive ego had Mawg in awe. "Still waiting for the apology, you narcissist."

"Getting there, chill out. And being powerful, it gives me some perks. Mainly, I get first choice of the pool of middle-aged women in the world. Out of almost a billion, I chose you, Mawg."

The confusion was clear on her face. "But why? Am I supposed to be grateful? All you've done is berate me all God damn day!"

"Mawg...that's because I see how much potential you have. You look at your life and see the same thing you've been

livin' for the past forty-four years. You see the routine and the safe choices."

Her annoyance grew. "Yeah, I didn't think there was anything wrong with my life until you showed up to tell me there was!" Mawg snarked with another eye roll. Peri shook his little head…face…whatever he had going on down there.

"There's things you don't know about yourself yet. I chose you because you're special, just like Tori's special. I need you to trust that I'm here to evolve your life into something amazing."

Her laughter dripped with sarcasm. "Trust you? All we've done since you got here is fight!"

"We're gonna argue and we're gonna fight, there's no opting out of that. But I chose you to fight with for a reason. I need you to trust that…and to trust I have your best intentions in mind."

Feeling overwhelmed with the turmoil of the day, and the demon in her toe asking for trust, had Mawg's eyes welling up in frustration.

Tori was bursting with happiness as she brought the dress up for Mawg. "Let's go try this on and see what you think!"

Shaking off the frustration of the conversation with Peri, Mawg walked into the dressing room as Tori hung the dress on the hook. "So just out of curiosity, did you know Peri was coming when he inhabited you?"

Tori chuckled at that as she straightened the dress on the hanger. "Absolutely not. In fact, our introductions to Peri are fairly similar. He got me fired, too."

Mawg's mouth dropped open in shock as she stepped into the dressing room. "What kind of work were you doing?"

Edging out of the dressing room, Tori said, "Go ahead and start trying this on and I'll fill you in," as she shut the door. "I was working at a finance firm, in the middle of a meeting with a client. Picture this: I looked phenomenal. The outfit was professionally on point, and the style said "don't fuck with me". But, I chose to wear open-toe heels that particular day."

Mawg heard her shuffling clothes outside the door as she continued. "I'm in the middle of a presentation with a room full of people in the conference room, when I happen to look down to the floor. There was Peri, on my toe. All he said was, "Hi Tori." I lost my ever-loving mind. I jumped up and started screaming like I was being murdered. Everyone in the meeting came over to help me and I kept pointing at my toe, because the little asshole was making faces at me. But they didn't see anything and thought I was having a breakdown. Eventually, someone suggested we end the meeting, and I went back to my office. I closed the door and the blinds, and that's when I had my first full introduction to Peri. I got 'laid off' a day later."

Halfway in the dress with one arm in the sleeve, Mawg couldn't believe what she was hearing. "Jesus, Peri, you have GOT to work on your first impression. Does scaring the shit out of women get you off or something?"

"I mean…kinda? We don't kink shame here, Mawg."

Mawg let out an exasperated sigh. "I'm sorry he did that to you, Tori. What an asshole."

"Eh, looking back now, it's all good. I hated that job and I despised the people I worked with. But yeah, at the time I was absolutely livid. Ok, hop out and let me see the dress." Mawg stepped out with a frown on her face, and Tori laughed. "Clearly you're not a fan of this one. Is it the color, the style, or the fit?"

With hands squishing her apron belly, Mawg studied her flaws in the three-way mirror and considered the question. One of the reasons she hated to shop was because she despised seeing her body. Clothing always looked cute on the rack, but terrible on her frame. "I don't know if it's the fit, or if it's me just hating how I look. The color is really pretty, you nailed it with that. But seeing my fat just makes me feel sad." Peri let out a loud sigh, and muttered something about stupid humans and meatsuits under his breath.

Tori looked at Mawg with empathetic eyes. "As women, we are notorious for obsessing over our flaws. You are absolutely beautiful. You've just been listening to the wrong tape."

Mawg turned to look at her, confused. "What tape?"

With her hands on Mawg's shoulders, Tori turned her to look in the mirror. "Here, let's see if I'm right about this…earlier in your life, someone you cared about said something hurtful about you. Your brain filed that message as a tape, and you've been playing that same tape over and over for years. Does that sound right?"

Thinking back to the awful kids in school and her first boyfriend, Mawg stared at Tori in the mirror and nodded, tears threatening to well up in her eyes.

Tori clapped her hands together. "Ok, soooo…It's time to throw that tape away and we're going to play a new one. A new tape for a new Mawg. Can we try that?" Mawg's eyes were now brimming with tears as she sniffled and nodded.

"I told you she was amazing."

Stepping back, Tori took another look to survey Mawg's shape. "Let's try an experiment just to get us started. You tell me what parts of your body you dislike the most, and we'll work tonight's outfit selection around that, okay? You can be beautiful and still be comfortable."

Wiping the tears away, Mawg nodded and sniffled. "I don't like going sleeveless because my arms are flabby. And obviously, I don't like my gut. My upper legs have cellulite, so short dresses are probably out."

Handing her a tissue, Tori perked up and said, "Excellent, now we're getting somewhere! Now tell me the parts of your body that you DO like."

Mawg didn't have an answer for that. Her self-esteem had been low for so many years, she couldn't answer the question. Staring in the mirror, she struggled to come up with an answer.

Patting her on the arm, Tori eased the uncomfortable moment. "I'll tell you what I see. I see knockout curves from your chest to waist to hip. You have an hourglass figure and many women would kill for that. I see a great booty that will look amazing in whatever you wear. Let's try emphasizing the hourglass and we'll stick with something that covers your arms so you don't feel self-conscious about that. Does that sound ok?"

Wiping her tears with the tissue and giving Tori a tentative smile,Mawg was feeling hopeful about trying on clothing for the first time in her adult life and murmured, "Yeah, that sounds great."

"Ok I have just the dress in mind. Give me one sec and I'll be right back." Tori took off to the back room.

"She wasn't always like this, ya' know."

Looking down at Peri, she noticed his face was surprisingly somber. "How so?" He took a moment to respond, more serious than Mawg ever expected. He clearly cared deeply for Tori.

"It's not my story to tell, but…trust me, the woman you see in front of you today is NOT the woman I encountered over a decade ago. I want you to take inspiration from her. Her change was personal to her situation, and yours will be to you. But I want you to see her thriving and know it's possible for you, too."

Sitting with that information, Mawg pondered her beige existence. Had she ever thought about what she truly wanted from life? Her adult experience to this point was centered around avoiding risk and embarrassment, keeping her head down and avoiding anyone or anything that could put her fragile self-esteem further at risk. So many years hiding and trying to blend in. Her entire adult life was built on avoiding judgement from the ghosts of her past.

"No more of that. We're done hiding, Mawg."

"Get out of my head, creeper."

Tori came bounding out of the back room with an exuberant smile. "I've got it! This is the one!"

Taking one look at the dress, Mawg's eyebrow raised significantly. It was a deep purple, silk maxi dress. The sleeves were full length and had a slit from the shoulder down to the cuff. The neckline was a DEEP v-neck, and the hem was almost to the floor. "It's stunning, but…I don't know if I can see myself in this."

Tori laughed. "Of course you can't. That's why I'm here. Go try it on and we'll look at it together."

Taking the dress into the changing room, Mawg stared at it momentarily before attempting to try it on. She pulled the silk fabric over her head and adjusted it. Never in her life had she exposed this much cleavage. Turning to look in the mirror, her eyes widened in shock. She looked…good. Like, really good. She might even venture to use the word 'sexy'.

"Well look at you! If I was a human male, I'd want to poke my meatsuit into your meatsuit."

With a tiny smirk on her face all she could do was shake her head. "Thanks Peri, you're such a sweet talker."

Outside the dressing room, Tori was anxiously waiting. "Girl, get out here and let me see it! The anticipation's killing me!"

Taking in a deep breath, she turned the door handle and walked out of the dressing room. Tori's eyes bugged out of her head. "Oh my God! Why have you been hiding this? You look PHENOMENAL!" She grabbed Mawg by the shoulders and turned her toward the three-way mirror. "Look at yourself! You are an absolute goddess!"

With a discerning eye, Mawg scanned her reflection Yes, there was a plus-size woman looking back at her who still had flaws. But the woman looked ethereal. The dress highlighted her curves in all the right ways, and muted the flaws so they weren't the first thing she noticed. For the first time in her life, she didn't see her body with hate in her eyes.

And that's when Mawg began to sob uncontrollably.

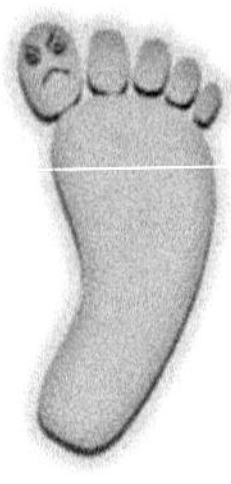

CHAPTER SIX

Stepping back into the dressing room, she took the dress off, slouched on the padded seat, and cried into her hands. She was crashing hard. Overwhelmed with emotions, the tears wouldn't stop flowing. She waited for Peri to make some sort of snarky comment, but he stayed surprisingly silent.

"Were your other cohabitants this much of a mess?" That made Peri chuckle.

"Yep. In a thousand years I've inhabited a hundred middle-aged women, and every single one was a mess when I arrived. Mawg, I've inhabited women all around the world. Do you know what you all have in common?"

Mawg sniffled and shook her head.

"No matter your social status, your physical attributes, your religions, races, sexual preferences, etc…you ALL have issues with self-doubt and self-esteem."

Her eyebrows lifted in surprise.

"Here, do something for me…grab your phone and use the googly thing to pull up supermodels from the 1970's."

Confusion spread across her face, but she grabbed the phone and did what Peri asked.

"There, that one in the top right photo. Do you recognize her?"

She looked at Peri like he was crazy. "Of course, she was iconic."

"Yeah, well she was also a wreck when I inhabited her."

Her eyes flew open wide. "Shut up! You did not inhabit her!" His little face was smug in a way that proclaimed how big of a deal he was.

"I absolutely did, demon's honor. And trust me when I tell you that her insecurity and self-doubt were some of the worst I'd ever seen. Way worse than yours."

Dumbfounded, she shook her head in disbelief. "I don't get that. She looks like she had everything…great career, stunning looks, gorgeous men on her arm…that makes no sense to me."

Peri took a long look at Mawg.

"That's because all this insecurity you have is based on your meatsuit. You think if your meatsuit looked like hers, you'd live happily ever after. Ya' gotta stop associating meatsuits with happiness. That premise is incorrect. Meatsuits are just houses, Mawg. Think of it like real estate…yeah, a pretty exterior might catch a potential buyer's eye. But if the entire inside is a wreck, it's gonna cost thousands of dollars and a lot of headaches to fix it. Sure, there might be somebody who likes a fixer-upper and wants to rehab that interior. But most people want a live-in ready home that's warm and inviting. Same thing with you humans. You all fixate on the meatsuits when it's the interior that's truly valuable."

Staring at Peri, her eyes welled up once again. She was annoyed at herself for crying so much today. She had shed more tears in the past six hours than she had in years.

"That's what I want ya' to learn, Mawg. The block to livin' the life you want is not external. It's inside your house. You built a beige wall of so many defense mechanisms that you no longer recognize your original colorful interior."

Tears continued to stream down Mawg's face as Tori knocked tentatively on the dressing room door. "Hey Mawg. I figured you and Peri were talking and didn't want to interrupt, but would it be okay if I join you for a minute? And don't worry about the tears, I shed plenty of them myself."

Wiping the tears from her face, she hesitantly opened the door. Tori stepped in, sat on the bench directly across from her, and leaned forward to grasp both Mawg's hands.

Taking a deep breath, Tori began. "Ten years ago, my life became a mess overnight. I was lucky enough to marry the love of my life, and we had a wonderful life together. Then the universe upended my world in one night and took him away from me too soon. I was devastated, and I spent the next year more or less catatonic. When Peri arrived at that meeting, he was the chaotic catalyst that threw my life down a different path. I was thirty-seven, a little younger than you when he came to me. I spent the first week of his inhabitation crying on my couch and eating snackies to sustain him, just so he wouldn't bitch at me."

That got a good sniffling laugh out of Mawg as she wiped her eyes.

"But once I finished crying, it was like a heavy weight had been lifted off my chest. It was a fresh start, and I could choose whatever path I wanted. I had a lot of hobbies, and I decided to pursue them more seriously. I took some sewing and crocheting classes and decided to enroll in fashion school. I wasn't that concerned about the degree. I just wanted to be a sponge and learn everything I could. I ended up creating an entire wardrobe for myself and that's when I realized I wanted to dress all kinds of women. There was a lot more that happened, and we can dig into that later, but eventually I opened this store. These are all my creations."

Mawg's jaw hit the floor as she gestured around the store with her arm. "All of this?"

Tori nodded with a smile. "All of it. I'm telling you because I want you to look at this and remember me crying on the couch that first week. What you're feeling right now is valid, but it's also fleeting. You're going to experience something amazing….if you open yourself up to it. That choice is ultimately yours."

Squeezing Mawg's hands, Tori gave her a hopeful smile. "Now, we're not finished with this outfit! Let's go look at shoes and accessories!" And with that, Tori bounced happily out of the dressing room. Mawg wiped the tears from her face and looked down at Peri.

"Will you trust me now?"

She felt a little of the weight lift from her chest and nodded. Walking out to meet Tori, they continued the shopping adventure until the proper accessories and shoes were attained. As Tori was at the front counter wrapping everything up, Mawg asked "how much do I owe you?"

Tori's eyes brightened and she said, "You owe me all the dirt after your adventure at The Church tonight. You can buy me a coffee tomorrow and fill me in. Deal?"

"Oh no, Tori, I couldn't—"

Holding out the bag to Mawg, she said, "Not another word of argument. Trust me, the stories you'll have tomorrow will be worth it." She gave Mawg a conspiring wink.

"Don't argue with her. Trust me on this one, it will get you nowhere."

Mawg's heart was full. "You are an absolute gem of a human, Tori. Thank you so much and I promise I'll be back with coffee tomorrow. Hey, out of curiosity, is there anything I should know about this club?"

Tori was taking a sip of water and almost choked at the question. "When you get there, ask for Gina. Tell her you're new and that you'd like "the tour". She's great, and she'll make sure you're comfortable."

"Ok got it, I can do that. Thanks again, Tori! I'll see you tomorrow!"

"Later, girl!"

Making their way back to the car, Mawg said, "She's like a ray of walking sunshine."

"Yeah, but I'm taking credit for that. She was kind of an asshole the first couple of years."

Mawg chortled. "That's the pot calling the kettle black!"

"Guess I better live up to my reputation, then. Can we please take these janky feet to get a pedicure? Maybe they can wash off the onion smell before you scare off everyone at the club."

Mawg was about to get snarky, but she thought of the amazing gift Tori had given her. "Sure, we've got a few extra dollars since Tori hooked us up." Peri's little eyes widened.

"Wow, I really thought you were going to put up more of a fight."

She gave him an incredulous look. "Are you complaining about my joyous countenance?"

"Nope, just surprised by it. Turn right up here, there's a nail salon around the corner."

They rounded the corner to the row of businesses, finding Happy Nail at the end of the block. They parked and made their way into the salon.

"For the love of demon, please get a color that ain't brown."

Mawg 'accidentally' banged her toe against the curb. Peri's little angry pug face scrunched up.

"Hey! Do it again and you'll have two chin hairs in one day. Keep it up and you'll be rockin' a full beard by the end of the week!"

Grabbing the handle of the door, she entered the salon. "You need to stop being so dramatic, it was an accident." The bell jingled, announcing their arrival.

The nail tech, working on a manicure, looked up at Mawg without missing a beat as she filed a nail. "What do you need?" She looked to be about seventy years old. The deep-set wrinkles around her mouth and eyes reflected a woman who had endured a tough life. Her name tag read Jessica. And friendly, Jessica was not.

"Just a pedicure, please."

Jessica seemed exasperated and said, "Pick a color, sit down, ten minutes." Mawg didn't fault her for the attitude. If she had to touch gross feet all day she would be cranky, too.

If she was being honest, surveying the wall of colors was a bit daunting and overwhelming.

"Since this is probably new for you, let me explain. These are colors, Mawg. See how they're bright and happy? Maybe let's try one of 'em."

Mawg mean-mugged her toe. "Lose the 'tude or I'll just paint them white." The laugh that came out of Peri would've shaken the room if anyone else was able to hear him.

"Oh, you DEFINITELY don't want to do that, especially tonight."

Having no idea what he was talking about, she ignored him and continued perusing the wall. She found a pretty light pink, took the bottle of polish to sit down, and waited her turn.

"So, what exactly is this club? Both you and Tori were pretty vague explaining it."

"Oh, I think you'll really like it. It's not a typical dance club vibe. The music and the atmosphere is geared toward middle-age adults, not young 20-somethings. Sexier music, grown-ass humans. It's your vibe. But we definitely wanna find Gina as soon as we get there. She's a concierge for first-timers."

"You ready?" Jessica yelled across the room at Mawg. She nodded, picking up her purse and following her to the pedicure station. Water was filling the bucket. "Take your shoes off and put your feet in." She pointed at the water.

Mawg removed her shoes and the smell of onion permeated the area. Jessica made a face of disgust and covered her nose and mouth. "Is that your feet?!" Mawg just stared at her feet with wide eyes, hoping she wouldn't throw her out.

"Bwahahahahahahahahahaha I told you that you'd regret the onions!"

Peri wouldn't stop laughing. He laughed so hard, he started crying. Jessica was staring wide-eyed at Mawg's feet and pointing to the bucket aggressively. "Put them in the water now! You'll scare off my customers!" Mawg hurried into the chair and shoved her onion feet into the water. It felt amazing, but she was too self-conscious about her foot odor to enjoy the moment.

A disgusted Jessica uttered, "I'll be right back," and ran to the back room. She came back a moment later, arm loaded with containers. When she got to Mawg's seat, various liquids and powders were tossed liberally into the water. The smell of lavender wafted up to Mawg's nose. Jessica frowned and said,

"That will be an extra five dollars on your bill." Mawg simply nodded. For what she just put the woman's nose through, five dollars was a steal.

While her feet boiled off the onion, Mawg pondered her upcoming club adventure. "So why do I feel like there's more to this club than you and Tori are letting on?" Peri's eyes got wide, the picture of innocence.

"Whatever do you mean? I'm just takin' ya out to have a good time."

Mawg's eyes narrowed, not trusting anything Peri was involved with to be innocent. "You better not be bullshitting me."

Jessica looked up as she grabbed Mawg's foot and froze with it mid-air. She stared at Mawg, then down at her foot, then back up to Mawg. Not knowing what to do, Mawg shrugged and said, "I'm sorry about the onion smell, it's a very long story." Peri continued to laugh.

"And I'll be savoring it for decades to come!"

Jessica's face froze as she looked down at Mawg's foot again. Mawg's internal alert system went off. Something was very wrong, but she didn't know what. "Peri…can she hear you?"

"I told you humans can't hear demons, Mawg."

With wide eyes, Jessica stared at Mawg's foot.

"I think this one can."

Her face flew up to look at Mawg, eyes still wide. Mawg didn't say anything out loud, but stared at Jessica with her mouth shut and thought "can you hear me right now?"

She nodded.

"Ohhhhhh…She's a demon."

It was Mawg's turn to look surprised. She and Jessica stared at each other, neither moving a muscle. The air was tense with the stand-off, both of them wondering what the other was going to do. Mawg thought, "Can you hear him, too?" and gestured with her eyes down to her foot. Jessica nodded, then went back to scrubbing the foot in hand. Mawg had another thought. "Can you see him?" Jessica looked at Peri and nodded, never missing a beat in her work.

Continuing to scrub, Jessica contributed a thought of her own. "You're not the first and you certainly won't be the last. Just act like nothing is unusual. I don't want to scare off my other customers." Then she grabbed a foot file and started sawing away on Mawg's massive calluses like nothing out of the ordinary just occurred. "And next time, don't use onions to shut him up. Use gelatin. I hear they hate gelatin."

"Demon dammit, I wish everyone would stop saying that!"

Mawg burst out laughing, and the lady next to her looked over like she'd lost her mind. "Sorry, it tickles when she hits my arches." Mawg turned back to Jessica and thought "Duly noted, thank you." Jessica gave a half smile. When she finished and put massage oil on Mawg's feet, she stuck her hand out, wanting the bottle of polish. Mawg handed it over.

"This is boring. Would you like me to add a flower?"

Mawg looked at the polish. "Oh, you don't have to do that. Just the polish is fine."

With a furrowed brow, Jessica said, "You really need the flower. I'll give you the flower. Men like the flowers. What color do you want?"

Realizing she wasn't going to win this fight, Mawg replied, "A white flower is perfect, thank you." Then she watched as Jessica used a steady hand and a tiny brush to create a very pretty flower.

Mawg looked at her and thought, "Thank you for being discreet. And for the flower."

Ambling back up to her feet, Jessica got up and barked instructions. "Ok you let that dry for five minutes, then you can go. That'll be eighty dollars." That made Peri's eyes bug out.

"Eighty dollars? For a pedicure?!"

Wiping her hands on a towel, Jessica thought, "No, fifty for the pedicure, thirty for the discretion." Peri's little eyebrows raised.

"Ahhhhhhh, I see how this works. I bet you're making a killin' with this racket, aren't you!"

Jessica winked and put her hand out.

"I ain't mad about it. That's a good game, well done."

Mawg handed her a hundred and told her to keep it. Then she gathered her things and headed to the car.

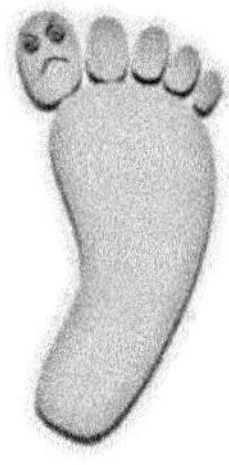

CHAPTER SEVEN

"I need snackies."

Mawg was rummaging through her purse looking for the car keys. "I wondered how long it would be before you brought that up. Hang on, we'll hit a drive-thru on the way home."

They picked up a burger and fries and got back to the house. Peri wasn't lying. He was a totally different person…demon…when he had something to eat.

"Hanger is no joke."

Relishing the last French fry, Mawg licked the salt off her fingers. "Oh trust me, I learned that the hard way." She looked down at her freshly pedicured toes. "So what time do we head to this club?"

"Most people don't arrive until after the sun goes down, so…maybe 9ish?"

She walked into the bathroom and looked at herself in the mirror. "Ok that works. Plenty of time to turn me into something presentable."

Peri started to say something snarky, but Mawg grabbed the toenail clippers and cut him off with a "Shut it."

"Geez, touchy! You do whatever it is you do and I'm gonna take a nap."

Confusion spread across Mawg's face. "Demons sleep?"

"We don't need to, but we can if we choose. Your breakdown and hormones were a LOT. I wanna gear up for tonight."

For the next few hours, she took her time primping, starting with a full shower, shaving everything. It had been a while, so it was a bit like trying to cut through a jungle with a machete. After applying her favorite moisturizers and body oils, it was time to paint her face. She normally wore a little makeup, but even she could admit it was a bit outdated. Taking a break on the bed, Mawg pulled up a couple of makeup tutorials on the internet and went to work on her face. The finished product was pleasantly surprising. She looked as youthful as a middle-age woman can look without surgery. The crow's feet and laugh lines were still there, but they were softened. She felt pretty.

Her hair was another story. She attempted beach waves, but it was a mess. After a minor meltdown, she said, "fuck it," and threw the hair into a loose updo. It wasn't her best work, but it was acceptable. Her upper arms were burning from trying to curl her hair, and she had to turn on the little fan on the counter to keep sweat from ruining her makeup.

It was about this time that Peri woke from his nap. Prepared for him to be cranky, she walked into the kitchen and pulled a mini charcuterie plate she'd made earlier out of the refrigerator. Peri's little face was mixed in with her toe flower, but he looked sleepy and pleased.

"Mmmmm…snackies."

Mawg felt a little bit of endearment for him in that moment. He was kind of cute when he wasn't being a sarcastic asshole.

"I heard that."

They finished their snack and it was time for Mawg to put on the dress and accessories Tori had suggested. The little teardrop earrings weren't fancy, but they looked perfect with her hair up. Mawg walked over to the full-length mirror in her closet and stared at herself. She didn't recognize the person looking back at her. What she saw was a sexy, curvy grown woman. This stranger appeared to have it all together.

"Get used to it. We're not going back, Mawg. Your rebirth begins tonight. Are you ready?"

Giving one last glance to the woman in the mirror, Mawg looked down at Peri and said, "Just one more thing." She walked toward her shoes in the closet and looked at the loafers, then down at Peri. His eyes widened in fear, and he was about to yell when Mawg reached over and grabbed her strappy sandals. She chuckled as she put them on.

"Not funny, Mawg. Not funny at all."

"Sorry, I had to do it," She grinned and booped his little nose. "Ok…let's go have an adventure."

In order to enjoy a few drinks without the risk of a DUI, Mawg decided to order a ride share. Peri gave her the address and she loaded it into the app. She wasn't familiar with that area of the city.

"It's kind of a hidden artsy area. The people in the neighborhood keep it quiet so they don't get gentrified and turned into live/work/play condos."

Mawg understood that. She bought her house ten years ago and her neighborhood had changed significantly in that time. It was unfortunate that anything unique with the tiniest bit of charm was always gobbled up and ruined.

As she walked outside to wait for the driver, Mawg started to feel self conscious about the amount of cleavage showing from the very deep neckline.

"Stop it right now. There has never been a time in the history of your world that boobies haven't been welcomed."

She couldn't argue with that. The driver arrived and she hopped in the car. He looked appreciatively at Mawg from the rearview mirror.

"See? I told ya'."

He verified the address in his GPS and they were off.

"Pick up your phone and act like you're callin' somebody. Say something like "we'll be there in fifteen minutes, honey."

Mawg looked confused and thought, "Huh? Why?"

"It's a safety precaution for women traveling alone. That way the driver thinks someone's waitin' for ya'. Makes them less likely to try and kidnap you."

Looking down at her lap, her eyes got wide. She thought, "Jesus, Peri! Are you purposefully trying to scare me? Do I need to be worried about this guy?"

"Not him specifically. But you should ALWAYS be aware, Mawg. You never know what kind of creepers are out in the world."

She thought, "Oh for fuck's sake," but did as Peri asked and pulled out her phone, pretending to dial someone. Waiting a few seconds, she said, "Hey babe, I'm almost there." Pause. "Yeah, I should be there in…." She looked at the driver. "Would you say about fifteen minutes?" The driver looked at the GPS and replied, "We should be there in eighteen minutes." Mawg focused back on the phone. "Did you hear that, hon? About eighteen minutes." Pause. "Ok sounds great, I love you too. See you soon!" She fake hung up, feeling proud of herself for pulling that off.

"I mean, you're not winning any Oscars in the near future, but it wasn't bad."

She thought, "Oh shut the fuck up."

As they continued the rest of the ride in silence, Mawg figured she would take a few minutes to doom scroll on her phone for the rest of the trip. When they arrived at their destination, the driver came around and opened the door for her. "Thank you, have a good night." She walked to the sidewalk, giving him five stars on the app before looking up at the building.

It looked like every other small shop on a city block, except towering back behind the storefront was a church steeple. Not at all what she expected. There was some sort of privacy film on the windows and she couldn't see inside, but there was a well-lit 3D sign above the door that simply said "The Church".

"This is a bar?" Mawg thought.

"Oh, this whole facade is purposeful. Remember, the neighborhood doesn't like attention. I think you'll be pleasantly surprised when we go inside. And don't forget to ask for Gina when we get in there."

A ginormous bald man with a goatee, wearing an all-black tailored suit and tie, welcomed her and opened the door.

"Let the adventure begin."

CHAPTER EIGHT

Nothing could have prepared her for what she found inside. Based on the storefront's exterior, she expected a local watering hole. The kind where cigarette smoke from decades before was baked into the walls, and people would cram around a small bar, asking for the channel to be changed to whatever game was important at that time.

What she experienced first was the smell. It was intoxicating, a mix of something woodsy (maybe cedar?) and something warm and spicy, like cinnamon and vanilla were splashed liberally on the mocha-colored walls. There was also a hint of cherry pipe tobacco. Not overwhelming like cigars can be, but floating lightly across the air. Instead of the traditional booth and table layout, there were dark leather couches and loveseats against the walls, and a few dark mahogany bar tables in the middle of the room with votive candles on them. The interior lighting was strategic, highlighting large black and white framed photos on the walls. Mawg had never described a room as seductive, but this room radiated a sexy, expensive energy.

"Hey lookie-loo, people are staring at us. We gotta move instead of acting like we've never been in public before. Head toward the bar in the back, get a drink and ask for Gina."

Mawg shook her head as if to wake herself out of a dream and walked back to the bar. The male bartender looked to be in his early twenties and had a face she would describe as adorable. If she was twenty years younger, he would be the perfect bar crush. He had sandy blonde hair, crystal blue eyes and a baby face with cherub cheeks begging to be pinched. Just like the man at the door, he was in all black head to toe, wearing pants, suspenders, and a button down with sleeves rolled up to the forearm. "Hey there, welcome to The Church. I'm Liam. Would you like a drink menu, or do you already have something in mind?"

It had been quite a while since Mawg's last alcoholic beverage, so she stuck with a classic that wouldn't go astray. "How about a gin and tonic with a lime?"

The affable Liam smiled. "Absolutely, one sec."

While he was mixing her drink, Mawg turned to survey the room. She was thoroughly enjoying the atmosphere. The jazz music was low enough that people could talk over it. This was a far cry from the clubs she remembered from her youth.

"No boots and pants here."

Mawg's face scrunched in confusion. "Boots and pants?"

"Yeah you know…say it really fast over and over. Boots and pants and boots and pants and boots and pants…"

Peri's little face bobbed to the beat as he emulated the music that was played in the clubs Mawg remembered from years ago.

She got a good laugh out of that, which caused a couple of patrons to look over. She'd forgotten she was talking to her toe. "Dammit, don't make me laugh. They think I'm crazy."

Liam returned with her drink. "That will be ten dollars." Mawg pulled fifteen out of her wallet, and as she handed it over said, "Oh, and I'm looking for someone who works here named Gina. Do you happen to know where I could find her?"

He put the cash in the drawer. "I can get her for you, no problem." He gestured over to another patron and said, "Give me one sec to pour his drink and I'll go find her."

"Thanks so much, I appreciate it."

Mawg resumed surveying the room, taking a closer look at the patrons for the first time. It was an interesting mix of people, ranging from 30-somethings to the 50ish-60ish crowd. The vibe in the room was loose, and everyone seemed to be relaxed and enjoying themselves. She felt comfortable in this place.

"See, that's why I chose it."

Mawg thought, "I've got to tell you Peri, I had no idea what to expect when we got here, but your selection was on point. This is exactly the type of atmosphere I like."

"Trust me. I wouldn't lead you astray."

"Hi, were you asking for me?"

Turning toward the smoky voice, she locked eyes with a middle-aged goddess. Her dark red hair was styled in a bob with blunt bangs. Her eyelashes went on for days, and dear God she was tall! The five-inch heels contributed a bit to her height, but Mawg's head barely came above her shoulders. Her body was bangin' and could only be described as statuesque. She was glorious.

"Um…yes, are you Gina?"

Tilting her head slightly, she fixed her gaze on Mawg. "I am. And who might you be?"

Mawg started to fumble her words at the woman's pointed gaze, in awe of the confidence she exuded.

"Get it together."

She took a deep breath and said, "I'm Mawg. My friend Tori recommended I ask for you since this is my first time here. She also told me to ask you about…the tour?"

Gina sipped her cocktail with the leisure of someone who rushed for no one. "I adore Tori. I'm one of her biggest fans…and probably her biggest client." She laughed, and Mawg fell in love with her low, raspy tone. She sounded like one of those cocktail lounge singers that would lay across a piano. "Tori custom designs my wardrobe. She also gave me a heads up that you might be coming here tonight."

"She did? Well, that was nice of her. And this is actually one of her dresses as well." Mawg gestured to the beautiful silk that clung to her curves in all the right places.

Gina eyed Mawg appreciatively. "I should have known. It fits you beautifully and it's absolutely gorgeous." She pointed toward a leather loveseat against the wall. "Let's go grab a seat and chat."

They walked to the couch and took a seat. Gina slowly crossed her insanely long legs as multiple men in the room took notice. "So, this is your first time at The Church?"

Adjusting her dress, Mawg said, "It is! I really love the vibe you have here. I walked in and was hit in the face with a feeling of warmth."

"That may have been a hot flash, just FYI."

Gina had a look of pride on her face. "Thank you, we're really proud of it. But, this is just a tiny portion of The Church." She gestured to the room around them. "Think of this space like a waiting room. See that door to the left of the bar? The one I came out of earlier?"

She glanced to where Gina was pointing. "Oh I didn't even notice it!"

With a nonchalant wave of her hand, Gina said, "When it's closed, it blends into the wall so it's difficult to see. Behind that door is a pass-through to an old church that's been converted. That's ours as well."

Mawg's eyes widened in surprise. "Oh wow, I never would have expected that! Do you host big parties back there, like receptions and events?"

The corner of Gina's mouth turned up and her eyebrow raised as she glanced over at the door. "We definitely have a lot of people back there, but we don't typically host formal events. So tell me, what brought you here tonight?"

Mawg explained the day, excluding the part about her talking toe demon. She told Gina about getting fired, meeting Tori, and how she was restarting her life. Then she mentioned it being her birthday.

With a smile, Gina raised her glass. "Oh, how wonderful, a birthday celebration! Let's see if we can make this a memorable evening for you."

"Thank you. And yes, cheers to an adventure!" Mawg replied, raising her glass to toast with Gina.

"Oh, the things we will see…"

Gina set her glass down and looked at Mawg like she was measuring her upcoming words carefully. "Are you on a solo adventure this evening or do you have someone meeting you?"

"Nope, not meeting anyone. This was a last-minute decision to get out of the house and have a little fun after a day of upheaval. I haven't had a night out in a long time, but I figured turning forty-five deserved a little celebration, so here I am."

"Yeah…a last-minute decision includes takin' three hours to prep your meatsuit, but okay."

Gina stared at Mawg with her head tilted to the side, listening intently. She was one of those people who gave you her undivided attention, no matter how many people wanted hers. Mawg admired that quality.

"I'm honored you chose to celebrate it with us," Gina said with slow smile. "So can I assume you don't know much about The Church?" Mawg nodded and Gina continued. "Would you like to take that tour in a little bit?"

Mawg smiled. "That would be wonderful, thank you." Mawg's eyes surveyed the room that was now getting busier. "I assume running a club that's as big as you described must take a lot of work. Are you the manager here?"

Gina sipped her drink. "I'm the operations manager, but I'm also a concierge. One of the highlights of my job is welcoming newcomers and showing them all that The Church has to offer. It's always a joy to open someone's eyes to the possibility of living out their fantasies."

It was Mawg's turn to tilt her head to the side, as a questioning look bloomed on her face. "Fantasies? What kind of fantasies are found at a bar?"

"A one-night stand with a guy named Chad who has beer breath and talks about 'giving you the business', but the booze gave him limp dick so he just gropes your boobies and passes out."

It took everything in her to hold eye contact with Gina when she was internally glaring at her toe.

Weighing her words carefully, Gina said, "That's what I wanted to discuss with you. The Church is much more than a bar, Mawg. I know we just met, but I'm going to ask you something. And if it's too invasive, or if I'm overstepping, you're welcome to tell me to mind my own business. In your past relationships…I assume you've had some past relationships?"

Taking a quick intake of breath before responding, Mawg gave a tight nod. "A few."

Gina uncrossed her legs and leaned in closer to keep the conversation quiet, as the volume was picking up in the bar area. "In those relationships, did you feel… fulfilled? As a whole, and also…you know…physically?"

She blushed, a bit taken aback by the question. "Are…are you asking if I've had an orgasm?"

Gina released a low, throaty chuckle and said, "Not just an orgasm. I'm asking if anyone has ever fully appreciated your beauty and treated it with the worship it deserves. I'm asking…" she gestured her outstretched hands at Mawg's body, "if you've ever been desired so intensely that just remembering that interaction sets your body on fire."

Leaning back and sipping her cocktail, Gina waited for Mawg to process the question. Mawg was gob smacked momentarily, shocked to be having this conversation with someone she just met. As the shock wore off, she was able to consider the question…and laughed. She laughed hard. Partly from nerves, and partly from the absurdity of the thought. She laughed so hard that she almost peed herself a little.

"Don't you DARE ruin Tori's dress."

Mawg sobered up and looked Gina in the eye. "Gina, what you see before you," she gestured toward her own body, "is a facade. Prior to Tori's glow-up today, I would be in the dictionary as the definition of the word 'frumpy'."

Sipping her drink, she gestured to her apron belly. "No, no one has ever worshipped this. And I wouldn't expect them to. Now if I looked like you…" she let the thought trail off but looked Gina up and down. "I see why men would worship you. You're absolutely lovely."

Gina sat in silence, a curious expression on her face. Worried her words might have offended, Mawg said, "I hope that didn't come across wrong. I just meant that you're what the kids would call a MILF."

"Do they still say that? I don't think they still say that."

Ignoring Peri, she smirked, "I can guarantee you there's not a man in this room who would look at us right now and say 'give me the chunky brunette over the gorgeous redhead'." Mawg shrugged her shoulders. "I don't mean that in a negative way, but I'm a realist." Now it was Peri's turn to roll his little eyes.

"You are very much a negative Nelly."

Staring at Mawg, Gina let the silence hang in the air with the cherry pipe tobacco. "You guarantee that?" she asked with a raised eyebrow.

Mawg shook her head. "No man would choose me over you, Gina. Yes I would 100% guarantee that."

"If you say one more negative thing about yourself, I'll give you IBS for the next week."

Gina leaned back in the loveseat and crossed her insanely long legs. With one arm lounging on the back of the loveseat and the other swirling her drink, a slow smile spread across her face. "Would you care to make a friendly wager?"

"This feels like a scene from one of those old mobster movies that you like."

Mawg chuckled. "Fired, remember? I can't afford to bet money. But sure, I'd be willing to make a friendly bet of some sort."

Gina sat for a moment in silence, contemplating. "Why don't we head to the main room, and that will give me a moment to determine the stakes of our wager."

Mawg finished what was left of her drink, stood up, and said, "Let's do this."

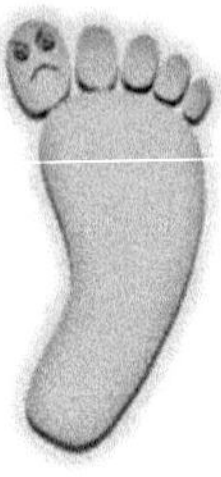

CHAPTER NINE

Using a special key card, Gina opened the door. As Mawg stepped in, she encountered a pass-through hallway that was approximately fifteen to twenty feet long. It was pitch black except for the lighting that was lining the path. There were luxurious green velvet curtains at the end of the hall that were set alight from the floor almost as if they were glowing, giving the impression she was walking into a hidden world.

"Now listen, no matter what you see when we go through those curtains, DO NOT react and make us look ignorant. You're a grown-ass woman. Keep the emotions off your face."

Mawg's eyebrow lifted and she thought, "Jesus, you act like I'm a rube. Give me a little credit, Peri."

As they reached the curtain, Gina grabbed Mawg's hand and turned to face her. "I'm about to show you a world that may surprise you. Please know before we walk in, you are under no obligation to participate in any of the activities you see. Nothing in this building occurs without consent. We'll plan to be observers only tonight, unless you desire to participate."

Taking Peri's advice, Mawg kept her face in a neutral expression and nodded, but internally she wondered what she had gotten herself into.

"Trust me, you're safer in here than you are in the outside world. I toured before with Tori, and there's absolutely no reason to be afraid. Remember, you're just an observer on an adventure."

Gina continued, "Pleasure is a funny concept, Mawg. Many people will deny themselves pleasure, even when they crave it deep down in their being. Maybe it's because of religious upbringing, maybe it's fear of being judged by society, or maybe they don't think they're worthy. If my intuition is correct, I think you fall in the last two categories."

Gina reached out, placing a hand on the curtain. "What you're about to witness is humanity releasing its inhibitions and experiencing pleasure without judgement. The Church is a safe place for adults to live out their fantasies…as long as they're legal and consensual, of course."

Gulping and nodding that she understood, Mawg realized she'd been wrong earlier…she was definitely a rube in this situation, completely out of her element. "Oh my God, what the fuck did I get myself into?!" That pissed Peri off.

"DO NOT JUDGE. Your exposure to the world has been very limited to this point. Gina's allowin' you a bird's-eye view into the broader world, and you will be respectful. If you have questions, you can ask me. When we get home, we'll do a full recap. But for now, please play it fucking cool."

Gina could see the hesitation on Mawg's face, and her expression softened as she reached out to grasp her hand. "You're safe here, Mawg. If at any time this becomes overwhelming, or if I've misjudged you, please tell me and we'll end the tour immediately. YOU are in control. Understood?"

Looking into Gina's eyes, Mawg's sixth sense felt she could trust her. "Understood. And thank you for being patient with me."

Gina nonchalantly waved. "No thanks necessary." She squeezed Mawg's hand and smiled. "Welcome to The Church, Mawg." As Gina pulled back the curtain, Mawg could feel her heartbeat in her neck and her palms began to sweat.

The architecture struck her first. The hardwood floors appeared to be original. She could tell the building was old because the craftsmanship was pristine. The cathedral ceiling had to be at least fifty feet high at its peak, and there were massive dark wood beams running across pitched slopes. Mawg wasn't great with dimensions, but she estimated the building was about half a football field in length.

"Closer to a quarter, but I appreciate your attempt at the football reference."

The front wall of the room was magnificent, boasting an old theater stage with massive velvet curtains. A crew was hauling props, lighting, and equipment up the stairs on the side, presumably preparing for the evening's entertainment. There was an open space on the floor in front of the stage, which she assumed was the dance floor.

The decor in the main area was similar to the front entry, with leather couches and bar tables spread throughout. Smack dab in the middle of the room was the circular bar, where two bartenders worked in tandem, both clad in black. The smell of vanilla, cinnamon, and cherry pipe tobacco intoxicated the room. Off to the left and right, she could see hallways that ran behind the wooden wall facades.

There were approximately a hundred people in the club, enjoying drinks and vibing with the hypnotic music playing over speakers in the background. The atmosphere was similar to what she experienced in the front entry, with one exception; the dress code was vastly different.

Various states of undress passed before Mawg's eyes, ranging from fully-clothed to completely nude. A balding, naked man with a pot belly sat on a nearby couch, having an in-depth conversation with a sixty-something year old woman sporting a see-through black lace dress. At the table next to them stood a well-dressed male couple speaking with a woman who was wearing nothing but stilettos and a collar around her neck. A tremendous amount of feathers, fishnets, leather, and lace were sprinkled across the patrons in the room.

"Where does one attain a matching pink boa and leather ass-less chaps? Asking for a friend."

Mawg thought, "You said not to judge."

"Oh, that wasn't judgement. I'd like to know so we can add them to our cart."

While Mawg was taking it all in, Gina was surveying Mawg. "So…what do you think?"

Mawg turned her wide eyes toward Gina. "You weren't kidding when you said it would be an adventure!" Gina threw her head back and laughed. Mawg continued to look around the room. "I can't put my finger on it, but outside of the initial shock of the naked people, the vibe you have here is fantastic. When I think of a 'club', my mind immediately goes to a rave setting. Strobe lights and never-ending techno music just aren't my thing these days."

With a hearty laugh, Gina said, "Oh dear God, that sounds like hell. I wholeheartedly agree, my boots and pants days are far behind me."

"Seeeeee!!! Boots and pants and boots and pants and-"

Mawg chuckled but thought, "Do not get that shit stuck in my head." She looked at Gina and said, "I definitely think this adventure calls for a drink. Do you mind if we hit the bar?"

Gina peered up at a clock on the wall. "We can, but we'll need to wait another forty-five minutes to order alcohol."

Face scrunched in confusion, Mawg asked, "Did they run out of gin?"

Gina smiled and replied, "We have a 'one alcoholic drink per hour' rule here."

Scrunching her brows and tilting her head in surprise, she said, "Forgive me for assuming, but that doesn't seem like a profitable business model for a bar. Why set it up that way?"

Gina gestured for Mawg to follow, and they began to walk toward a server wearing the all black uniform. "Given the activities that occur within these walls, our top priority is safety. Consent is the most important tenet of The Church. If someone is overly intoxicated, their inebriation could cause them to consent to something they don't actually want. We want members to be relaxed, but they MUST have their wits about them." They reached the server and Gina said, "Luca, can you bring us two waters, please?" Luca nodded and off he went.

Mawg was curious about how they were able to keep track of how many drinks a member had. "So, how does the bartender know when to serve someone?"

Gina's chin raised, a light coming into her eyes at Mawg's astute question. "Once a member orders from the main bar in this room, their keycard is scanned before the drink is served. We track based off the last swipe."

Finally feeling comfortable enough to ask, Mawg said, "Gina, I think I'm starting to get the idea, but just to clarify…what specifically are the activities that happen here?"

"The naked boobies and weiners aren't clueing you in yet?"

Gina guided them to a nearby loveseat, where they sat. "Before I describe it any further, let me ask you a few questions. Have you ever read dark romance books?"

Mawg's brow furrowed, thinking. "I've read romance books but I don't know what dark romance is, so I'm going to say no to that one."

A thruple passed by as Gina asked, "Have you ever watched porn?"

Mawg immediately blushed. "I mean, I've seen a few, but I don't actively seek them out."

Gina had a knowing look on her face, although Mawg wasn't sure why. "So, you may not be aware that pleasure and sex can come in many different forms. What turns one person off will turn another on. The Church is an adult club where people can explore erotic fantasies in a safe environment. Those hallways you see behind the walls?" She pointed to each side. "In those hallways are rooms, and in those rooms, people choose to…enjoy each other's company in a manner they've both agreed to."

Mawg's eyes were wide.

"The naked dude on the couch really didn't give it away? I'm a little concerned about your contextual skills, if you're shocked."

Gina tilted her head to study Mawg. "I assume this is a bit of a surprise, but let me ask you this…is it an unpleasant one?"

It wasn't the topic that was unpleasant. It was the idea of discussing sex so openly with a stranger. While Mawg's parents were quite affectionate, her home wasn't a place where sexuality was a comfortable topic growing up. Her mom seemed almost embarrassed any time Mawg brought up questions and would tell her, "Just wait until you're married, honey." And she'd never felt comfortable being vulnerable with her ex. She'd always had questions and curiosity, but no safe outlet to ask. Even though her sexual past was a bit limited, she didn't consider herself a prude. "It's not unpleasant, just…very surprising. Whenever I've heard of what you're presenting, it's always been described to me as deviance."

Mawg could see that word clearly upset Gina.

"Hey, thanks for welcoming me to your club full of deviants. Excellent way to say that, Mawg."

She immediately felt awful. Gina had been nothing but kind to her. "I'm so sorry, I didn't mean to imply—"

Gina cut her off with a wave of her hand. "Don't apologize. We live in a civilization that has continually hammered home the idea that sexual pleasure is 'dirty', especially here in the states. We shouldn't be surprised that a country built by Puritans has a Puritanical view on sex. I'm not upset with you, Mawg. I'm upset that adults experiencing consensual pleasure are still considered deviant in this day and

age. Unfortunately, I don't know if that will ever change."
Luca returned with their waters, and Gina took a sip before
continuing. "But, we can begin to rectify that here and now.
Would you like to begin the tour and we can discuss it as we
go?"

She felt a wave of relief wash over her that Gina wasn't
upset. "That would be great. And thank you again, Gina. I
appreciate your patience with a noob."

Gina smiled and patted her on the arm. "We've all been
a noob at one point or another. I started this adventure five
years ago, and I remember very clearly the feelings you're
experiencing right now." She rose and led Mawg toward the
hallway on the left.

Before they reached the hallway, Gina stopped and
turned to Mawg. "About that bet…here are the stakes I have in
mind. If you walk away from this experience tonight without a
single man showing interest in you, I will cover your bar tab.
BUT, if at least one interested man has an eye for you, then
you come work for me here…if you find yourself feeling
comfortable in the atmosphere, of course."

*"Ooooh…you'd get to wear suspenders if you bartend.
Suspenders are fun."*

Mawg's jaw dropped and an awkward laugh came out of her mouth. "Work for you? I don't know anything about bartending, Gina. I think that would be a bad investment for you."

Gina laughed and waved a hand nonchalantly. "Oh, I don't need bartenders right now. What I do need is someone to help me with operations, and to learn the concierge position so they can fill in when I can't be here. We're in the process of expanding to more cities, and I need someone to be my backup. Would that potentially interest you?"

"Ask if you can still wear the suspenders."

Mawg stared at her water that now had condensation running down the bottle. "So just to clarify, if a man likes me, I get a job. And if no man likes me, you'll cover my bar tab?"

"Correct."

It was highly probable this was one of those "too good to be true" situations, but tonight she felt a stirring inside and didn't want to be practical, so she shrugged. "I feel like I'm winning this either way. But if that's what you want, then deal." Mawg stuck out her hand.

Gina shook on it and smiled. "Alright then, let's begin our adventure." She turned and headed down the hallway.

"Next time I take over your body, we're adding suspenders to your cart."

As Mawg caught up, Gina said, "Before we start, let's go through some protocol and basic rules of courtesy. If you are able to view the people in these rooms, they have given consent to having an audience. If the blinds are open, you are welcome to watch through the window. If the door is open, you're welcome to enter the room and either watch or join the activity. If both the blinds and door are closed, it's a closed session. Under no circumstances are you allowed to enter the room."

Mawg felt a mixture of excitement and nervousness in her stomach as they passed by two attractive men making out against the wall. "Ok, understood." She wanted adventure, and she was about to get it. Meanwhile, Peri was singing.

"Boobies on the right, boobies on the left, hope these boobies gonna give you consent…"

Chuckling internally, she thought, "I guess I should have asked instead of assuming. Are demons male and female?"

"Demons don't have genders. I just find boobs more pleasant to look at. Weiners are weird."

The first room had a viewing window with the blinds open and the door closed. Mawg peered through the open blinds while she sipped her water. The walls of the room were a deep chocolate and the floors were hardwood. There was a ledge around the edge of the room with candles, keeping the mood soft and the lighting low. In the middle of the room was a padded full-size bed with a thick blonde woman laying on it wearing absolutely nothing.

She was flat on her back, and her aged breasts fell to the side near her armpits. A tall, athletic, sandy-haired man kneeled in front of her on a padded, wooden ottoman at the end of the bed, wearing only jeans that currently sported an impressive bulge. Mawg watched him pick up the woman's left foot and place it on his bare, muscular chest. His left hand reached down to the inside of her knee, and he lightly trailed his fingers from her knee to the arch of her foot. She heard the woman's guttural moan as she watched the man, and it stirred something inside Mawg. The man grasped her ankle with his right hand to lift her foot near his lips. His eyes darkened as he began to suck on her polished toe. He continued to lick and suck her toes while reaching down with his left hand to massage the bulge in his jeans that was growing larger by the second.

Watching two random people arouse each other warmed Mawg's blood in a way she wasn't prepared for.

"Abso-fucking-lutely not. Don't even think about puttin' me in some dude's mouth. Who knows where it's been?"

Mawg thought, "Weren't you the one who said DO NOT JUDGE? And shut up, I don't need your commentary."

Gina leaned over and chimed in. "Most people don't use their real names here. Anonymity is offered and welcomed if one prefers it. Men are Dick and women are Jane, unless they specify otherwise. Those who choose not to identify with either male or female are Chris. This particular Dick adores feet. He's not interested in traditional sex, he simply wants to worship feet."

"For all she knows, he could have eaten anchovies earlier and that poor toe is being suffocated by fish breath."

She was trying her best not to react but all she could do was watch as he continued to stroke himself through the jeans, his eyes squeezed shut. The woman in the mask was gripping the sheets, her breathing becoming more intense as his tongue licked the sensitive skin between her toes. She rolled her head toward the window where they were standing, and her eyes were glazed over in pleasure. He licked the arch of her foot slowly, making Jane buck uncontrollably, and now it was Dick's turn to moan.

Something deep in his moan triggered a tingle deep inside her beginning to build. She had heard of foot fetishes, but to watch a foot be the source of sexual pleasure live was an entirely different experience.

"Nope, don't even think about it."

Interrupting her thoughts, Gina turned to Mawg. "That Jane is what's known as a pillow princess. Her fantasy is to be pleasured without reciprocation. She doesn't give, she only receives."

Mawg's face showed her surprise. "Wait…that's a thing? Just receiving?"

With a hearty laugh, Gina's lips curled into a smile. "It absolutely is, especially here. Erotica is helpful for people living out fantasies, and also for those dealing with trauma. Many people come here for what they're missing in life, or to heal a part of themselves."

The fantasy aspect made sense, but the trauma healing did not.

Sensing the confusion from Mawg's face, Gina explained. "For example, a woman who has survived an abusive situation where she had no one to help her but herself…that woman might be able to heal part of that wound by being worshipped and shown how precious she really is."

Mawg reflected back about her past experiences while she continued to watch Jane moaning and gripping the sheets. The concept was slightly baffling. Not because a woman would want that, but because she'd never encountered a man who didn't expect something in return. She turned to Gina. "And…there are men who are okay with that?"

Gina's face softened and held a tinge of sadness that the idea was so foreign. "Not only are there men who are okay with that, but there are men who love that." Mawg's eyes were still wide with disbelief as Gina continued. "Erotica is about pleasure exploration, Mawg. Is it safe to assume that your past experiences were fairly traditional?"

"Is the two-pump chump experience considered traditional? If so, then yes."

Still deep in thought, Mawg tried to grasp what it would be like to have someone treat her like she was desirable. The sound of Jane on the table breathlessly begging, "Oh God, yes…please don't stop," pulled her out of her thoughts.

"If that, Gina. If I'm being completely honest, I don't think I've ever experienced that kind of reaction." She gestured toward Jane. "I always assumed what I was experiencing was an orgasm, but I have never felt like that."

Complete glee spread across Gina's face. "And that's exactly what The Church is for!" Gina continued smiling and clapped her hands together. "Ok, shall we move onto the next room?"

"Oh thank Demon, if we watched one more toe be tormented, I was gonna give you a chin hair for the mental anguish."

Mawg laughed internally at Peri and smiled at Gina. "Let's do it!"

The next room had the blinds and door closed, so they skipped it and continued on. Before they came to the third room, Mawg noticed the door open and people standing in the doorway. As they approached the window with the blinds open, Mawg was about to drop her jaw when Peri piped in.

"Be cool."

In the middle of the darkened room with a spotlight shining down from above was a large, free-standing wooden X. It was solid wood and had to weigh a few hundred pounds. There was a naked Dick strapped to it, splayed out in the shape of the X. Another Dick was standing in front of him wearing only boots and pan—

"Boots and pants and boots and pants and bo—"

"Don't start!" Mawg thought internally as she tried to process what was in front of her.

Standing Dick was about 6'5 and probably three hundred pounds, and he was holding a feather between his fingers. Standing Dick would stalk around Strapped Dick and stop to run the feather along his body. Meanwhile, strapped Dick was very erect with a ring squeezing his actual dick and pleading for release. "Please…please let me cum!" Standing Dick shook his head, and instead ran the feather along Strapped Dick's balls. Strapped Dick broke out giggling so hard he began to cry.

Mawg tried her best to keep her expression neutral but her shock must have shown, because Gina noticed it. She lightly pulled Mawg away from the window and said, "In regular life, the Dick that's strapped in has a career that bears a tremendous amount of responsibility. He comes here because the weight of that responsibility wears on him. In The Church, he gets to be completely powerless and not be responsible for the outcome of a situation. It's a release."

While she wasn't fully prepared to see a grown man tickled and crying, Mawg understood what Gina was saying. "I think I'm starting to get it…the fantasy concept, I mean." What she didn't grasp was how all of these people were comfortable being so vulnerable while others watched, and subconsciously clasped her hands in front of her belly.

"I'm not a fan of the feather. Can we move on from Tickles before he gets to the toes, please?"

Mawg asked, "So, is he ever allowed to…um, release?"

Gina shrugged her shoulders. "That depends on what rules they've set up in advance. There's no one right answer to that question, because it depends on what the individuals have agreed upon. Because I've known them for a long time, yes, I know he will get to release. But he won't be in control of when that occurs."

Mawg didn't like the idea of having no control. Maybe it was her Capricorn nature, maybe it was her need to ensure her own safety, or maybe it was because she was afraid of what would happen if she let go. "I get it, but I don't think that's something I'd be comfortable doing."

Gina noted Mawg struggling with the concept and gave her a gentle smile. "And that's absolutely fine. The purpose of the tour is exposure to all of the possibilities. It's actually responsible to acknowledge that you don't enjoy something."

"Oh my Demon, he's almost down to the toes! Can we please move along?"

They turned to move further down the hallway. As they were walking, Gina asked "Sooooo…how are you feeling so far?"

"Horny. She feels horny."

Doing her best, Mawg ignored Peri and considered the question. A memory of her toxic ex flashed in her mind. Mawg had been online searching for lingerie for their upcoming vacation when he'd walked up behind her. "What are you looking at that for?" Mawg had been excited to try and woo him out of the funk he'd been in lately. "I thought it might be fun for our trip…you know, spice things up a little." His eyebrow had raised as he'd looked her up and down and said, "I don't think they make them in your size," then shrugged and walked off.

"Hey! Snap out of it. Look around you. Clearly he was a piece of shit, and we're throwing that tape away, remember?"

Pulling herself out of the painful memory, she surveyed the hallway and the wide variety of bodies around them. Peri was right. He *was* a piece of shit, and she wasn't going to let toxic reminders ruin her evening.

She turned and replied to Gina, who was still waiting on an answer. "I'm feeling a mixture of things. Ignorant, for not knowing these things existed. Curious, wondering what other options are out there. And if I'm being completely honest, a little naughty."

Gina got a good laugh from that and raised an eyebrow. "Naughty can definitely be fun."

They arrived at the next room, and the blinds and door were open. Mawg could hear a woman's voice raised like she was irritated. Gina's eyes lit up as she grabbed Mawg's hand and said, "Ooooh, I know who this is just by that voice! Let's go stand in the doorway, I have someone I want to introduce you to."

Allowing herself to be led, Gina brought her over to the open doorway. If she thought her face was in shock before, she couldn't hide it this time.

"Fuck yeah, this is more like it!"

On a wide table in the middle of the room laid the balding man she saw sitting on the couch earlier. He was strapped down, buck naked with a full erection. Standing on the table, straddling his hips and wearing a leather catsuit and knee high black boots was a tiny, muscular woman with blonde, curly hair. If she wasn't in her current position, Mawg would have described her as adorable. But in this particular moment, she was terrifying.

"She scares me…but I like it."

The woman squatted down so she was perched just inches above Dick's very erect dick. She scowled, staring down. "Look at it. LOOK. AT. IT." The Dick looked at his dick and whimpered. She hopped off the table and bent so she was eye-level with it. "Never in the history of micro-penises has there been one this small."

"Daaaaaaaaaaaaamn!"

Unable to hide the complete shock, Mawg's hand flew up to her mouth as she watched the Dick's dick get so hard that it twitched, and he began to plead. "I have the tiniest dick in the world, Mistress Nikki. It could never please any woman, let alone you. I am not worthy of you, Mistress!"

Mistress Nikki walked to stand by his head, the heels of her boots clacking against the hardwood floor. She leaned forward to stare directly into Dick's eyes and said, "No, you are not. And that's why you'll never have me." Then she slapped his face.

The sound of Mawg's gasp echoed around the room, and Mistress Nikki turned around to see them standing in the doorway. Making eye contact with Gina, her face immediately morphed into the biggest grin. She mouthed "one minute" and turned back to Dick. Leaning down, she looked into his eyes and whispered menacingly, "You're going to lay here and think about how unworthy you are, and when I get back that tiny dick better still be hard."

The man whimpered, "Yes Mistress."

"Will you let her slap me? I really want her to slap me and call me a naughty demon."

Mistress Nikki turned and came over to the door, shooing them out into the hallway. She pulled the door shut and her countenance immediately changed. "Oh my God, Gina! It's been almost a month, where have you been!" She grabbed Gina in a bear hug, then turned her smile to Mawg. "Hi! I don't think we've ever met. Are you new?"

"Oh we have a lot of catching up to do! Nikki, this is Mawg. Mawg, this is Nikki." Gina quipped as she introduced the two.

Stretching out her hand to shake, Nikki stopped her with a twinkle in her eye and said, "Ooooh, let's save that for after I wash my hands."

"Bwahahahaha you almost got sweaty bald guy juice on your hand!"

Pulling her hand back with a smile, Mawg said, "I'll definitely take a raincheck on that."

"Nikki, this is Mawg's first time at The Church. I'm taking her on the tour." Gina explained.

"Oh how fun," Nikki said, her eyes lighting up. "I hope you're enjoying it so far!"

Mawg laughed. "My eyes are truly being opened." Then a thought came to her. "Hey just out of curiosity, how come the other women go by Jane but you use your real name?"

"Oh Mistress Nikki is the pseudonym I use for work, it's not my real name. I'm a dominatrix by trade."

Mawg's eyes widened. "Wait…I don't understand. You get paid to treat men like that?"

With a bit of pride in her laugh, Nikki explained, "If that's what they want. I'm not a sex worker, if that's what you're thinking. Doms can fulfill desires without sex being involved. Normally, it's not this performative, but that's what the client likes, sooo…" She trailed off and shrugged.

Mawg's face scrunched in confusion. "So that man in the room wants you to belittle him?"

Nikki nodded. "He does. He gets pleasure from me degrading him. It's known as a humiliation kink. He wants me to degrade him, and he enjoys it even more when he has an audience."

"Whichever demon inhabited her is going to have the best stories to tell at the next gathering."

Face frozen in awe, Mawg said, "So he pays you to treat him horribly and expects nothing in return?"

"If it's a one-on-one experience outside the club, then yes the client pays me. But when I'm here, I'm a paid contractor for The Church." Nikki winked.

Turning to Gina with eyes enormous and full of wonder, she blurted out, "I've been going about this career thing all wrong!"

Unable to hold back, Gina and Nikki burst out laughing. "This is a pretty extreme version of what I do. If you'd ever like to sit down and discuss it sometime, I'll gladly give you a more in-depth rundown of the Dom/Sub dynamic. There's a lot more nuance than what you see here." Nikki took the time to explain.

Nikki seemed like a genuinely nice person, and Mawg took an instantaneous liking to her. "I would love that, thank you."

With a warm smile, Nikki said, "I've got to get back in there, but can we catch up later?"

"Of course! Go play with your Dick and we'll see you in a bit." Gina replied.

"Nice to meet you," Mawg said, giving her a wave.

Nikki grinned. "You too! And that offer is open any time you want to talk!" Then she opened the door, heels clacking on the hardwood as she walked back in the room and yelled, "That tiny dick looks flaccid to me!"

Mawg and Gina turned to each other and burst into laughter as they walked away. Mawg said, "If I saw her on the street, I would NEVER have expected that."

"I think I'm in love."

With a mischievous chuckle and tiny nod Gina kept walking. "Nikki is amazing, and a complete professional, too. This is actually a good intro to a conversation about the Dom/Sub relationship. Are you familiar with that outside of what you've seen in movies or books?"

Shaking her head, Mawg thought about the few examples she'd seen on TV and in movies. "No, I always assumed it was people wearing a lot of leather straps, and one person would be mean to the other. It looks kind of scary, if I'm being completely honest."

"I bet it would be less scary if we got the leather straps in pink. I'll be on the hunt for those and the ass-less chaps...don't think I forgot."

Gina smiled at the description. "I mean, I don't blame you for your misunderstanding of it. That's often times how it's portrayed by the outside world. But in the world of kinks, the sub actually has power."

Mawg's brow furrowed in confusion. That didn't make any sense to her.

Gina noted the confusion and continued. "The Dom may be the one initiating the activity, but the Sub is the one who wants to be in that position. So from the outside, it might look like the Dom is in charge. But in reality, the Dom is responding to what the Sub wants or needs. Before any Dom/Sub relationship begins, a tremendous amount of trust must be built up, and clear communication is vital."

She paused, gauging Mawg's reaction. "The Dom can continue to push and test boundaries, but the moment the Sub invokes their safe word, everything stops immediately. It's a balance of power."

"I think I get the concept…I just don't understand the desire. Maybe I'm just too independent to enjoy the idea of giving someone control over me."

Gina stared silently with a knowing look, then sauntered in front of her until bare inches separated them. Because Gina was taller, she looked down on Mawg, her gaze locked on Mawg's eyes. Mawg felt her heart speed up and heat ran up the back of her neck. In a low tone, Gina leaned down near her ear and said, "Maybe someday you'll discover the right teacher, and you'll learn that giving up control can bring freedom. If you ever want to learn, I know someone who would be perfect. I've been a Dom for years, and so has he. He's a great teacher."

Mawg gulped. She envisioned Gina dressed like Mistress Nikki, and couldn't determine if she was terrified or turned on.

"That might be my fault. I was dreaming about one yelling at me while the other slapped me. Sorry 'bout that."

Gina stepped back to a more comfortable social distance and said, "I do want to give you some homework, though. After you leave here, watch the movie *'Secretary'* with James Spader. That's a good introduction to the Dom/Sub relationship, in my personal opinion. Then come back and let's talk more about it."

Mawg loved James Spader, so that didn't even feel like homework. She smiled and said, "Deal."

They neared the end of the first hallway and Gina asked, "Do you want to continue, or would you like to take a break and have that drink before we hit the other side? We've been here long enough for another round."

Processing everything and sitting for a minute sounded like a good plan. "Let's grab a drink first." They wandered back to the main area of The Church and found a sofa where they could rest. Gina caught the attention of a server nearby and requested their drinks. While they were waiting, Mawg noticed the main stage had been set up and there was now a gorgeous burlesque dancer performing a bawdy number that had the crowd roaring.

Settling into the couch, Gina asked, "So what questions do you have so far?"

Mawg continued to watch the burlesque dancer remove a glove as she thought about the question. "I guess if I were going to be a participant in any of the activities, I'd want to know how you guarantee the safety of everyone involved. How do you know someone isn't a creeper?"

"Excellent question," Gina replied. "In the past five years since I've been here, there's been one incident of someone getting out of line and it was handled immediately before anyone got hurt. This club has a membership. We don't let anyone come into the main room off the street. Anyone can have a drink in the front reception bar, but this back room is reserved for members only, and requires an assigned key card to get in. That's another reason why you didn't immediately see the door to the back. Anyone who applies for membership goes through a vetting process and an extensive interview with myself and the owner. And we also have anywhere from three to eight security personnel scheduled at all times."

"Oh wow," Mawg said. "I don't mean to look a gift horse in the mouth, but how did I get approved to get the tour without the vetting and interview?"

"Actually," Gina smiled and said, "you did get vetted. When Tori called me earlier, she gave me your first name and I did a little research about you online. Your name is unique so you were easy to find."

Mawg's eyebrows raised. "Ahhhh, so you already knew I was pretty boring then."

Tilting her head, Gina gave Mawg a soft smile. "Mawg, you are anything but boring. Most people would have walked in, seen the activity in the first room, and walked right back out. You have a curiosity about you. Curious people aren't boring."

"Don't wear the loafers or she'll change her mind."

Mawg thought, "Say one more thing about my wardrobe and I will find the person with the funkiest smelling mouth and let them have their way with you."

"Hag!"

This might be the first time in her life that someone thought she was curious. Mawg's heart warmed at Gina's comment, and she continued to people watch as the server returned with their drinks. She was still blown away at the variety of body types roaming the floor. There were people who were thick, thin, and somewhere in-between.

Gina noticed her surveying the room. "Penny for your thoughts?"

Mawg contemplated as she watched a short, heavy-set brunette, wearing only pasties and a thong, give a lap dance to a woman with purple hair and a matching catsuit. "As someone who has spent the past forty-four years of my life battling self-esteem issues, it baffles me to see people of all shapes and sizes running around buck naked without a care in the world." She turned to look Gina in the eye. "How does one become confident enough to do that?"

Gina sipped her wine and said, "Confidence is a by-product. A member must first feel they are safe. Once safety has been established, they can open themselves to being vulnerable. Everyone with a membership is here for their own reason, and no one judges that reason. They spend their hard-earned money to come here and find fulfillment they don't have in the outside world. We all have needs and desires, Mawg. And the size or shape of a person shouldn't determine if they deserve to have those needs fulfilled."

"See, meatsuits don't matter."

It sounded so simple the way she explained it. Mawg tried to envision herself standing naked at the bar, having a random conversation with a stranger about the weather while waiting for a gin and tonic. She subconsciously laid her arm across her apron belly while playing out the scene in her head.

Continuing to study Mawg, Gina said, "I'm going to ask you a very personal question. Once again, if it makes you uncomfortable just tell me to mind my own business." Mawg gulped her cocktail nervously and nodded.

"Do you have a fantasy? You know…something you think of when nobody's watching and you're home alone with your vibrator?"

She choked on her drink and began to cough. Gina patted her on the back while she attempted to regain her composure. As she wiped her mouth with a napkin, Mawg blushed to even consider speaking the words aloud.

"If this involves anything with feet, we're outta here."

Gina could see her hesitation and said, "Mawg, there's no need to be embarrassed here. Anything you see happening I've tried at least once. I'm the last person in the world who would judge you."

Mawg thought about it for a moment and closed her eyes. She already had the picture in her head, because it was always the same fantasy.

"Ok," she said in a small voice. "It's almost always the same visual. I'm in a dark room, lit only by candles. I'm naked on a bed, tied down, spread eagle, and wearing a mask so I can't see. There's a very sexy man with dark hair and dark eyes in the room. He's teasing me, touching every part of my body except the one area that is screaming to be touched. He relentlessly runs his fingertips lightly over my skin, over and over again. He replaces his fingers with the tip of his tongue and continues the assault. Between trips up and down my body, he whispers filthy, delicious things in my ear. With the mask on, I can't see anything so my senses are heightened, and every touch is lighting me on fire. He gets me so aroused that..." Mawg trailed off, embarrassed to finish the sentence.

Gina clapped her hands together and said, "No seriously, please proceed. This is really steamy and I'm here for it!"

"Yeah, finish it. I'm learning a whole new side of naughty Mawg!"

Mawg's lips turned up in a small smile, then she closed her eyes once more. It was more comfortable to describe it without seeing Gina watching her. "He gets me so aroused that I'm wet without him even touching me…there. That turns HIM on, and when I beg him to touch me, he kneels before me and buries his face between my thighs. Then he pulls out one of those vibrating massagers…you know, the ones that look like a microphone with a cushioned ball on the end of them? And then all hell breaks loose as he's going to town on me with his mouth, fingers and the vibrator. I cum over and over, so many times I can't walk when he's finished. He has to carry me to the shower and wash me off."

Mawg nervously opened her eyes, hoping Gina wouldn't be laughing at her. Instead she found Gina's eyes fixated on her. She waited for Gina to laugh, but the laugh never came.

Gina leaned in with a smile on her face and began to speak conspiratorially. "Mawg…remember earlier when you said you couldn't understand why a Sub would want to be a Sub?" Mawg nodded, and Gina slowly raised an eyebrow and gave her a smirk.

Mawg's eyes widened as Gina said, "Sometimes Subs enjoy being tied up. I didn't expect that to be your fantasy, based on what you described to me about needing control. Why does it feel more comfortable to you in this scenario, just out of curiosity?"

In her mind's eye, Mawg immediately envisioned the man. "Because it's my fantasy and I made the man up, so I'm still in control of what he does. He doesn't try to coerce me into doing things I'm uncomfortable with."

Gina leaned her chin on her hand and her eyes lit up, like she had a secret that she wasn't sharing. Mawg was feeling a little hot and bothered and didn't notice the knowing smile. As they both grabbed a drink to cool down, Mawg took a moment to scan the room. It was much busier now, with groups of people milling everywhere. Naked bodies were grinding on clothed bodies, hands were groping, mouths were kissing, licking, and sucking.

"It's starting to smell like musty meatsuits in here."

Peri wasn't wrong. The mood in the room was palpable and the sexual desire was like a heavy fog, floating across the air. As she continued to scan the area, a pair of staring eyes caught her attention.

She wouldn't say he was literally the man from her fantasy, but he was damn close. He was leaning with one arm on the bar, but if he stood up straight, she'd estimate him to be about 6'2 or 6'3. He was wearing all black, the top two buttons of his shirt unbuttoned and his sleeves rolled up. From this distance she couldn't see a lot of details (thanks, deteriorating eyesight), but he seemed to be built like a swimmer with broad shoulders and a lean, muscular form. She knew his eyes were as dark as night, because he was staring at her. Staring hard. His tousled dark hair and beard made him look just the right amount of dangerous to be sexy, but not scary. It was hard to tell from this distance, but she pegged him to be somewhere in his thirties. When he noticed Mawg returning his stare, he slowly nodded his head and raised his glass as if to say hello, never breaking eye contact.

"Oh my demon, I can feel your lady bits tingling all the way down here!"

Mawg blushed and nodded back to the sexy stranger, then turned to Gina who had witnessed the entire interaction with a knowing smile on her face. She took a sip of her drink and said, "I think you're about to lose our bet."

Mawg peeked back over at the man, hopeful, but he finished his drink and walked off with the glass toward the other hallway.

Disappointed but not willing to show it, Mawg turned back at Gina and laughed. "I wouldn't count your chickens quite yet."

Both ladies finished their drinks and Gina asked, "Ready for round two?"

Mawg nodded and they took off for the hallway on the other side of the room. The first room had the door shut, but the blinds were open. As they neared the window, Peri chimed in.

"You know what I'd like to see? A pegging. I haven't seen a good pegging since the 80's."

Mawg peered through the window and saw a giant bed that was actually three full-sized beds put together. On the bed were six naked people entangled with each other, two Dicks and four Janes. The two Dicks were laying side by side on the bed, with the four Janes working together above them. Each Dick had a Jane kneeling between his legs performing oral, and another sitting on his face. The Janes straddling their faces were positioned so they were facing the Janes performing oral. One of the Janes that was straddling a man's face turned her head toward the window and made direct eye contact with Mawg. Mawg's eyes widened and her jaw dropped.

It was her now former co-worker, Shannon.

Shannon's eyes flew open wide as she recognized Mawg. Peri chuckled.

"It might be awkward, but clearly not enough to stop smushing her meatsuit into that man's face."

Mawg turned on her heel and scurried away from the window so she was out of Shannon's view. Her breath was caught in her throat, but she wasn't sure if it was because she saw Shannon, or because Shannon saw her. She'd forgotten to respond to her text after Julie's phone call this morning, and this was not how she envisioned their next interaction.

"Oh you saw her alright."

Mawg face was disgusted as she glared down at Peri and attempted to keep that image out of her mind. "Shut up or I'll ask Gina if they have gelatin here."

"I bet you a week's worth of snackies they do. In a place like this, it's probably guaranteed."

Noticing something spooked Mawg had Gina concerned. "Is everything okay?"

Mawg laughed and nervously began straightening her dress. "I know someone in that room. We weren't… um…expecting to see each other here."

"Ahhh," Gina said, her eyes sparking with understanding as she nodded. "Yes, that can be a bit of a shock. Is it a friend, family member, or foe?"

Mawg was looking off at the wall. "She's a work friend…er, former work friend. From the job I got fired from today."

"Hmm," Gina murmured and clasped her hands behind her back. "It is completely up to you to decide how you'd like to handle this. However, if you want my two cents, I suggest having a conversation with the person. You're both adults, and you're both here, so…" She let the sentence trail off and watched Mawg, who was wringing her hands together.

"Oh for fuck's sake, you're an adult. She's an adult. It's not that big of a deal."

About that time, Shannon, now clad in a robe, popped her head out the door. "Mawg?"

Gina squeezed Mawg's arm and said, "I'll give you two a minute," and took a few steps down the hall.

Shannon strode over to Mawg, a look of concern on her face. Mawg couldn't get the visual of what she'd just seen out of her mind, and was looking anywhere except at Shannon's face.

"Mawg…honey are you okay? Do you want to go sit down?" Shannon reached out and touched her upper arm, her brow furrowed with concern.

Looking up to meet her gaze, she realized she was being ridiculous. Peri was right, they were both grown adults and they were both here. It might be surprising, but it was no reason to be rude.

"Shannon, I…I'm sorry. That just caught me off-guard and I wasn't prepared. I didn't realize…" She let the sentence trail off, not sure how to finish her thought.

Shannon grinned. "You didn't realize I like to get a little freaky. It's ok, Mawg. If our roles were reversed, I would have felt the same shock."

Mawg's awkwardness started to dissolve and she chuckled. "I mean…I…ok, I have so many questions right now!"

Shannon's smile morphed into a huge grin. "I bet you do! I remember my first time touring and all the wild things running through my head! Listen, go finish your tour with Gina, and then call me this weekend. I'll gladly answer any questions you have."

She reached out and hugged Mawg, whispering, "And have yourself some fun tonight. You deserve it after putting up with Julie's bullshit for so long." As Shannon pulled back and grinned, Mawg's awkwardness toward the situation melted away. Her friend was living her best life, and Mawg was happy for her.

As Shannon walked back to the room, Mawg turned to find Gina watching her. "Everything okay?"

She paused for a moment as she listened to the sounds of the people passing by in the hallway. Everyone seemed so comfortable here. Mawg smiled as she met Gina's eyes. "Yeah. Yeah, everything is great, actually."

Gina grinned and said, "Wonderful. Shall we continue?"

The next room had closed blinds and doors, so they moved along to the last room in the hallway. Before they got near the window, Gina stopped Mawg and said, "Wait here and give me one sec." She disappeared into the open doorway.

While she was gone, Mawg leaned against the wall and reminisced about her day. In less than twenty-four hours, she'd woken to learn demons were real, gotten fired from her job, been gifted a beautiful dress, met two new friends, and found herself at an erotic club watching people have sex. This was so wild and unrealistic, she expected to wake up any moment.

"But you're having fun, aren't you."

It wasn't really a question, more of a statement because he already knew the answer. Mawg looked down at her toe. "I am, as unexpected as that is. And don't get all cocky. Tori and Gina were a huge part of making this day a success."

"And you wouldn't have met them without me, so happy birthday."

As Mawg sighed at Peri in exasperation, Gina came back out to the hallway. "Let's watch this next one in the room. Are you okay with that?"

Palms sweaty as the nerves kicked in, Mawg said, "I am…as long as I'm not expected to participate."

Gina's eyes were empathetic as she reached out to Mawg's clammy hand. "Not at all. Remember, you're in control and you set the boundaries. Observing is perfectly welcome and acceptable." The blinds were closed as they passed the window. Gina noticed her confusion. "This will be a private viewing party."

Eyebrows raised in curiosity, Mawg stepped into the room as Gina closed the door behind them.

It was pitch black, save for a small light centered directly above the padded table in the middle of the room. The table looked custom made, with two leather straps on one end spread about three feet apart, and two leather straps on the other end, but much closer together. Currently in those straps were a woman's hands and feet. With her body bare except a pair of red stiletto heels, she was stunning. Her frame was voluptuous and her skin glistened. Her arms were strapped together above her head and her feet were split apart, locked in leather. Her eyes were covered in a black blindfold.

Dark and primal music was piped in low over the speakers in the corners, and Mawg felt something begin to stir inside of her…this was very reminiscent of the fantasy she'd just described not fifteen minutes before. With the right partner, she would love to be the woman on the table. Her palms began to sweat, and she felt that familiar tingle in her "lady bits" as Peri would say.

Mawg was staring at the generous curve of Jane's hip when she noticed a shadowed movement in the corner. A small night light flickered on, and there in the shadows sat the mystery man from across the bar. Leaning in a chair with an arm draped across the back, he held the glass which now contained nothing but melting ice. Now that she was closer, Mawg could see the corded muscles in his forearm as his long fingers grasped the glass. From far away, she had pegged him to be in his early to mid thirties. Up close, she noted the wrinkles etched in the corner of his eyes and the sprinkle of grey in his beard and near his temples. He had to be at least forty. Either way, he had no business looking this damn good. Mawg's underwear were already damp and they hadn't even begun.

"Oh demon dammit…if you ruin the dress, it's on you to explain it to Tori."

Mawg thought, "Shut. The Fuck. Up."

Their eyes locked.

He stood up.

Her heart raced.

Mawg's face was flushed, and she felt a warmth spreading through her body.

"Um…not to ruin your moment, but I think that's another hot flash."

The man broke eye contact and walked over to Jane on the table. Placing a hand on her shoulder, he asked, "Are you ready to give these ladies a show?"

Dear God, he had an Irish accent.

Jane smiled and nodded. The man pushed the hair back from her brow and put earbuds in her ears. "The usual playlist?" She gave a thumbs up. He set the music up for Jane, then glanced over to Gina and Mawg.

Gina took a moment to interrupt. "Mawg, this is Declan. Declan, this is Mawg. It's her first time visiting The Church."

Mortification set in. Her name sounded so clunky in this particular moment. The self-esteem she'd gained throughout the day took a dip.

Declan sauntered over and stood in front of Mawg as he continued to gaze into her eyes. She was flushed and awkward, not knowing what to say or do. He leaned down to her ear and said, "We're going to do a study in sensuality tonight, Mawg. I hope you'll enjoy the lesson as much as I'll enjoy watching you learn." His voice was deep and raspy, and that accent… He surprised her, lifting her hand and kissing the top of it like she was some high lady in an English court.

She felt his fingers slide against her palm as he released her hand, and every cell in her body woke to his touch. Mawg was in complete shock, unable to move.

"Things I learned about Mawg today: She's a whore for an accent."

She had no idea what to say, so she stared, caught in his gaze. The combination of the accent, his cologne, and those chocolate brown eyes were causing new and strange sensations in her body.

With a devilish grin, he turned his attention to Jane. His fingertips grazed the left side of her neck down to her shoulder, causing the blindfolded Jane to gasp in shock at his touch. He worked his way down the left side of her body at a torturously slow pace. When he reached the first stiletto, he rounded it and continued to travel up the inside of her thigh. His fingers danced across her lower lips, but never entered. Jane inhaled sharply at the teasing promise of that touch. He continued the feather-light assault, stalking around the table and outlining her entire body ever so slowly. By the time he got back up to her right shoulder, the pace of Jane's breath had increased and she was beginning to release little moans.

Mawg's eyes were glued to Declan's hands.

"What is it with you and phalanges?"

Ignoring Peri, Mawg focused on the show before her. Declan strode back to his corner to grab something, slowly turning on his heel to return to the table. In between his fingertips was an ice cube that he was now dangling above Jane's body, allowing icy cold droplets to drip on her smooth skin. She gasped, unprepared for the unexpected cold. Mawg watched as he grazed the ice cube across Jane's very hard nipple. Her back arched involuntarily as she mumbled, "Oh god". Mawg looked up from the display to find Declan's eyes locked on her as Jane's noises were progressively getting louder. He removed the ice cube from the nipple and slid it down the center of her body until he reached her apex. Jane was fully waxed, and Mawg watched her hips buck as Declan picked up the ice cube in his hand to squeeze water on her lower lips and inner thighs.

With her nipples hard as diamonds, a panting Jane was clearly having an enjoyable evening. Removing the ice cube, Declan replaced it with his lips.

"He looks like he's bobbing for apples."

Not taking her eyes off Declan, Mawg slammed her toe into the ground.

"Hey! You'll pay for that when we get home!"

She didn't care if Peri gave her fifteen chin hairs. Jane's nipple was alternating back and forth between the ice cube and his mouth. Over and over, he continued the barrage. All Jane could get out was "Oh God, Oh God!" as she continued to arch her back, begging for the sweet torture.

Moving to the other side of the table to even out the torment on Jane's body, Declan looked up to meet Mawg's lust-filled eyes. The devilish smile returned and he held out the dripping ice cube in his fingertips. "Would you care to assist me?"

With eyes wide, Mawg looked over to Gina who smiled and raised an eyebrow saying, "You're the one who decides your boundaries."

"Just do it, you know you wanna."

"Is…is she okay with that?" Her voice was shaky as she pointed to Jane. Mawg had no idea what she was doing, but curiosity got the best of her.

"She is." Declan replied. "We discussed it before you came in, just in case." He gave her a little wink.

As if she was about to walk on broken glass, she paused and then took one step forward. Declan's eyes lit up and he gestured for Mawg to stand in front of him. As she did, he lifted her right hand palm up and placed the ice cube in it. His cologne enveloped her as her wet palm began to chill. She felt his chest against her back as the raspy voice murmured in her ear, "Hold it with your fingertips." He needed to stop whispering to her like that, or she was going to melt into the floor. "Good, now circle her areola with it, but don't run it across the nipple quite yet." Mawg was nervous, her hand shaking as she reached it toward Jane. Sensing her hesitation, Declan laid a calming hand over hers. "We'll do it together." The ice cube, pinched between her thumb and forefinger, touched down on Jane's sensitive skin. His hand guided Mawg's in a circle, and she felt the edge of her thumb brush Jane's nipple.

"Boobies!"

Mawg was a little out of her element. She had never touched a woman's body in a sexual way.

"Wait…this is your first booby?! Aw, I feel so honored to be here for this moment!"

Declan gently pulled Mawg's hand back and said, "Let's repeat what I was doing on the other side. I'll warm it up, and you'll cool it down. Sound good?" He tilted his head and smiled.

"If he asked you to chop up a body and bury it right now, you'd do it."

Mawg wanted Peri to be wrong, but…Declan gestured for her to run the ice cube over Jane's nipple. She did, as Jane arched and moaned once again. He gently pulled Mawg's hand back. Leaning down and turning his head slightly to look at her, Declan ran the tip of his tongue over Jane's nipple…never breaking eye contact with Mawg. Jane cried out, and so did Mawg's hormones.

"Unholy shit! Do you have any idea how loud your pheromones are?! It's like your meatsuit is screaming "ME, ME….PICK ME!"

Continuing to ignore Peri, her eyes locked with Declan's. The lust in the room was as thick as she was. Declan removed his mouth, then it was Mawg's turn with the ice. This went on for three more rounds, until Jane was moaning and begging for the torment to descend lower. Declan stepped back and turned Mawg around to face him. Reaching down for her now wet hand, he kissed the top of it once again. "You can be my assistant anytime, Sweet Mawg." She could see Gina in her peripheral vision, mouth agape.

Gina! Jesus, Mawg had completely forgotten she was in the room. Turning her back to walk away, she looked over as Gina's wordless expression screamed, "Oh my God, we are

SOOOOO going to gossip about this later!" Mawg just grinned, falling back in line beside her to observe the show. Peri piped up in his best attempt at a Valley girl accent.

"Oh my demon, let's stay up all night and talk about cute boys!"

Mawg thought, "What did you expect when you brought me to a sex club, a discussion about current world events? It was YOUR idea to come here. You obviously knew what this place was, so don't get all pissy that I'm starting to enjoy myself. Deal with it, and we'll get extra snackies when we leave." Peri sighed and his little face pouted, his annoyance showing.

"Oh I get a reward for being a good little demon. Lucky me."

They continued to watch as Declan grabbed a vibrator off the corner table. Mawg thought, "Is it just me, or do all women react like Pavlov's dog and get excited when they hear that buzz?"

"Fair question. All my cohabitants loved those things. You shoulda seen the wild shit you all were shoving inside yourselves before those were invented."

Declan lightly trailed the vibrator along the inside of Jane's thighs, and she had a sharp intake of breath. His other hand lightly slapped her hip. Mawg could think of nowhere she'd rather be right now than watching this man go to work.

"That's a bold lie, you'd rather be ON the table."

Declan watched Mawg as he continued to tease around Jane's most sensitive area, never touching it. The more Jane moaned and begged, the more Declan's eyes bore into Mawg. Slowly, he slid two fingers down the slit and spread Jane wide open, letting the cool breeze from the fan overhead dance across the warm, wet skin.

"I just realized why they call them meat curtains…he parted the curtains."

Mawg looked down at her toe with a glare and thought, "Do not EVER use that stupid phrase again or you'll bathe in gelatin every night for a week."

Jane was almost in tears, begging Declan, "Please…oh god please, I can't take anymore." With one hand holding her open, the vibrator in the other hand was placed lightly against Jane's very wet and swollen clit.

She bucked so hard, Mawg thought she was going to break the straps and bounce off the table. Declan, knowing it was time to give Jane the release she wanted, slid the vibrator inside Jane. She begged, "Yes! Yes, more!" He removed the now soaked vibrator and continued teasing it against her swollen clit. Jane was feral, bucking and screaming "Fuck me! Oh God, please fuck me!"

"For fuck's sake, Dicklan…put the poor woman out of her misery."

And dear sweet Jesus, he did. Keeping her open with one hand, Declan began the assault Jane yearned for with the vibrator. Over and over again, he slid it into her. When he knew she was close to release, he removed it and placed it against her swollen clit. Then he slid three fingers inside her. Jane was wild, trying to use the little leverage she had to bury the vibrator against her clit as Declan slid his fingers in and out of her, each thrust faster and reaching deeper. With one final, primal scream, Jane came so hard that the entire bottom half of the table was drenched.

As Jane lay panting, Declan removed his glistening fingers and looked from them to Mawg. Jane continued breathing hard on the table and whispered "Oh my god, thank you." He squeezed her shoulder affectionately, stepping back from the table. Mawg's eyes were drawn to the impressive bulge in his pants momentarily. Raising her gaze, she realized he caught her staring. His dark eyes smoldered, like he could read the filthy thoughts running through her head. He sauntered over to stand directly in front of Mawg, bare inches separating them.

Gazing into her eyes, he raised two of the still-wet fingers to his lips. He placed the fingers in his mouth, slowly drawing them out as he sucked them clean, never breaking eye contact.

"Unholy fuck!"

Mawg's eyes clouded and she whimpered. Declan smiled and leaned down to her ear.

"Until we meet again, sweet Mawg." He turned and walked out the door.

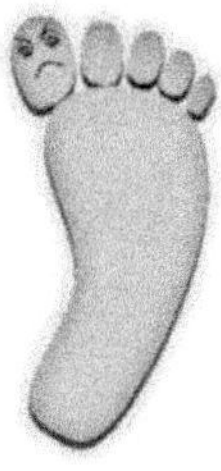

CHAPTER TEN

"I'd like to officially welcome you as the newest employee of The Church." Gina clapped Mawg on the back with a huge smile.

Finally recovered, Jane rose from the table. Removing the blindfold and earbuds, she said, "Oh hey, Gina! I didn't know you would be here." She looked at Mawg and winked with a cheeky grin. "Welcome to The Church." Gathering her things in her arms, Jane strode out the door, buck naked and ass swinging as her stilettos clacked down the hallway.

Mawg was too stunned to speak. Her mind couldn't stop replaying the visual as he'd stared into her soul and licked his fingers. She felt wild, like a caged animal that needed to be released was prowling inside her. Never had Mawg experienced desire this intense, and the sensation overwhelmed her like an unexpected tidal wave.

"Easy there, cougar. You look like you're gonna pounce on the next man that walks by."

Peri's voice shook her out of her reverie and she looked at Gina, who was still grinning from ear to ear. "I….I don't think I've quite processed what just happened."

Gina laughed and replied, "Honestly, I don't know if I have either! I know Declan very well, and I have NEVER seen him look at someone the way he looked at you tonight. That was intense, Mawg!"

In the past decade or so, Mawg had stopped searching for romantic or sexual fulfillment from men. She was tired…so tired of trying to fit into the box of what was "acceptable" or "desirable". It had been made clear to her time and time again that who she was, at her core, wasn't what they wanted. And instead of trying to contort herself to fit into those pre-approved boxes, she'd found herself ensconced in projects and hobbies. For her mental health, she'd thought it was better that way.

"But it wasn't better. Do not lie to yourself to stifle your feelings. You gave up because a few people said awful things, and you allowed that to marinate in your brain."

Maybe she had. But tonight, the way Declan looked at her like she was a tray of desserts to be devoured…it woke something within Mawg. Something that felt wild and untapped. She felt desired for the first time in her life.

"And she also discovered a fetish for fingers."

Mawg looked down at Peri. "Eat a ginormous bag of dicks." She turned to Gina and pulled herself together. "I think that might be a good finale for tonight's tour." Gina threw her head back and laughed. "Fair enough, there's a snack bar in the back. Let's go grab a bite and we'll chat about your new career adventure."

"SNACKIEEEES!!"

Her growling stomach confirmed it was a good time to feed Peri before he turned into an asshole. They walked over to the charcuterie-style snack bar, grabbed a few things and found a seat. Mawg was surveying the area and noticed Mistress Nikki and the Dick with the humiliation kink sitting away from the crowds on a couch in the corner. Her arm was wrapped around him and he leaned into her, crying as she stroked his hair.

Mawg's eyes were wide and Gina must have felt her distress. She leaned over and whispered, "Remember when I said there's much more to the Dom/Sub relationship than what you've seen in movies? One massive part of that relationship that is always overlooked is aftercare."

Mawg's head tilted to the side and her face scrunched in confusion as Gina nodded her head toward Nikki and the Dick. "Both parties have a responsibility to each other. Yes, the Sub wants to be in that position, but they're also opening themselves up to a tremendous amount of vulnerability. Try to imagine what you would feel like if you were in his position on that table."

Immediately, she felt a sense of panic at the thought of being humiliated in front of a crowd of people. She watched as Nikki stroked the man's hair, comforting him the way a mother would comfort a child.

Gina continued, "In the same respect, the Dom requires aftercare as well. You've met Nikki. Do you think she's someone who enjoys demeaning people in her day-to-day life?"

Mawg shook her head vehemently. No, that was the last thing she would picture Nikki doing.

"It's a role for her as well. She has to walk a tremendously fine line between doing what the client asks and not breaking them. They come to her to feel better…to heal. That's a huge responsibility on her, and she will need time after she's done comforting the Dick to release the weight of that responsibility."

Mawg sat back, absentmindedly playing with the hem of her dress, trying to process all this new information. Everything she'd assumed about this world was wrong, and that hit her hard. This was not deviance, as she'd been taught. It was raw human vulnerability on display. And it was beautiful.

As she was placing a piece of ham and Swiss on a cracker, Gina switched gears and asked, "Ok so, that last steamy moment aside, how do you feel about your first Church experience?"

Mawg chewed and held up her finger to signify *let me finish this bite*, then said, "If you asked me this morning if I would feel comfortable being in a sex club, I would have been so mortified that we probably never would have spoken again. But after tonight's experience…I'm quite surprised at how comfortable I feel here."

"You're comfortable with gettin' that Dicklan in ya."

She internally snarled at Peri and indicated that he should shut the fuck up.

"That's wonderful, Mawg! This place is a unique world that allows vulnerability and no judgement. To be quite honest, that's overwhelming for a lot of people. I'm glad to hear you find comfort in it. Now, with that being said…How do you feel about starting on Monday?"

"I can't believe you're serious about the job offer. How do you know I'd be any good at this? What if I'm a terrible concierge?" Mawg chuckled.

Gina shrugged. "Then we agree to mutually part ways, no harm no foul. Besides, I know you'll be good at the operations side. I vetted you, remember? I already dug through your work history, it's solid. Now it's just a matter of teaching you the concierge side of the business."

She pondered Gina's statement. "I mean, if you're willing to take a chance on me, then I'm willing to give it a go. But don't you need to run it by the owner? Or do they give you carte blanche to make those decisions?"

Gina smiled. "I showed the owner your history and the stamp of approval has been given, as long as I feel like you're a fit…which I do."

"Do it, kiddo. Adventure, remember?"

"Kiddo? I'm a forty-five year-old woman."

"I'm a thousand years old. You're still a kiddo to me."

Mawg looked Gina in the eye, raised her bottle of water and said, "Cheers to a new career adventure." Tapping the bottles together, Gina looked up at the clock.

"This has been so much fun, but unfortunately I've got a few things I need to take care of tonight. Feel free to explore and meet people if you'd like. The Church doesn't close until four o'clock. Just remember the rules about closed blinds and doors and you'll be fine. Oh, and I almost forgot…as an employee, you automatically get full membership status."

"Ohhhhhh, the fuckery I see in your future…"

Mawg's eyes widened. "Oh wow, that's definitely an unusual perk! Gina…I can't thank you enough for tonight. I will forever be grateful for everything."

Smiling as she rose to leave, Gina said, "We'll see how you feel after your first day," she laughed. "Nine a.m. good for you on Monday?"

"Nine a.m. is perfect, I'll see you then."

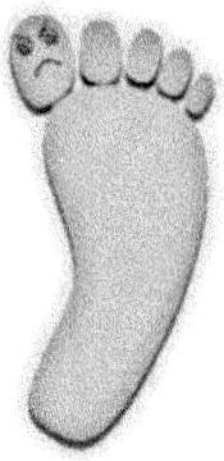

CHAPTER ELEVEN

As Mawg and Peri exited the ride share at her house, her phone read two o'clock in the morning. She couldn't remember the last time she was out this late.

"That's because all the loafer stores close at six o'clock. The average age of their shopper is seventy-two, so they're in bed by seven."

Mawg smiled and put the key in the locked front door. "You know, even your smart ass can't ruin my mood right now."

"Oh my demon, are you still swooning over that man's phalanges?"

Turning up her nose in disgust as the key clicked in the lock, she entered the house. "Would you stop saying phalanges? It sounds icky coming out of your mini mouth."

"I just don't get the human fascination with fingers and toes. It's weird."

Mawg immediately envisioned Declan's fingers buried inside her while those dark and broody eyes stared at her.

"Ew, that's enough. Point made."

"Jesus, is there a way to block you from my thoughts? That's so intrusive and annoying."

"Trust me, I wish there was. But unfortunately, no."

Mawg sighed. As she got to her room and started to remove the beautiful dress and her very wet panties, she couldn't get the image of Declan out of her mind.

Peri also sighed, because he knew what needed to be done.

"Ok listen - let's make a deal. You're clearly not gonna stop thinking about that man until you can...remedy the situation. So I'll try to take a nap while you grab that vibrating mechanism from your drawer and get this out of your system. You won't hear a peep from me, and I'll do everything possible to ignore you. Once that's done, can we PLEASE sleep or think about something else?"

For once, they were fully in agreement. "Deal." Mawg walked over to her sock drawer and grabbed a sock to throw over Peri's face.

"That doesn't prevent me from seeing anything, you know."

"It's not for you. I need to forget you're there."

"Ahhh, understood. Get it done, then."

She put on her socks and nothing else, grabbing the vibrator out of the drawer. She put in her headphones and found a sexy songs playlist. Then she turned on the vibrator, thinking of nothing but Declan for the next twenty minutes.

Apparently she'd fallen asleep the second her late-night adventure reached its peak, because the vibrator was laying between her thighs and she still had her headphones in one ear. This might be the first time Mawg had slept through the night in over a month. She felt glorious.

Sunlight peeked through the curtains, and her phone display read ten o'clock. Holy shit! She scrambled up, forgetting there wasn't a job to rush off to, and realized her pillowcase was soaking wet. So was the hair clinging to the back of her neck.

"Jesus, I know I had a little moment there, but I didn't think it was that good!"

"Good morning, Sunshine. That was me. You left me in that damn sock all night and I was screamin' at ya' to let me out. But apparently floatin' your boat knocked ya' out. I got overheated. And when I get overheated, you get night sweats."

Pulling the sweaty hair off her neck, she stepped into the bathroom where Tori's dress hung on the wall. Memories of the previous day's activities came flooding back, and she looked in the mirror. Normally, she would pick apart every flaw in that reflection. The cellulite on the back of her legs, her apron belly, and her flabby bat wing arms were still there. But today, she saw them with a softer focus. After watching women of all shapes and sizes being confident and pleasured last night, Mawg was feeling more confident about herself. It was a brand new day, and a brand new Mawg.

"Oh...before I forget, here you go."

Peri squeezed his eyes shut. Bam! Mawg watched in the bathroom mirror as a rough and wiry chin hair sprouted out of her skin.

She stared at the hair, peeled off her socks and snarled at her toe. "What the hell, Peri?!"

"That was for slamming me into the floor last night while you were drooling over Dicklan's phalanges."

Mawg grabbed the tweezers to pluck the hair. "Stop calling him that. And it was your own fault. You were being an ass!"

"Some people like to learn lessons the hard way, Mawg. You seem to be one of those people. Those never go away, just FYI. So maybe next time you'll think before you 'stub' me."

She scowled down at Peri. "Someone woke up on the wrong side of the bed this morning."

"I spent my night in a sock while you floated your boat! Of course I'm cranky!"

"Ew, please don't ever call it that again. 'Float the boat' is guaranteed to make the boat sink."

"I don't wanna be anywhere near the boat, for future reference. Now quit being all mad and let's go eat. You still need to take coffee to Tori and fill her in on your shenanigans."

She'd totally forgotten about bringing coffee to Tori. "Shit, we need to get moving." She hopped in for a quick shower, sped through her morning routine, and headed out the door.

They stopped at a drive-thru coffee shop to grab caramel lattes and a croissant breakfast sandwich. Mawg ate on the way to Torific while she listened to Peri lecture about the dangers of eating while driving. When they arrived and entered the front door, the bell alerted Tori and she came out from the back with a ginormous smile on her face.

"Girrrrrrrrrl, I don't know what you did last night, but you must have been impressive!"

"Oh, you don't want to know what she did last night. Buuuzzzzzzzzzzzzzzzzzzz."

Mawg handed Tori the latte with a quizzical look on her face. "Huh? What do you mean?"

Sipping the coffee, Tori groaned in happiness. "Thanks, you have no idea how much I needed this. I'm talking about the phone call I got this morning from Gina. She told me about your new job. Congratulations!"

Chuckling, Mawg said, "I swear I didn't do anything that would impress anyone. But Gina was amazing, and thank you so much for introducing me to her!"

Tori gave her a quick hug and said, "She's fantastic, isn't she? But I was talking about you being my newest client!"

Mawg continued to stare at her with a confused look. "Tori, I have no idea what you're talking about."

"Gina wasn't just calling to say hi. She was calling to set up an account for you. If you work as a concierge, you have to look the part. The Church is paying for a custom-designed Torific wardrobe for you!"

"Hallelujah, we're burnin' the loafers!"

Mawg's jaw dropped. "You're fucking kidding me!"

"I am not. So, finish that coffee and let's start trying things on!"

Mawg was absolutely speechless. She sat sipping her latte while Tori ran around the store grabbing different articles of clothing. She was a whirlwind, yelling from across the store, "we'll need both daytime and evening outfits. You'll be meeting with vendors and members, depending on what time of day you're there."

As Tori made her way to the dressing room to drop off an armful of clothes, Mawg sat down, cradling her coffee with both hands. "Tori…..what am I doing? I have no idea how to be a concierge."

Tori stopped running around and took a moment to look at Mawg's worried countenance. "Hey." Mawg looked up at her. "I've known Gina for a long time. She's confident in her decisions and knows what she wants. If she thinks you can do this, then you can do this."

"I'm not worried about the operations work, but seeing the way Gina handled me last night, I don't know if I would be very good as a concierge. She made me so comfortable there, Tori."

Tori smiled. "Gina will teach you how to explain the club to new people. What will make you good at this is being empathetic. I think you're good at reading the room and reading people. Plus, you have a leg up that other people don't…you have Peri."

"Yeah Mawg, what am I, chopped liver?"

Looking down at Peri, Mawg rolled her eyes. Then looked back at Tori and said, "Why does he give me a leg up?"

"I bring that BDE…Big Demon Energy."

Tori looked at Mawg's toe. "I know you're running your mouth. Shut it."

Mawg almost spit out her coffee laughing, and Peri's little face scrunched up as he pouted.

"One of the effects of Peri inhabiting you," Tori continued, "is you will naturally become more confident. Over the next decade, he'll remove that desire you have to please people. He will also decrease your tolerance for bullshit, which will drive your communication to become more direct. Part of the concierge job will be determining if someone has the right temperament for The Church. While you're in the early stages of this change, Peri can give you insight if you're unsure."

Mawg frowned. "So, you're saying I have to be nice to him then?"

"Hey!"

Tori laughed. "I know this is hard to believe right now, but you're eventually going to love the little shit."

"Listen you hags, I can hear ya! I am glorious and you should be grateful that I selected you. It's a damn honor!"

Tori looked at Mawg. "Is he ranting about how amazing he is?"

Mawg laughed hard, fighting not to spill the coffee. "He is."

"Demon Dammit!"

Tori looked at Mawg's toe and laughed, knowing full well that Peri was still bitching. Then she said, "Come on, let's go create your brand new wardrobe!"

CHAPTER TWELVE

Mawg spent the weekend bouncing back and forth between being so nervous she could vomit, and so excited at her new adventure. She walked into the closet multiple times to stare at the massive pile of clothing she'd brought home from Torific. For the first time in years, she felt alive.

The doorbell rang, which was odd. She wasn't expecting anyone. Mawg opened the front door, curious to see who stopped by, but found no one. Instead, a small pile of packages in RainForest packaging were piled to the left of the door.

She glared down at her toe. "And when exactly did you order from RainForest?"

"Oooh! They weren't lying about the overnight Nile shipping! I took over while you were sleeping and picked up a few things we needed."

Mawg rolled her eyes as she picked up the packages and brought them in. Tearing into the first box, she said, "Please stop buying things without consulti—"

Her eyes got wide as she removed the bubble wrap to reveal a pair of pink assless chaps. Her eyes shot down to her foot. "You did not!" Peri grinned innocently.

"I really thought those were going to be more difficult to find, not gonna lie."

Mawg rubbed her temples as she inhaled deeply, counting to ten. Without responding, she grabbed the other package and began to rip it open. "Is this going to piss me off?"

"Why would fun clothing piss you off?"

She stared at his little eyes as she continued to tear into the packaging. "Peri, I swear to God, I will—"

Suspenders. He'd bought the fucking suspenders. She held them up in the air and stared at her toe, who was now getting defensive.

"Hey, don't get pissy with me. I told you I was going to get them. If you didn't believe me, that's on you."

She gave one last sigh as she rolled her eyes and gathered up her unrequested purchases. Throwing them on the bed, she went back to the living room to start her research.

Taking Gina's advice, she watched '*Secretary*' and took notes so they could discuss it later. Peri shook his little head as she pulled out her legal pad.

"You're the only person I know who watches sex movies and takes notes."

When the movie was finished, she was in the mood to continue her research.

"Oh, I bet ya are."

Googling things about bondage and BDSM didn't give her the results she desired. Deciding to take another new step in life, she grabbed some snacks to keep Peri quiet and pulled up some porn sites. She was blown away at how many categories were available.

"You're about to get quite the education."

She recognized a few things, but others were uncharted territory. She attempted to watch one video from each category, and experienced a wide range of emotions and questions throughout the process.

"Ya know I can help you, right? What kind of questions do you have?"

Mawg thought about it before she looked down at her toe and asked, "I don't understand the whole stepmother, stepsister, stepson category. Absolutely nothing about that turns me on. AT ALL."

"That's somethin' you'll have to come to terms with in this position. There's different strokes for different folks. Whether you personally like something or not, it's not up to you to judge it as long as it's a legal consensual act. Although to be fair, I don't get that one either. I don't think that's gonna be something you see a lot at the club, so I wouldn't get too worried about it. What else ya' got?"

Mawg ate some popcorn and pondered. "Ok, this is more of a life question but it applies here, too. The "barely eighteen" section gives me the absolute ick. Like, I get it if young people want to look at each other, but it feels soooooo gross to see someone that young with a fifty-ish year old man."

"Being that I've got about a thousand years on you, a thirty-year age gap isn't that much to me. However, knowing the societal standards of your species, I can understand why it gives you the ick. BUT, it's legal. And if two consensual adults are fine with it, then how you feel doesn't matter. Working in a job like this, you gotta let that judgement go."

Trying to overcome three decades of misconception in a day was a bit overwhelming to Mawg. "I know, I know…controlling my face may quite possibly be the biggest challenge in this job. Peri…am I doing the right thing, here?"

"Sorry kiddo, but it's not about what I think. You have to decide if this is the right path for you. Here's the thing…I think you should at least give it a try. What's the worst that happens? You find out you don't like looking at weiners all day and you resign and find something else. Easy peasy. But if you don't take the job, I think you'll always wonder about it."

Mawg sighed. "Yeah, you're probably right. Ok, I think that's enough research for tonight. Let's head to bed early so we're ready for this tomorrow."

"Weiner row awaits."

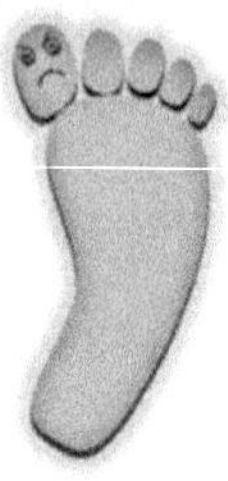

CHAPTER THIRTEEN

Mawg buzzed the doorbell to The Church at five minutes before nine. She chuckled internally, remembering how her mom would always tease her about being early to everything. Mawg would say, "I just think it's rude to be late," even as a young girl. It was ingrained in her Capricorn nature to be responsible.

"You watched way too many of those 80's movies where the hard-workin' girl tried to make it in the big city."

She ignored Peri. She was wearing a black pencil skirt that hit just above the knee and a tailored baby blue button down top. Mawg had no idea how Tori did it. Her clothing fit Mawg like a glove, even without alterations. She really had a gift for dressing women.

The door opened and someone from the cleaning crew let her in. She asked for Gina and they led her through the door to the main room. Once inside, the cleaner directed her to a set of stairs she hadn't noticed the other night. With all the lights on in The Church, it was a stark contrast to the vibe she experienced on her first visit. Noticing the office with the lights on upstairs, she thanked the cleaner and headed up.

Reaching the top of the stairs, she could see Gina through the window, sitting at her desk. She was talking to someone on the phone while staring at her laptop. Noticing Mawg, she smiled and waved her into the office. As Mawg entered the doorway, Gina put up a finger and mouthed "One minute".

Taking a moment to survey the office while Gina finished her call, Mawg noticed five large, framed black and white canvas photos on the surrounding mocha-colored walls. They were all erotica. One had a woman with ropes wrapped all over her body in intricate knots. It was a stunning piece of art. Another was a portrait of a man from the waist up wearing a blindfold with a ball gag in his mouth. As she turned to the next canvas, it struck her like a lighting bolt. It was a middle-aged woman staring at herself in the mirror using one hand to masturbate. The actual woman was average, with cellulite and saggy boobs with stretch marks. Her expression was pained, like she didn't want to see herself. She stood stiff and looked uncomfortable. The image in the mirror was the same woman, but she looked relaxed, softer…happy. Her expression was that of confidence, not a care in the world.

"It's quite bold, isn't it?" Gina asked, as she walked up beside Mawg, startling her. So engrossed in the artwork, she missed the end of Gina's call. "It is. Gina…have you ever felt like the woman staring in the mirror?"

Gina studied the canvas, then looked back to Mawg. "I think we can all empathize with her insecurity on some level. I don't feel that way about my body, but there are plenty of reasons I've felt insecure."

She couldn't imagine Gina being self-conscious about anything. "I wish I had your body confidence. I feel like her every morning when I'm getting ready."

Gina's eyes softened. "By the time you're finished with training, that feeling will dissipate. I promise you that. Ok, let's get your paperwork done and get that stuff out of the way. Then we'll walk through an overview of how this place runs. Sound good?"

Mawg smiled and gave a little salute. "Ready and reporting for duty."

The morning passed quickly, full of all the boring paperwork that happens at every new job. They had breakfast sandwiches while Gina explained the daily routine. The Church closed at four AM every day, so the cleaners would show up at five AM. The sanitation process was intensive due to the nature of activities occurring nightly. Gina explained there was storage behind the stage where all the props were kept; beds, tables, toys, costumes, lubricants, candles, lighting, etc.

"Ask her about the gelatin. I guarantee they keep gelatin on hand."

Anything a member could possibly want for their evening was available. Members could call ahead and reserve a room for up to two hours. The room would be set up according to their request prior to arrival.

"Hey Dick, the usual? Two thigh-sized dildos and a gallon of lube in room four? Done deal, buddy."

"That will be part of your role," Gina said to Mawg. "Taking those phone reservations, noting everything requested, and conveying that to the prep team. Reservations can be made no later than three o'clock the day of their visit. That allows the prep team plenty of time to ensure the room is set according to their liking. With you being new, members will try to bullshit you to get reservations last minute. That's a polite but absolute no."

"Yeah, don't be a pushover. We'll practice saying 'no" when we go home since I can already tell you're not great at it."

Completely ignoring Peri, Mawg continued taking notes so she didn't miss anything, and Gina was smiling at her diligence. "Any questions so far?" Mawg stopped writing and said, "Not really a question, just more of an observation. It seems the service we provide when someone gets a membership is heavily customized to their needs. That type of customization usually comes with a hefty price tag."

"Did you SEE the size of that wooden cross the other night? Somebody's definitely paying for that to be moved around."

Gina nodded. "You are correct. And astute." She smiled at Mawg and continued, "There are differing levels of membership within The Church. The bronze package allows members access to the main area. They are welcome to play on the main floor or they can be invited into a room activity, but rooms are invite only for them. They have access to the entertainment we provide nightly. We don't charge for drinks or the snack bar. Those are also included in their package."

"Free snackies!!"

Gina gestured for Mawg to follow her, and they headed down the stairs while a cleaner was sanitizing the hand rails. "The silver package includes everything in the bronze package, plus the option to participate in private activities in the rooms IF they aren't reserved." They reached the bottom of the stairs and headed toward the stage while Gina continued. "Gold memberships are the top tier. That allows full access, including the ability to reserve rooms as long as they're available for a max of two hours a night."

She flashed back to Declan standing in front of her in that room, licking his fingers. He must be a silver or gold member. Duly noted.

"Hey! Focus on the work, not the fingers."

They walked behind the stage to a storage area full of shelves that held props, costumes, toys, etc. There were stacks of approximately twenty unwrapped mattresses, some tables and chairs, and a door to a utility room. Mawg said, "I was curious about the bedding options the other night. With all the bodily fluids, I wondered how you keep them sanitized."

Gina smiled. "That's an excellent question because sanitation is vital in this business. We don't want members to feel like they're in a shady motel. They can do that on their own. We spend quite a bit on mattresses, but we also buy them in bulk so we get a discount."

"So THAT'S how the mattress stores stay in business!"

As she continued to peer around the room, she noticed a box of doggie pee pads. Gina saw her confused look and gave a low, throaty laugh. "Would you believe me if I told you those are fantastic for keeping messes off a bed? Once we set a bed up in a room, we lay down the pee pads on the mattress, then cover the bed with a plastic sheet before putting the bedding on. It's just an extra layer to protect the beds." She saw Mawg's wide-eyed surprise and chuckled again. "You'll be learning all the tricks of the trade before training is finished."

"You'll also be thankful for those when somebody wants to go full golden shower."

Gina looked up at the clock and said, "I'm starving. Let's go across the street and grab a bite to eat."

"Oh thank God, I was starting to get cranky."

The little neighborhood cafe was quaint, and the owner seemed friendly with Gina. Mawg got the impression Gina spent a lot of time there. They ordered a couple of big salads and settled in to wait.

Gina sipped her water and said, "we don't have a lot more scheduled for this afternoon. The bulk of the Monday work happens in the morning. How do you feel about cutting out after lunch and then coming back tonight? I don't have any potential newcomers on the books, so it will give me a chance to walk through what the concierge role truly is."

"Weiner work!"

"Sure, that would be great," Mawg replied. "Do you typically have a regular schedule or does it fluctuate depending on business needs?"

"Once we get you through training, you and I will create a set schedule that works for both of us. It might be a little crazy for a couple of weeks while you're training, but after that we'll fall into a routine." Gina said, as Peri took it upon himself to create a new song.

"Administration in the morning, masturbation in the evening…"

Their salads arrived and the chit-chat slowed as they ate. Then Mawg said, "By the way, the clothing allowance was completely unexpected. Thank you so much for that."

Gina paused, holding her forkful of salad. "Oh, don't thank me. That's a perk of the job. When I first started five years ago, I was completely broke and showed up in the only clothes I had. This role required me to look confident, so that became part of the compensation package. Just FYI, you'll have a five hundred dollar monthly allowance going forward now that you've got your wardrobe started."

Mawg almost choked on her arugula. "Five hundred dollars per month?! Holy shit!"

"Hallelujah! The loafers are going in the trash tonight."

Gina laughed heartily. "You'll find it spends faster than you think. But Tori is an absolute lifesaver and I would happily pay her more."

"She's an absolute gem of a human. I'm looking forward to working at The Church, Gina. It seems like everyone is taken care of, whether they're a member or employee." Mawg agreed.

"Oh they're getting taken care of all right…"

Gina gave a knowing smile. "They absolutely are. With any small business, owners put their heart and soul into it, and they treat their employees well so they'll do the same."

Mawg understood that. "Makes absolute sense. If I put my time, finances, and heart into building something, I'd want to ensure it thrives."

"Absolutely. Dildos depreciate fast."

The cafe owner came by and Gina handed her a credit card. Mawg tried to pull out cash but Gina shooed it away. "Lunch is always covered, too."

"Thank you," Mawg replied.

"Free lunch snackies?! Fuck yeah!"

Grabbing her purse, Gina motioned to the door. "Let's pop back in across the street for a minute so I can grab some information for you, and then you can head home."

"Sure, sounds good."

As they entered back into The Church, Gina said "Come up to the office with me and I'll send some homework with you for whenever you have free time."

"Did you ever envision sex being homework?"

They went up into the office and while Mawg was looking over the artwork again, Gina gathered some pamphlets for her. Mawg called over her shoulder, "So when do you think I'll get to meet the owner?"

"What if you already did?"

She whirled around, hearing the raspy voice with the Irish accent and froze.

"Bwahahahahahahaha……… Dicklan's your boss!"

He was leaning on the door jamb, those damn laser eyes staring at her again. It probably wasn't normal to feel mortified and turned on at the same time, but that's what Mawg was experiencing. Seeing him with normal, overhead lighting didn't lessen the impact. His dark hair was slightly mussed, like he'd been running his hands through it.

"Mawg wants to fuck her boss, Mawg wants to fuck her boss, Mawg—"

Mawg thought, "You will shut the fuck up right now or I will buy gelatin on the way home and this will NOT end in your favor."

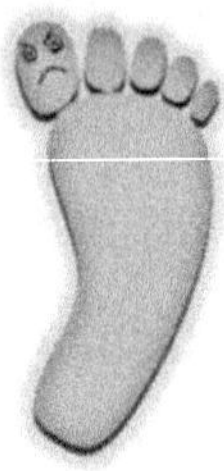

CHAPTER FOURTEEN

"Your face is absolutely priceless right now."

Declan tilted his head and continued to look at her. Gina, sensing Mawg's mortification, said, "Don't be a shit, Declan." Then she turned to Mawg and said, "I probably should have mentioned that sooner, but someone asked me not to." Then she looked directly at Declan with a glare.

Mawg was still trying to find the right words, but the awkwardness of the moment won out. "Thank you for the opportunity."

"Thank you for the opportunity?! Do you know what you sound like? Remember that dancing movie from the 80's you love? You know, where the girl meets the hot guy and all she can say is, "I carried a watermelon"? You just carried a watermelon, Mawg."

Her tongue was tied and her heart rate had to be significantly higher than it was a moment ago.

Gina broke in, trying to lessen the tension that overwhelmed the room. "Mawg spent the morning learning the basics of our operations. You'll find as quickly as I did that she's sharp. We decided to break and come back tonight to focus on learning the concierge role."

Declan looked over to Gina and nodded, then back to Mawg. "I look forward to seeing you ladies this evening then." He backed out of the door and was gone.

She glanced over at Gina, whose expression was sheepish. "So yeah…probably should have mentioned that. I'm so sorry."

Mawg put out her hands to take the documents that Gina had been gathering for her. "It's probably good I have a few hours to process this before tonight." She was so embarrassed, she could barely get the words out. "What time do you want me here?"

"We can do nine o'clock. And Mawg…I really am sorry. He asked me not to say anything. I wanted to tell you the other night."

"I understand." Mawg gave Gina a half-hearted smile and said, "I'll see you at nine." She fumbled with the documents as she rushed out the door, hurriedly walking to the car so she could experience mortification without an audience.

Except she still had an audience of one.

"Bwahahahahahahaha Dicklan OWNS Dick-Land!"

He was a very tiny and snarky audience. His little face was scrunched and she could have sworn it was making her toe red from his laughter.

She got in the car and sat in the driver's seat for a moment, still in shock. Then she felt it…the rage beginning to simmer.

All those times when kids would make fun of little Mawg.

All the times her ex would make some little dig about her weight.

Julie making her feel incapable at work.

Every humiliating moment of her past came to the forefront to taunt her, ending with the smile on Declan's face as she realized who he was. Mawg was livid. She turned over the ignition and took off like a bat out of hell.

"Whoa! Hey, calm the fuck down! You're gonna get us in an accident!"

She continued to drive, not acknowledging Peri. Racing home, she slammed the door getting out of the car. Her anger was boiling, and trying to put the key in the lock was a frustrating mess of fumbling fingers. Finally entering, she launched her purse onto the sofa and stomped to the bedroom. Tearing her beautiful new clothes off in a flurry, she tossed them on the floor and fell face-first into the bed. Mawg closed her eyes and inhaled until she felt full like a balloon, then released a furious scream into a pillow. When the air from her lungs emptied, she inhaled and screamed again. She laid in silence, allowing the rage to subside.

Peri said nothing as Mawg released. Rage he understood and welcomed. He gave her a few minutes to calm down.

"Feel better?"

Mawg made an unintelligible sound, her face still buried in the pillow. She came up for air, rolled over and looked at Peri. "Why do I always have to be the butt-end of someone's joke? Jesus, Peri, it's been years since I've felt this humiliated! Julie firing me wasn't half as embarrassing as this!"

"Ok, I get that he didn't tell you who he was, and he should have. Gina should have as well. But…is it really that big of a deal?"

She slammed her fists into the pillow. "He's my fucking boss, Peri! Gina already knew before we made that bet that I was going to work for her. They set that up, Peri. He only paid attention to me to help her, and now I feel like a fool." Peri listened to the rant and waited until she was finished.

"Or, and hear me out…maybe he was actually attracted to you. You know I don't want to encourage more thoughts of Dicklan, but Gina looked completely surprised at the way he was ogling you that night. I don't think that was planned."

Mawg sighed in frustration. "Ok hypothetically, let's say you're right. Even if that is the case, starting off a flirtation with a deception isn't the best way to go about it. He knew who I was, and he knew Gina wanted me to work there."

"Just one small clarification. I wouldn't call licking another woman's meatsuit juice off his fingers as he stares at you a flirtation. That was a straight up invitation."

Mawg sighed again, her head flopping back against a pillow. "I don't know what to do, Peri. I feel…humiliated." Peri's little face looked aghast.

"Wait, why are YOU feeling humiliated? You were an innocent bystander in all this. HE made that decision. You knock this shit off right now. I know what you're gonna do. You're a grown-ass woman, and you're gonna make him treat you like one. "

She laughed half-heartedly. "Oh really? And how, pray tell, am I going to accomplish that?"

"By pulling your grown-ass woman card and calling him on his bullshit. Let him know you don't have time for games. Be the ultimate professional, but be firm. He'll either respect it and take you seriously, or he won't and you'll know The Church isn't the place for you."

Mawg sat on that for a minute. Calling people out wasn't her nature, but it sure sounded cathartic.

"Oh…and when you have that discussion tonight, wear one of those outfits of Tori's that makes you look badass. Not pretty. Badass."

She was getting onboard with the idea. "Badass. I think I can do that."

She went to work transforming herself by channeling the most badass woman she could think of…a killer of vampires from her favorite show. She put some product in her hair and played with it a bit to get a sexy, messy look. A tutorial online coached her to add a wing to her eyeliner and a smoky look to her eyes. She tried on the cigarette-style fitted brown leather pants that highlighted her curves and ass, and paired it with a fitted long sleeve tee. Then she stared at her badass self in the mirror.

"Feeling better?"

Mawg looked down at Peri and said, *"Five by five."* She took one last look in the mirror, smiled, and headed out.

"I don't know what that means."

"Don't worry, we'll watch the show."

CHAPTER FIFTEEN

With the air of complete confidence, Mawg strode through the main door of The Church, her nerves concealed under a calm, collected mask. She was about to step far outside her comfort zone, and with that came intermingled feelings of trepidation and power.

"This is what we're training for. These are the situations that will change the caterpillar into the butterfly, Mawg. Keep your head up and walk through here like you own the place. Do not apologize."

She glanced down at Peri, took a deep breath, and gave an acknowledging nod. She raised her chin and strode back to the entry room bar toward adorable Liam, who was bartending again. He was washing glasses when he looked up at Mawg, one eyebrow raised in appreciation. "Well, well…don't you look absolutely fierce! Are you here on business or pleasure tonight?"

Mawg smiled. Liam's affable demeanor could break down any woman's walls, no matter if she was twenty or eighty. "I'm actually here to train with Gina. Should I wait for her out here, or head on back?"

Liam nodded to the hidden door. "Go right ahead. She'll probably be on the main floor, doing rounds and greeting members." He smiled at Mawg, cocked his head and said, "For what it's worth, Mawg…I think you're going to be a great concierge."

Breaking into a warm smile, she dipped her head in acknowledgement and said, "Appreciate that, Liam. I wish you a gazillion dollars in tips tonight."

"I'll take it!" he said, laughing as he turned to help a customer.

She took a deep breath, swiping the key card to open the door.

"Remember: Polite, professional, no reaction. You're here to work. Grown-ass woman shit."

"Grown-ass woman shit," Mawg whispered. Making her way down the hall, she pulled the curtain aside to enter the main room. Being a Monday night, it was a bit slower than her last visit. There were about eighty-ish people wandering around. On stage was a jazz trio providing a laid-back atmosphere. Mawg scanned the room for Gina, and found her standing in front of a couple seated on a leather couch. The conversation seemed intense, based on their serious expressions.

"Incoming."

The intoxicating cologne breezed by her nose and her peripheral vision caught a hand holding a gin and tonic on her right. Before she could turn her head, she felt his breath against her ear. "I was told this was your preferred poison."

That damn accent was going to be the death of her. She blushed, noticing his fingers wrapped around the glass, remembering what they could do.

"Focus, dammit!"

Peri shook her out of the cloud of lust. With a tight, but polite smile she accepted the glass and said, "You would be correct, thank you." Mawg hoped to practice run her spiel with

Gina prior to bumping into Declan, but the universe decided she would have to jump in with both feet. "I want to thank you for the opportunity and the job. You seem to have a solid business with a great reputation. I look forward to being part of the team."

"Nice. Very HR-appropriate and boring. Well done."

Declan took a couple of steps and stood in front of her, studying her face intently. "You're absolutely stunning when you're annoyed." Oh God, the fucking accent was melting her facade at a rapid pace.

"There will be no melting!"

Thank God for Peri or she would have spread her legs for this man in thirty seconds flat.

"You're welcome, now keep those knees together and stand your ground."

Mawg lifted her chin in a slightly haughty expression. "Thank you. But why do you assume I'm annoyed?"

Declan smiled and took a step closer. Leaning down to speak softly with his breath teasing against her ear, he said, "Because I can't get you out of my mind, Marvelous Mawg. I remember every single emotion displayed on your face the other night. That beautiful face is quite expressive. So the fact that you're stiff tonight tells me there's a wall up, and that you're upset or annoyed with me."

He couldn't get her out of his mind…did she hear that right? Ignoring the warmth building inside, she kept her expression cold. "Your decision to hide who you are was a bit deceptive, don't you think? I don't appreciate someone embarrassing me for their own amusement."

"Attagirl, let him have it!"

Surprise registered on Declan's face. "Embarrassing you? You thought I was purposefully attempting to humiliate you?"

Mawg was getting mad, and she could hear Peri cheering it on. "I didn't until today. How else would you describe it when a man eye fucks you the entire time he's performing intimate acts, but neglects to say, 'Oh by the way, I'm your boss'? That's deceptive, Declan! It made all the things I felt the other night seem icky now."

"I am so fucking proud of you right now."

Declan looked like he'd been slapped across the face. "What things did you feel the other night, Mawg?"

Seeing his surprised expression, she realized her faux pas. "Mawg…" he stepped directly in front of her and lifted her chin, holding it in place. "Tell me what you felt." Mawg scrambled for an answer, trying to think of how to get out of this awkward conversation.

"You're a grown-ass woman, remember? You will tell him the truth. No more hiding."

She took a deep breath and looked him directly in the eye. "I felt a lot of things. Sexy, vulnerable, desirable, terrified, turned on, curious…but most of all, I left feeling confident. And now the magic of that moment is tainted." She didn't back down, she didn't look away, and she didn't say another word. The ball was in his court.

Standing there they stayed locked in the stare for what felt like eternity, her pounding heartbeat the only acknowledgement that time was passing.

"There are many things I want you to feel, Mawg." He began to walk, circling behind her. He leaned in, body so close she felt the front of his shirt brush the back of hers.

His lips grazed her ear as he whispered, "I want you to feel ecstasy." She shivered and goosebumps appeared on her arm.

He slid to the other side of her body, his warm breath teasing her other ear. "I want you to feel brazen." She could not confirm nor deny that a moan escaped her lips.

His voice dipped and he was on the verge of growling. "I want you to feel wanton." Ohhhh, how she wanted to be wanton for this man.

He whispered, "And above all else, I want you to feel like the powerful goddess that you are."

"Does anyone care what I feel? Because I feel like this conversation went way beyond HR-appropriate. No? No one cares what I feel? Ok, I guess I'll go fuck myself then."

He circled back in front of Mawg. The heat radiating between them could be felt by anyone walking by. His hand reached down and grasped her fingers, his thumb brushing across the top of them. "What I never want you to feel is hurt. And clearly I have hurt you. For that, I am ashamed and I am sorry." He raised her hand to his lips, and she felt a sweet fire burn through her body at his touch.

"Fuuuuuuuuuuuuuuck…you're forgiving him, aren't you."

Mawg panted internally as she thought, "Wouldn't you?!"

"As much as I hate to admit it, that was kinda smooth. One point for Dicklan."

Declan released her hand as Gina walked over. Her brow was furrowed and her fists were clenched. Something had her agitated, and her eyes were darting around like she was distracted. "Mawg, I am so sorry. I've got a bit of a situation happening with the Whitneys and I need to deal with it."

Declan rolled his eyes and sighed as he ran a hand through his hair. "And what, pray tell, is bothering the Whitneys tonight?" His demeanor stayed calm, but Mawg saw a spark of agitation in his eyes.

Gina waved her hand like it was no big deal. "Just the usual, complaining, arguing with each other, etc. But it might take a few minutes. Declan, if you don't mind could you take Mawg through the viewing rooms? She needs to learn the different classifications of erotica so she can speak to it with potential members."

Oh shit.

"Oh shit."

Giving Gina a nod, he said, "Of course. Go on and deal with the Whitneys. And if they become too much of a pain in the ass, just come get me. I'm one step away from revoking their membership if they keep causing problems."

Gina rolled her eyes and waved her hand nonchalantly. "I'll keep you posted but I think it will be fine. Mawg, you're in good hands." Then she winked at Mawg as she walked off.

Declan turned to study Mawg, anticipation hanging in the air between them. "Before we watch anything live, it would be best to gauge your understanding of the erotica world. That will give me an idea of where to begin this lesson."

Mawg's face turned beet red.

"Hey kiddo, you need to get over the embarrassment about sex stuff real quick. This is your job, and ya gotta be able to explain things to new people. You're a grown-ass woman."

Peri was right. If she was going to work in this industry, she needed to be professional about it. She straightened her shoulders and looked up into his eyes. "Prior to the other night, I had very little exposure. I guess I've always been…what's the term, vanilla?" Declan nodded, listening. "After my visit here, I went home and started researching."

Declan's eyebrow raised, and he seemed to be attempting to hold back a smile. "Researching?"

"Watching various categories of porn to try and understand a bit more. Oh, and I watched '*Secretary*', too."

He peered at her over the whiskey glass he'd just raised to his lips. "Ahh, I see. So your visit here was your first time seeing anything like that in-person?"

Mawg nodded, hoping he wouldn't find her lack of knowledge to be a problem. "It was."

He paused momentarily, then asked the question she knew was coming, but wasn't excited to answer. "And as far as personal experience…what knowledge do you have from that?"

She was nervous and it was making her mouth dry.

"I know he's your ooey gooey crushy poo, but he also built an adult club from the ground up, Mawg. He's probably heard and seen it all."

Obliging both Declan and Peri, she took a deep breath. "I've had five male sexual partners in my lifetime. None of those instances involved anything from the erotica world. They were your most standard, basic interactions."

Declan tilted his head to the side, his expression perplexed. "You're telling me five men had the chance to be with you, and the best impression they left you with was 'standard and basic'? Sounds like they really blew it."

"Technically I was the one blowing things," came flying out of Mawg's lips before she thought about it. Her eyes got wide and she covered her mouth in shock.

"Maaaaaaaan, I was gonna say that but you beat me to it. Well played."

Declan's face lit up and he chuckled. "Sexy and funny? Those guys really messed up."

Mawg was mortified, but was grateful he wasn't making a big deal out of it.

Declan continued the questioning, his voice dropping low. "Do you understand the difference between being sexual and being sensual?"

This seemed too easy…was it a trick question? "I mean, not the standard dictionary definitions, but I think I grasp the basic concept. They're tied closely together."

Declan smiled and said, "Not necessarily. The basic root of sex is procreation for the species. All manner of animals have sex to procreate. Take ducks for example. I'm not going to describe that because it's not pleasant, but look it up when you go home. Ducks, no matter how gruesome the process, are still procreating. Sex can be performed without pleasure."

Mawg thought back to her previous sexual encounters and realized how on point that was. How many times had she performed the act without true enjoyment? Most of them, if she was being honest.

Declan watched her swirling the straw in her drink as she processed that information, then continued. "On the other hand, sensuality is all about pleasure, which can be derived without sex at all. Your body experiences pleasure through your brain. It's just a matter of determining what triggers your pleasure center and feeding that."

"Did he say feeding? Are we getting snackies?"

Mawg ignored Peri and tried to focus, but the hot Irishman who kept saying 'pleasure' wasn't helping one bit. The sexy accent was distracting, but she was able to catch the main point of his message.

"Here, let's do a quick example." His hand brushed hers as he took her drink and placed it on a nearby table, then came back to stand in front of her. "Close your eyes."

Mawg looked at him with a raised eyebrow. He met her gaze, lowered his voice, and took a step closer. "Close your eyes, Mawg." The rumble in his voice made her breath hitch, and she closed her eyes.

He said nothing for a few moments, allowing her senses to acclimate to the surroundings. Her brain began to cue in on the sounds and smells around her. Her body was taut with tension knowing that something was about to happen, but having no clue what that would be. She felt fingertips sliding her hair behind her right ear as his cologne wafted into her senses. In his deep, raspy tone he whispered, "Sensuality is all about anticipation, Mawg." The hair on her arms raised and she could feel her nipples hardening as his warm breath caressed her skin. Then the warmth was gone, like he disappeared. Her body waited anxiously for whatever would come next.

Walking up behind her, he pushed her hair to the left, letting his fingers trail along her now fully-exposed neck. His lips were close enough that his beard brushed against her jawline, and she let out a small gasp. "Does that make your brain anticipate pleasure, Mawg?" Slowly, he began to run his fingertips lightly up her arm as his beard continued to tickle her jawline. The scent of his cologne was intoxicating her. She was ready to throw her clothes on the floor and pounce on this man like an animal.

And then he stepped away.

"Open your eyes." She did, and they were fully dilated. Her breathing was thick and every inch of her body radiated, feeling alive. Was it sad that this tiny moment was even better than her past sexual encounters? Probably. Declan watched her intently, his expression that of a predatory cat. He finally broke eye contact and murmured, "That, dear Mawg, is a small, yet meaningful, example of a sensual experience."

He reached over to the table and picked up her drink, handing it back to her with the hint of a grin and a feigned innocence in his eyes. "Does that help clarify the difference?"

She took a gulp of her drink and nodded. She didn't trust herself to speak quite yet.

Declan finished his whiskey and gestured over to one of the hallways. "Shall we continue our lesson?"

Mawg nodded again.

"Does having a lady boner leave you unable to speak? Hellooooooo?"

Mawg thought, "Go away."

"I will not. If I wasn't here, you'd be spread eagle naked on the floor in five minutes. Pull it together."

Declan stood with a puzzled look on his face. Realizing she'd been looking down at her toe while internally chatting with Peri, Mawg said, "Sorry, just, um…gathering my thoughts."

They walked toward the hallway, and as they neared the first room, he put his hand on the small of her back and stopped. He turned toward her and said, "Don't be afraid to ask me questions as we walk through this. Also, when we're done with each room, I'm going to ask you two questions: Number one- How did you personally feel about what you saw? And number two- Why do you think someone would choose to do that? Full honesty, ok?"

She smiled up at him. "I think I can handle that." He placed his hand on her back and guided her to the open window.

She was caught off guard, first by his touch, then by what was displayed in front of her. Standing in the middle of the room was a stunning Jane with caramel colored skin. Her long hair was in a slicked back braid that reached down to her ass. She wore a skin-tight black lace bodysuit with a halter top neck. Mawg guessed her stilettos to be five or six inches tall, and she looked like an amazon warrior goddess. In her left hand was a leather leash, and attached to the leash by a collar around his neck was a Dick on all fours, next to her on the floor.

"Sit," Jane commanded. The man raised up to a kneel with his hands draping in front of him like a dog would. Jane petted his head. "Good boy." Then she handed him a morsel of food from her other hand. Dick accepted the food and rubbed his head against Jane's leg. She commanded, "Lay down," and the Dick laid down flat on his stomach on the floor. "Roll over." The Dick complied, rolling onto his back and putting his bent arms and legs in the air. The Jane leaned down on one knee and rubbed his belly. "That's a very good boy," she said, handing him another treat.

Mawg felt Declan's gaze sizing up her reaction.

"Should I be jealous that he's getting snackies? 'Cause I'm kinda jealous."

Mawg thought, "If you responded to commands and didn't act like an ass, you'd probably get more of them." She turned to Declan, and he gestured to move down the hall, away from the window. Stepping a few feet away, he leaned one arm against the wall and said, "Ok, so how do you personally feel about that?"

Mawg pondered the question and attempted to answer it as objectively as possible. "I'm experiencing a few different emotions. The Jane struck me as sexy and powerful. I can't decipher yet if that's because of her role, or simply because she looks stunning. The Dick's role made me feel uncomfortable. Seeing a human on a leash seems quite demeaning."

Declan's eyes lit up with excitement and he smiled. "Ok so question two- Why do you think someone would desire to do that?"

"Clearly, because there are snackies involved. Duh, Dicklan."

She walked back over to the window to study the couple again. "Gina explained there's a shifting balance of power that happens between a Dom and a Sub. I get why a Dom would want to be a Dom. What I don't grasp is why a Sub wants to be in their role."

Declan's eyes were kind as he ingested Mawg's words. "The Dom/Sub relationship is very easy to misunderstand looking at it from the outside. But it's also one of the most intimate relationships there can be. It requires honest communication, ultimate respect for boundaries, and the highest level of trust." He took a step toward Mawg and held out his hand. "It might actually be easier to give you a situational example. Would you humor me and role play with me…for training purposes?"

"Oh, that's fucking smooooooooooth, Dicklan. Very smooth."

Mawg hesitated, placing her hand in his. He led them down the hall to an empty room with just a chair in it, then closed the blinds and the door.

Her pulse was racing, but she wasn't sure if it was with trepidation or lust. Probably a mix of both. Declan gestured for her to sit in the chair. She sat, and he adjusted the lighting so the room was dark except for an overhead light shining down on Mawg. She sat nervously with her hands in her lap, no idea what to expect.

He slowly walked over and stood in front of her. She looked up at his face, vulnerable as he towered over her. Her chin was raised, leaving her neck stretched and exposed. She wiped her sweaty palms nervously on her pants and felt her breath coming in short bursts. Without breaking eye contact, he dropped down to his knees directly in front of her, and now she was looking down on him. She felt her heart race as his eyes softened. "Do you notice the difference in how you feel when I'm standing above you versus kneeling below you?" Mawg nodded, unable to speak. The combination of this powerful man on his knees, mixed with the smell of his cologne and that god damn accent was overwhelming her.

Declan uttered, "We're going to role play. You, Sweet Mawg, are a queen that rules over thousands of loyal subjects. You've had to fight and claw to retain your power as your enemies continually try to dethrone you. You take shit from no one. You just discovered that I, one of your subjects, have committed treason against you. I've been spying on you, and now you need to make me pay. Are you with me so far?"

Mawg replied, "I'm the queen, you're spying on me. Got it."

"Now, before we begin, we need to establish boundaries. Normally, a safe word would be agreed upon as well. We can do that, but I don't plan to go that deep tonight…that's a lesson for another evening." And then he winked at her.

Her mouth was dry as the desert. She nodded in understanding.

"Good, now I'll go first so you can get an idea of the boundaries. Mine are as follows: No marks on my face since I have a meeting first thing in the morning." He sat there kneeling, staring at her.

"That's it?"

Declan's eyes pierced her. "That's it."

"Oh you are in sooooooooo much trouble with this one."

She swallowed, trying to get rid of the lump of anxiety that was lodged in her throat. He said, "Now it's your turn, Mawg."

With no experience in this situation, she had no idea what her boundaries were. Declan sensed her hesitation and said, "A few things that people might say could be 'no choking', 'no pain', 'no external objects', 'no other parties are allowed to participate', etc. Ultimately, it comes down to you. In this world, it's important to be very specific with your boundaries. Since you haven't experienced any of it yet, it's okay to not know what those boundaries are. Just realize that going forward, you shouldn't get into a situation like this until you have those boundaries locked down, okay?"

Mawg breathed a sigh of relief. "Ok, thank you."

Declan readjusted his kneeling posture to be right in front of her. "You know my boundaries, and you know the scene. Now it's time to act. You are not Mawg. You are the queen. You are the Dom. I am the traitorous Sub who wants you to punish me. Now take charge of this situation and punish me."

Closing her eyes and taking a deep breath to get into character, Mawg calmed herself. She envisioned herself in a throne and tried to put herself in the mindset of a queen. A queen was confident. She wouldn't care about her flaws. She was strong enough and smart enough to be in charge, and she wouldn't doubt herself. A queen wouldn't give a shit about the opinions of others. She would expect her word to be law.

Opening her eyes, Mawg fixated her stare on Declan with a haughty expression as he looked up at her. "Avert your eyes." Declan dropped his head so he was looking at the floor. Mawg felt a little rush of adrenaline, and she began to find power in her voice. "Did you really think I wouldn't find out? Did you take me for a fool? Answer me."

Declan, kneeling with his head down replied, "Never, your majesty." Getting fully immersed in the character, Mawg raised her voice. "Lies! How dare you lie to your queen!" Then she did something she'd wanted to do since she first laid eyes on him. She leaned down from the chair, grabbed a fistful of his silky dark hair and lifted his face up to look at hers. Surprise sprung up on his face, then his eyes turned dark and smoldered. She leaned in, her face bare inches from his and demanded, "Who is your queen?" Declan's chest was rising and falling.

Mawg was baffled. Was he actually turned on by her right now? She stared into his eyes, watching his pupils dilate and felt the tension hanging heavily in the inches between them. His lips were slightly parted and she desperately wanted to feel them on her skin. She thought, "He's…he's as turned on as I am!" Peri rolled his eyes.

"I am shocked. Absolutely shocked."

She felt emboldened, leaning even closer to his face. Almost nose to nose, she stared deep into his eyes. "I asked you a question. Who. Is. Your. Queen?"

The lust was burning between them as he whispered, "You have always been, and will always be my queen, Your Majesty."

Mawg embraced the power of a queen. She released his hair and leaned back to bring the space back between them. "I don't believe you. You, sir, are a liar. I demand you show me your allegiance or I'll have you hung outside the castle."

Declan, aroused and fully in character whispered, "Let me honor you in the only way I can, Your Majesty. May I…may I please you, Your Grace?"

She had no idea where this train was going, but she was fully onboard and ready to ride. "You may."

"Chugga chugga choo choo!"

He bent down, unstrapped her sandals and took them off.

"Hey, hey, hey…what the fuck is he doing?"

Mawg thought, "Honoring his queen, now shut the fuck up."

Now on all fours, he began kissing the tops of her feet. She was shocked, frozen in place. Here was a powerful, successful man literally worshipping at her feet. He paused, head still bent down and asked, "May I continue, Your Majesty?"

Mawg's reply was breathless. "You may," she whispered.

He reached up to her knees, grasping the inside of them with his hands, slowly spreading her legs apart. Mawg's breath caught in her throat at his touch. He put a hand on each of her wide hips and drew her forward to the edge of the chair as she let out a small gasp. He kept his hands on her hips and his head bent, but he brought his head forward so his nose grazed the center of her leather pants. He took a long inhale and murmured, "Let me apologize to you properly, Majesty."

She melted, losing all sense of where she was. All she wanted in this moment was his mouth on her. The rest of the world evaporated. She whimpered, "Please." The queen was gone in that moment, replaced with a woman who wanted to be ravaged. She didn't care.

The knock at the door shocked them back to reality.

Declan sighed, laying his face on Mawg's lap, still holding her hips. He looked up at her and said, "That's probably Gina. She only knocks if there's something urgent that needs to be handled."

Mawg was still pulling herself out of the fantasy. Declan raised up to place his body in between her legs and got so close his nose touched hers. "This is a to-be-continued, Your Majesty." He placed a very light, very soft kiss on her lips and rose up. Realizing he was fully erect, he cracked the door and peeked his head out. It was Gina. They whispered for a moment, and then she left. Declan closed the door and ran his hand through his hair as he turned to Mawg.

"Unfortunately, I will have to apologize to Her Majesty another evening. I have to go deal with the Whitneys. Fucking Whitneys," he said as he shook his head and walked back to Mawg, who was still sitting in the same position where he left her on the chair. He bent down so he was in front of her. "I meant what I said. This WILL be continued…that is, if that's what you want?" He looked at her with a hopeful expression.

Disappointed but understanding, Mawg smiled and said, "Your Majesty commands it." That got a big smile out of Declan. "Ok then, feel free to stay around if you want, or if you need to go home, that's absolutely fine, too. Will I see you in the morning?"

"No," Mawg replied. Declan's expression deflated, then she said, "You have your meeting, remember?"

He smiled. "You are correct, and thank you for the reminder." He chuckled. "Good night, Your Majesty."

CHAPTER SIXTEEN

The next two weeks passed in a blur. Some might think learning the operational side of a business would be tedious, but Mawg took to it like she was born in the role. Her practical nature and appreciation for organization and timeliness were a perfect match for managing what she now called "member services". By the end of the two week training period, Gina was comfortable handing off operational tasks to Mawg.

The concierge training was another story. Seeing naked human bodies in various states of arousal was no longer shocking, so that was progress. But she still wasn't sure how to broach the topic with potential members for tours. She shadowed Gina the past four or five sessions, but Mawg still couldn't grasp how Gina made it look effortless.

"I'm absolutely baffled at how you make this look so easy. I really struggle with broaching the initial conversation with someone. Like, 'Hi, nice to meet you. How would you like your orgasm today?"

Gina burst out laughing. "I mean, we could create a fast food menu of ideas for them. I'd like the number one with an extra side of foreplay, please."

"I think a buffet of bouncing boobies would be better. That's it. Just boobies."

Mawg didn't laugh. Instead, she stared at Gina like a lightbulb was turning on in her brain. "Ok wait, hear me out…Not a fast food menu, but what if we had a guide for first timers? Something that would explain basic etiquette, some of the most common kinks and fetishes, the offerings at each member level, etc. We could provide it to them right before the tour begins."

Gina looked off in the distance, pondering. "I like the idea, but I don't want them taking a pamphlet home with them. It may sound silly, but what we have here is pretty special and I don't want someone getting the bright idea to copycat. BUT, we could keep the guides available on-site and potential members can review them before we tour. I actually love that idea."

"Look at Mawg with the big brain!"

That perked Mawg up. "Awesome! That would be a helpful tool for me giving the tours as well. If you can select the kinks and fetishes that are most common here, I can put all of the info together."

"What exactly are you ladies changing?" The voice came from behind them and startled Mawg. She turned to see Declan smiling, one hand in his pocket and the other holding a rocks glass of whiskey. His dark eyes looked tired and his shirt was slightly rumpled.

"Oh joy, Dicklan's back in town. And just when we managed to keep our underwear dry for two weeks straight."

Mawg's face was smiling but internally she thought, "Actually, that's incorrect. Remember when we sneezed the other night and a little pee came out?"

"Joke's on you, I'm the one that made that happen. Just another of the fun little gifts I bring."

"Dickbag."

"Hag."

Disregarding Peri, she asked Declan, "How is the expansion coming along?"

He took a swig of his whiskey and replied, "Ugh, challenging. We're waiting for the building owner to get the permits." Then his laser eyes focused a soft smile on Mawg and he asked, "So what new idea did you come up with?"

Gina piped in, "Mawg thought it would be helpful to provide a guide for newcomers who are touring that explains etiquette, common kinks/activities, our packages, etc. They will be guides that stay here so they don't walk out the door."

Thinking about it, Declan nodded. "That's an excellent idea. The more information people have in a situation like this, the more comfortable they feel." Then he gazed intently at Mawg and said, "And we want every member of The Church to feel comfortable enough to experience real ecstasy." His deep, chocolate gaze never left hers as he took another swig of whiskey.

Mawg's eyes widened and she gulped.

"Aw fuuuuuck, here we go again...."

Seeing what was developing in front of her, Gina said, "Declan, I know you just got back and apologies for springing this on you…but do you mind taking over Mawg's training for the rest of the evening? I've got a backlog of things to catch up on for the expansion."

Declan pulled his hand from his pocket and ran it through his hair. "I'm fully invested in ensuring Mawg has a comprehensive training program. No problem at all."

Gina thanked him and turned to Mawg to give her a hug before she walked off. Leaning in, she whispered, "May your education be…hands-on." She gave Mawg a wink and walked off, leaving Declan looking at Mawg, and Mawg looking anywhere but Declan's face.

"The man had his nose rooting around in your leather pants like he was sniffing for a snackie the last time you saw him. I think the time for being shy is long past."

Internally she sighed at Peri. He was annoying, but right. Mawg finally made eye contact with Declan, who was still watching her intently and said, "I can see work has been keeping you busy. If you need to take a raincheck, I completely understand."

Declan didn't say anything, but looked down to her feet and slowly brought his eyes back up to meet hers. "Rest is the last thing on my mind right now."

"You two just need to merge your meatsuits and get it over with already."

He asked, "Shall we take a stroll down the halls and see what activities we can study tonight?"

"Sure. Although it's been a little slower in the rooms tonight so I'm not sure how much activity there will be."

He smirked. "If that's the case, then we'll just have to do some…hands-on training." He winked at her. Dammit, he totally heard Gina. Declan gestured over to the hallway and they embarked on their journey.

There was one room in use and the blinds and door were open. As they walked up, Mawg noticed the foot fetish Dick from her first tour had returned. He was setting up the room with supplies, and Mawg assumed he was waiting on tonight's Jane to join him. Declan walked into the door but the Dick didn't see him. Declan stood behind him and said, "You know, this usually works better with a partner, but whatever gets you off." Mawg's eyebrows raised and the Dick turned around. "Declan! Jesus man, it's been forever!" The Dick walked over and he and Declan proceeded to engage in the official bro hug, shaking hands with their right and slapping each other on the back shoulder with their left.

Declan turned to Mawg and said, "Mawg, meet Jake. We've known each other for…shit, how long has it been, man?"

She watched Jake calculating in his head. "Wow, I think we're going on ten years now? Crazy how time flies!" Then he reached out his hand to Mawg and shook hers. "Very nice to meet you."

Declan turned to Jake. "Mawg is new to The Church and she's been training to learn more about the erotica world as a whole." Then he turned to Mawg. "Jake is a lawyer and a very good friend."

Mawg said, "I actually saw Jake on my first tour. You were in a room with a blonde woman while I was touring. Gina mentioned that Jane was a…pillow princess, I think she called it?"

"Ahhhh, yep," Jake said, "I know exactly which interaction you're referring to. That was fun. I was supposed to meet another partner tonight, but she just texted that she can't make it. I was hanging onto the room for my scheduled time, hoping someone would be interested in playing."

Declan turned to Mawg.

"ABSOFUCKINGLUTELY NOT. I swear to all that is demon, I will give you a full fucking beard, Mawg!"

She risked a quick peek down at her toe and thought, "Hey, you're the one that said I need to be a professional and understand what I'm doing like a 'grown-ass woman'. That *was* the expression you used, wasn't it? Nut up, this is for science."

"You hag!! You hateful, spiteful hag! I'm going to make that chin hair extra pubey!"

Switching her gaze between Declan and Jake, she said, "I have absolutely no idea what I'm doing and I've never done this before."

Declan said, "Jake has been doing this for years. He'll explain everything before he takes any action. If at any time this doesn't feel right or you want to stop, you just say your safe word."

"Safe word. I'm saying the safe word now."

"And since we don't know each other well," Jake chimed in, "you're welcome to have Declan stay in the room if that makes you feel safe. I want you to have a good first experience so you know what to expect if you choose to do this again in the future."

"You will NOT be choosing to do this again."

Mawg thought about it while Peri continued to rage at her. She thought, "Just take a fucking nap. I'll get you an extra dessert on the way home." That shut him up.

"What should I choose as a safe word? I've never used one before."

Declan replied, "You want to pick something that has nothing sexual tied to it. Something random that would never come up in an…intimate setting. Something easy to remember in the heat of the moment. A favorite among the community here is meatloaf."

Her head tilted to the side. "Why meatloaf?"

Declan chucked. "Think of the singer, not the food. One of his popular songs."

Mawg was confused, then she burst out laughing as it came to her. "Ok that makes sense. Meatloaf it is." She smiled at the two men in front of her.

"Why don't you feel nervous about this? I figured this would freak you out."

Mawg thought, "I don't know…because it's just feet. Outside of you bitching, what harm can it do?" That raised Peri's little eyebrows.

"It's not going to harm anything, but…this is erotica, Mawg. Feet can be very erotic. The torment I'm about to face might just be worth it to see you learn that."

Tapping the bed, Jake gestured for Mawg to have a seat. Then Declan asked, "Do you want people to watch, or do you want me to shut the blinds and door?"

Mawg thought for a moment and asked, "Am I going to be naked during any part of this?"

Jake shook his head and said, "Not if you don't want to be. You can pull your dress up to your knees so I have access to your lower legs and feet."

She looked at Declan and said, "Let's go with door shut, blinds open, and I'll keep the dress on." He nodded and moved to close the door.

"Oh you don't want anyone seeing your bare ass but they're welcome to watch my torment?! That's great…way to sacrifice MY comfort, Mawg."

Mawg looked down at Peri and they stared each other down. She thought, "Just take a fucking nap already." He scowled up at her, huffed, then closed his little eyes.

Walking over, Jake stood in front of Mawg. "Ok, so the first thing I always do is wash your feet. That way you don't feel insecure about foot odor and I'm comfortable putting them in my mouth. Is that okay with you?"

She nodded. "Solid starting plan, I'm good with it."

While Jake prepped the wash water with a lavender soap, Mawg peered over at Declan. He was lighting candles on the ledge that wound around the room, then he walked over to the lights and dimmed them low. Suddenly, the air in the room felt warmer to Mawg.

"That's just you being in heat."

Mawg glared at Peri.

"No, I'm not being sarcastic this time. That's literally your body acknowledging that fuckery is coming."

"Shush," she thought.

Declan walked over to Mawg and said, "Would you like music on? I've found that it helps when experiencing something new." She nodded, and he sauntered over to the portable speaker that was sitting on a table in the corner. A slow, sultry song began to play.

Jake finished prepping the wash water and brought it over to the foot of the bed. Declan took a seat in what she had recently learned was the spectator chair in the corner behind Jake. It was set up for those who enjoyed voyeurism and viewing the activities rather than directly participating. Declan would be able to experience Mawg's facial expressions and body reactions from the chair.

With one last look up at Mawg, Jake smiled and said, "Ok I'm going to start now. And remember, say meatloaf the minute you feel uncomfortable or feel like we've reached a boundary. Ok?"

Mawg smiled and nodded. "Understood."

Jake had her sit on the bed with her legs dangling off the edge. He began by unstrapping her sandals. Noticing her pedicure (thank you Jessica!), he said, "You have beautiful feet. Your arches are so high." And then he made a little moan when he dipped the washcloth in the lavender soap and began to wash her left foot.

"Nope, nope, nope.....not one bit happy about this!"

Instantaneously, Mawg realized she'd sorely misunderstood what she was going to feel during this experience. She originally thought it wasn't a big deal because hey, just feet, right? She did not expect to feel turned on as she watched Jake run the washcloth over the top of her foot. And then her eyes drifted to her big toe and the pissy face that was staring at her.

Acknowledging she did NOT want to think about Peri during this experience, she raised her eyes to look first at Jake, then at Declan. Jake's face was hyper-focused on her foot, and his expression was one of arousal. Declan, on the other hand, was watching her face to gauge her emotions. Jake reached the arch of her foot and she gasped and twitched, the sensation tickling her skin. Jake groaned at her response and ran the washcloth over her arch two more times. Each time, she would gasp and twitch and she could tell it was arousing him. She peered over at Declan, and his eyes were locked on hers. It was difficult to tell because of the low lighting, but she swore he was breathing harder. Then Jake began to wash her painted toes.

"Dude, I already had a shower today, thank you very much. Move along."

But Jake continued, sliding her toes apart and slowly running the washcloth between them. When he finished, he moved over to her right foot and repeated the entire process. When finished, he stepped back in front of Mawg and said, "Do you mind laying flat on your back with your legs straight out so your feet hang off the edge?" She had no problem with that and complied. Jake walked to his table of supplies, grabbed something and came back to stand in front of her. In his hand was a jar of chocolate sauce.

"And what exactly does he plan to do with that?"

Mawg chuckled internally and thought with feigned innocence, "Looks like a snackie to me."

"That's not fucking funny, Mawg."

238

Jake came up to the side of the bed so he could speak with her. Mawg noted his very kind eyes, and from the interaction she'd had so far, he seemed like a decent guy. "I want to pour chocolate sauce all over your feet, then lick and suck it off."

"Oh yeah, he's a real sweetie."

His bulge was at eye level while she was laying there and she could see that he was already turned on from the foot washing. "As you can probably tell, this is going to arouse me. I'd like to pleasure myself throughout the process as well, but I won't touch anything other than your ankles and feet. Would that be alright with you?"

Mawg had no feelings about it either way, but she was curious what Declan was thinking. She looked at him in the corner and could see that he was now leaning forward intently in the chair, his elbows on his knees and his hands clasped together under his chin. His expression was unreadable, but his eyes never left her. Catching Declan's staring eyes, she looked directly at him as she replied to Jake. "I'm fine with that. Who can turn down chocolate, right?" Their roles were switched from her first tour, and she was going to do to him exactly what he did to her. Determined with her plan, she kept her eyes focused on Declan.

Jake began to pour the warm chocolate sauce over her feet and toes. Peri's little face was dripping with chocolate.

"Demon dammit, Mawg!"

Ignoring Peri, she continued to keep her eyes locked with Declan's when she felt Jake's tongue run across her sole. She didn't know what she was expecting, but this was intense. And then her brain randomly pulled up a fact from her high school science class, remembering that the foot has approximately twenty thousand nerve endings.

"And you're on my LAST nerve, Mawg! End this torture!"

Jake licked her arch as she continued to stare at Declan. Her eyes widened in shock and she gave an audible gasp. Declan, still in the same position, began to bounce his right leg unconsciously and it felt like his eyes were drilling into her. Jake moaned, louder this time. "Your feet are a work of art, Mawg," he said breathlessly between licks.

"I mean...I guess there is kind of a Picasso vibe going on down here."

Jake's left hand reached down to massage himself while he held her foot in his right hand and continued the assault with his mouth.

Mawg felt everything in her core begin to warm and tingle. Jake moved his mouth higher on her foot, licking the area where the toes connect to the foot. Mawg's eyes rolled back as she breathlessly said, "Oh my God," and jerked involuntarily. That made Jake moan and massage himself faster as he continued to lick her. "Yes Mawg, yes." She couldn't control what she was feeling in her body. She was so turned on she was on the verge of vibrating.

Holding her foot with his right hand, Jake began to suck on her pinkie toe. She could feel the suction of his mouth against her skin and it made her come undone. Forgetting her plan to stare Declan down, she closed her eyes and grabbed the sheets to ground herself.

He continued to suck on her toes, one by one. Mawg continued to moan and gasp. When he got near her big toe, Peri lost his shit.

"This is fucking bullshit, Mawg!! Don't let him do it! I don't want it, I don't want it!"

But Mawg couldn't stop the flood of pleasure that was coursing through her. This feeling was so intense, and she'd been repressed for so long. It was like the universe was begging her to let go.

She looked up at Jake, whose erection was absolutely massive now. She saw his eyes light up as his mouth descended to take the big toe in his mouth.

"MAAAAAAAAAWWWWWWWWG!!!!!!!"

And then Peri disappeared into Jake's mouth.

"Demon dammit, Maaaaaaaaawwwg!"

Mawg's moans were getting higher pitched. She continued to grip the sheets and thrash about, making Jake suck even harder. She felt a change in the air flow to her left and turned her head and opened. Declan was standing next to her, also fully erect. He knelt down, his face next to her ear. As Jake proceeded to mouth fuck her foot, Declan whispered, "I could listen to you moan a thousand times, and I'd still want a thousand more."

He stood up, and she got a very closeup view of the absolute weapon he was packing. Jake had released Peri and was now furiously licking her foot all over, getting close to his own release. Peri was glaring at her furiously. Mawg closed her eyes again and she reached out her left hand to touch Declan. Her hand grazed his erection through his pants and his entire body stilled. Jake, finally reaching his apex, came in his jeans at the end of the table with his tongue licking her heel.

Jake's head drooped for a minute as he gathered his breath. Then he whispered, "That was incredible." Looking up, he saw Declan eyeing Mawg like she was a meal and realized this party was going to continue without him. Jake looked at Declan and said, "Are you good if I…" and he gestured his head to the door. Declan nodded, his eyes never leaving Mawg.

The corner of Jake's mouth turned up in a smile. "Will do." He walked up on the other side of Mawg, lifted her hand and kissed the back of it. "It was an absolute pleasure to meet you, Mawg. Thank you for a most lovely evening." And then he turned on his heel, walked out, and shut the door.

Declan immediately walked over and shut the open blinds. He double-checked that the door was closed. Turning on his heel, he stared at Mawg lying on the bed. Her face was flushed, still trying to comprehend what she just experienced.

Feeling sexy and confident after a man got off by having her foot in his mouth, she sat up and her eyes connected with Declan's.

"I hope his weiner is flaccid and your experience is awful! Do you know what you just did to me, you hag?! Have you ever seen the inside of a human mouth, Mawg? Nothing but bacteria and food particles. You humans are disgusting! You're gonna sanitize me as soon as we get home and this IS NOT the end of this discussion!"

Mawg continued to stare at Declan but thought, "I will give you every fucking snackie in the world when we get home if you will shut up and take a nap right now."

Peri sighed in exasperation and closed his little eyes.

Not breaking eye contact, Mawg stood up. The nerves were kicking in but she wasn't about to stop. She began to walk toward Declan, watching his eyes cloud with desire as she got closer. As she stood directly in front of him with her legs spread apart, Declan opened his mouth to speak and Mawg placed a finger against his lips. Her voice was sultry when she said, "Your Majesty is eagerly awaiting the apology she is owed for your treasonous acts."

The surprise that appeared on Declan's face was replaced with lusty eyes and a devilish grin. He lowered himself to a kneeling position in front of her. Mawg was wearing a silk maxi dress, and as he grabbed the front hem with both hands he looked up to meet her eyes, the dress dragging in his lap. "May I make amends for my grievous error, Your Majesty?"

"You may," Mawg replied in her haughty queen voice, happily falling into character. Declan gave her one last lusty look as he lifted the dress and disappeared beneath it.

"Argh matey, Dicklan's diving for treasure…and his knee is touching me. Does that make this a threesome?"

Mawg thought, "If you say one more thing, I'll gladly take the chin hair and stomp you into the floor. Go back to your nap."

The beautiful fingers she dreamed about glided up the bare skin of her legs. She gasped at the sensation. When he reached the curve of each hip, his fingers dug in, squeezing and kneading. The reverberation of his breath against her thighs caused her knees to feel weak. His beard grazed her inner right thigh as he began kissing his way up to her center. He was going to realize in about two seconds that her thong was completely soaked. She thanked the sexy gods that she'd chosen the thong instead of the granny panties tonight.

"Arrrrrgh, this treasure is buried in grandma's pantaloons!"

She ignored Peri as Declan's hands slid from her hips to cup her very generous ass. He began to knead her cheeks while his beard and lips continued to torment her inner thighs, and she moaned. "You have no idea how much I've dreamed about this ass the past two weeks."

Mawg wanted her hands in his hair, but the dress was in the way. "Your Majesty wants to touch you."

He groaned. "Begging your pardon, Majesty, but I am too lowly to have earned your touch."

Mawg replied in her haughty voice, "Remove this dress at once and let Your Majesty watch as you apologize."

Declan paused for a moment and Mawg's insecurities returned. Maybe she'd taken it too far. Maybe he didn't want to see her cellulite. Declan removed his head from under the dress. When he peered up at Mawg, his dark eyes were smoldering.

"Your Grace, you are the most stunning woman in the land and you deserve much more than this humble abode." His eyes locked onto hers.

"My traitorous transgression was so dastardly that it will take weeks," his left hand came around and one finger slid underneath her thong to graze her lower lips.

"Months," his other hand smacked her ass lightly.

"Even years to make it up to you," his eyes were still locked on hers.

"And when I do, it will be in a manner that's fit for a queen." Very slowly he slid one finger in between her lips and ran it oh so lightly across her very wet and throbbing clit on its way down to enter her.

She locked her hands in his hair and threw her head back with a gasp and a moan. Her delicate skin was drenched, and he slowly began a pattern. He slid the finger inside her, then all the way back out to graze her. Over and over he continued, keeping the same slow and torturous rhythm while he reveled in her moans and gasps. "Sweet, sweet Mawg, you get so wet for me, baby."

She looked down into his eyes while he continued to torment her, creating an incessant ache that begged for release. Her eyes pleaded and she whispered, "Declan, please…oh god, please…" Keeping his finger inside her, he rose so he could watch her face. A second finger joined the first and she came unglued in his hands. Her eyes widened and she panted and moaned, feeling the pressure of the orgasm beginning to build. She closed her eyes and her head fell back. He used his other hand to clasp the nape of her neck to bring her head back up. "I want to see that beautiful face when I take you over the edge."

They were both panting and his speed was increasing. The pressure was building in a way Mawg had never experienced. She felt like her body was out of her control. The final straw was when he looked her in the eye and breathlessly begged, "Let go for me. Be a good girl and let go, Mawg."

She let go. Her body had a mind of its own and she felt wetness running down over his hand and down her legs as she gripped his shoulders and tried to catch her breath. She clung to him for minutes after, still experiencing the reverberation of the orgasm. His eyes never left hers as he removed the two fingers from inside her. He brought them to his lips and sucked every bit of her off of them. And when he finished, the hand wrapped around the nape of her neck dragged her forward. He devoured her mouth with a kiss so passionate, her knees began to buckle. He wrapped his other arm around her back to hold her steady and continued the assault on her mouth.

When they parted, both were wild-eyed and breathless. Declan let her go and took a step back. Mawg noticed his erection was very visible in his pants, and she looked from it up to his face. She pointed down at it. "Would…um, would you like me to help you with that?"

"Ya' just carried another watermelon, Mawg."

Declan got a huge grin on his face. He stepped forward and placed a light kiss on the tip of her nose. "With everything in me. However, this is not the time nor place. I meant what I said earlier. When we truly explore each other, it won't be here. I will not be rushed or concerned about someone knocking on the door with an issue when I have your body laid out in front of me. You will have my full and undivided attention." Then he kissed her gently and whispered, "I'm going to go home and enjoy a cold shower, fall asleep and dream of my face buried in between the thighs of a very lovely Rubenesque Venus." He pushed a straggling strand of hair behind her ear. "My Venus should head home and get some rest, too. Can I walk you to your car?"

She had no idea if her legs would even work, but she nodded. He grabbed a clean towel that had been set to the side, kneeled before her and wiped the evidence of their activity from her inner thighs. He rose up and tossed the towel into a hamper she hadn't noticed before and reached out his hand, seeking hers. Together they walked out of The Church across the street to the parking lot where her car sat. As they reached the door, Declan put his hands on each side of her face and drew her in for a much softer parting kiss. Then he opened her door and uttered, "Goodnight, my Venus."

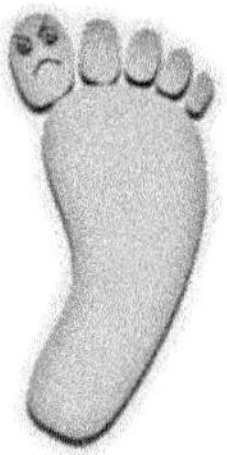

CHAPTER SEVENTEEN

Turning over the ignition, she watched him walk down the street to where he parked. Mawg's body was still vibrating from tonight's events, her mind not believing what she just experienced. A throat-clearing noise from her toe interrupted the reverie. "I know, I know, I owe you big time."

Silence.

"How many desserts do you want?"

More silence.

"Peri, are you just going to ignore me all night?"

"We are not speaking until I've had my snackies."

Mawg rolled her eyes, put the car in drive, and headed to a late-night bakery that was still open. Pulling into the parking lot, she asked, "Shall I assume that you don't want any more chocolate tonight?" She was holding back a laugh at Peri's glaring, pouty face.

The bell dinged over the door as she entered the bakery, and the smell of carbohydrate heaven wafted around her. There were breads baking and the aroma of cinnamon rolls filled the air. A bakery case that extended the width of the building was filled with cakes, pies, doughnuts, rolls, and breads. Mawg waited in line to order. When it was her turn, she selected a cinnamon roll with cream cheese icing and a cake doughnut with pink icing and sprinkles. Paying and thanking the cashier, she took the bag of goodies out to her car and they drove home in silence.

Entering the house, Mawg dropped the desserts on her bed and hopped in the shower. After washing off the evidence of the evening's events, she completed her nighttime skincare ritual and sat down on the bed with the desserts and a fork. The cinnamon roll tasted like heaven, and Mawg swore she heard Peri moan in pleasure. They ate in silence, both enjoying how delicious gluttony can taste.

"We will speak now."

Mawg rolled her eyes. "I take it I'm forgiven, then?"

"Forgiven? One dessert and you think that makes up for what you did to me? You're out of your demon-damn mind, Mawg. You put me in a random man's mouth! Do you have any idea how terrifyin' that is? We don't know him! If Dicklan's known him for ten years, then I want you to imagine how many toes have been in that mouth. That's foul, Mawg. Absolutely filthy."

She began to cry, quickly realizing they weren't her tears. Peri was truly upset with her. And now she felt like an ass.

"You should! You will get no argument from me. You are a certified ass. And a hag...you're an asshag."

She sat quietly while Peri ranted. He was absolutely right. She was an asshag. "I am so sorry, Peri. I was so wrapped up in the moment that I didn't listen to your boundary." She shook her head in disappointment. "It's literally my job to be the person who makes people comfortable and I completely ignored your feelings."

Peri sniffled through his tears and looked up at her like a dog that had been reprimanded. His little eyes were so sad. Mawg felt like garbage. "I know this won't make up for it, but do you want to try the pink sprinkle doughnut?"

"That would be a good start."

They ate the pink sprinkle doughnut in silence and Mawg felt the tears slowly subside. She was full of desserts and her demon seemed placated for the moment. "Are we okay?"

Peri thought about it and squeezed his little eyes shut.

"Now we are."

Mawg, fully expecting a new chin hair, walked to the bathroom mirror. Not a chin hair in sight. She looked down at her toe. "What did you do, Peri?" Suddenly she began to experience cramps and back pain. He got an evil little grin on his face.

"Mawgerite, congratulations! You are the grand winner of a shiny, brand new menstrual cycle!"

"Whaaaaaat?!?" Mawg disrobed and sat on the toilet. Yep, there was her period arriving in full force. She scowled down at her toe, grabbing toilet paper off the roll and crumbling it up angrily. "I just finished last week. That isn't fair!"

The little smirk on Peri's face was the first time Mawg truly saw the demon that he was.

"Oh it's absolutely fair after your shenanigans tonight. And now that your estrogen supply is depleting, I'll be the one who initiates your cycle. Guess I forgot to mention that. Oopsie."

"Oopsie?! This is a dirty, rotten trick. You take it back this instant!" He smiled smugly at her.

"No can do, Mawg. Once it's started, it has to play out. We have no idea how long it will continue or how heavy it will be. It might stop by for a day, or it could hang around for two weeks. I can only control when it begins."

Mawg glared down at her toe as she pulled out her tampons. "This is fucking garbage."

"And we learned a valuable lesson about boundaries today, didn't we?"

As she finished and pulled her pajamas back on, she hopped into bed and grabbed a heating pad and a bottle of ibuprofen. Then she turned on her favorite show, preparing to hibernate and pout. They settled in and began to watch.

"How does that vampire have bleached blonde hair? Is that his natural color? Vampires should look the exact same as the moment they were turned."

"Different storytellers use different lore, so apparently in this lore they can change their look. Now ssshhhhh…just watch the sexy vampires."

Peri was about to argue, but decided to leave it alone. Ten minutes later, he got a curious look on his little face.

"Do you love him?"

Mawg, fully engrossed in the show, looked confused. "Which vampire are you talking about, the broody one or the blonde?" Peri sighed in exasperation.

"Demon help me, not the TV vampires. Dicklan! Do you love Dicklan?"

She was taken aback. "Love him? I've known him for a grand total of…what, two and a half weeks? And our conversation has been limited to a lot of moaning, if we're being honest. No, I don't love him…I don't even know him."

"Don't get all defensive, I was just curious. I've seen some of my past cohabitants fall for a partner faster than that."

She thought about it for a moment. "Had this happened fifteen or twenty years ago, I probably would have said yes, I love him. But I'm old enough and wise enough to know the difference between love and lust now. I want that man to do absolutely filthy things to me, but that doesn't mean he would be a great partner for life. He might be, but I don't know him well enough to discern that yet. Does that make sense?"

"Mawg the Practical. Of course that makes sense to me. I just wasn't sure if we should prepare for wedding dress shopping anytime soon."

Mawg let out a laugh that reverberated in the room. "Oh my God, no. Peri, the past decade or so I've become way too independent to jump into a relationship. My house is decorated the way I like it. My schedule is determined by me and me alone. My money is mine. I have no desire to jump into a relationship and then find out it's the wrong person. If I end up in a relationship with someone, it's going to be a slow burn because we need to really know each other before we make a commitment."

She hunched over with the heating pad on her abdomen, her cramps now in full force. "As of this moment, yes. Could that change? Sure. But I don't really know anything about him, Peri. You're also making the assumption that he wants a relationship, and he's given me no indication of that. This man owns adult clubs. Maybe he's just happy in the single life, enjoying an occasional dabble with the lady of the month, ya know?" Peri's grin was so wide she thought he would break out of her toe.

"Do you know how much this pleases me? You have no idea how many cohabitants I've watched make life decisions based on lust, and then fall to pieces when that relationship fell apart. I knew there was a reason I chose you."

"And here I was, thinking it was because of my fashion sense." That got a solid laugh out of Peri.

"Can we please go get another pedicure tomorrow? I'm still traumatized and that would help wash away the filth from that random mouth."

Mawg rolled her eyes, but replied, "Yes Peri, we'll get another pedicure."

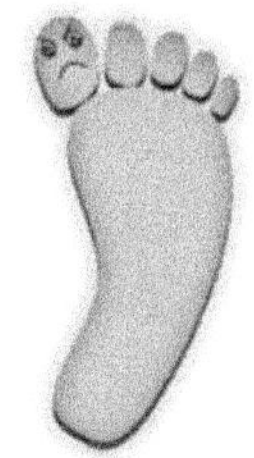

CHAPTER EIGHTEEN

Mawg was off the next day, so they rolled into Happy Nail. Jessica was standing with her hand extended out to a customer, waiting for payment for her services. She turned to see Mawg enter, shooting her an annoyed glance, and pointing to the wall of polish. "Pick a color." Mawg had hoped after the last visit that Jessica might have warmed to her, knowing they shared a secret about demons.

"Yeah, fat chance of that. She doesn't strike me as someone who enjoys the girl talk very much. I don't see any happy hours with her in your future."

Mawg was feeling bold and grabbed a dark, blood red polish. Peri's eyebrow raised.

"Making a statement, are we?"

She chuckled and thought, "Having my period makes me feel awful, so I'm going to treat myself to fancy toes."

"There's a fine line between fancy and hooker. Let's walk that line carefully, shall we?"

Mawg ignored the judgmental little shit. She woke up this morning feeling combative due to the raging hormones. The dark red toes were a reflection of her current emotional state. Bottle in hand, she turned and saw Jessica gesturing her over to the pedicure stations in the back. As Mawg reached her, Jessica said with a disgusted face, "Do I need to get the lavender again, or did we learn our lesson about the onions?"

She normally would have laughed, but Jessica's expression was all business. Taking off her shoes, Mawg looked at the annoyed nail tech. "Lesson learned." Nodding in satisfaction, Jessica began to prepare the water. Mawg grabbed a magazine off a nearby table to skim through. Once the water was ready, she hopped into the chair and submerged her feet. She was happily relaxing, reading her magazine ten minutes later when Peri piped up.

"Don't move your magazine away from your face. I need you to see who just came in, but I don't want them to see

you. Wait for me to say when, and then peek your eyes over the magazine."

Scrunching her face in confusion, Mawg wasn't sure what to make of Peri's request, but she did as she was told. A few moments went by.

"Peek."

She brought the magazine down so the top was just barely below her eyes. Straight ahead were Gina and that woman from the other night, Mrs. Whitney. There was also a third woman with them Mawg didn't recognize. Pulling the magazine back up to cover her face, Mawg thought, "Why do we need to be secretive? If the Whitneys are members of The Church, it's quite possible she and Gina could be friends."

"I don't buy it. The other night both Gina and Dicklan acted like the Whitneys were a huge pain in the ass. Plus, she just looks bitchy."

Jessica looked between them and thought, "Are you talking about that sex club? I've heard the bitchy lady talk about it before. And the redhead looks familiar, too. Hang on, I can hear the thoughts of anyone with a toe demon. Bitchy has one, I can listen in. Just read and stay quiet so I can focus in on them."

Concerned, Mawg asked, "Wait, but if I can hear your thoughts, can Mrs. Whitney?"

Jessica shook her head. "I can hear any toe demon within a thirty-foot radius. But they can only hear my thoughts if they're within about five human steps of me. Their radius is much smaller than mine."

"Ooh, what's the toe demon's name? I wonder if it's my cousin Eddie."

Jessica continued to work on Mawg's calluses and glared at Peri.

"Again…if you shut up, I might be able to find out."

She continued to hold the magazine up, no longer interested in it. Peri had her curious about the relationship between Gina and Mrs. Whitney. She was also wondering about Mrs. Whitney's toe demon. After about five minutes, Jessica thought, "Ok, the bitchy one is telling the redhead it's time for the next service. The redhead said Sunday was the earliest she could do it."

Mawg's eyes widened in surprise. What service would Gina be providing to Mrs. Whitney? Maybe she had a side business?

"Nah, this is fishy, they —"

"SSSSSHHHHHHHHHHHH!!" Jessica thought as she stared at them pointedly. "Shut up and I'll find out." Another couple of minutes passed until Jessica said, "The redhead is heated. Something about wanting out. Bitchy isn't having it and told her she'll keep up her end of the deal or else."

"What the fuck?" Mawg thought.

"What the fuck, indeed."

Jessica continued to listen in as Mawg tried to wrap her brain around why Gina would be involved in an agreement with the Whitneys. She thought back to her first night of concierge training and remembered the Whitneys arguing with Gina at the club. Then how she pawned Mawg off on Declan to "handle" something with them. Peri was right, something was definitely off.

"Duh, I already told you that. Are you gonna say something to her?"

Mawg thought, "And how would I go about that? 'Oh hey Gina, my nail demon friend conveyed to me and my toe demon that you might be doing some shady shit.' Yeah, that's absolutely believable."

"The sarcasm isn't really necessary. Hag."

Jessica held Mawg's foot in a vice grip and glared at them. "If you two would shut up we might find out what's going on." They shut up and waited. A few moments later Jessica thought, "Bitchy lady's husband owns the building for that sex club. Oh, and the other woman with them is her sister, and the toe demon's name is Mac." Peri's sharp intake of breath and panicked tone caught them by surprise.

"Mac? Did you say Mac?"

Jessica squeezed Mawg's foot. "For fuck's sake, if you people would SHUT UP, I wouldn't have to repeat myself. Yes, Mac."

Mawg peered down at Peri's very concerned little face. She didn't even realize he had a brow until this moment, but he did, and it was now furrowed with worry.

"Who's Mac, and why do you look like you're about to freak out?" Peri's little eyes darted over toward Mrs. Whitney and for the first time since arriving in Mawg's body, he seemed speechless. "Peri! Who is Mac?"

"Shhhhh, he might be able to hear you! Mac is short for Climacteric, and he is the only toe demon more powerful than me. He's two hundred years older than I am, and he HATES ME…for real, Mawg. He's always wanted to have first pick of the middle-aged women because he's the most powerful. But he's kind of a dick, so the clan gave me that right instead. He's never gotten over it."

Mawg stared at her toe, still completely confused. "Ok, sooo…he doesn't know you're here, does he? Like, can you hear each other?" Peri shook his face vehemently.

"No, and thank Demon! If he knew I was here, he could take over Mrs. Whitney's body and attack you. He doesn't have to wait for her to be hungry…that's why he's the strongest. He's just an angry little demon with a lot of power to control his human."

Mawg's eyes sprang wide open. She had no desire to get into a fist fight with an older woman, no matter how much of a cunt she was. Mawg's knees and back were not in fighting shape. "Let's just wait them out and get the fuck out of here. We'll do some research when we get home. We need to know more about Mr. Whitney and the lease, and start researching how to get Declan out of it."

"Yeah, if he's the landlord, he's got Dicklan by the balls."

Jessica began painting Mawg's toes, but was still trying to listen in. "I think Bitchy lady and her husband are blackmailing the redhead. She told her, 'you know the stakes'. Red looked pissed but she nodded." Peri looked up at Mawg while Jessica painted blood red polish over his face.

"I think you should say something to Gina…later. You two are doing the same job, and if she's doing something illegal or unethical, you don't want any blowback. And if she's in trouble…she might need help."

Mawg pondered that and agreed. "Jessica, can you tell me if they mention a location for Sunday?" Jessica continued painting on her toes with a bored expression and thought, "Yes I can…if you will SHUT UP long enough for me to listen. You two are terrible at taking direction." She looked pointedly at them. Mawg and Peri shut up and waited. "They're meeting at the sex club at ten o'clock. No idea if they're staying there or not."

"Ok thank you," Mawg thought. "Neither of us works Sunday night because we don't tour that night. Gina said it's too slow and there's not as much to watch. Maybe we should go and be a fly on the wall to see what happens."

"Ooooooh, we get to spy? I love a good spy adventure! Can you get me a fedora and some sunglasses?"

Mawg rolled her eyes. "Yeah, dressing up my toe to look like Inspector Gadget is an excellent way to stay incognito."

Jessica snorted. "You two are weird," she thought. "Ok, they're leaving. And you're almost finished, you just need a flower." Mawg had given up arguing about the painted toe flower. Besides, it made Peri look kind of cute.

"I don't need a flower to be cute, kiddo. I'm a hot commodity in the demon world."

That made Mawg curious. "Do demons have relationships? Like, with a monogamous partner?"

"No, at least not my particular species. You humans and your sweaty meatsuits are driven by love. We don't feel what you consider 'love'. We'll merge ourselves together and allow our power to surge. So I guess we identify more closely with what you consider 'lust'. We don't cling to one particular member. It's more like a demon power orgy."

"Interesting," Mawg considered.

Jessica piped in. "My species doesn't do any of that. I don't understand what all the fuss is about stabbing a meatsuit sword into a meatsuit scabbard for pleasure. We thrive on transactions. Getting paid is my love language. I want money."

"Ok, I think I can grasp that," Mawg replied.

"No," Jessica said, shaking her head and holding out her hand, "I want my money. Your toes are finished. Seventy-five this time since I didn't need to quarantine your feet."

Now that Gina, Mrs. Whitney and her sister had left the salon, Mawg put down the magazine and pulled out a hundred for Jessica. "Keep it. And just curious, can you hear anyone with a toe demon out in the world?"

Jessica separated the money, stuffing the discretion cash into her bra. "I can hear everything his kind says," she nodded toward Peri, "and the thoughts of the person they're inhabiting."

A thought struck Mawg. "Did the redhead by chance have a toe demon?"

Jessica shook her head no. Mawg said, "Weird…I think she's about my age, so I assumed she might have one as well."

"Not all women experience my kind at the same time in life. Some of you hit earlier, some later. Her time either hasn't come yet, or it's already passed by."

Mawg shrugged as if to say "whatever", and they began to walk out of the salon. Before they hit the door, she heard Jessica say, "Be careful of that Bitchy one. I'm supposedly evil, and she gave me the heebie-jeebies."

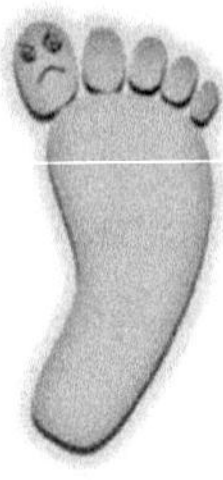

CHAPTER NINETEEN

"So are you gonna confront her?"

They made it back home, and Mawg was chomping on chips and salsa to keep Peri happy while she pulled open her laptop. "I want to do some research first. It's too soon to make assumptions, and I want to learn more about Gina and the Whitneys before I make any accusations. I like Gina and she's been nothing but kind to me. We're giving her the benefit of the doubt."

"Mawg the Practical strikes again. Fine, just keep the snack bucket full. I can't think on an empty stomach, and all that worrying about Mac made us hungry."

She was going to do a search for Gina first, but realized she didn't know her last name. In all the times they'd talked, that never came up. She pulled up the website for The Church to see if Gina was listed as the manager. No such luck.

"I wonder if Gina is her pseudonym? Like, that's her alter ego for the job? You know, safety and all that."

Mawg hadn't considered that, but now realized she should do the same, especially since her own name was so unique. She decided to put the search for Gina off and moved onto the Whitneys. That search brought up a ton of information about the Whitney Group, but not much about them individually. Mr. Whitney was apparently a very powerful real estate mogul across the country. There were photos of him and Mrs. Whitney at various fundraisers and galas, shaking hands with some of the more well-known elites. Mawg was becoming increasingly concerned about Gina the more she looked into the Whitneys and their influential friends. "What could they possibly want from her?"

"They clearly have money, so I don't think it's financial. Let's just say hypothetically that Gina was skimmin' off the top at The Church. Even doin' that wouldn't be a drop in the bucket to these people, so that doesn't make sense."

Sitting deep in thought as she continued to scroll through photos of the Whitneys, she said, "We need to find out more about Gina. I'll try to think of a creative way to learn her name. Maybe that will reveal more search info for us. In the meantime, I definitely want to be a fly on the wall for this meeting they're having Sunday."

Peri started humming the Inspector Gadget theme song. "You're not getting a fedora," Mawg said as she rolled her eyes. While surfing the internet for more information, her cell rang with a number she didn't recognize. Picking it up, she muttered "Hello?" She wasn't super friendly over the phone because it was usually a scammer or telemarketer.

"Is this my Venus?"

The unexpected deep voice with a lilting Irish accent almost made her dump the laptop onto the floor. She tried to compose herself, not wanting to sound rattled. Giving what she hoped was a light-hearted chuckle and not the laugh of a crazy person, she said, "I guess that depends on which Irishman this is."

"Not bad, not bad...you pulled it together."

The amused voice on the other end of the phone replied, "It's the one that wants to nibble on those thick, juicy thighs, and who can't stop thinking about how your ass felt perfect in his hands. It's also the one who wants to cook you dinner tonight so he can get to know the woman underneath the irresistible curves."

Mawg pulled the phone away from her ear and stared at it in shock. Was…was he asking her on a date?

"Has it been that long that you don't remember what a date is? Oh my demon, I'm glad I got here when I did."

She had assumed the "training" they'd been conducting at work was a dalliance for him…a way to pass the time. But inviting her to his home? Mawg felt a giddy little rush that he wanted to see her.

"Oh, I think he wants to do a lot more than that."

Realizing she hadn't responded, she said, "Ahhhh, I think it's coming back to me now. The one with the magical fingers and enviable hair? You can cook?"

Declan laughed on the other end. "I guess you'll have to be the judge of that. Can I send a car for you at seven o'clock?" Mawg pulled the phone away and looked at the time. It was currently two o'clock. It would be a tight schedule, but she could make it work.

"Five hours is a tight schedule to get ready for dinner?! It's not like you have to sew the outfit together, good grief!"

"Seven o'clock is perfect. Do you need my address?"

"The perks to being the boss…I have your address on file," Declan replied.

"Oh yeah, duh."

Mawg chuckled. "Valid point, I should've thought of that. Ok, seven o'clock it is. Can I bring anything?"

"Just yourself and that beautiful ass. I'll see you tonight, Venus." He hung up.

Mawg went from frozen and stupefied to whirlwind in a matter of seconds. Picking the phone back up, she called Tori. "We've got a five-alarm outfit fire and I need your help! What do you wear when a man wants to cook you dinner at his place?"

She heard Tori laugh as she said, "Ok calm down, we've got this. First off, who's the guy? Spill it!"

Mawg laughed and replied, "My boss. My very sexy, Irish, hottie boss that I want to do filthy, filthy things with."

Tori literally squealed. "DECLAN?! I didn't know you were dating Declan! Oh girl, that man is fine! How did that come about?"

Mawg paused for a moment and said, "Um…Well, we're not dating. He's sort of been giving me lessons on erotica. Like, hands-on lessons." Tori squealed so loud that Mawg had to pull the phone away from her ear. "Ok, ok, calming down now…one second, I was NOT expecting that. Let's see…are we going for demure or blatant invitation?"

That's when Mawg froze, remembering that she was having her period. "Oh fuck, Tori…FUCK!" She glared down at Peri.

"Hey don't blame me. I told you not to put me in that mouth. You fucked around and found out."

Mawg sighed. "I'm having my period. I guess we better shoot for demure. God dammit!" She threw a pillow from the couch in pure frustration.

Being the voice of reason, Tori said, "Ok, ok, don't panic. The man runs an adult club, this isn't going to be a foreign situation to him. Let's just get the outfit picked out, and then you can spend all the time you want getting ready. Put me on video and let's go into your closet."

They continued the video call and rummaged through Mawg's closet, settling on a green milkmaid dress that made her eyes pop and her boobs look ginormous. She was feeling too bloated for pants and didn't want to be uncomfortable all night. As they got ready to hang up, Tori said, "Even if you don't think anything will happen tonight, I would go ahead and do the full prep. It will make you feel better, plus…you never know."

In Mawg's entire life, no man had ever wanted to be with her in this state. They treated her more like a leper, to be quarantined for seven days until her monthly 'disease' disappeared. She couldn't imagine any man, let alone this particular man, wanting to fuck her in this condition. But she would do as Tori asked, at least to make herself feel better.

They hung up and Mawg started the full prep. Hair washed and deep conditioned with a coconut conditioner, body scrubbed and shaved top to bottom, she felt fresh getting out of the shower.

"Put on that greasy stuff that smells good. Put it everywhere. And I mean EVERYWHERE."

Peri was talking about her special massage oil that was a mix of citrus and tea tree. She loved that oil and used it for special occasions. Head to toe, she massaged the oil into every ounce of her skin. Once completed, she began the hair and makeup process that always took the most amount of time. Her makeup was light and emphasized her eyes. She was determined to figure out the beachy waves that had been elusive for years. With no time to waste, she found a tutorial video with three million views and followed the instructions. By the time the tutorial was complete, Mawg was in shock. It actually worked!

"Save that so you can find it again."

Before putting on any clothing, she took a moment to look herself over in the mirror. She never really paid attention to her curves before meeting Tori. She'd been so focused on hating her flaws that she completely overlooked the beautiful parts of her body. Never again. Mawg felt sexy. Really, truly sexy.

"See, I told you….caterpillar to butterfly. You really are lucky to have me."

Mawg put her foot up on the tub and leaned down to get close to Peri. "You know what? You're right, I am. Mark that down, because it's probably the last time you'll hear me say it."

Shocked with her statement, Peri's little mouth hung wide open. For the first time since they'd known each other, he was speechless. Mawg grabbed her fanciest matching bra and panty set and put them on.

"You better be prepared for whatever happens tonight, 'cause if Dicklan sees that, he's not gonna care what's coming out of your vagina. He'll be too intent on getting inside it."

Mawg stared at the green milkmaid dress and considered that. She'd been so concerned about how he would react to her period, that she hadn't taken time to consider how she would feel. Would she be comfortable enough to let him touch her intimately? "I guess we're going to find out." She slid the dress over her head, adjusted it, then grabbed some small silver hoops and her strappy sandals to complete the outfit. It was 15 minutes until the car was supposed to arrive.

"Can we have a small snackie? I'm gonna starve if dinner's not ready when we get there."

Mawg pulled a granola bar out of her purse and began to unwrap it. "This will have to tide you over." She finished the bar and brushed her teeth one more time, then reapplied her lip gloss. Just as she was grabbing her purse, the doorbell rang. Meeting Peri's eyes, they both said, "Here we go," in unison.

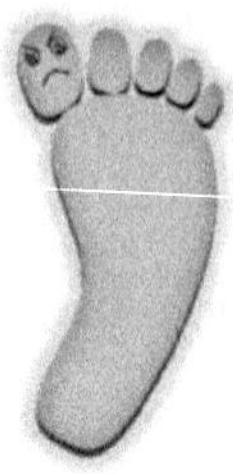

CHAPTER TWENTY

The driver greeted her, then went back to the black Cadillac Escalade to open the door while Mawg locked the house. Approaching the vehicle, she thanked him and he assisted her into the back seat.

"Daaaaaaamn, Dicklan's out here throwing out the red carpet. Good first impression for a first date. Hopefully he's a good cook. If he is, I must insist you marry him."

Mawg chuckled internally and thought, "Oh now you're warming up to him since you know he'll feed you. I see how it is."

"Delicious snackies are the way to my non-existent heart, Mawg. You ought to know that by now."

The drive was quite nice. They wound through some back roads that Mawg didn't recognize, but it was beautiful scenery. As they got further out of town, she watched the setting sun against the horizon. She'd pegged Declan to be a city boy and was surprised to find them heading out to a more rural area.

"If he's taking us to a cabin to chop us up, I'm going to be so pissed. He better feed us first."

Mawg looked down toward her foot and with an arched brow. "Ten minutes ago you were marrying me off to the man. Now you think he's a murderer? It's hard to keep up with your mood swings."

"Ohhhhh get used to it, there's a lot more of that coming your way."

The car made a right turn and as they passed a large grouping of trees, a beautiful, rustic ranch home came into view. It was a single story, but spread wide across a plot of land that was at least three to four acres. The property was surrounded by a wooden split rail fence and the long concrete driveway ran from the end of the property to the front of the house.

"Pick your jaw up off the floor, please."

Mawg realized her eyes were wide and her mouth was definitely open. She relaxed her face into a neutral expression, but continued to survey her surroundings. It was so peaceful. As they continued up the driveway, she noticed an in-ground fire pit with built-in seating on the left side of the front yard. The porch was a wrap-around. Mawg was a sucker for a wrap-around porch. From the Escalade, she could see some potted flowers hanging, but it was difficult to see what was on the porch. The driveway curved when it reached the front of the house, and wound to the right side where there was a large shop that could probably hold a fleet of vehicles.

They pulled up to a stop in front of the house and the driver came around to let Mawg out. As she exited the vehicle, Declan emerged from the front door of the house, wiping his hands on a dish towel. His face lit up with a warm smile as he walked toward her. Gone was the business attire, replaced with jeans and a dark blue fitted t-shirt. Mawg's mouth watered.

"I can't even fault you this time, that's a fine-looking meatsuit."

This relaxed version of Declan was unnerving. He always looked sexy, but she'd only seen the city version that dressed immaculately for work. She envisioned this Declan chopping firewood or riding a horse and herding cattle. Those weren't gym muscles. He looked like he earned that body through physical labor, and damn if it didn't set her on fire.

"Easy there, Annie Oakley."

He turned to the driver as he reached her and said, "Thanks Jim". Jim tipped his hat, got back into the car, and drove off. They were left standing in the driveway, staring at each other. Declan shoved the dishtowel in the back pocket of his jeans and ran his hand through his hair. He seemed different, almost…nervous?

What Mawg didn't realize was the sun setting behind her, casting a glow that made her look ethereal. Declan strolled over and enveloped her in a welcoming hug. "You truly are a goddess, Venus." Being wrapped in his arms while his cologne entranced her was heaven.

Releasing her, he asked, "Did you have a nice drive? I could see the sunset out the window, it looked beautiful. Not as beautiful as you, but still enjoyable." He smiled at her and moved a piece of hair behind her ear. She felt a shyness she hadn't felt in probably twenty years.

Mawg finally found her words. "It was gorgeous, I got to watch it descend the entire drive." Then she gestured to the property. "Declan, this is absolutely stunning. And so peaceful! I can see why you must love living out here."

The crickets were already starting to chirp, and she could see lightning bugs out in the yard. As she observed them twinkling like fairy lights, Declan watched her take delight in their dance. "They usually come out in the spring and summer seasons, but they're a little early this year. It's brilliant, isn't it? Like watching nature's little light show." Then he grabbed her hand and said, "Come on in and I'll give you the twenty-cent tour."

Continuing to hold her hand, they made their way onto the porch. Mawg saw a set of rocking chairs with a little table off to one side, and a long picnic-style table on the other. She said, "I have to tell you, I'm a sucker for a wrap-around porch. I'd be out here every evening to watch the sunset if I were you."

He smiled with a touch of sadness. "Whenever I have the opportunity to be home, I absolutely do that. Unfortunately, that's been few and far between the past few weeks with the expansion happening."

They reached the front door and he stood to the side and put his hand on the small of her back as he gestured for her to go ahead of him. "Ladies first." She passed through the doorway and took in the surrounding space.

Her first impression was that he designed The Church to bring the same vibe of comfort that he had in his own home. There was not a white wall to be seen, but rather rich earth tones. The space was an open floor plan, with the kitchen, dining, and living areas all flowing together. Normally Mawg hated open floor plans, but in Declan's home, they felt right. All along the walls were more of the large black and white canvas prints of erotica, just like they had in the office. There was also dark brown leather furniture in the living area. She turned to him and asked, "Now I'm curious…did you design The Church after your home, or your home after The Church?"

He smiled. "This was our family home when I was growing up. My family immigrated here when I was ten years old and we lived here the rest of their lives. Once my parents passed about thirteen years ago, I inherited it and updated the design in this style. I opened The Church ten years ago and decided if I was going to spend a lot of time there, I wanted it to feel like home."

Mawg nodded and said, "I'm so sorry about your parents. I lost both of mine as well in my twenties and thirties. I know it's something we all go through eventually, but I wouldn't wish it on anyone."

Declan gave her a soft, understanding smile. "Thank you. Yes, that was definitely a tough time in my life. And I'm sorry you went through it as well." He looked empathetically at her for a moment and then his eyes widened. A noise from the kitchen had caught his attention. "Shit!"

He took off toward the kitchen and she laughed as he dealt with an overflowing pot on the stove. "I'm glad I'm not the only one who has pots boiling over. Whatever it is, it smells amazing!"

"It does. Wouldn't it be amazin' if we could actually eat the food? That would be just swell."

She gave a snarky look down at her toe, then wandered over to one of the erotica prints on the wall while Declan cleaned up the mess on the stove. It was a man lying on a bed and a woman straddling and riding him. But the photo was taken from the point of view as if the man was holding the camera. The woman's hands were in her hair and on her face, her expression conveying that she was enjoying her night.

Mawg looked over to Declan in the kitchen just as he finished cleaning the flat-top stove. Their eyes connected and they both laughed as he shrugged his shoulders. "This is why I own an adult club and not a restaurant."

Mawg walked over to him in the kitchen. "Ok so I have to ask, how does one find themselves owning an adult club? I don't recall seeing any classes like that available when I was in college."

Declan chuckled as he opened the oven door to check the food inside. Whatever it was, it smelled heavenly and made Mawg's mouth water.

"Can we fucking eat already? This small talk bullshit's torture. You humans and your societal customs are so annoying sometimes."

Mawg thought, "We're going to eat, just calm the fuck down. Do NOT cop an attitude tonight, please."

At the same time, Declan said, "You are correct, there is no career path for those who find themselves in this lifestyle. I'll have to back up a little bit to give you the full story." He shut the oven door and moved over to a bottle of wine on the counter. He popped the cork, poured two glasses, and handed one to her. Then he walked over and pulled out a barstool for her to sit on.

"I was in my mid-twenties and was your typical young guy. At that age, most of us felt lucky just to be having sex, and we had no idea what we were doing. Wham, bam, thank you ma'am. But I had an experience that most guys my age didn't, and it gave me a leg up. I met a middle-aged woman one night at a bar. One thing led to another and we ended up back at her place. I was in such a rush to get down to it." He shook his head and laughed thinking back on it. "I immediately stripped down, thinking we were going to hop into bed so I could give her the business." They both chuckled at that.

"The ol' dickin' by Dicklan."

"There I was, dick hard and standing by her bed naked as a jaybird. I assumed she was going to disrobe and join me. She just stood there in her red dress, wine in hand and a smirk on her face. Then she turned my world upside down." He paused to drink his wine, then leaned down and sat his forearms on the counter. "She looked me dead in the eye and asked, 'Do you want to get your dick wet once, or do you want to learn how to please every single woman you meet for the rest of your life?' The twenty-something boy in me wanted to

288

get my dick wet, but something about what she was offering made me think more long-term."

Mawg's eyes were wide, fully invested in the story. "I'm guessing you chose the latter?"

Declan chuckled. "I absolutely did. I didn't get my dick anywhere near her that night, or for the next month. Instead, she started teaching me about women….where your pleasure spots are, things that turn you on, things that turn you off. When I tell you that I received a hands-on education, I mean I could have received a degree. I was still young and green, but I was leaps and bounds ahead of my friends by the time she was done with me."

Fascinated, Mawg leaned in. "So was she teaching you the actual erotica, or was it more about understanding women?"

Declan drank his wine and replied, "My education with her was more about paying attention to your cues. The fascination with kinks didn't start until about five years later. A friend told me that he and his wife were going to a big gathering at a campground for people who were in the kink world. He described it as a place where anything goes, as long as it's legal and consensual. I was single and wanting to mingle, and he told me I was welcome to go. So I did."

He reached his hand across the table to grasp hers. "Mawg, when I tell you that my eyes were opened," he laughed, "I mean OPENED. We drove into this campground toward our campsite and all down the road were naked people. We passed by a tent, and I will never forget this," he took a swig of wine, "there was a woman buck naked on a plastic fold-out table on her hands and knees, and a man was standing on the ground next to her whipping her ass with one of those little leather whips…right out in the open! No doors, no rooms, no hiding in the tent. Just right out in the middle for everyone to walk by and see!"

The shock showed on Mawg's face as her jaw dropped. Declan said, "Yep, that was the same expression I had! So we set up camp, and my buddy and his wife immediately strip down to nothing. I'm standing there in my shorts and tee and I'M the one feeling out of place, because everyone around me is naked. So…if you can't beat 'em, join 'em." He shrugged and his eyes twinkled.

Mawg almost spit out her wine she was laughing so hard. "Oh my God, so you did it?"

He smiled. "I absolutely did. And for the first day, I felt so self-conscious, like everyone was staring at me."

Mawg got an appreciative grin as she looked him up and down. "To be fair, they probably were, but not for the reasons you were concerned about."

"I think you just made a grown man blush."

Declan was smiling and indeed, he did look a little red in the cheeks. "Thank you. But I think they could smell the newbie on me," he chuckled. "The next morning I unexpectedly hit a turning point that completely changed the direction of my life. There was a communal area, like a main office that had a kitchen, bathrooms, etc. As I walked up there, I was standing in line waiting to reach the coffee when a sixty-ish year-old woman in front of me was pouring hers. She needed to get to the sugar, which was on the other side of me. We exchanged some random pleasantry about the weather as I handed her the sugar. There we were, buck naked having the most mundane conversation in the world. It was surreal. And it was in that moment I realized how comfortable she was. She wasn't worried about what people thought about her body. She was in a place where everyone there was in the same situation, and it just felt…normal."

Mawg was absolutely fascinated.

"Blah, blah, blah, we get it. Naked bodies good. Now can we eat?!"

He continued, "That's when it hit me like a ton of bricks. These people, no matter where they came from or what they looked like, were stripped down to nothing. No finery to hide behind, no facades. They were literally at their most raw and vulnerable. And because it was safe for them to be vulnerable, their inhibitions disappeared. They could be whoever they really wanted to be."

He took another swig of his wine. "My name means 'man of prayer', but I'm not really religious. So when I stumbled upon an old run-down church, the idea came to me. Why not create The Church and turn it into a place where a different type of worship occurred?" He gave her a knowing wink.

Mawg was sipping her wine, ingesting all this information. "I wish I could envision myself being as comfortable as you were in that camping environment, but I fear I'd be too self-conscious. But going the direction you did with The Church…that's brilliant."

Declan came around the counter and turned her chair so she was facing him. Setting his wine down, he put one hand on the arm of the barstool to hold it steady and used the other to graze her cheek with his knuckle. He leaned in and whispered into her ear, "Your only flaw is your vision, because I see nothing but a goddess, Venus." Then he kissed her softly and pulled his head back. "Let's eat before I say 'fuck dinner' and take you right here."

"It's about fucking time!"

She could feel the heat rising up her neck at Declan's comment and stumbled with her words. "Uh, yes dinner…dinner would be great." He held out his hand to help her down from the barstool and pointed over to the little round nook table. "Feel free to have a seat and I'll bring it over. Oh and if you need the washroom, it's down the hall, second door on the right."

"Now you have to wash your hands whether you were planning to or not. Otherwise, he'll think you don't have basic manners and you eat with dirty pee hands."

Declan's back was turned as she scrunched up her nose in disgust and looked down at Peri. "Ew! Don't be gross!" She made her way down the hall toward the restroom, passing a room with the door cracked open. It was his bedroom. The bed was ginormous and had a solid oak frame.

"Anyone with a frame that sturdy plans to do a lot of heavy pounding on it."

Mawg rolled her eyes. "Enough with the commentary, I'm nervous enough as it is."

They reached the bathroom, entered, and shut the door.

"Why are you nervous? He's already probed your guts with his phalanges. You know he wants to do it again, and he wouldn't have asked you out here if he wasn't interested. Relax and quit dissecting everything."

As she pulled down her thong and sat on the toilet, she whispered, "Exactly! He wants to do it again and I've got to tell him about this situation!" She pointed toward her vagina. "How the hell am I supposed to bring that up?"

"Listen, if shit starts heading that direction, which it will, you just say 'Are you a fan of the Red Wings? 'Cause you will be after tonight!' You'll find out real quick what that answer is."

"Jesus, you are so crass sometimes. I'll figure it out. Just cut it out with the commentary." She pulled the panties back up and flushed the toilet, then went over to the sink to wash her hands. She had never seen the brand of soap that was on the counter, but the smell was amazing. The man had a love for vanilla and cinnamon, that was for sure.

As she exited the bathroom and headed up the hall, she found him standing next to the two-person breakfast table. He looked up and said, "Perfect timing," and smiled at her. As she neared, he pulled out her chair.

"Dicklan knows all the gentleman shit. That's pleasant. A couple of my cohabitants dated dudes who would sit out in the car and honk the horn. That was absolutely maddening."

Once she sat, he returned to the kitchen and came back with one plate of food. There were no other plates, nor was there silverware on the table. Slightly confused but not wanting to make it weird, Mawg said, "That smells phenomenal." Declan placed the plate on the table and smiled at her. "Have you ever experienced how erotic food is, Mawg?" Seeing the quizzical look on her face, he picked up the bruschetta on the plate and came to stand behind her.

Heat radiated between their bodies as he leaned in to speak softly in her ear. "Food and sex have long been tied together." His left hand slid up her neck and his fingers lightly gripped her hair, causing her head to arc back slightly. Her hair fell back and he began kissing along her jawline. Mawg's eyes closed and her body lit on fire at the touch of his lips. He groaned hearing her little gasp and said, "Open your mouth, Mawg." Parting her lips, she opened her eyes and saw him holding the bruschetta with his fingertips, ready to feed her. Turning her head slightly to look into his eyes, she bit in and both she and Peri moaned. It tasted heavenly. Declan's eyes darkened with desire. "Do you have any idea what you do to me, Mawg? Your little moans of pleasure are a drug, and I am the addict."

"You know what would cause more moans, Dicklan? If we could actually EAT THE FUCKING FOOD!"

He let go of her hair and placed a kiss on her forehead. Gesturing at the bruschetta, he said, "Please, eat. I'll go plate up dinner." And then he walked over to the stove.

"Eat the fucking bruschetta before I black you out and start running this shit. Dinner's gonna take a quick turn if you don't."

She ate the bruschetta and thought, "Is it normal for men to be this…giving?" Peri groaned as she ate.

"I can't speak for the billions around the world, but there have to be a few. Based solely on the experience of my previous hundred cohabitants, no."

Mawg contemplated that while she continued to eat, wondering what good karma had been earned in a past life to be blessed with this type of unicorn experience.

"Just enjoy it. Quit overanalyzing everything."

Declan returned with two steaming plates of food and silverware. "I hope chicken is ok. I just realized I didn't ask if there are any foods you don't like or are allergic to."

She smiled as he set the plate in front of her. "The only foods I don't like are texture-based. I don't like anything that feels…slimy? Oysters, anchovies, etc. I think you're safe."

Declan had a sly grin as he sat down at the table. "I'll be sure not to slide anything slimy between those lips." Mawg had been sipping her wine and almost spit it out. She looked over at the shit-eating grin he was wearing and burst out laughing.

"Ha ha ha, aren't you two so clever with your innuendos. Get back to the eating, dammit."

Picking up her knife and fork to cut the chicken, she took her first bite. Moaning involuntarily as it melted in her mouth, she said, "Oh God, that's amazing. What is this?" She continued to cut up the chicken, putting the second bite in her mouth when he replied, "Marry Me Chicken."

She choked on the chicken. Eyes widening, Declan jumped up and began patting her on the back. She was able to get the bite down, her eyes watering. Grabbing a glass of wine to wash it down she said, "I'm okay, I'm fine. Just slightly embarrassed."

"I bet he's got another chicken you can choke on..."

Declan knelt down so he was eye-level with Mawg. He put his hand under her chin so she would look at him. "Mawg…Never, and I mean never, feel embarrassed with me. There's absolutely no reason. Ok?" He pushed the hair behind her ear and gave her a gentle smile.

"You don't have to feel embarrassed with Dicklan, but I will absolutely be giving you shit about that for a while."

Staring into his eyes, Mawg whispered, "Thank you." He stood up and went back to his chair, settling back in. They continued to eat when he asked, "So I know your work history from the vetting, and you told me about your past relationships and losing your parents…what else should I know about Sweet Mawg?"

She paused to think about it while stabbing another piece of chicken with her fork. "I have an unhealthy obsession with vampire shows and cheesy horror movies. I also dabble with a lot of grandma hobbies, but nothing seriously."

He tilted his head to the side with a curious expression. "Grandma hobbies?"

Mawg chuckled. "Sewing, crocheting, reading, baking bread…you know, things that grandmas like to do," she replied as she shrugged.

"Bread?" He asked, eyes perking up. "If you tell me you make sourdough, you are never allowed to leave this house. I love sourdough."

That got a good laugh out of Mawg. "I've dabbled with the occasional sourdough. I actually made an apple pie from scratch once, too. I see now why we buy them frozen. It took all day and was a pain in the ass."

"Pie? You make pie and you didn't think to share this information?"

"So you're a multi-talented woman, is what I'm hearing," Declan replied. Mawg pondered that and said, "I guess I always thought of it more like I'm not really good at any one thing. But I like your description better." She smiled at him as she finished her wine.

His eyes narrowed in on hers with a feral expression. "I can think of a few things you're very good at." She felt the heat rush up her neck.

"You need to tell him. Dinner's done and shit's about to go down."

"I, um…. I probably should have mentioned this before you invited me over tonight." While Mawg fumbled over her words, her hands unconsciously played with her dress. "I'm…um…I'm physically a bit unprepared for what I think you have planned tonight."

His head tilted to the side. "Meaning?"

Oh god, she was going to have to say it out loud.

"Hey…grown-ass woman, remember?"

Mawg looked up at Declan and gestured with her hands toward her torso. "I'm unfortunately cycling right now." She waited for his reaction. Would he be pissed that he went to all this work for the evening and she hadn't told him?

Wine in hand, he stretched his arm across the back of the chair. With his focused dark eyes centered on her, he said, "I can see the wheels turning in your beautiful head. Do you really think I would be mad about that?"

Still feeling overly awkward having this conversation at all, she said, "To be fair, we don't really know each other that well. And working off the sum total of my past experience, that would be a predictable response."

He broke eye contact with her and got up from the table. She thought, "Shit, maybe I misjudged him."

"Nah, Dicklan's got good vibes. I think he's gonna surprise ya'."

To hear that from Peri was unexpected. She watched Declan walk over to the entertainment center in the living room and start messing with some sort of electronics. A few seconds later, slow, sexy music she'd never heard before piped into the room across the surround sound. He turned around and began to walk toward her, reaching out his hand when he got near. She accepted, rising as he said, "Dance with me, Venus."

Fingers entwined, he turned and led her to an empty spot between the kitchen and living room. Taking her right hand in his left and putting his right arm around her waist, he pulled her close. They began to sway with the music, eyes locked on each other. There could have been a five-alarm fire and neither one would have noticed. Declan wrapped her in closer and she rested her head on his chest. She felt his heartbeat as his cologne wrapped around her like a blanket of safety. She couldn't help herself. Leaning her head up to his neck, she began to place slow, soft kisses on his skin. She felt their swaying slow, and heard him take a deep inhale. He released her, bringing both hands to her face and gazing into her eyes.

She recognized the moment his resolve snapped, and his lips crushed down onto hers. The dam of inhibition broke between them. Her hands slid up his chest, the muscles beneath the t-shirt tightening at her touch. His left hand found its way to the nape of her neck where his fingers entwined in her hair.

She was desperate for the taste of him. More…she wanted more. "Declan," she whispered breathlessly.

The desire in her voice as she breathed his name must have broken the last ounce of Declan's reserve. Mouths and bodies still entwined, he began walking them back toward his room. He stopped at the wall inches from the doorway and backed her up against it. His palms were against the wall on each side of her head, his flushed face an inch from hers. With clouded eyes and a voice that was low and gruff, he said, "If we walk through this doorway, there will be no doubt what I desire. I want you to tell me now, Mawg…is this what you want?"

There was nothing she wanted more. "It is, but what about—"

His mouth came crashing down on hers and their hands frantically groped, entangling in each other. He walked them into the room and closed the door. He must have had the surround sound in his bedroom too, because she could hear the music here as well.

"Aren't ya supposed to wait thirty minutes after eating before you do this shit? Don't come crying to me tomorrow if your little tummy hurts."

He pulled his mouth away from hers. Pushing the loose strands of hair behind her ear, his fingers trailed down her neck to the center of her cleavage. Mawg involuntarily shivered. Circling behind her, his arms wrapped around her waist. He leaned in and began to nibble and kiss on her earlobe and neck. Mawg reached her arms above her head to run her hands through his hair. His hands slid up from her waist to her breasts. She arched her back, feeling the hardness of him against her ass. His breath intake was sharp, emboldening her. She began to sway her hips to the music, sliding her ass back and forth against the length of him. He was breathing heavily and growled, "Mawg". He swung her around, his eyes pools of lust. Taking a step back to gather himself, he said, "If you keep that up, I can only promise you a solid five minutes of our evening." He took her hand and walked her over near the master bathroom, gesturing toward it with a nod. "Take your time and do whatever you need to feel comfortable."

Realizing what he was saying, she blushed. Declan saw the shyness creeping back in and lifted her chin. "Hey…if you don't want to do this, you can tell me. But if you're worried about what I'll think…" He reached around and grabbed her ass hard with both hands, causing her eyes to widen first in shock, then desire. "There's nowhere else I'd rather be right now than here. With you. Exactly how you are in this moment."

"Oh my demon, if I had a meatsuit it would be a flood down there. Dicklan's good, he's very good."

Mawg looked into his eyes and said, "Give me a few minutes and I'll be right back." She kissed him quickly, then walked into the master bathroom and shut the door.

"Ok soooo…do your business, then take off the dress before you go back out. Trust me on this."

Mawg thought, "Completely naked?!"

"No, leave the underclothes on. You wore the fancy ones, remember?"

She went over to the toilet and began the process of removing her tampon and cleaning herself up, feeling vulnerable in this state.

"Mawg. Trust that Dicklan meant what he said. This is all gonna be fine. Just clean yourself up and lose the dress. I've seen enough human males to know…he's gonna lose his mind."

She finished cleaning up and stood in front of the bathroom mirror. With a deep breath she said, "Grown-ass woman shit," and dropped the dress to the floor. The woman in the dark green lace lingerie looking back at her was flushed, ready to be rightfully and properly fucked.

"Ooh, ooh! When you open the door, lean against the doorway and just wait for him to see you."

Mawg rolled her eyes and thought, "You'd think YOU were the one getting fucked with how invested you are in this."

"If that man is willing to feed us on a regular basis, I fully support this. And besides, I'll be here the entire time, soooo..."

She pushed that visual out of her mind and focused on trying to be sexy. Folding up the dress and putting it on the counter, she took a deep breath and opened the door. She leaned against the doorway as Peri suggested and waited.

Declan had lit candles around the room and was straightening the bed when she came out. As his head turned, he froze mid pillow fluff. Straightening, his eyes went into predator mode, and she took a moment to understand what prey must feel like.

"Told ya."

His expression was dark, his eyes burning a hole through her. He crooked his finger and his voice was guttural. "Come here, Mawg." She walked toward the side of the bed to stand in front of him. He reached for her hand and held it in the air, gesturing for her to twirl around. Back turned, he put a hand on her arm to stop her from circling any further. She felt his eyes burning into her back, surveying her form. She jumped as his fingers traced from the nape of her neck down to the top of her thong. He turned her back around and she stared into eyes that were now burning with golden flecks. Reaching out, he slid his fingers underneath her bra straps, pushing them down her arms. She shivered as his fingers grazed across her skin. Leaning down, he began to kiss from her neck down to her shoulder. Mawg's heartbeat raced as she felt the softness of his lips contrast with the roughness of his beard on her sensitive skin.

Declan paused and stepped back for a moment. Tilting his head, he asked, "Do you trust me enough to try something?" Mawg felt her throat go dry and nodded. He gestured for her to lay on the bed. She sat on the edge awkwardly and he said, "In the middle please." He walked over to the bureau while she got situated in the middle of the bed. When he returned, he was already erect and Mawg's mouth watered at the thought of removing his jeans. She noticed something in his hand and asked, "What's that?"

He smiled a devilish grin. "This, my Venus," he said, holding up a black eye mask, "is going to introduce you to a whole new world. Are you nervous?"

She laughed awkwardly and said, "a little," as the pitch of her voice raised about two notches. Apparently, that turned him on because he said, "Good," and leaned onto the bed to place the mask over her eyes.

"Oh shit! I think he's gonna do the thing…you know, the thing you think about when you use that vibrating mechanism!"

Mask on, she laid in complete darkness, her breathing unsteady. Unable to see, her other senses took over. She noticed the dryness of her throat, a cool breeze of air across her skin, presumably from the ceiling fan. The music was a sexy, rhythmic instrumental. She focused on her breath to slow her racing pulse. The comforter was soft and cool, causing a slight chill on her heated skin. The smell of his cologne wafted lightly around her. Her body was aching in anticipation.

"You're about to get a dickin' from Dicklan."

She felt movement on the bed to her right as warm breath whispered against her ear. "Do you have any idea how alluring you are?" She shivered, causing her nipples to harden. He adjusted his position and took her by the wrists, placing them together above her head. The breath returned to her ear. "Don't move those. If you do, I'll have to tie them up." His fingertips ran down the underside of her arms and he nipped her jawline with his teeth. She gasped, the unexpected sting catching her off-guard. Her senses were on high alert now, her body aware this man was about to feast on her.

"Hehe…you're Dicklan's snackie."

He backed off for a moment, then she heard him moving down by her legs. She felt fingers on the inside of her thighs, prompting them to spread open. She complied, and he growled, "Wider." She shuddered and widened the distance between them. "That's my good girl," he said, as she felt the sting of his hand slapping her hip. She gasped, then felt him grip the hip as he began to kiss and lick the inside of that same thigh.

She was losing herself in a world of sensations. He must have dropped to lay on his stomach between her thighs, because he slapped both of her hips at the same time, then followed that by gripping them. She felt his beard against both inner thighs and realized his lips were poised against her entrance. He was breathing her in and she was losing her mind.

He brought his right hand off her hip and slid two of his fingers sideways under her thong. He began to run them up and down her closed lips and she bucked at his touch. "If I slide my fingers inside you, are they going to be soaking wet, my Venus?" She was throbbing and knew that if he opened her, he would find a lake. She could only moan. Words wouldn't form, but he wouldn't let it go. "I'm not going to touch you until you answer me, Sweet Mawg. How wet is that beautiful pussy?" Then he took the front of her thong and pinched it together. He slid it inside of her lips so it ran across her swollen, wet clit. Mawg cried out, "Oh god!"

She moved her hands down to grip the sheets. He saw it, and stopped what he was doing. He got off the bed and made a 'tsk tsk' sound and shook his head. "What did I tell you would happen if you moved your hands, Mawg?" She heard him rummaging around in the bureau, returning a moment later. His hands drew her wrists back above her head. "Clasp them together."

She panted desperately, "I'm sorry, I couldn't help it. It was too much."

He continued tying her wrists together. "You're going to learn something about me, sweet Mawg. When I say to do something in this bed, I mean what I say." He finished tying her up and she inhaled sharply when he pinched her nipples. He wasn't hurting her but instead causing her body to feel used…alive. In all of her wriggling, her thighs had come back together. He tapped them with his hand and asked, "What did I ask you to do with these?" She immediately spread her legs back open as wide as she could.

"I wouldn't spread those much further or you're gonna get a cramp."

With an evil grin he said, "Good girl, thank you for listening. Now…where were we?" A moment later his face was back between her thighs. "Ahhhhh, now I remember." Once again he pinched her thong and rubbed it against her wet clit. The sensation was intense and she was throbbing. He removed the thong from inside her and pulled it to the side. His tongue began to tease the outside of her lips. She was writhing, pushing her hips up. Her body begged him to enter, but he did not.

"Can you flip over so you're on all fours? Or would you like some assistance?"

It wasn't a question of "do you want to turn over". It was a statement. Mawg rolled over until she was on all fours, her hands clasped together so it looked like she was kneeling in prayer. He hopped onto the bed behind her, his hands sliding up the inside of her thighs again. "I still want these spread apart, please." She widened the space between her legs, causing her ass to arch into the air. "Sweet Jesus," he said as he grasped his hands onto her bountiful hips. "You are my drug, Mawg." She felt his right hand begin to massage and grope her ass. He planted kisses along her back.

Just as she was relaxing, he smacked her ass.

She jerked, and he began to massage the spot, then kissed it. "You still owe me an answer," he said, smacking her ass again, this time on the other cheek. The tormenting cycle continued…smack, massage, kiss, smack massage, kiss. "I can do this all night, Mawg. I'm not stopping until you give me an answer." Smack, massage, kiss.

She was in a puddle of sensation beneath his hands, debating if she wanted it to stop. "I…I forgot the question."

That caused him to chuckle. Smack, massage, kiss. "How wet is that beautiful pussy?" Smack, massage, kiss.

"I would answer before you can't sit for a week."

She craned her neck to look back at him and whispered, "Drenched."

Declan's eyes turned fierce. "That's very good, Mawg…very good." She felt his hand slip down from her ass giving the reddened skin a moment of relief. His palm cupped her lower lips, massaging them without entering her. She moaned and arched against his hand wanting more. Torturously slow, he slid one finger along each side of her thong and said, "Let's find out, shall we?"

The two fingers slid in between her lips with the thong trapped between them. The devil's doorbell was begging to be rung, but the devil refused to comply. He teased her, running his fingers around her entrance the way one would absentmindedly circle the rim of a wine glass. She was coming undone, everything in her body begging to feel him inside her again. He barely dipped one finger inside her and then removed it. She could hear him sucking on the finger and he groaned.

She whimpered in desperation, her body crying out for his touch. "Declan… please…"

Her plea woke the beast, and he unraveled her. She felt the smack on her ass, then he was dragging the thong down until it sat stretched just above her knees. One hand gripped her hip for leverage while the other began the assault she'd been waiting for her entire life. Gone was the gentleman. The devil had arrived. She cried out and jerked against his hand as the pressure built. But the hand wouldn't yield. Harder it began to pound, and she could no longer speak. The room was filled with nothing but heavy breathing, moans, and cries. She tried to cry out, "I can't control it…oh god, I can't—"

With one final smack of her ass, he moaned, "Let go, Mawg…let go for me."

She let go. Never in her life had she experienced anything like this. Her back arched and her face buried in the pillow as she released a primal cry. She had completely lost control of her body. It was on a journey of its own and there was nothing she could do to stop it. Nothing mattered. He shattered her in the only way a woman should be shattered.

Declan came undone. Her cries and her body's reaction to him were too much. He released his fingers from inside her, then flipped her onto her back. Removing the mask and untying her hands, he stood above her watching, a lion ready to pounce on a gazelle.

She watched as he hurriedly removed his shirt and jeans.

"Holy shit…I was joking before, but you might actually choke on that particular chicken!"

Peri wasn't wrong. Declan was male perfection. She knew that was shallow, but she didn't care in this moment and instead, thanked whatever gods created this fine piece of man.

"Something that delicious has to come from demons, not angels. Just FYI. We've cornered the market on the naughty stuff."

He crawled onto the bed. Prowled was probably the better word. His eyes never left hers as he positioned himself between her thighs, which were now the consistency of gelatin. She still hadn't recovered fully from the first orgasm. Eyes locked, he slid down onto his flat, muscular stomach.

Mawg thought, "Oh my demon, is he about to do what I think he's about to do?"

He wrapped his arms under her legs and grabbed her by the hips, dragging himself up to plant his face right at her apex. Looking up slowly, she saw the predatory grin spread across his face as they locked eyes.

"Maybe Dicklan's like those vampires you like to watch...you know, 'I vant to suck your bl—'"

And then he did it.

"—oooooooooood, holy shit!"

All she could see was his eyes looking up at her. At the touch of his tongue, her body jerked. She was unable to pull away, his hands still gripping her hips. Slowly and torturously, he licked and sucked. Her eyes rolled back in her head and her toes began to curl, gripping the comforter.

"You would never make it as a vampire slayer, just FYI."

He moaned against her sensitive skin and her hips raised, begging to bury him deeper. He obliged. The sensation was too much, too alive. She tried to pull away but he used her hips to keep her in position. She could feel it building, much faster this time. She tried to warn him. "Declan…Declan I'm going to—"

He growled and locked his face in to drive her over the edge. When she came, it felt like a dam broke and he groaned, gripping her hips and lapping her up. "Sweet, sweet Mawg" he murmured. Her legs were shaking and bucking with no control whatsoever.

When she was able to open her eyes, she saw the feral look in his. He released her hips and crawled back up onto his knees. She tried to shimmy to sit up, but he yanked her legs back down. "You're not going anywhere, Venus." Her eyes widened, trying to figure out how she could survive any more sweet torture. He lifted her left leg and positioned himself so his right was poised under it.

"Hey! Hey, there's no need for me to be up here!"

Keeping her leg in the air, he grabbed his very erect dick and began to tease her entrance. Her breath caught in her throat as he slid inside her. It had been a long time since Mawg had felt a man inside her body. She didn't recall any of her previous experiences feeling this good. She clenched, making Declan groan.

317

"Put me down, dammit!"

She couldn't take her eyes off him. She was dancing with the devil and his slow, torturous rhythm pounded deep into her. Mawg began to pant, feeling him hit her G-spot. All inhibitions gone, she began to beg, "More…oh God, more…Declan…"

"All this shaking is gonna give me vertigo!"

Hearing her call out his name was all it took. He thrust into her with reckless abandon and pace, losing his control. Realizing she had the power to do to him what he had done to her, she said, "Look at me." His clouded eyes looked into hers and she dropped the hammer. "Let go for me, Declan…let go."

He gave one final thrust and groaned, "Mawg," and let go.

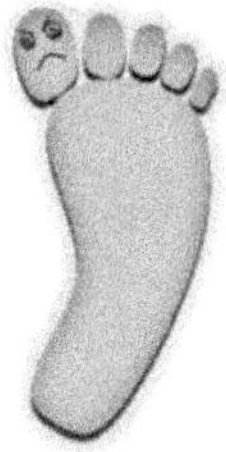

CHAPTER TWENTY-ONE

"Can we smoke in here? I feel like we need to smoke after that."

Still recovering from the explosion of sensations, Mawg laid with Declan's head on her chest. She was overwhelmed with emotions. Never had a man made her feel alive, desired, used, delicious and filthy like this.

"Hey, hey, hey…I can already see the path your brain is going down. Don't get dickmatized."

Mawg's face scrunched in confusion as she looked down at Peri. "Dickmatized?"

"Yeah, that's when the dicking is so good you start doing stupid shit like mistaking lust for love. Just because he dicked you properly, don't start making wedding plans."

She ran her hand through Declan's hair, thinking about that. As much as she hated to agree with the little demon, he was right. Just because this man made her legs shake, it didn't mean anything more than amazing sexual chemistry. Love and relationships required so much more than chemistry.

"Of course I'm right. I'm not saying it won't come to that eventually, you're just not there right now. Keep your head on straight."

Mawg agreed, the activities of the evening finally taking their toll as she fell asleep. Six hours later she woke to the smell of coffee brewing and bacon cooking.

"I've changed my mind, we love him….as long as he keeps feeding us."

She chuckled and sat up in the bed to take stock. Her bra was strewn across the floor. The thong was still hanging around one of her ankles, bringing back memories of last night. She smiled with the satisfaction of a woman who finally knew what it meant to be ravaged. Stretching her hands behind her on the comforter, she felt a spot that was…crusty?

Horrifying realization came over her in the morning light. She'd fallen asleep with no underwear on or tampon in.

With the sunlight peeking through the curtains, she could now see the carnage of the previous night's activities. Luckily his comforter was a dark blue, so it wasn't immediately obvious, but she looked closer and realized the bedding was demolished. It looked like someone had been murdered in the bed.

"He should hang that in a museum. 'Death by Dicklan's Dickin'."

Hopping out of the bed in a panic, she bent over and fumbled with the thong, trying to get her now very sore leg to lift so she could get the damn underwear on. Her stupid hip was locked up and stiff after having her legs spread wide all night. She was hopping on one leg, fighting to get the other leg in the hole and almost toppled over on the bed. She angrily whispered to the fabric, begging it to comply. "Just fucking work with me, would ya?"

"I thought I was with the coffee and breakfast, but if you have other things in mind…" came the lilting voice from the doorway.

Startled by his voice, Mawg lost her balance and face-planted on the bed, ass in the air and thong half on. Squeezing her eyes together in hopes this was a horrible dream, she realized he was about to see beyond the fantasy of last night.

She raised her head to find him holding a cup of coffee, leaning against the door frame with an amused look on his face. Peri was laughing so hard, tears ran from his little eyes and he could barely speak.

"Oh my demon…I wish…I wish you could see your face…because it's fucking priceless."

He'd showered this morning and was wearing nothing but a pair of black sweatpants. Despite the ridiculously awkward situation, she couldn't help but ogle him openly. The sweats were sitting low enough that his hip bones were showing and her brain flashed to visuals of him driving those hips into her last night.

"Can we forget the part of the night where I was flailing around like a wind sock in front of a car lot?"

"Ten more seconds of you looking at me like that with your ass in the air and we're going to skip breakfast and go straight to dessert."

Her cheeks flushed as she met his gaze. He was smiling, but his eyes were dark and she realized he meant it. She got up and managed to fumble with the thong one last time and got it on. Looking back to him, she said "Good morning. I, ah…sorry, you caught me a bit out of sorts."

"I like you out of sorts. I also like you out of dresses. And lingerie." He looked her up and down like he was sizing up an opponent he was going to pounce on.

Her cheeks were heating up and so was her core. "Um…would you mind if I use your shower and clean up?"

Clearly enjoying her awkwardness in the moment, he said, "I gladly offer my services if you'd like the help." His rogue-ish smile was about to drive her wild.

"Um…raincheck?"

Placing the coffee on the bureau, he walked over and wrapped one hand around the nape of her neck while the other grabbed her ass. Thoroughly was the best way to describe how he kissed her. With a light smack on her already sore ass cheek, he whispered in her ear. "Go shower and breakfast will be waiting." Then he kissed her again, picked up his coffee, and walked out, closing the door behind him. She stood there, unable to wrap her mind around how he could melt her in seconds.

"Get your horny meatsuit in the shower and cool off there, Cougar."

Mawg shook her head to clear her thoughts, walked into the master bath and shut the door. Her dress had been hung up, and on the counter were towels, a washcloth, a brand new toothbrush, toothpaste, and a wrapped tampon. Mawg leaned against the counter, eyes wide as she stared at it.

"I know last night I said not to get dickmatized, and I still stand on that. BUT…he's doing a damn good job of making that difficult."

This was one of the few times they were in full agreement. As her mind replayed everything about the past twelve hours, Mawg began the process of cleaning herself up. When she emerged from the bathroom 30 minutes later, the bedding had been changed and the aftermath of last night's activities had disappeared.

"AND he cleaned up the crime scene?! More points."

She wandered out to the kitchen to see him leaning on the counter over his laptop, still no shirt on. Hearing her footsteps, he turned. She stood with no makeup and wet hair falling on her shoulders. Keeping things light, she smiled and said, "You've got to share where you get your soaps. They smell amazing." He stood staring, not saying a word. She tried to fill the awkward silence. "Thank you for setting everything up for the shower, that was really sweet."

In a flash, he was standing in front of her. Placing his hands on her waist, he hoisted her onto the counter. Surprise registered on her face at what he'd done, but also that he was able to lift her like that. He stood between her spread legs and braced his hands on her hips. "How do you do that?" he asked.

Her confusion showed. "Do what?"

"Walk in the room and make me forget everything else exists."

"Just don't forget the bacon exists. Because I haven't."

His hands were in her hair and he was kissing her again. She couldn't get enough of this man. He kissed the tip of her nose and asked, "How do you take your coffee?"

She smiled a cheeky grin. "Hot and sweet, like you."

"Ewwwwww. Oh that's just gross, knock it off."

Declan put her coffee together and brought it to her on the counter, along with a plate of bacon. They snacked on it as she pointed to the laptop and asked, "How is the expansion coming along?" He sighed and replied, "Slower than I'd like. The Church is mine, but the building is not. I lease that from the owner, so when it comes to anything to do with the building, my hands are a bit tied. Right now we're waiting on city permits."

Thinking back to Gina and Mrs. Whitney's conversation at the salon, Mawg asked, "So will it be the same building owner for the new locations?"

Declan rolled his eyes. "Unfortunately, yes. Do you remember the people that Gina was talking about the other night? The Whitneys?" Mawg nodded while she chewed a piece of bacon and he continued. "They're the building owners, much to my dismay."

Mawg tried her best to look surprised. "Oh wow…so that's why you put up with their antics, then?"

"I'd prefer to never deal with them again, but they make it difficult. When I first opened The Church, someone else owned the building. About five years into that arrangement, he sold the building to the Whitneys and I've been dealing with them ever since."

She tilted her head to the side, considering what he said. "So, if you don't like working with them, why expand the business through their properties?"

"Remember when I said they make it difficult to ignore them? Well, they made it virtually impossible to walk away. Contractually, it's written in that I get a 25% discount on the normal lease rate as long as they are members at no cost."

Mawg almost spit out her coffee. "Twenty-five percent?! And you'll get that rate for the new leases, too?"

Declan nodded. "Yes, with the caveat that their name is never associated with The Church, outside of their company owning the building. Their membership requires strict anonymity because of their high-profile life. So, if you have to deal with them, be sure to call them Dick and Jane like everyone else."

The wheels were turning in her mind, but she said, "Understood. Now Gina's frustration with them the other night makes more sense."

"We gotta find out what their deal is with Gina. Something about this situation is very sketchy. Nobody in real estate gives twenty-five percent discounts on rent. Nobody."

He chuckled at that. "Yeah, Gina can't stand them. It's absolute murder getting her to put on a pleasant expression around them. I think it physically pains her."

Mawg laughed, but her brain was working overtime trying to put pieces together. Deciding not to take this conversation any further until she had a chance to gather more information, she hopped off the counter. Her forty-five year-old knees did not approve of that decision, and she would pay for it later. She walked behind him and encompassed him in a body hug with her head laying against his back. "Thank you," she said, placing a kiss on his back.

"For what?"

She smiled against him. "For everything. For making me feel alive. For dinner. For just being you."

"Thank him for the bacon. We want to ensure more bacon in our future."

He turned around in her arms and lifted her chin. "Oh we're just getting started, sweet Mawg. I fear you've turned me into a fiend, and there are soooooo many experiences I want to have with you."

She shivered, imagining the possibilities. "Experiences that require safe words?"

His grin was devilish. "Safe words, toys, ball gags, paddles…I'm going to show you a whole new world, Mawg. But first, I'm going to get you home because I know you need to go into work. And I hear the boss is a real stickler about being on time." He winked at her.

"Are you two always gonna be this gushy and cheesy? If you continue to torment my ears with this crap, I'll make your ears itch. Knock it off."

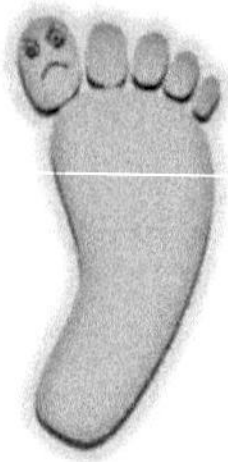

CHAPTER TWENTY-TWO

There were a lot of things to keep Mawg busy at The Church for the next couple of days. It was time for monthly inventory, in addition to the flood of room reservations that were coming in. She was also deep in the process of creating the welcome guide for new potential members. She and Gina were like ships passing in the night, so there wasn't much opportunity to probe for information. Declan had been traveling all week for meetings. She hadn't seen him since the drive back to her home, where he kissed her like a man going off to war. But he would text her random filthy messages throughout the week. Mawg had never sexted before and was thoroughly enjoying it.

"How many times can one person text the word throbbing? I think you need to get a thesaurus."

Sunday rolled around and Peri was imploring her for a costume for the night's spying session.

"You gotta figure something out. Gina will absolutely recognize you, and what are you gonna say if that happens? She knows you're all googly about Dicklan. It'll be suspicious if you're just hanging out there looking for a Dick on your night off."

"You're so presumptuous…what if I was looking for a Jane?"

"Don't try to distract me with boobies…actually, I take that back. Do try to distract me with boobies."

She sighed. "And what kind of costume do you have in mind, Peri?"

"Have you never played dress-up? Isn't that a thing you female humans do when you're little? Use a little imagination and figure it out!"

She was slightly intrigued at the idea of pretending to be someone else in that atmosphere. Maybe she could work on creating an alter ego.

"Yeah, that's the idea! Dicklan calls you Venus...why don't you create an entire persona for her?"

Getting on board with the idea, Mawg picked up the phone and dialed. "Tori? Yeah, I'm gonna need your help with something."

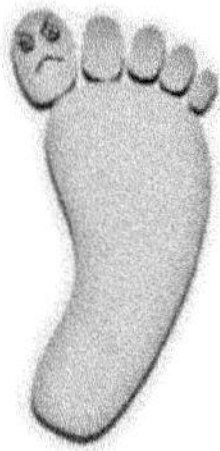

CHAPTER TWENTY-THREE

Mawg discovered pretending to be a fictitious person was fun. This was valuable insight into why people enjoyed cosplay so much. She could be whoever she wanted. The little girl that still lived inside her was having a ton of fun playing dress-up.

She'd parked down the street to avoid being recognized getting out of her car. Passing a shop window and catching her reflection, she adjusted her posture. Venus wouldn't slouch. She was in a slick one-piece black catsuit with a halter top that hugged every curve and felt fucking fierce. Tori worked a miracle and hooked her up with a friend who owned a wig shop. The jet black wig was long and straight, reaching down to the small of her back. It had bangs that just touched her eyebrows, and she was wearing black sunglasses.

"I'm honestly shocked about the heels. You caught me off guard with that."

She wasn't sure how long the heels would last. She had a pair of flats in her bag, just in case she couldn't hack being a heels girlie.

"Ok, before we get to the door, let's chat. You are not Mawg. You are Venus. Venus is a bad ass. She doesn't apologize. She doesn't move out of the way for people. Venus will be responding to people, not Mawg. Got it?"

Mawg paused before she got to the door and took a deep breath with a little nod down to Peri. There was no Mawg here.

The first test was to get past John at the front door unrecognized. She held her breath for a moment as she walked up to the door that he held open. "Welcome to The Church, have a great night." Venus, head held high, gave him a curt nod of acknowledgement and she was in.

Next up was the Liam test. This might be slightly more difficult. She'd developed a good rapport with Liam, and they chatted regularly. She walked up to the bar and waited silently as Liam finished serving another customer. He turned, and she saw nothing register on his face that signaled recognition. "Welcome to The Church, I'm Liam. Would you like to see a drink menu, or do you know what you'd like?"

"Whiskey on the rocks, please."

"Whoa there, slugger…you sure you can handle that?"

Mawg thought, "Venus can."

Liam looked at her with a questioning expression for a moment and she feared she'd been discovered, but then he said, "Any particular kind?"

Ahhhh, it wasn't recognition. He was giving her a double take because she didn't know how to order whiskey. Amateur. She needed to play this off.

Venus leaned an arm onto the bar and purred, "Surprise me." Liam's eyebrow raised in appreciation. "As the lady requests." He filled a glass with ice and grabbed a bottle to pour. Once finished, he grabbed a coaster and placed the drink in front of her. "That'll be fifteen dollars." She gave him a twenty, picked up the drink to head to the main room, and said, "Thanks, sugar." Peri looked up at her with his little face all crinkled up.

"Sugar? Is Venus a waitress from an 80's sitcom who smokes long cigarettes and has a husband who eats TV dinners in his recliner?"

She glared down at her toe and thought, "Patience, toe boy. I'm still figuring out the character." Peri began shaking his little face back and forth vehemently.

"Nope, nope. Absolutely not, we're not doing toe boy."

Realizing how much it annoyed Peri, she grinned and said, "Ok, Toe Pesci." One tiny eyebrow raised slowly.

"You wanna keep it up? Cause we can fight tonight if ya wanna fight."

Venus grinned as she used Mawg's key card to open the door to the back room. Hearing the familiar click, she opened the door and stepped into the hallway. Thankful there was no one there, she took a moment for another deep breath and pulled herself together. She took a sip of the whiskey and immediately felt the burn ignite her throat.

"Yeaaaaaaaaah, I don't think Venus is gonna be a whiskey drinker in the future."

"We'll figure that out." They walked to the curtain and she took stock of herself before walking through.

"You got this?"

She closed her eyes, inhaled the vanilla and cinnamon in the air, and called on the visual of Declan's predator eyes before he went down on her. She wasn't the prey. She was the predator.

"Yep." Venus lifted her chin and pulled back the curtain to enter. It was surprisingly busy for a Sunday night. She recalled Gina saying Sundays were slow, so the volume of people in the club caught her off-guard. The air was thick and the bodies were already grinding. Normally it was later in the evening when the main floor got wild, but that was not the case tonight.

"We need to be in a strategic spot to see Gina and the Whitneys come in."

There was a small two-top table near the front of the stage that gave her a good view of the entrance without being seen herself. She sat and sipped on the whiskey that was still burning her lungs, surveying the room.

There was only one rule in The Church about activities on the main floor: they had to be legal and consensual. Sex is a legal and consensual act in a private establishment as long as money isn't being exchanged, and there was plenty of that happening currently. A group of ten people were on the dance floor laying on what looked like gym mats that had been brought out. Laying wasn't the right word. They were fucking on the mats. All of them. Together. It was one massive bundle of entwined limbs, moaning noises, and bodily fluids. Men were with women, men were with men, and women were with women. No one seemed to care who they were touching, as long as their hands were on skin.

Venus observed through her sunglasses as a couple approached the mat and were welcomed with open arms…and vaginas. Peri popped off in a TV announcer voice.

"Come on down to MeatSuit Mania! We've got so many weiners and vaginas, we're practically giving them away!"

Venus almost spit out her drink and shushed him internally. "Jesus, don't make me laugh! We're going to blow our cover." But he wouldn't relent.

"We won't be the only ones blowing things, don't you worry about that!"

She knew he was trying to break her character, but she wasn't going to let him win. She sat cool as a cucumber, resting bitch face in place. A loud thump on the stage grabbed her attention. She looked over to see the set-up crew hauling what looked like a padded massage table to the middle of the stage.

"Don't be obvious, but I think the Whitneys just arrived."

Slowly turning her head to survey the room, Venus peered out over her sunglasses. Sure enough, there were the Whitneys appearing through the curtain. As they entered the main floor, they grabbed the attention of a server walking by. Venus sat sipping her whiskey as they ordered, then found a high-top table to stand at. A few minutes passed before the server returned with their drinks. Venus continued to sip and watch as their heads were huddled together, a quiet conversation being had. Dressed like they were heading out to an upscale dinner with their fancy friends, they looked rigid and stiff, completely out of place with the half-naked bodies gyrating around them.

"Something about them gives me the fucking heebie-jeebies. Him especially."

Venus didn't argue because she felt the same. Mr. Whitney looked like every rich, old businessman that had ever been portrayed in movies. But his eyes…something about his eyes bothered her.

"They're dead. He has those serial killer eyes, ya know…the ones with no emotion."

That was an accurate depiction. And Mrs. Whitney wasn't much better. While her eyes weren't lifeless, they were constantly scanning, and Venus could almost see the scheming going on behind them. As Venus continued to survey the Whitneys, the curtain moved behind them. In walked Gina with a very handsome, fifty-something year-old man on her arm.

"Is she married? Or does she have a partner of some sort?"

"Not that I'm aware of. Then again, we don't gab about her personal life, either." Venus took a sip of whiskey, keeping her face hidden behind the glass. She watched a server walk up to Gina and the man, and they placed an order. They were less

340

than ten feet away from the Whitneys, but neither party acknowledged the other.

The hair on Mawg's…er, Venus's arm was standing on end. Her gut was telling her this was something bad.

The server returned with their drinks, and Gina and the man wandered off toward the nearby hallway to the private rooms. Venus watched the Whitneys, who were still sitting and drinking. Mrs. Whitney's expression had turned more serious, and Venus assumed the whispered conversation had taken a turn.

From the corner of her eye, she saw the set-up crew hanging some sort of rack contraption from the ceiling, centered right above the massage table.

"Sundays are weird here. The vibe is more…animalistic."

She understood what Peri was trying to describe. The energy was palpable, like lust was floating across the air. That vibe was always at The Church, but it seemed enhanced tonight. This was the first night she'd seen people openly fucking on the main floor. Whoever made the music selections for the evening was driving the atmosphere. The sounds were very rhythmic and ethereal, like one would hear in a movie about Vikings.

The Whitneys were now on the move, taking the last sips from their glasses and walking toward the hallway where Gina and the gentleman were.

"Showtime."

Venus finished her whiskey with a final swig and looked around for one of the servers. When one stopped by, she said, "I need to step out for just a minute. Please reserve my table and I'll be back momentarily." Then she walked off.

"Wow. That was really rude. But kudos for getting into the character, that's totally what Venus would do."

The corner of her mouth turned up in a small smile. She thought, "I'll make sure I'm extra nice to him next time I see him. But thank you, I was really feeling like she would be cunty."

They were near the entrance to the hallway. Venus peeked around the corner and saw the first two rooms had open doors and blinds. The last two rooms were both closed up.

"Betcha a snackie they're in a closed room."

She inched up to the window of the first room. There was a naked Jane in the middle of the room that lined with mirrors. She was beautiful, all curves and softness as she danced in front of the mirror. Holy demon, she was sexy! Venus looked over as another Jane was in the spectator chair in the corner, pleasuring herself under her skirt as she watched dancing Jane.

"Booooooobiiiiiiiiessssss....."

Peri was in his happy place. "Stay focused, there will be plenty of time to watch boobs later." His face smushed into a little pouting expression as she continued down the hall. Nearing the next open window, she saw Jake on his knees, his back to her. In front of him was a woman standing with her feet in a container of what looked like squished fruit.

"I don't ever want to see that man again. I'm still pissed about that. Move along."

She chuckled internally. He wasn't going to let that go easily.

"No, I will not. Filthy bacteria boy."

They moved down the hallway to the next room where the door and blinds were closed. She could hear muted voices. There was a small crack in the blinds, and she gave it a quick peek. They were in there. Gina's deep red hair would be noticeable anywhere. Venus thought to Peri, "keep an eye out for anyone coming down the hall and give me a heads up."

Venus tried to look nonchalant, but it was difficult standing next to closed blinds in an environment where that was a no-no. She peeked through the small crack to see Gina stepping out of her dress. She wore nothing underneath and looked like one of those insanely tall amazon goddesses. Venus couldn't see, but the man must have been standing in front of her. She walked forward out of the view of the crack. Venus leaned her head to a better angle and could now see the man, naked on his knees in front of Gina, a dark red circle surrounding him on the floor. She could also see Mr. Whitney in the corner spectator chair looking on. Even watching this, he still looked dead in the eyes.

Gina took two long steps forward and grabbed the man by the hair forcefully to yank his head back. He was now kneeling between her feet, his nose grazing her lower lips.

Listening through the window made it muffled, but it sounded like she said, "Eat." She shoved his face into her, bringing her arms up to rest on top of her head. Her face showed no pleasure, but rather, annoyance. The man was making an attempt, and came up once for air as Venus noticed his eyes. He looked scared. Not scared in a "oh this is kinky" kind of way. Scared in a "someone help me" way.

Gina grabbed his hair once again and this time she bent down so her face was inches from his. "I said, EAT." Then she shoved his face back into her pussy.

In the corner, Mr. Whitney had a snake-like grin with those empty eyes. Mawg couldn't see Mrs. Whitney, and assumed she must be against the near wall, outside of the small window of sight she had.

"Is…is she forcing that man??"

Venus thought, "That's sure what it looks like. What do we do?"

Suddenly, Venus heard a woman's low, muffled voice and the man's temperament changed instantaneously. His hands reached behind Gina, fingers digging into her ass. He buried himself even deeper and moaned.

They were so caught up in the scene in front of them, they didn't hear the footsteps behind them. "What do you think you're doing?"

Venus froze. Fuck.

"Fuck."

Putting on her best attempt at acting yet, she turned to the security guard and said, "I'm looking for my friend. She asked me to meet her in a room, but I wasn't sure which one. I'm new and they all look the same."

The security guard gave her a wary look. "If doors and windows are closed, they're off-limits. I don't care what your friend might be doing in them."

On one hand, Mawg was thrilled that security was coming down on her because it meant The Church was serious about ensuring everyone was safe here. On the other hand, her sleuthing was done for the evening.

Donning her alter ego, she lifted her chin and said, "Well where can I get a drink while I wait on her?" The security guard took her by the arm and pulled her back into the main room. "The bar is over there," he said, pointing. She looked at the bar, then down at the hand on her arm, then back up to the guard's face with an expression of annoyance. "Are you buying? Or can I please go get my own drink now?"

He released her arm and said, "Familiarize yourself with the rules here. We don't play around with them and you'll get yourself banned if you do that again. I'll be watching you." Then he gestured toward the bar as if to say "you're free to go."

She turned away from him with a haughty expression, like dealing with him was beneath her.

"Should I be worried that you're taking to this cunty personality like a duck to water?"

Her heart was beating ninety miles per hour and she definitely needed that drink now. That was way too close. She stood in line at the bar, waiting her turn.

"Ok...let's recap so I understand. Those evil people watch Gina, what...suffocate men? That doesn't make sense. Why would she do that if she hates them?"

It was a great question, and she didn't have an answer. It was her turn to order, and she requested a gin and tonic with a lime this time. The whiskey wasn't doing it for her.

"Much better choice. We'll figure out a signature Venus drink on a later date."

The bartender handed her the drink, and she walked back to the table that had been reserved for her earlier. Sipping her drink, Venus tried to put the pieces together from what she just saw, but was left perplexed. And who was that man with Gina?

"That might be a good starting point to research. Didn't you tell me once that all the member files have their photo in them?"

She had, and thought, "Excellent point. I'll take a dig through those on my next shift, if I can get away from prying eyes."

The lights suddenly dimmed across The Church, and deep, heavy bass drums began to pound. The crowd that was already getting wild began clapping and yelling. Apparently the entertainment was about to begin. She was sitting in the front near the left side of the stage. The set-up crew had been busy while she was snooping. The massage table was still centered in the middle of the stage, and the rack they had been hanging now had at least six cameras hanging from it. They were all focused on the massage table.

More drums pounded through the speakers. Even the MeatSuit Mania, as Peri had called them, stopped to catch the show. The ball of bodies and limbs had grown to somewhere between 15-20 people. It was hard to get an accurate count with all the intermingling body parts.

A roar came from the crowd as six very muscled, masked and shirtless men emerged onto the stage. Three came from the left, and three from the right. They wore black cargo pants and army-style boots. Slowly, they walked in unison to the beat of the drums to form one massive unit of muscle in the back middle of the stage.

They stood shoulder to shoulder with two in the back, two in the middle, and two in front. A moment later, they parted down the middle as a woman appeared, emerging from the curtains behind them. Venus judged her to be somewhere in her late twenties to early thirties. Her long, silver blonde hair touched her very naked ass. She was shaped like a delicious pear, with smaller breasts that would fit easily into a palm and hips as wide as her shoulders. In her right hand was a shiny, red apple. She was Eve.

Eve raised her arms out to her sides, and the two muscled men in the back lifted her up by her arms. The two men in the front reached down to her feet to swing them in the air, holding her legs above their heads. The two men in the middle supported her back. She was suspended in the yoga corpse pose. The men walked her forward until they held her hovering above the massage table.

The cameras that were hung from the rack earlier displayed a birds-eye view of Eve on the video screens that came to life around The Church. The room was filled with various images of her, depending on the camera's view. Her face was angelic and the little makeup she wore made her look like a shimmery fairy.

The muscle men gently laid Eve on the table, then knelt down on one knee surrounding her. The drums and music continued to build, and Venus became immersed in her surroundings. It was hard not to succumb when her senses were being overtaken. She had seen plenty of entertainment at The Church, but nothing that compared to this.

The drums began to beat faster and the crowd became more frenzied, waiting with baited breath for what was to happen next. Suddenly, the music stopped and the room hushed. Eve sat up on the table, holding the apple out with her bent arm, showing it to the crowd. All eyes were on her as she looked directly at the crowd, then bit into the apple. Out walked a man from behind the stage. He was wearing the mask of a snake, leaning into the Garden of Eden theme. Something in Venus's gut churned.

"Wait…is that…??"

She would recognize that beautifully toned swimmer's body and those hip bones anywhere.

Declan. That was Declan. Her Declan.

"…I mean…technically he's not yours…"

Peri may have been right, but that didn't make one bit of difference to the pain that burned inside her.

A new song and a new batch of beating drums began. The snake sauntered up to Eve, and she feigned a shocked expression at seeing him. The snake plucked the apple from Eve's hand, turning and throwing it into the crowd, causing them to whoop and holler. He turned back to Eve and placed his widened palm on her chest, guiding her to lay down on the table. He sauntered to stand at the head of the massage table, Eve's head precariously close to the bulge in his cargo pants.

"Hey, we don't have to watch this. Come on, let's get out of here."

Venus was frozen to her chair. Maybe she was a glutton for punishment, but she wasn't going anywhere.

"I really don't think this is a good idea."

She didn't care. She was caught between a strange mix of emotions. Mawg wanted to vomit. Venus wanted to fuck.

A small instrument table had been rolled out onstage. The snake picked up a wine glass from the table and began to pour clear liquid into it. Once finished, he held up the glass above Eve and gestured at the crowd. Again, they went wild. He tipped the glass and a small bit of liquid dripped onto Eve's breasts. Then he handed the glass to the muscled man next to him, who stood up and poured a bit more on her body. This continued, the glass being passed from one muscle man to the next as they poured the liquid on Eve.

When the last man was finished, all seven men reached their hands out to Eve and began to massage a part of her body. Eve's eyes closed and her mouth opened slightly. She had the face of a woman who was living out a fantasy. The massage continued until every bit of her skin had been touched.

The snake hunched down so his head was next to her ear. There must have been a microphone under the mask, because his voice came over the speakers above the music.

"Goddess. Mother. Giver of life. How may we celebrate you on this night?"

His hands were slowly gliding up and down her arms, his head still next to her ear.

Eve whispered, "Release."

"Then release you shall have."

As if they'd done this a thousand times, all seven men began attending to Eve in a practiced routine. Seven sets of hands began to run fingers lightly across whatever part of her body was closest to them. The two near her breasts leaned down, each taking a nipple into their mouth. The snake continued to purr in her ear for the crowd to hear.

"What a very good girl you are, Eve…your beauty will drive men mad for thousands of years. They'll worship you. They'll hate you. They'll want nothing more than to bury themselves deep inside you."

One of the men closest to her legs reached over and spread her lower lips wide. Eve was now gasping and moaning, her body overwhelmed with sensations. The other man near her legs took one finger and began to circle her very wet clit. She went mad, releasing guttural moans and screaming for more.

"More? You want more, Eve?" the snake purred into her ear. The muscle men, who were now erect and also turned on, began to go to work. While one tormented her clit, another slid his fingers inside her. The two men at her breasts had released her nipples from their mouths and the snake handed them vibrators. They ran the vibrators over her nipples.

Everyone in the room had stopped what they were doing to watch Eve. Various parts of her body were on the screens surrounding the room, and they got a very up-close and personal view into her experience.

Her body was writhing in ecstasy. She was unable to form words and her breath was coming in short, staccato pants.

The sounds she made were the envy of every woman in that room, Venus included.

The pace began to pick up. The fingers inside her drove harder. The ones on her clit picked up speed. The men holding vibrators to her nipples used their other hands to run fingertips down her sides.

Meanwhile, the snake was still in her ear. "You are the fruit that nourishes us. You are mother to the Earth and we worship you. Release, Eve…let go and release."

There was nothing Eve could do to hold back the earth-shattering release. With a primal scream, she came so hard that she squirted. The crowd, seeing the up-close view on the monitor, lost their ever-loving minds.

Venus thought the show was done, but she heard the snake whisper, "Again."

The men continued to push the threshold of pleasure. Eve breathlessly cried, "Oh god, oh god…" over and over, and then she released, squirting again.

Eve laid there, her body continuing to shake long after the beautiful torment had stopped. The men had stepped back from the table and everyone watched silently as Eve's body reveled in the pleasure it had just received. The snake walked over to the side, slid his arms under her back and legs, and picked her up. She hung limp like a lifeless doll as he walked in front of the table, standing in front of the crowd with Eve in his arms.

To the crowd, he said, "Tonight we celebrate you, mother of all the Earth."

The crowd roared, raising their arms and cheering. A chant of "mother" began. Venus stood with the crowd as they celebrated Eve. The snake surveyed the crowd as they cheered, and his masked face turned her direction. She could've sworn he froze for a moment, but before she could tell, his head swiveled to the other side of the audience. And then, carrying Eve's limp body, he walked back behind the curtain.

The lights went back to normal and music piped throughout the club. The show was over. Venus finished her drink and decided to make a pit stop before heading back home.

In the stall of the empty bathroom, Venus sat for a moment, gathering herself.

"Soooo…how are you feeling?"

She stared at the stall door, zoned out. "I'm feeling a whole bunch of things, and I haven't processed any of it yet."

"Well, I know we're feeling hot and bothered, so you don't have to describe that one."

That she definitely was. Watching the sheer pleasure radiate from Eve made her think of the night at Declan's house and how she'd felt. She wanted more.

"Are you mad at him?"

She thought about it for a little while, finally saying, "No, not mad. I think I am jealous, though. And I'm struggling with that. I have no right to be. We haven't claimed any rights to each other. I think I was just hopeful that our night together meant as much to him as it did to me, considering he went to so much trouble to make me comfortable. Seeing him up on that stage made me consider that might not be the case." A single tear rolled down her cheek and she sniffled and wiped it away.

"Hey kiddo…you know I'm the first person to give you shit about Dicklan. But after a thousand years hangin' around

your planet, I've become pretty good at judging your kind. Dicklan has a good vibe. Sure, tonight was a shock but did he really do anything other than put on a show? Think back to that first time you saw him with the Jane. He was puttin' that show on just for you. Tonight, he was puttin' it on for the crowd. He's literally the central figure in a world of kink that he built. Of course he's going to be involved in it."

Mawg sniffled again, wiping her nose and nodding.

"He brought you to his home. You know what your own home means to you. That's your sacred place. And he let you into his. I don't think he's just playing with you, Mawg."

CHAPTER TWENTY-FOUR

Mawg no longer felt like Venus. She might still look like Venus, but Mawg realized no matter how much she changed her outward appearance, she would always be just Mawg underneath the costume. Feeling better after Peri's talk but also emotionally overwhelmed, she cleaned herself up and walked out of the bathroom door to head home.

And ran straight into Declan's bare chest. Gone was the snake mask, and the chocolate brown eyes that looked her up and down were concerned. Remembering she was still in costume, she tried to play it off and mumbled, "Oh sorry," and moved to walk around him. He caught her by the wrist as she tried to pass, then leaned down by her ear. "You could wear a burlap bag twenty years from now and I would still know those bitable hips, sweet Mawg."

She froze, realizing she'd been caught. Still holding her wrist, he asked, "Can we go somewhere and talk?" A lump caught in her throat and she nodded. He walked her over toward the stairs, but the security guard from her earlier interaction was standing in the way. Declan nodded and said, "Hey Steve," and started to walk past him, but Steve piped up. "Is she causing problems again, boss?"

"Fuck."

Declan had a quizzical look on his face and looked at her, then back to Steve. "Again?"

Steve nodded, "Yeah, I caught her peeking in one of the closed rooms earlier. She gave me a story that she was new and looking for a friend."

"Fuuuuuuuuuuck."

Declan turned a surprised eyebrow toward Mawg, then told Steve, "Nothing to worry about, I'll handle it. Appreciate you, Steve." He gestured for Mawg to walk up the stairs in front of him as they headed to the office. They entered the room and he closed the door and blinds behind him. She stood awkwardly in the middle of the room, her brain scrambling to decide what to say.

Standing by the door, he watched her nervously squirm. "I see the wheels turning, Mawg. Whatever is going on, you can talk to me."

"Just tell him. Don't play games with Dicklan, not if you want something real with him."

Mawg let out a big sigh and said, "I want to tell you everything, but part of this concerns someone else, and I don't want to throw them under the bus when I don't have all the facts yet."

Declan's face got a confused look.

As she wrung her hands, Mawg nervously let out another sigh. She started back at the conversation overheard at the salon, omitting to mention the demon variables. Then she explained the disguise and what she saw with Gina and the Whitneys in the room.

He stayed silent, but his face looked surprised at hearing that. She could clearly see that whatever was going on, he'd had no idea about it.

Mawg continued, "And then when Steve found me, I played it off and went to the bar for a drink to calm my nerves. That's when your…er…show began."

He ran his hand through his hair and then over his face, trying to process the information she'd just given him. He sat on a loveseat in the corner and patted the couch for her to sit with him. She did and he wrapped his arm around her shoulders. "So you've been carrying this around for the past week?"

"I didn't want to bring it up in case I was wrong about what I heard. I adore Gina, and if I was wrong, it would hurt everyone involved. I was hoping to get some truth tonight, and then talk to you when my understanding of the situation was more concrete."

"I'm not mad at you, Mawg. You wanted to give her the benefit of the doubt."

"Yes, and I still do. I don't think she's doing this voluntarily, Declan. In every single interaction with these people, she seemed angry. Even tonight in that room, she wasn't experiencing pleasure. She wasn't happy. I'm concerned they're blackmailing her for some reason."

His face was still disappointed. "I just don't understand why she wouldn't come to me. We've worked together for five years now. She should've known I would help her."

Mawg's eyes widened as a piece of the puzzle fell into place. She pulled away to look at him. "You said she's been with you for five years?"

He nodded. "Yeah, we've worked together a long time."

The wheels were turning in her brain again. "Declan, did you meet Gina before or after the Whitneys bought the building?"

He sat with a thoughtful look, trying to recall. "I believe she came right after they bought it."

Mawg gulped at the realization. "Do you think she knew the Whitneys before she came here? Like, maybe they wanted to plant her here with you?"

Declan's eyes widened in surprise. "But why? I know our books are clean, I audit them regularly. She's not skimming from me."

"I think there might be something else going on," Mawg replied. "I didn't recognize the man that came with Gina tonight. Do you know if she has a significant other?"

Declan shook his head. "Not that I'm aware of, but she doesn't share about her personal life very much. She's always kept that to herself and I've respected that."

"Ok, and I noticed the same thing," Mawg said. "What do you think about taking a look through the member files? I'm curious if he's actually a member."

He stood up and held out a hand to her. "I think that's an excellent idea…for tomorrow." She took his hand and stood up, and he wrapped his arms tightly around her, breathing her in. They stayed in the embrace, lightly swaying for the longest time. Then he leaned back to look in her eyes. "About what you saw tonight…"

Mawg's heart dropped a little, not fully prepared to hear whatever he was going to say next.

"We've had a long-standing tradition of performing that particular piece for the past three years. There is a sign-up for women who want a night to experience being Eve. Once a month, the Eve is selected and we play out this same performance."

Mawg stood in his arms quietly, continuing to listen.

"My role is always the same. It is not a matter of attraction for me. It's strictly a role."

"I knew it. I knew he wasn't some slimy guy."

He lifted her chin with his finger to look in his eyes. "I know we still have a lot to learn about each other, but please don't ever doubt my desire for you, sweet Mawg."

She felt her eyes welling up and wanted to kick herself for getting emotional right now.

"Sorry, that's not you. It's me."

"I told you before, but I will reiterate it as many times as it takes to stick. There are a world full of things that I want to make you feel, baby. But hurt is never one of them." He wiped the tear that was threatening to run down her face.

"I think I was jealous. And I know I shouldn't be, because we've never discussed what this is," she gestured between them, "but I was. And I feel dumb about it because we're literally in a place where everybody's touching each other and I knew what I was getting into. But I saw you whispering into her ear the way you do in mine and—"

He swung her around so she was facing the office desk and stepped forward with his chest against her back. The forward motion caused her to brace her hands on the desk to steady them. In a deep, gravely voice he bent over and whispered in her ear, "Listen you raven-haired vixen. I only have eyes for one woman. One very sweet, delectable goddess with thighs I would happily die in-between. Try as hard as you like, but you'll never be her." And then he smacked her ass hard. "You need to be punished. Not only are you pretending to be her, but you broke the rules tonight."

"Ooooh, naughty Dicklan's kinda fun."

Naughty Declan was very fun. And very hot.

"What are you waiting for? Get into character!"

Venus smiled with a cat-like grin. "And what kind of punishment do I deserve?"

His eyebrow raised. "The worst kind. The kind that will leave you panting and unfulfilled because you tried to be her.

You could never be her. Sweet Mawg is my goddess." He smacked her ass hard again and she cried out at the sting.

Venus was feeling fierce now. "I'm so much better than her, I'll make you forget her name before the night is done." Smack. Her ass was on fire but she wanted it. She wanted more. "She'll be nothing to you when I'm finished." Smack. Then she felt his hands at her neck, untying the halter top of her catsuit. Letting it drop, her breasts spilled out. He reached under her arms that were still braced on the desk and began to squeeze and massage her breasts that were now hanging freely. "You are not her." He smacked her right breast, then immediately began teasing and torturing her nipples. She was falling apart underneath his hands. If she thought the devil arrived on their first night together, she was sorely mistaken. He was still leaning into her, and she began to rotate her hips to stroke against him with her ass. She didn't want sweet tonight. She wanted fire. His groan came from deep within and she could feel his dick straining against the cargo pants on her ass.

"Your words may belong to her, but your body betrays you."

"Rawr! Get him, tiger!"

Venus kicked her hips back into him, catching him off guard and pushing him back a couple of steps. Freed, she turned to face him. He stood, unmoving. She took two steps forward looking him directly in the eye, and grabbed him by the balls without breaking eye contact.

His eyes were wild. It was her turn. He was at her mercy, and she turned them around so his back was against the desk. Refusing to let go of his balls, she said, "Unbutton your pants. Now." His eyebrow raised, and ever so slowly he unbuttoned them. Balls still in hand, she leaned up to his ear and began to lick and nip at his earlobe. "Hands behind you on the desk." His breathing was uneven, but he complied. She continued the onslaught. "If you remove them, I'll get up and walk out that door."

Then she got down on her knees in front of him. His eyes widened. "Mawg, you don't have to—" She gave a sharp "ssh" and looked up at him while her hands reached up to drag the pants off him.

"Where are his underpants?"

"Where indeed," she thought, a hungry look in her eyes. She dragged the pants down around his ankles, then sat momentarily staring at his dick like it was the most beautiful piece of artwork she'd ever seen. He moaned, catching her expression. He was fully erect, and she marveled at how veiny and thick he was.

She had his balls back in her hand, and began to lightly massage them. He groaned and his head rolled back. She placed light, feathery kisses on his tip, teasing him with sensation. She ran the tip of her tongue down the length of him while continuing to massage his balls. He was straining, and she continued to tease. Finally, she looked up to his eyes, holding eye contact while her lips slid around him. He moaned, "Maaaawg…". She worked the tip with her lips until he looked like he would burst, then slid him all the way to the back of her throat. Her eyes began to water but she continued with a slow repetitive pace, still massaging his balls.

"Mawg…Mawg you have to stop. Oh god, you have to stop or—"

Meeting his eyes, she dug her fingers into his ass to hold him in place and took him all the way in. He was beyond being able to stop it and thrust forward, hands coming off the desk and into her hair and he cried out breathlessly, "There's only Mawg," as he released himself into her.

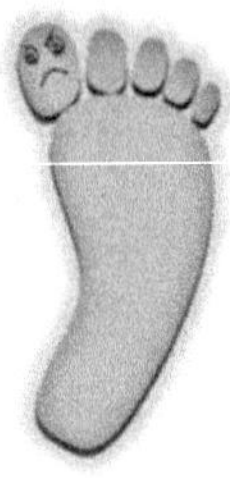

CHAPTER TWENTY-FIVE

Declan stayed at her house that night instead of driving back out to the ranch. Mawg woke to his arm laying across her waist in her bed and thought about how lucky she was.

"Being in a relationship with a good person is not luck. You're fixing both the interior and exterior of your meatsuit house. I told you early on, once you do that the right person will take notice."

"What are you, my spiritual advisor now? Just let me revel in the moment."

"No. You're gonna acknowledge right here and now that you're worthy of a good, healthy relationship."

Mawg rolled her eyes. "Ok, I'm worthy."

"I'm not fuckin' around, Mawg. Look at all of the things you've experienced in the past few weeks. Think back to the day that we met. Do you even recognize that woman anymore? Because I don't. That woman was a caterpillar. The woman I see right now is on her way to becomin' the butterfly."

She thought back over the past few weeks. She'd made new friends, stopped hating her body, learned how to dress, spoken up for herself, started a new career…yeah, she'd changed a lot.

"Say it for me and mean it."

She felt a lightness in her spirit and looked down at the beautiful man lightly snoring on her chest. She thought, "I am worthy, and I really do deserve this."

"That's better. Now, figure out how to either extricate yourself or wake him, because I need snackies."

Declan, half in and out of sleep mumbled, "Lemme guess, he's hungry."

Mawg and Peri froze, staring at each other. Mawg stroked Declan's hair, hoping he was just dreaming. She asked quietly, "Who's hungry?"

He rolled his head up to look at her. "Your little toe guy. I assume you have one?"

"What the fuck?!"

She stopped stroking Declan's hair and scrambled out of the bed to stand beside it. "How do you know about him? Can you hear him? See him??" Mawg started to panic. Humans can't hear toe demons.

Declan sat up, realizing she was freaking out. He held up his arms like a man being held at gunpoint. "Easy, baby…no, I can't see or hear him. Remember that middle-aged woman I met when I was in my twenties? The one that taught me so much? She also told me about the little toe guys. I just assumed based on your age and the way that you're always looking at your feet that you have one."

"Ok, we're not doing 'little toe guys'. That's just rude."

She was standing with her hands on her hips. "So you've known about him the entire time?"

Declan shrugged. "I didn't know for sure, but I assumed. I figured if you wanted me to know, you'd tell me."

She took that in for a moment. "But you can't see or hear him?"

"No, I cannot."

"Oh thank demon."

She stood there, deciding what to share. She looked down at Peri and he shrugged.

"That's totally up to you. I don't mind Dicklan."

She sat down next to him, propping her left foot on the bed. "His name is Peri, and he's at least a thousand years old. And he lives in the big toe of my left foot."

Declan looked down at her big toe in fascination. "So, is he looking at you right now?"

Peri started making faces at her.

"He's always there. He talks with me internally all day long, too."

Declan perked up like a kid who just learned superheroes were real. "That's so cool!"

Mawg chuckled and Peri rolled his eyes. Then Declan's face changed into one of horror. "Wait…he's ALWAYS with you?"

"Every single second," Mawg replied.

Declan's eyes were wide. "Even when—"

"Yep. Even then."

His face was frozen in horror. Mawg began to laugh, and she said, "If it makes you feel any better, he's very impressed with your upgraded meatsuit."

"Hey! You're such a hag!"

Declan just sat there, staring at her toe as he asked, "Can…can he hear me? Like, can I talk to him?"

"You're actually hungry enough that I could take over and talk with him."

Mawg thought, "Don't you dare. I don't want you fucking this up for me."

"Oh my demon, give me a little credit here."

Mawg gave him a snarky look. "Forgive me, but the last time you did that I ended up without a job."

She said that last part out loud, and Declan looked over at her, then back down to Peri, fascinated. She turned to Declan and said, "When I'm really hungry, which apparently I am right now, he can take over my body and run the show."

The loud noise that erupted in her ears the first night they met happened again, and she slammed her hands over her ears even though it did nothing. "God dammit, Per—"

Then she blacked out.

She came to about 20 minutes later, lying on the bed. She smelled coffee brewing and could hear Declan in the kitchen rummaging around. Looking down at the smug little face on her toe, she thought, "What did you say to him?" His expression turned innocent.

"Nothing! We had a nice little man to demon discussion. Oh, and I emphasized how important it is for you to have bacon. We negotiated two bacon days per week."

Mawg's eyes narrowed. "So you manipulated him into getting you snackies?!"

"How dare you attack my character that way! I was lookin' out for you. Now he knows how important it is for you to have three meals and a few snacks each day to keep this from happening."

She thought, "You little shit. Don't manipulate my boyfriend or it's gelatin day for you!" Peri's little eyebrow raised.

"Boyfriend?"

She threw her hands in the air in frustration. "Whatever, you know what I mean!" Annoyed with Peri, she walked out to the kitchen to find Declan cooking something that smelled amazing on her stovetop.

"Did he manipulate you for food?"

Declan turned and smiled, walking over to kiss her. "Not at all. He explained what happens when you don't eat.

That doesn't sound pleasant for you, so I'll make it my goal to see that doesn't happen in the future."

She stared down at Peri. "I know exactly what you did." He and Declan both laughed. Then Declan said, "I won't lie, I was really surprised that he sounds like Danny DeVito, though. That voice coming out of your mouth threw me for a loop."

She looked at Peri. "Wait….you didn't sound like me?"

"I normally do, but since we're letting Declan in on our little secret, I showed up as myself."

She looked back to Declan. "You got DeVito? I pegged him for more of a Pesci." That got a laugh out of Declan. "Both could work," he said as he flipped something in the pan.

"How many times do I have to say this? I'm a thousand years old, you hag. They sound like ME."

Mawg watched him working at the stove and was flabbergasted that he was acting like this situation was entirely normal. "So, you're not freaked out about the demon in my toe?"

Still facing the stove, he said, "Not at all. I'm Irish, love. Our history is full of lore and mythical creatures." He slid an omelette on a plate and turned, handing it to her with a smile.

She looked at him in disbelief, then down at the omelette. "And you swear he didn't try to manipulate you?" That got a laugh out of Declan, who placed a kiss on her forehead. "My sweet Mawg, he's looking out for you. We're on the same page, I promise."

"Told you."

Declan smiled at her and said, "Oh…he also showed me something most intriguing." He leaned down next to her ear and whispered, "I would very much like to see you in those pink chaps."

Her cheeks turned five shades of red as she stared wide-eyed down at Peri.

"Oh, you don't get to be mad when he's lookin' at you like you're his fucking dinner. I did good and you know it."

They took the plates over to her dining table and ate, TV on in the background. She brought up the situation with

Gina. "Are you still okay if I dig through the member files today to see if I recognize that man?"

Declan nodded but was frowning. She could tell he was still upset that Gina hadn't come to him. Mawg understood his frustration and put her hand on his arm. "Hey…I could be totally wrong and this could be a simple miscommunication. That's why I didn't want to bring it up and worry you yet. Let's give her the benefit of the doubt."

Mawg was lifting a forkful of omelette to her mouth when something on the TV caught her ear. Turning, she saw him. There was the man that arrived with Gina at the club last night. He was standing next to Mr. Whitney and they were shaking hands, getting ready to cut the ribbon in front of a brand-new building.

She squeezed Declan's arm…"Look," and she nodded toward the TV. Hopping up, she grabbed the remote to turn it up.

"Garrett Smithton, CEO of Synergis Industries, announced a massive move that will relocate the Synergis headquarters to the newly constructed Avian building, owned by The Whitney Group. This move will

<u>bring **20,000** jobs into the city by next
summer."</u>

Mawg's jaw was hanging open and Declan's looked at her. "Is that him?" She nodded. Neither spoke as they processed what they just saw. She grabbed the remote and turned the volume back down. Turning, she said, "I don't think this is a coincidence, do you?"

Declan was resting his chin in his hand, looking off in the distance like he was still trying to process. Running his hand over his face in frustration, he said, "Unfortunately, no. I don't think it is." She watched him push the rest of his omelette away, no longer hungry. He looked up at Mawg. "I hate to leave you like this, but I need to get some air and think this through."

She walked over and hugged his head to her chest, placing a kiss on his head. "Of course. Do what you need to do. I'm going to head to The Church in about an hour. Just call my cell if you need anything." She crouched down eye-level with him. "Anything, ok?" He ran his hand through her hair and kissed her, then nodded. He got up and gathered his things, then headed to the door. Turning back, he gave her a long, lingering kiss and said, "My Sweet Mawg," as he walked out.

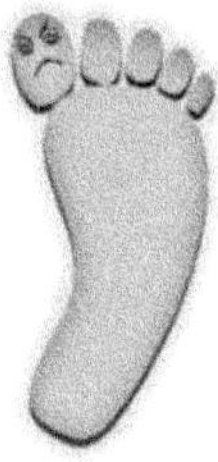

CHAPTER TWENTY-SIX

The Church was bustling with activity. Monday mornings were always full, between the cleaners scrubbing away the remnants of the previous night's orgy and delivery drivers bringing in the week's supply of alcohol.

"Did you know that glitter was created by demons?"

She watched the bristles of the cleaner's broom shimmer, as it glided across the floor. "That doesn't surprise me one bit. Glitter is evil."

Keeping herself busy with tasks, she still found herself distracted with this morning's newly discovered information. Hands on the keyboard, she stared off toward the wall. Declan had looked so hurt when he heard the news. Mawg couldn't imagine what it would be like to work so closely with someone for five years, and find out they were lying the entire time.

Wrapped up so deeply in her own thoughts she didn't hear Gina walk into the office.

"Aren't you a busy little beaver," Gina said as Mawg jumped, startled. Gina's eyebrow raised. "Jumpy this morning, are we?"

"Play it off, quick."

Mawg laughed and said, "Sorry, I was buried in inventory." She turned in the chair to face Gina. "How was your weekend?" Gina walked over and sat her purse on the loveseat in the corner. "Quiet, thankfully. I caught up on a lot of errands. How about you?"

"Same, just binged some shows and did laundry. One of these days, I'll come in with a wild story for you."

Gina laughed at that as she sat on the couch and pulled out her laptop. "I figured Declan might be giving you some more…er, lessons," she said, giving Mawg a conspiratorial wink.

"Actually, I had dinner at his place last week."

Gina had been pulling things out of her purse and stopped, her mouth opening wide in surprise. "You went to his house?"

Mawg nodded. "He asked if I wanted to come over for dinner, then he sent a car over to pick me up. It was very sweet. And he's actually a really good cook."

"Yeah, both chickens he presented you were perfection."

Gina was still frozen with her mouth open. She gave her head a little shake and said, "Mawg…. I've known that man for five years and he has NEVER brought a woman to his home. EVER." Mawg's face turned red and she pushed a piece of hair behind her ear, saying nothing. Gina continued, "I assumed you two were having a good time, but I didn't realize…" She continued to stare at Mawg and said, "I think he really has a thing for you."

Then it hit her. Deep inside, Mawg desperately wanted that to be true. And that tiny realization scared the shit out of her. She said quietly, "The feeling is mutual."

Gina's hand was covering her mouth and her eyes welled up. She stood up and walked over to Mawg, leaning down to hug her. "You have no idea how happy that makes me. For both of you. Declan's been like a big brother to me, and I've come to adore you as well."

Mawg hugged her back, but there was a pit in her stomach. "Thank you."

Gina stood up and said, "Let's go celebrate during lunch and you can give me all the naughty details!" That sparked an idea in Mawg.

"Actually, I was planning to get a pedicure. Do you want to come with me?"

Gina smiled and said, "That would be great, I'm overdue for one anyway."

One of the cleaners popped his head into the office. "Hey ladies, sorry to bug you but can you come take a look at this? We've got a weird situation in one of the rooms."

Mawg and Gina looked at each other with confusion, but got up to follow. They trailed him down the stairs as he said, "I've never seen anything like it before." At the bottom of the stairs, he turned down the hallway toward the room where Gina had been with the man and the Whitneys the night before.

Mawg watched her out of the corner of her eye. Gina's eyes widened in realization a moment before she adjusted her face back to a neutral expression.

They followed the cleaner in the room to the spot where Gina and the man had been last night. On the floor were the remnants of the circle, drawn in what looked like dried blood with symbols in the middle of it. Mawg thought, "Was last night a ritual? That looks like something out of a horror movie."

"That's exactly what that is. Trust me on this one. Do you have your phone on you?"

She did.

"Try to snap a picture if you can. You'll wanna show that to Dicklan later. Mawg...I hate to tell you this, but someone in that room last night was not human. And based on what we watched, my money's on Gina."

Her eyes got wide as she put her hand on the phone in her pocket. As the cleaner was explaining what he found to Gina, Mawg quietly stepped behind them to the side and snapped a few quick photos with the phone down by her leg.

Turning just as Mawg got the phone back in her pocket, Gina had a quizzical expression on her face. "Have you ever seen anything like this since you've been here?" Mawg kept her wide-eyed expression and shook her head. "No, but should we call Declan?"

Gina stood like she was pondering the idea. "Let's go look at the books and see who was reserved in here last night. We can reach out to them first before we worry Dec. He's got enough on his plate with the expansion going on."

Turning to address the cleaner, Gina said, "I think we have some peroxide in the back. If it's blood, that will clean it right up." Then she turned to walk out the door. Mawg's eyes narrowed as she followed her, pissed about the lies Gina was weaving.

"Easy...you can't let on that you know anything. We're dealin' with some serious shit here, Mawg. Play it cool."

They got back to the office and Mawg pulled up the room reservations from last night, knowing there would be nothing. She was correct. Gina, looking over her shoulder said, "So someone without a reservation was in that room. It's going to be difficult to figure out who, considering we don't keep cameras in the rooms for privacy purposes." She walked back over to her laptop on the sofa and said, "let's keep an ear to the ground over the next couple of days and see if we hear any rumblings."

Mawg felt the rage beginning to build. How the fuck could Gina be so nonchalant while she lied through her teeth? Mawg watched her pull out a lip stain and a little mirror, applying a layer like she had no care in the world.

She quietly steadied her breath and pushed the rage down deep. "Do you want me to reach out to the members and start asking questions?"

"We don't want it getting around if there was a situation. That will cause people to lose trust in our security and safety protocols. Let's just keep this quiet for now and we'll dig into it."

"She's shifty as fuck."

Mawg nodded as an idea came to her. "Ok." Then she looked at her phone and said, "How do you feel about getting out of here and doing our pedicures now? That gave me the creeps and a break might do us both good."

"Excellent idea," Gina agreed. They gathered their things and walked to Mawg's car.

On the ride over, Mawg attempted to make small talk that really wasn't small talk. "Hey, I forgot to ask, what's your last name? I was on Facebook last night and I was going to shoot you a friend request."

Gina waved her hand and said, "Oh, I don't do social media. I may work hard to look young, but I'm an old soul at heart. I prefer interacting with people in person."

"Nice dodge on the question."

But Mawg kept at it. "Ugh, I totally get that. I get sucked into it sometimes trying to keep up with who has a birthday and who's dating who. Speaking of, we've never really talked about you before. Do you have a partner? Boyfriend? Girlfriend?"

"No," Gina replied, with a bit of a sad look on her face. "I've become too independent over the years. Having to share my time, space, and life with someone sounds suffocating. I enjoy my freedom and just dabble at The Church from time to time if I need to scratch that itch."

Mawg appeared to empathize with her. "I feel you. I've spent the past ten years living by myself. This whole situation with Declan is one I haven't dealt with for a very long time."

They pulled into the parking lot of Happy Nail. Mawg looked over at Gina and saw her eyes widen momentarily, then revert back to normal. "I discovered this place a few weeks ago and the main lady does a great job. Have you ever been here?"

"I had no idea this place was here," Gina said, shaking her head.

Mawg seethed and Peri told her to calm down again. As they walked in the door, Jessica was walking out of the back and saw them. Before she could say anything, Mawg thought, "Please play it cool and don't act like anything is weird. I'll throw in an extra twenty bucks." Jessica looked her in the eye and gave a short nod.

Jessica called to them. "What do you need?"

Mawg replied, "Pedicures, please."

Jessica gestured over to two open pedicure chairs. "Grab a color and sit."

Mawg turned to Gina and whispered, "She's not super friendly, but she does good work." They walked over to the wall of colors.

Jessica looked over at Mawg and thought, "I heard that." Mawg raised her eyebrow and thought, "And you know it's true." Jessica glared at her for a minute, then shrugged.

Colors selected, they walked back over to the pedicure stations. Jessica already had the water started, and they sat. With their feet in the water, Jessica called over another nail tech so both pedicures could happen simultaneously. Jessica took Gina, and Mawg got the new girl.

"We should do this more often," Mawg said as she turned to look at Gina and smiled. Gina nodded, not saying anything.

"Yeaaaaah, that's the brush-off she just gave you, in case you were wonderin'."

Jessica lifted Gina's foot out of the water and gasped. Realizing all eyes were on her, she schooled her face and said, "You have the prettiest feet I've seen in years. Do you want to remove the ring?"

Mawg looked down at the golden toe ring with some sort of inscription on Gina's big toe. Gina looked slightly uncomfortable and said, "No, no, that's ok. It's sentimental. I don't take it off." Jessica shrugged and said, "No matter to me, price is the same."

As she began to scrub Gina's feet, Jessica thought, "Pick up a magazine so she doesn't see your face." Mawg picked up the three month-old fashion magazine from the table next to her and began to skim it. Then Jessica said, "Your friend is in trouble. She's also a demon."

Mawg's eyes widened, but she kept skimming and thought, "You said she didn't have a toe demon last time we were here!"

Jessica replied, "She doesn't HAVE a demon. She IS one. A succubus, to be exact." Peri inhaled sharply, his little face now worried.

Mawg was confused, and thought, "What is a succubus?"

"There's been a lot of mixed lore about them, but big picture, they can literally suck the life out of people…through sex."

Mawg was shocked. Jessica piped in saying, "And this particular succubus is being controlled. That ring on her toe has a spell written on it."

Everything came crashing into place. The timing of Gina and the Whitneys coming into Declan's life, the deal they gave him on the property, the scene she witnessed last night, the news story today.

The Whitneys were controlling Gina to manipulate business deals in their favor. And they were doing it using Declan's clubs.

Mawg wanted to vomit. Her eyes began to swim and she felt like she was going to pass out. Suddenly, she heard the awful alarm in her ears and she blacked out.

When she came to, she was sitting at the desk in the office of The Church. As the grogginess began to fade, it all came flooding back and panic set in.

"Calm down, you're safe and you're fine. Take deep breaths and get your heart rate under control."

She started to ask questions and Peri stopped her.

"Sssshhhh…We'll talk as soon as we get home and I'll fill you in. Just breathe, dammit!"

Mawg inhaled and exhaled, over and over until she felt herself steadying. She looked around the office and noticed Gina's things were gone. "Did she leave?"

"Yeah, she left for the day. You're good, I made sure to lock the door when we came in here. But we should leave. We've got a lot to talk about, and you're still looking green."

She continued the breathing exercises for another minute or two and got herself under control. She agreed, nothing else was going to get done here today. Picking up her purse and gathering her things, she noticed her toenails were painted black with pink polka dots. She raised an eyebrow at Peri.

"Hey, at least I stopped the flower nonsense."

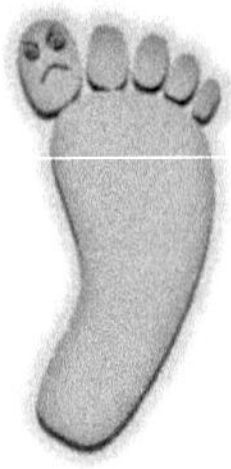

CHAPTER TWENTY-SEVEN

Mawg grabbed a glass of Chardonnay and the mini charcuterie plate Peri requested when they got home, and flopped down on the couch. She propped Peri up on the ottoman and said, "Ok, spill it."

"Well, I could tell you were crashing out when Jessica told you about Gina being a succubus. Luckily, you were hungry enough that I could take over, so I did."

Mawg's eyebrow raised. "Yeaaaaaah, I'm gonna need a little more detail than that."

"There really wasn't much more to it. I took over and kept the conversation light so Gina wouldn't suspect anything. Jessica knew what was going on, and she played along. I paid Jessica the hundred and we drove back here with Gina."

Both Mawg's eyes and her mouth were wide with shock. "You DROVE back here with Gina? You…you know how to drive?"

"Enough to get us back here safely. Although, Gina may not want to ride with you anymore. You did hit a couple of curbs on the way back."

Mawg shook her head, bringing her hand up to rub her brow. "I mean…thanks, I guess?" He didn't acknowledge the sarcasm and his little face smiled.

"You're welcome. But enough about that. What are we going to do about this succubus situation?"

Mawg sighed and began to pick off the charcuterie plate. "I have no idea. Since I had no idea a succubus was a real thing prior to this afternoon, I should probably research." Peri sighed in annoyance as she reached for her laptop.

"The googly machine isn't going to help you. Hello…you have an actual talking demon here. Maybe use me as a resource?"

Her annoyance registered on her face and she said, "My apologies for not assuming you were an expert about every demon species. Fill me in."

"Ok, so succubi are female demons that prey on men. They're normally stunning, which tracks. You thought Gina's meatsuit was beautiful."

Mawg nodded. "It absolutely is."

"Right. So anyway, a succubus will seduce men in order to drain their vitality, in some cases, their lives. They're driven by pleasure and power."

Her jaw dropped. "So that's why she's so natural at being a concierge!"

"Again, another thing that tracks with what I know about succubi. But here's the thing…a succubus can be controlled by a spell. It sounds like that toe ring she's wearin' is probably how the Whitneys are controlling her."

She began putting it together in her head. "So the Whitneys use Gina to get these men into The Church, and using sexual activity, she gets them to enter into business deals that favor the Whitneys?"

"That seems most likely to me."

Her expression turned to horror as she had a realization. "Declan is in a contract with them." Peri didn't say anything, his little face unusually stoic. She looked down at him. "Do you think—"

"Highly likely. Two humans with upgraded meatsuits that work closely together in an environment surrounded by sex for five years...maybe not recently, but I would bet tonight's snackies they definitely hooked up at some point."

If Mawg was being honest, that thought had crossed her mind before. Two single, attractive people hooking up at the adult club they work at would be a reasonable assumption. "We need to ask Declan. If they hooked up when they first met, it's highly likely that contract has something nefarious buried in it."

"You gonna be ok if he confirms that?"

She waved it off with her hand. "He's an attractive man who owns a sex club. I fully expected him to be sexually active before we started our thing. That honestly doesn't concern me." Peri's eyebrows raised in surprise.

"Wow…that's very adult and mature of you. Are you sure you're feeling well?"

She chuckled. "I feel fine. I just think it's silly to be jealous of someone's past. Now, if he's been fucking her recently, that's a different story. But my gut says that's not the case."

Reaching for the phone, she decided to call Declan. No ring, straight to voicemail. Weird. She hung up and texted him, "Hey babe, I found some more info. Give me a call when you get free."

Waiting on him to text her back, Mawg began to search more about The Whitney Group. They were publicly traded, so all of their financials and business deals were available. Over the past five years, thirty major businesses had moved their headquarters to a Whitney Group building. Massive industry leaders in insurance, health care, robotics, fashion & beauty, automotive, oil & gas…the list went on and on.

"I don't mean to be the demon downer, but what exactly do you think we're gonna do with this information, kiddo? I think we've stumbled onto somethin' way above our pay grade."

As she took another sip of the Chardonnay, she ruminated on that. "I don't think we can do anything about the Whitneys specifically. They're too powerful and connected. But…"

"But?"

"If all of this power is coming because of Gina, wouldn't it make sense to try and get her spell broken?"

"Oh sure, let's just roll into the library and find the book of spells section and hop right on that."

Narrowing her gaze on him, she was starting to get a bit annoyed. "I thought you were supposed to be some sort of powerful demon. Shouldn't you know about this type of shit?" Peri raised an eyebrow like he couldn't believe her audacity.

"I'm a powerful Change demon. Peri, man of pause…remember? Do you just assume all demons are omniscient? I'm not Lucifer, for demon's sake. Do you know everything about humanity on your little planet? Like, tell me this…name all the countries in Asia."

Her brow scrunched as she tried to think of an answer. Geography was not her strong suit. "Okay, okay, I get your point. The sarcasm isn't necessary."

"It really is. We're way out of our league here, Mawg."

"Well we can't just let them continue to manipulate Declan and his business! There has to be something that can be done." Mawg looked down at her phone. Still nothing from Declan. She was beginning to worry.

"I'm sure he's just processing all this. He got slammed over the head with his closest co-worker runnin' massive scams through his business. Give him some room, he's probably feeling raw right now."

Sighing in frustration, she knew Peri was probably right. What exactly did she think she was going to do? Save the day? She didn't even know if she believed in spells and magic. It all sounded crazy.

"You have a talkin' demon livin' in your toe, a nail tech that's a demon, and you work with a succubus...how could you not believe magic is real?!"

"I don't know, Peri! For fuck's sake," she took a swig of wine, "you of all demons should know I would find that challenging. Mawg the Practical, isn't that what you called me?"

She picked up the remnants of the charcuterie plate and her wine glass and took them into the kitchen. She was going to look at her phone one more time in hopes that she'd missed a call from Declan, when she remembered the photos she took at The Church. That ritual symbol was in her camera roll. Pulling it up, she enlarged it. There were no letters, just symbols.

"Jessica seemed to recognize the spell on Gina's toe ring today. Maybe she would know what this is."

Mawg looked up the number to the salon and called. Someone answered on the second ring, "Happy Nail," with a very unhappy tone. Mawg asked, "Can I speak to Jessica?" The voice on the other end was silent for a moment, then said, "This is. What do you need?"

"It's me, the girl with the toe de—"

"I know who you are. What do you need?"

"She's so sweet. Maybe you will have that happy hour someday."

Mawg glared down at Peri and said into the phone, "I have a photo of something we found in the sex club, and I was wondering if you could tell me what it is."

Jessica was silent for a moment. "I don't want to see gross dildos, no thank you."

"No, no, nothing like that. There was something drawn on the floor and I want to see if you know what it is. Can I text you the photo?" She could hear Jessica's annoyance through the phone. "555-624-8731. And I'm adding this to your next bill." She hung up.

"You're gonna be handin' over your paychecks to her at this rate."

Mawg texted her the photo and waited. Her phone dinged a moment later with a response.

"Contract spell, sealed in blood."

Mawg replied, **"Do you know anyone who knows how to break spells?"**

Ding. **"Maybe. I'll reach out if I do. Now go away."**

Mawg put the phone down, feeling frustrated. Declan was hurting, Gina was in a bad situation, and Mawg was at a loss of how to help either of them.

"There's nothin' else you can do right now. Let's go crawl into bed and watch the vampire show. Maybe it will come to you in the morning."

He was right. And that's exactly what they did.

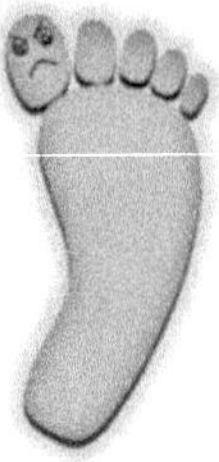

CHAPTER TWENTY-EIGHT

Three days had passed since Declan had walked out of her house. She sent a text and left a voicemail every few hours to check in, but received no response. He hadn't been to The Church, either. Mawg was now beyond worried. Even when he was busy with meetings, he always managed to find time to send her a quick message. Something was very wrong, and Mawg gathered her things.

"Where are we going?"

Grabbing her keys and sunglasses, she said, "To his house. This isn't like him, Peri."

"You don't think that's a little much?"

"No!" Mawg yelled, slamming her purse on the counter. "He was wrecked when he left here and apparently we're dealing with otherworldly shit. He always returns my calls and texts, Peri. I don't care if I'm overstepping. I care that he's safe."

She locked up the house, got in the car, and drove. While the scenery hadn't changed since her last visit, this trip was much different. Her adrenaline was pumping and her teeth were clenched as she white-knuckled the steering wheel. She had finally discovered some excitement in her life with the dream man she'd fantasized about for years, and now some greedy assholes were ruining it. Fuck them. Fuck them for dragging Declan into their deception. Fuck them for climbing a ladder that ruined everyone in their path. And most of all, fuck them for trying to ruin a place where people felt safe. Fuck them all.

Peri sat in awe. This was the first time since their initial meeting that Mawg had dipped a cup into the well of rage that he provided. He reveled as she let it pour out of her into the universe.

They arrived at the long driveway of Declan's beautiful home. She drove in and parked right in front of the house, not seeing any sign of life or a vehicle. Stomping up the porch, she pounded on the door. No response. She pounded again and yelled, "Declan! It's Mawg, please answer me." Again, no response. She pulled out her phone and dialed his cell. He must have connected it to the surround sound with bluetooth, because she heard it ringing inside the house. Still, he did not come to the door. She began to pound with all her might. "Declan! I'm not leaving until I know you're okay!"

"Maybe he isn't here?"

"That's even worse! Where would he go without his phone?" Mawg walked over to the windows on each side of the door and peeked through. She could see the interior, just as she remembered, but there was no sign of Declan.

"Mawg…look."

She turned. In her rage coming up the porch, she had missed it. There was a trail of what looked like dried, dripping blood that ran from the doorway down to the driveway. Even Peri's little voice sounded scared now.

"When he left your house…do you think he confronted the Whitneys?"

The horror of that thought struck her to the core. "Peri, he's in trouble. We've got to find him."

She turned back to get into the car.

"Where are we going?"

She turned over the ignition and put it in reverse. "To the one person who can tell us what the fuck is going on."

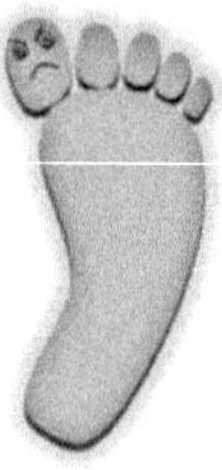

CHAPTER TWENTY-NINE

The sound of the door slamming against the wall as Mawg barged her way through startled Liam. He was setting up the bar for his shift and gave her a wide-eyed expression of surprise. Seeing the rage on her face, he immediately asked, "What's wrong, Mawg?"

"Where's Gina?" She seethed. Slowly, he set down the glass he'd been drying, realizing the signs of a middle-aged woman who was about to lose her shit. He nodded his head tentatively toward the door heading to the main floor. "I think she's in the office."

She swiped her key card and stormed through the door, hearing him call out, "Are you okay?" She was not, but there was no time to stop and chat. She made a beeline for the storage area behind the stage and found what she was looking for. There was a pile of random items that had been collecting, left over the years. In the pile was a wooden baseball bat.

"Mawg...what are you doing, Mawg?"

She didn't answer, but grabbed the bat and swung it around in her hand. Turning, she made her way across the main floor, stomping up the stairs. She could see Gina sitting at the desk with her ear buds in, her back to the door as Mawg rounded the corner. Entering the room, Mawg shut the door and closed the blinds. She turned, swinging the bat overhead and slamming it on the desk.

"AAAAAGGGHHHH," Gina screamed as she turned, yanking out her ear buds. She pushed back in the chair and was about to stand when Mawg blocked her path, trapping her in the seat.

"WHERE IS HE??" Mawg yelled, holding the bat in the air, ready to bring it down on Gina's head at any moment.

"What the fuck, Mawg?! What's wrong with you?"

Mawg leaned down placing one hand on each side of the chair, her face inches from Gina's. "Where. Is. He?"

Panick poured over Gina's face. "I don't know what you're talking about! Back up, Mawg, you're scaring me."

The rage radiated off Mawg as she pointed the bat at Gina's chest. "I know what you are, Gina. I know what you've been doing and I know about the Whitneys."

Gina's eyes widened in shock, but she tried to play it off. "I…I have no idea what you're talking about."

Mawg turned and slammed the bat on the desk again. "Do NOT fucking lie to me you filthy succubus!"

Terrified, Gina froze, but Mawg just let loose. "Yeah, I know everything. I know you've been using Declan and The Church for years to do shady business shit for the Whitneys. I know it was YOU that was in the room with the Whitneys the other night. I saw you with that man. And I know you're helping them fuck Declan over!"

White as a sheet, Gina was unable to form words.

"And now you're going to tell me what they've done with Declan, Gina. You're going to tell me right now, or I swear to all that is demon, I will knock the teeth right out of your lying mouth." Mawg raised the bat.

Raising her hands in surrender, Gina said, "Ok, ok, put the bat down and I'll tell you everything."

Her eyes grew dark and Mawg shook her head. "Nope. You're gonna talk first, then I'll decide about the bat."

Tears began to run down Gina's face, but Mawg didn't give a shit. "Cry all you like, but you're not leaving until you tell me everything. I can fucking wait." Mawg sat one ass cheek on the edge of the desk, bat still raised.

"I know this isn't the right time, but this version of you is giving me a massive ragegasm."

Gina, sniffling and crying, began. "I never wanted to hurt Declan. He was never supposed to find out."

Mawg continued to glare at her, saying nothing.

"Ok, ok…it started seven years ago. I was at a party with this guy I was fucking. It wasn't serious, and I was just feeding off him to pass time. We were in the back hallway of this house and things got hot and heavy. It must have gotten too hot, because the next thing I know, he was dead at my feet. I'd sucked the life out of him. I panicked. I'd never killed a human before, you have to believe me!"

Mawg stood listening, her expression stoic.

"I turned to run, and there stood Mr. Whitney in the shadows. He saw everything. He gave me a choice: He could either turn me in to the police, or I could keep my secret safe and become his 'assistant'. I was so freaked out that I left with him. He took me back to their home, and that's when I met Mrs. Whitney. He told her what happened, which shocked me. I figured she would freak out and want to turn me in."

Wiping the tears from her face and taking a tiny breath in, Gina continued. "But instead, she went all 'mother bear' on me. 'Oh, sweet girl, how scary that must have been. Here, let me make you a drink.' I felt safe, like she would make it all go away. I didn't realize that she spiked the drink. The next thing I knew, I was waking up on a floor naked, my hands and feet spread eagle and locked down. I was laying in the middle of some sort of circle they had drawn, and there were candles all around it."

Taking another deep breath as she relived the terrifying moment, Gina said, "Mrs. Whitney stepped into the circle with me and started chanting. I still have no idea to this day what she was saying. When she finished, she took a ring from the palm of her hand and put it on my toe." Gina looked down at her feet and scowled. "Ever since that moment, I've been at the mercy of the Whitneys."

"So, take the ring off, Gina."

Gina's voice raised in frustration. "Don't you think I've thought of that? I've tried, but it won't come off! I even tried to chop off my toe one night, but it's like there's some sort of force field around it!" She began to cry again.

Mawg leaned down and grabbed the sides of her chair again. "Who's idea was it to bring Declan into this shit show, Gina?"

Head in her hands, the muffled reply came in breathless spurts. "…Mrs….(sniffle)…Whitney."

Mawg was livid. "And what did you do to Declan, Gina?"

She began to sob. "Mr. Whitney heard about the club and mentioned it to Mrs. Whitney. She realized it would be a prime spot where my talents would blend in. So, Mr. Whitney called the current building owner at that time and had him come to their house for dinner. When he got there, I seduced him into selling the building to the Whitney Group. They signed the contract in a blood ritual that night. Two weeks later, when all the paperwork had cleared, Mrs. Whitney had me go to The Church and approach Declan for a job." She hesitated, looking fearfully at the bat in Mawg's hand.

"Say it, Gina. Say the words out loud."

Gina was wracked with overflowing tears. "I…I seduced him. I walked in to ask about a job, and he was so nice. I didn't want to do it, but they were there watching me. I got him to create the concierge job for me."

"You fucked him."

"I didn't fuck him, but it was the same thing you saw the other night. Mawg, I'm so sorry! I didn't want to do it. He was so nice to me and I knew it was wrong, but I couldn't stop it!"

"What shady shit did the Whitneys put into the lease agreement, Gina?"

"There's a copy of the lease in the drawer," she pointed toward the desk, "but basically, if Declan ever leaves the lease, the Whitney Group will take ownership of The Church."

Mawg's eyes bugged out of her head. "That's fucking robbery! Declan's smarter than that, why would his lawyer let him sign that?"

Gina looked sheepish, her eyes dropping down to her lap.

"You got to his lawyer, too."

Slowly nodding, Gina confirmed the worst. Mawg sat back on the edge of the desk and let out a frustrated sigh. She stared at Gina now crumpled in front of her, sobbing with her head in her hands.

"Um…I know this isn't gonna be a popular opinion, but Gina's not the one you should be angry with. She's a victim in this, too."

Mawg glared down at her toe.

"Hey, don't shoot the messenger. But deep down, you know I'm right."

Now wasn't the time to process that. "Gina, where is Declan right now?" Gina looked up at her with confusion in her teary eyes. "I don't know, I haven't seen him for a couple of days."

Mawg continued to glare at her. The overwhelming frustration of the situation had her fighting the urge to swing the bat.

"He's been missing, Gina. I've been texting and calling with no answer. He found out you were in some sort of shady business with the Whitneys three days ago."

Gina's eyes widened in alarm. "You told him?"

Mawg's jaw clenched and her eyes widened as she gripped the bat so hard her hand hurt. "You don't get to be aghast, or defensive, or whatever the fuck you're feeling right now. He's fucking missing, Gina!"

Gina dropped her head and began nervously shifting her weight back and forth.

"He doesn't know about you being a succubus. We put together what was going on after I saw that man here with you and the Whitneys. We watched the TV announcement the next morning. He left my house upset, and I haven't seen or heard from him since."

Gina raised her head, looking genuinely perplexed. "Mawg, I swear I have no idea. It's not uncommon for him to be gone for a couple days then show up here. I assumed he was traveling…I truly had no idea.”

“I went to his house before I came here, Gina. He wasn’t there, and there was blood running from his doorway to the driveway. I think he confronted Whitney, and now he’s missing. I need you to think. Where would Whitney take someone if he were going to hide or harm them?”

Gina sat rubbing her temples, trying to think of where they could have gone. “He’s got buildings all across the country, Mawg. He’s never had me go anywhere with him except The Church or his house. They could be anywhere.”

Fear struck Mawg’s heart. The images of Declan flipped through her mind like an old slide show. Standing at the stove, smiling as he cleaned up the mess. His hand sliding up her arm while his breath was on her neck at The Church. Hovering shirtless over his laptop on the counter in the morning, bacon on the counter waiting for her.

Mawg wanted to crumple in a ball and sob. She wanted to…but she wouldn’t.

Sometimes being practical can come in handy. A crisis situation is one of those times. Like every strong woman in the history of the world, Mawg pushed her overwhelming emotions deep down and went into project management mode.

"How do you normally communicate with the Whitneys, Gina? Do they reach out to you, or do you check in with them?"

Gina looked unsure if she should reveal that information. Mawg slapped her and ignored the sting in her palm. "We do NOT have time for this. Declan is in trouble, and if you have ever cared even the tiniest bit for him as your friend or boss, you'll start talking. NOW."

"I was not prepared for Mawg the Enforcer, but it's givin' me a demon chubby."

Gina rubbed her reddened cheek. "I…they…they normally text me."

Mawg sat on that, thinking. "You're going to text them. Tell them Declan was asking a lot of questions then disappeared for three days. See if they give you any information." Then she got in Gina's face and pointed a finger into her chest. "You will act like nothing is out of the norm. DO NOT give them any indication we had this discussion today. Then you will keep me closely updated on what they say. Understood?" Gina nodded.

Mawg took a deep inhale. "Ok. In exchange, I'm going to find someone who can break the spell on the ring…or figure out how to get it off you. One or the other. We're going to find a way to free you from the Whitneys."

Gina's eyes widened, then filled with more tears. "Why would you help me now that you know what I did?"

"Did you enjoy hurting those people?" Gina shook her head no.

"Did you feel good when you hurt Declan?" Gina began to cry again, but continued shaking her head.

"If I figure out how to free you, are you going to spend your days making it up to Declan?" She nodded.

"Then that's why. Now, go text the Whitneys and keep me informed. I'll be working out a way to help you." Mawg started to walk out of the office, then stopped and turned back toward the woman hunched over in the chair. "And Gina?" The shame-filled succubus raised her tear-stained face.

"You've been the victim, and you've been the villain.
Now it's time to be the hero."

421

CHAPTER THIRTY

"Where the fuck did that come from?? Oh, I wish you coulda seen yourself. Your face glows when you rage! You were absolutely magnif—"

"We don't have time for this," Mawg chastised, looking down at her toe. They were in the car on their way to Happy Nail. "But," she said, pulling into the parking lot, "thank you."

The little bell dinged as they walked through the front door. Jessica was in the middle of a manicure and said, "What do you need?" Looking up and seeing Mawg, she frowned. "It's a 30-minute wait for a pedicure."

"I don't need the pedicure today," Mawg replied. "I can wait." She plopped down in a chair near Jessica's station and grabbed a magazine. Jessica's annoyance was plastered on her face. Mawg was impressed she was able to glare at her and not miss a beat on the manicure.

Picking up the magazine, she heard, "Why do you keep bothering me at work?" Jessica was not happy.

Mawg thought, "It's serious. That bitch lady and her husband kidnapped the sex club owner. And they're the ones that put that ring on the succubus."

Jessica's eyes never left the manicure in front of her, but they did widen momentarily. "Again, why is this my problem?"

Mawg thought, "Because I need to find someone who knows about spells and I think you probably know who can help me. Just put me in contact and I'll let you get back to work." Jessica paused filing a nail and gave Mawg a look from the corner of her eye that could cut through steel.

"Ain't no side eye like a demon side eye."

Mawg sighed, knowing how this was going to go. "How much?"

"Fifty dollars and I'll give you the name and number."

"Fifty dollars?! Do you know how many snackies we could buy with that?"

Her eyes turned murderous as she looked down at her greedy little toe.

Jessica's eyebrow raised. "How much is saving that man worth to you?"

She opened her purse and dug around for her cash. Jessica shook her head and thought, "Don't be obvious! Just meet me out back in five minutes. I need a smoke anyway."

Mawg put down the magazine and walked out the front door. As they wandered around the side of the building, Peri cleared his throat dramatically. Mawg stopped and looked down at him. "Yes?"

"I know you're hell-bent on rescuing Dicklan, and I'm here for your hero vibe. BUT…"

Mawg sighed. "But what?"

"Let's just play this out for a second. You find a person who has a spell that will release Gina. You, the woman who doesn't know if she believes in magic, will know how to conduct a counter spell? But let's say you figure that out and you discover where Declan is. Ok…now what? What exactly are we gonna do to save him, Mawg? I mean, I can provide

you plenty of rage, but your middle-age knees aren't gonna let you ninja kick us out of a hostage situation."

No longer running on adrenaline, Mawg leaned against the side of the building. Tears welled up in her eyes and she slammed her fist against the brick wall. "Ow! Dammit!" Peri shook his head, just glad she didn't use her foot to kick it.

"I don't have an answer for that, Peri. I have no plan. All I know is I'm falling for Declan, and he and The Church have changed the way I see life. I'm not willing to walk away from that. For the first time in my life, I have something I want to fight for, odds be damned." The desperation rang in her words and her heart.

"One of these days I'd like some thanks for also changing your life. But we'll come back to that another time."

A "psst!" whispered from around the corner. Mawg shook out her wrist that was now throbbing and stepped behind the building. The cigarette hanging from Jessica's mouth had the longest and most impressive ash she'd ever seen. Her outstretched hand was holding a piece of paper, which Mawg took. Fishing the fifty dollars out of her pocket, Mawg handed it over.

“How do you know this person is the real deal?” Mawg asked. Jessica rolled her eyes and flicked the cigarette, annoyed at being questioned. “Because he is. You don’t need to know how I know. That’s my business.”

Mawg looked down at the piece of paper. “This is potentially a life or death situation.”

Jessica tossed the cigarette on the ground and stomped it out, turning on her heel to walk back inside. “It always is.”

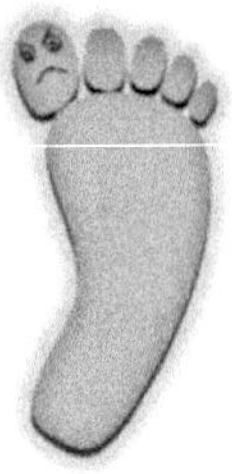

CHAPTER THIRTY-ONE

They got back to the house and Mawg dialed the number. It rang a few times before the voice of a very cranky old man answered.

"Yeah?"

"Hi, uh… I'm looking for Sal, of Sal's Cleaners. Do I have the right number?"

"Yeah."

"Oh great, um…I was referred to you by Jessica from Happy Nail. My name is Mawg."

"Yeah?"

Peri sighed in exasperation. Mawg ran her hand through her hair. "Yeah, so…I've got a cursed item that we need uncursed."

"Can you break it?"

"The curse? I don't know, that's why I'm calling."

"No, the item. Sometimes that will break the curse."

"No, it's a ring on a person. They tried to take it off but it won't budge. They even tried to cut their toe off, but it wouldn't allow it."

"Why they cuttin' their toe off?"

"To get the ring off."

"They should try cuttin' the finger."

"The ring is on their toe."

"I could shove a flaming pen in my eye and it would be less painful than this conversation."

Mawg replied, "It's a toe ring."

"Oh…ok, that makes more sense."

Mawg was trying hard not to laugh at Peri. "So do you know how to remove a curse or spell like that?"

"Yeah."

Peri was losing his ever-loving mind. She'd never seen him so annoyed before. If it hadn't been for the gravitas of the situation, she would have been rolling on the floor laughing.

"Ok…can you please tell me how?"

"There are lots of spells, depends what it is. Who's wearing the ring?"

"A succubus."

"Ahhh, a control spell then."

Mawg called on every ounce of patience she had. "If you have one of those, could you share it with me?"

Sal said, "Hang on one minute, lemme look." She heard him grunt like he got up from a chair and there were shuffling noises. She could hear Sal rifling through papers.

"I bet you a week's worth of snackies he's a hoarder."

There was a loud thump in her ear and she heard Sal say, "God dammit!" as he picked up the phone he'd just dropped. "You there?"

"Yes I'm here."

"Ok you got a pen and paper handy?"

"You…you want me to write down an entire spell?"

"How else would you get it?"

Mawg held the phone away from her face and silently screamed at it, then took a deep breath. "Would it be easier if you took a picture and sent it to me?"

Sal was quiet for a few seconds. "Oh….yeah, that might work. One sec."

Both Peri and Mawg rolled their eyes as they waited, then they heard him get back up.

"Wait, why is he getting up? Where is he going?"

Mawg said into the phone, "Sal? Sal, can you hear me?"

More noise, then Sal answered, "Yeah, I can hear ya. What's the matter?"

"You can just take the photo with the camera on your phone."

Sal said, "Oh, I don't have one of those. I've got one of those disposable cameras."

Mawg put the phone down, buried her head in the pillow next to her, and screamed. She picked the phone back up. "You know, don't worry about the photo. How about if I swing by? Would that be easier?"

"Sure that's fine, I'll be here all night."

Perfect, what's the address?" Mawg asked, breathing a sigh of relief that the conversation was ending. Sal gave her the address and she promised to be there within the hour. Then she hung up.

"Please chop your toe off before ever calling that man again. That was torture."

CHAPTER THIRTY-TWO

"Um….if we walk out of that apartment and your car is still here, I'll be shocked."

Sal's apartment was in the most run-down section of the city. Walking through the small complex, they heard a variety of noises. A couple stood on their patio screaming at each other. Another had all their windows and doors open, their TV blaring across the complex. A sad excuse for a pool full of green water was in the middle of the courtyard. The community trash area was overflowing and full of flies.

"Please make this the fastest interaction you've had all month."

They made it to the door and Mawg knocked, waiting. She heard shuffling inside, then the door opened. Sal was exactly how she pictured him. He looked to be in his seventies, and what little combed-over hair he had left was white. He was tall with a pudgy belly, and his stained t-shirt that said 'I love boobies and beer' was about two sizes too small. The smell of rotting food and dirty man coming from the apartment almost knocked her over.

"Do we really need to release Gina? Is her freedom worth getting tetanus in this shit hole?"

"Hi Sal, I'm Mawg."

Sal looked her up and down in the grossest way an old man could. "Well hi there, Mawg. Come on in," he said, stepping back and waving her inside.

"Actually, I'm in a bit of a rush. If you can show me the spell, I'll take a quick photo of it and be out of your hair."

Sal shook his head and said, "It's gonna take me a minute, I've been digging through my files for it. Come on in."

"You still have that pepper spray handy?"

Mawg thought, "Yep, on the keys in my hand."

"Good. Keep your hand on it."

She took one step inside the door and went no further, realizing she owed Peri a week's worth of snackies. Sal was a hoarder. Piles of papers, books, boxes, trash, and food encompassed the room. A narrow pathway lead to a couple of rooms in the back, which she assumed were a bedroom and bathroom. Looking in the little kitchen area that was covered with leftover food and dirty dishes, she noticed a roach crawling across the edge of the sink.

"You can have a seat," Sal called out from behind one of the piles.

"Oh absofuckinglutely not."

"I'm good, thank you. I'll get out of your hair as quick as possible, sorry to disturb your evening."

Sal peeked around a pile and looked her up and down. "I'm never disturbed by a beautiful woman."

"BLECH! Don't make us vomit, creeper."

Fist encircling the pepper spray, Mawg waited for Sal to dig through the pile. He shuffled through papers for the next five minutes. Finally, Mawg heard him say, "Wait…I think this is it." He held up a sheet in his hand. She could see the stains on the paper from what looked like spilled coffee. Or at least, that's what she hoped it was.

He extended his arm, paper in hand, as he waited for her to take it. Mawg tiptoed three steps across the clutter and reached out her hand to take the paper, keeping a pile of junk in between them. His dirty hand reached for her fingers as she grabbed for the sheet. She pulled the pepper spray out with her other hand and aimed it at him. "Not gonna happen."

Sal's eyes widened as he released the sheet, arms in the air in surrender. "Geez, you women are so dramatic. I was just seeing if there was a possibility."

"There's not," Mawg said, her expression stoic. Pepper spray pointed, she stepped back and found a surface near the door to set the paper down. Grabbing her phone, she snapped the photo as fast as possible and slid it back into her pocket. Mawg handed the paper back to Sal, never dropping the pepper spray.

Backing out the door, she said, "You know…you didn't have to make it weird. That was a choice. And it was the wrong one." She turned and hightailed it back to the car, getting back on the road as fast as possible.

Windows down to diffuse the stink of Sal's apartment from her nose, Mawg turned into a gas station and parked, pulling out her phone. She'd been in such a rush to get out of Sal's apartment, she never stopped to read the paper. She enlarged the photo, a piece of paper with two words written faintly on it:

Release it.

She'd been duped, and her heart sunk. "Mother fucker!"

"Don't freak out, kiddo. We'll figure this out."

The phone rang, scaring the shit out of Mawg. It was Gina. She answered and sighed, shutting her eyes and leaning back against the headrest. "Please give me good news."

"I wish I had more. I did what you said and texted Whitney, but he hasn't responded. Any luck on your end?"

Mawg fumed. "I met the spell guy and he fucked me over. Total waste of time."

"He didn't give you a spell?"

Mawg let out a sarcastic laugh. "Oh he did, but it was garbage. He was just some creeper that wanted to grope me."

"What did it say?"

"Release it."

Silence hung on the line, until Gina finally responded. "Mawg… I think I know what we need to do."

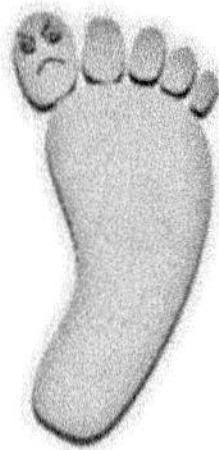

CHAPTER THIRTY-THREE

Mawg sat, stunned. "But that doesn't make sense. Wouldn't the spell have broken anytime you had an orgasm in the past seven years?"

The response from Gina was quiet. "Possibly, but I wouldn't know. I haven't had an orgasm in the past seven years."

Mawg's jaw dropped. "What? How is that possible?"

"It's one of the boundaries I set. The last time I engaged in actual sex, a human died. If I accidentally did that to someone at The Church, I would have lost the job. And if I lost the job, there's no telling what the Whitneys would have me do."

Mawg sat quietly, letting her continue.

"When I told you I've done everything you see, I meant it. Just not at The Church. I've dabbled a little in there to keep up the image, but only in a Dom role. Not receiving. I would give or direct, unless I was with one of the Whitney's marks."

"Can I call her the dommubus instead of the succubus since she's clearly not sucking anything?"

She glared down at her toe and thought, "Don't start." Pondering the information Gina just shared, a memory nagged at her brain. "Gina, when the Whitneys enslaved you, did you say it was Mrs. Whitney that cast the spell?"

"It was."

An idea began to formulate in Mawg's mind.

"I don't like where you're going with this."

"Gina, set up a meeting with Mrs. Whitney at the nail salon before Sunday. Tell her you've got someone she needs to meet."

"Okaaaaay….who do I say she will be meeting?"

"Their next mark."

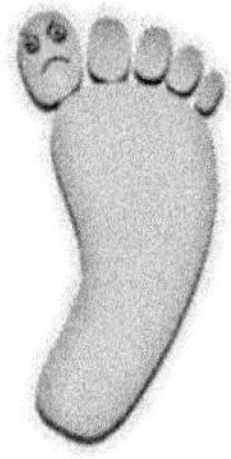

CHAPTER THIRTY-FOUR

Forever grateful to Tori's beautiful collection, Mawg was pulling together pieces of her wardrobe to find the right combination for Evelyn, her newest fem-boss cosplay character. She wore a black pencil skirt that hit her just above the knee, with a tucked white cotton button-down shirt with a large collar. The top two buttons were undone, and her hair was pulled back into a loose bun.

"You need a wig. It's possible Mrs. Whitney has seen you walkin' around the club and she might recognize ya'. But otherwise, it looks fine."

Fine was okay, but she needed it to be convincing. She dialed Tori. "Hey Tori, could you put me in touch with your friend with the wigs again? I've got another character to put together." They talked for a couple more minutes and an idea began to form. Mawg said, "Awesome, I'll meet you at the shop in an hour. You're a lifesaver!"

She puttered around in circles, trying to recall where she left everything she needed to leave the house.

"Oh, I probably should've mentioned that. Another side effect of our relationship. Your memory's gonna be shit for a while."

"Great. Love that for me."

Continuing the middle-age scavenger hunt, she finally gathered her things. They made it out to the car and headed to Torific. When they got to the store, Tori greeted them at the door. "Oooooh, who are we going to be today?" She enjoyed creating Mawg's cosplay characters almost as much as Mawg.

"I need to be a bad ass business leader that looks like she has her shit together and could command a board room. Think we can pull that off?"

Tori clapped her hands and laughed. "Oh I have the perfect outfit for this! Can we add a little age to you? I feel like you should be in your fifties."

"You can just pull the loafers out of retirement. That should help."

Mawg glared down at Peri, then told Tori, "I think that would be amazing. The less I look like me, the better."

While Tori was pulling the outfit options together, she was multi-tasking on the phone with her friend who owned the wig shop. With the idea coming together, Tori shoved Mawg in the dressing room with an armful of clothing.

She was pulling on the black stretchy cigarette pants when she heard the ding from the main door opening. Tori's friend with the wigs had arrived. Mawg got the pants on, tucked in the shirt, and put on the black fitted jacket. Emerging from the dressing room, she heard Tori give her a wolf whistle.

"Love that on you! It's professional, but contemporary so you look sleek. Hang on one sec." She ran to the back of the store to grab shoes from the rack on the wall. Her friend with the wigs came over and they discussed the look Mawg was going for. Tori came back with a pair of pumps with a low heel and Mawg's nose scrunched in distaste. "I know, I know, you don't like heels. Just give them a try. And while you're at it, put this on." She held out a chunky red necklace.

Mawg took everything back into the dressing room and pulled the look together. She had to admit, Tori understood the assignment. She looked like a ball buster. Showing Tori and her friend, they agreed. The last piece was the wig, a chin length white bob. It was the perfect complement to the outfit. Mawg looked at herself in the mirror.

"Hello Evelyn."

CHAPTER THIRTY-FIVE

Mawg sat nervously in the rental van, lurking in the Happy Nail parking lot.

"Are you sure you wanna do this? This is even outside MY comfort zone."

She took a deep breath, looking down at Peri. "Of course I'm not sure. I have no idea how to be a kidnapper."

"The van is a bit cliche, if I'm being honest."

"Yeah, well it's a classic for a reason. It's a helluva lot easier to shove someone through the door of a van instead of a four-door sedan."

Her palms were sweaty at the thought of what they were about to do, and the wig was itching along her brow line. Mawg didn't break laws, as a rule. Sure, she would speed when driving or jaywalk across the street. But as a whole, she abided the law. This could land her in jail…or prison…she didn't know which one was applicable for this particular crime.

"Yeah, orange definitely isn't your color. Let's stay out of the pokey."

She saw Gina pull in and wait in her car. They made eye contact, acknowledging each other. Moments later, Mrs. Whitney arrived. Mawg let the two of them enter the nail salon before stepping out of the van. She texted Jessica, who was in on the scheme (for a price, of course) and let her know it was about to begin.

"Ok, one last time. Who are you?"

Mawg rolled her shoulders back, getting into character. "I'm Evelyn Masters, the head of an international escort service."

"And why can't she find your business online?"

"We require the highest confidentiality due to the nature of our clients. Discretion is of the utmost importance."

"Excellent. And how is Evelyn gonna present herself?"

"Like a no-nonsense, badass bitch."

"Yeah she is. Ok, let's do this."

With one final steadying breath, Evelyn strode slowly and purposefully toward Happy Nail, the bell above the door dinging as she entered. With a disdainful look, she surveyed her surroundings and her eyes fell on Gina and Mrs. Whitney at the pedicure stations. Her heels clacked on the tile as she made her way toward them. As she neared, Evelyn stated, "What an odd venue choice for a meeting. Do they even provide cocktails?"

Standing in her foot bath, Gina reached out to shake Evelyn's hand. "Evelyn, thank you for coming. Yes, the atmosphere here is a bit…lacking. My apologies. But the need for discretion brought us to a neighborhood where we wouldn't be recognized."

Evelyn looked at Mrs. Whitney, then back to Gina like she expected to be introduced. Gina fumbled and said, "Ah, um yes, Evelyn, this is Miranda Whitney. She and her husband own The Whitney Group that I was telling you about."

Evelyn peered down at Mrs. Whitney in the chair and gave her a curt, "Hello." Mrs. Whitney responded in kind.

"Ok sooo, the tone of the meeting is gonna be cunty, I see..."

Trying to fill the awkward lull of conversation, Gina said, "Mrs. Whitney, Evelyn's business is expanding and she might need to find new office space."

Mrs. Whitney gave Evelyn a once over and said, "That's nice. What do you do, dear?"

"Dear? Oh what a bitch."

Recognizing the condescending tone, Evelyn matched it. "I run the world's largest international escort service...hun." Mrs. Whitney's eyes narrowed at being addressed in such a way.

"Oooooooh, you pissed her off! That was fun."

Reading the room, Gina hopped in and said, "Evelyn has outgrown her current headquarters and needs space for..." She turned to Evelyn. "How many employees would be at this location?"

"Approximately 400 for this location. But we have 8,000 employees across the United States and 15,000 overseas. Companionship is a business that's always in need."

Mrs. Whitney's eyebrow raised, and Evelyn knew she was intrigued. Mrs. Whitney pulled out her phone. "What's the name of the business?"

"Remember the story."

"The business is Just For Tonight, but you won't find it online. We don't do traditional marketing due to the need for discretion among our clients and employees. We rely heavily on referrals from current clients."

"Good job."

As Mrs. Whitney was weighing the benefits of having a tenant like Evelyn, Jessica had her staff getting busy on their pedicures. She thought to Evelyn, "Let me know when you're ready." Evelyn dipped her head in acknowledgement.

When Evelyn raised her head, she noticed Mrs. Whitney studying her curiously.

"Oh fuck...Jessica is standing too close. I think Mac heard her."

"Any particular area of town?" Mrs. Whitney asked smoothly, her face back in the usual resting bitch expression. Evelyn pretended to consider it while her nerves started to fray internally and said, "As long as it's a safe neighborhood with good security for my staff, I'm flexible."

Mrs. Whitney looked off in the distance at the wall of polish colors, like she was having an internal dialogue. "I'll bring this to my husband and have Gina get back to you."

"We need to get the fuck out of here before Mac figures out what's going on."

Evelyn lifted her chin and said, "I'll need to make a decision by the end of the month."

"You'll have an answer by then," Mrs. Whitney nodded. "Now if you don't mind, I'd like to relax and enjoy my pedicure." She was dismissing her.

"Come on, quit fuckin' around and let's go!"

Evelyn looked down at Mrs. Whitney's feet that were currently in the hands of the nail tech and couldn't resist. "You might try that koi fish treatment. I hear it works wonders for difficult calluses." She gave a nod to Gina and said, "Have a deserving day, ladies," then turned on her heel to leave. Catching Jessica's eye on the way out the door and making sure she was far enough away that Mac couldn't hear Jessica, she thought, "Give me three minutes, then go." Evelyn strode out the door, bell dinging behind her.

"Oh I wish I could see her face right now. I bet she's fuming over that."

"I guarantee she is. I want her to be a little flustered and riled up when Jessica comes in."

"That was way too fucking close, we almost got caught."

Mawg got into the van, turned it on, and waited. She could see inside the salon windows from her position in the parking lot. Jessica came out of the back room looking panicked. Walking over to Gina and Mrs. Whitney, she whispered something to them and disappeared in the back. While Gina and Mrs. Whitney scrambled to put their shoes on, Jessica appeared from behind the building. She ran over and hopped in the side door of the van. "Go!"

"Showtime."

Mawg shifted into drive, pulling the van in front of the salon as the ladies exited the building. She stomped on the brake when the women were directly in front of the side door, which Jessica swung open.

Surprise registered on Mrs. Whitney's face. Gina shoved her into the van as Jessica grabbed her shoulders to haul her in. Mrs. Whitney was too stunned to realize what was happening…initially. When her fight or flight kicked in, she chose fight and morphed into a rabid animal, twisting and raging, scratching and swinging.

"Shut the fucking door!" Mawg yelled. Gina, with one hand holding off the rabid Mrs. Whitney, grabbed the side panel and slammed it shut as they tore out of the parking lot.

There was no hiding from Mac now. Jessica was too close to both Mrs. Whitney and Mawg, and anything she said or thought would be picked up by both toe demons. Mrs. Whitney was still flailing wildly as Jessica climbed on her back like a spider monkey. Using the strength of her demon, she fought like her life depended on it. While Gina tried to corral her kicking feet, scrappy Jessica was able to avoid her flailing arms and put Mrs. Whitney's neck in a chokehold.

"Isn't she like seventy years old? That's fucking impressive."

"I'm older than you, toe boy," Jessica thought, locking her arms and squeezing tight to get the old bat to go to sleep. Mrs. Whitney was putting up a helluva fight, but after two minutes of struggling and clawing at Jessica's arms, she finally went limp.

"We are not doing toe boy!"

Jessica grunted as she slid out from under Mrs. Whitney while Gina grabbed the rope they brought. Throwing some to Jessica, they began to tie Mrs. Whitney's legs and arms together. Mission accomplished, Jessica slid an eye mask over her face for the final touch.

Mawg, doing her best not to freak out with her Evelyn wig now slightly askew, was focused on getting to their destination undetected. "She's not dead, is she?"

"She's fine!" Jessica yelled. "Just get where we're going so I can be done with you people."

"Hey you never told me, what did you say to them in the salon?"

Mawg looked in the rearview mirror and saw Jessica produce her first full smile. "I told her that her Mercedes was being towed." That gave Peri a good laugh, until Jessica paused momentarily.

"Yeah, the other little toe guy doesn't find that as amusing as you do."

Peri's little eyes bugged out as Mawg continued driving to The Church. It wasn't the most ideal place, but there was a bay area in the back where the liquor delivery drivers would pull in to unload their products. They could get Mrs. Whitney inside and locked away in a room until they could hatch the next part of their plan.

When they arrived, Gina went in first to scout. She came back about five minutes later and said, "As long as we move quickly, we can get her from the back storage area to the utility closet."

Jessica and Mawg hauled Mrs. Whitney by the arms while Gina carried her feet. They made it inside the bay and over to the storage room before they realized how difficult it was to carry dead weight. Everyone's arms were burning. Mawg's eyes scanned the room and fell on a dolly. "Put her down for a second, I have an idea." They laid Mrs. Whitney on the ground as Mawg grabbed the dolly. She placed it flat on the ground like a gurney and said, "Ok, let's lift her the way they lift ER patients on TV." Fumbling, they hauled Mrs. Whitney onto the dolly as Gina ran to the utility closet to prop the door open.

As Mawg lifted the dolly, Mrs. Whitney began to slide. "Jessica! Lay on her and wrap your arms around the back of the dolly so she doesn't fall off!" Jessica's eyes shot daggers at Mawg. "Oh this is soooooo going on your bill." She spider-monkeyed onto the front of Mrs. Whitney and clung onto the dolly for dear life as Mawg rolled them to the utility closet.

"That image will forever be burned in my brain."

Jessica leaned around the body to glare down at Mawg's foot. "Fuck off, toe boy."

"Demon dammit, we're not doing toe boy!"

They entered the utility closet and sat Mrs. Whitney on the floor, propped up against a shelf. Mawg checked her pulse, ensuring she was still alive. She was. Her hands and feet were tied and they were going to stay that way. Mawg found a roll of duct tape on a nearby shelf. She ripped off a piece and placed it over Mrs. Whitney's mouth, ensuring nothing obstructed her nostrils.

Jessica stood staring at Mrs. Whitney for a moment, then turned to Mawg. "Her little toe guy is losing his shit right now. And he knows it's you," she said, pointing to Peri. "If I were you two, I would lock her down securely. She'll have his rage to use against you."

Mawg looked down and immediately felt the weight of what they'd done. She could tell by Peri's terrified expression that Mac was not a demon they wanted to fuck with.

Mrs. Whitney was starting to mumble and come around. Mawg turned to Jessica and Gina. "You two drop off the rental van and get Jessica back to the salon. Don't forget, her purse is in the back of the van. Use her keys to move the Mercedes far away from the salon…like, miles away. Just put her purse in the trunk before you dump the car. I'll stay here and deal with her."

Jessica pulled a pack of smokes and a lighter out of her back pocket as she turned on her heel. "You don't have to tell me twice." Gina started to follow her out, then looked back to Mawg. "Are you sure you're okay?" Mawg waved her hand nonchalantly, although inside her nerves were fried. "I'll be fine. Just make sure to send me Whitney's cell number."

Gina nodded and they left Mawg standing next to the crumpled woman.

"Well, now you can check kidnapping off your bucket list."

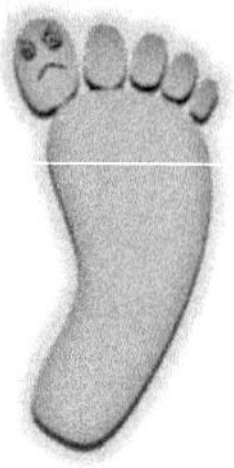

CHAPTER THIRTY-SIX

"Oh my demon, I think she farted."

Peri was right. She had. And the putrid odor of rotten egg immediately burned Mawg's nose. "Gah!" Channeling the essence of a terrified skunk, Mrs. Whitney had produced a defense mechanism so powerful it rendered her enemies helpless.

"My eyes!! It burns, it burns!"

Peri's little eyes watered as he made gagging noises. Mawg gathered the edges of her collar together and buried her nose down inside, seeking relief.

Mrs. Whitney groaned, finally coming around.

"Ohhhh, Mac, you asshole! I know that was your doing!"

With the eye mask still on and her arms and legs tied together, Mrs. Whitney was alert enough to realize something in her world was very, very wrong. She began to yell against the tape.

"MNMPHFMMPHNF!!!!"

Leaning down with her face still buried inside her shirt, Mawg was able to grunt, "Shut. The Fuck. Up."

Mrs. Whitney got quiet momentarily, assumably to gather her wits about the situation she'd found herself in. But that moment passed quickly, and she began to rage against the rope tied around her wrists and ankles. Her muffled screams were bound to attract attention if they didn't do something quickly.

A wave of guilt hit Mawg as she was plotting how to shut up a kidnapped woman. What the hell was she doing? She didn't even recognize herself.

"Hey! You're not the bad guy here! Did you forget what these people did? They're garbage, and they have your man. No mercy."

Peri's words made sense. But there was still a piece of her humanity screaming at her.

"We don't have time for your misplaced pity."

The loud noise rang in Mawg's ears. "Peri, no!—"

Mawg woke in the office, the clock on the wall showing she was out for a good thirty minutes. When she came to, she was sitting at the desk in the office with a sharpie in hand and a white piece of paper in front of her. "What the fuck, Peri?!"

"Just fucking relax. She's fine in the closet. We're makin' a sign to post on the door to keep people from goin' in. We don't want the cleaning crew stumbling onto her in the morning."

"Is she still trying to yell in there? Jesus, Peri!"

"Mawg. Relax. I shut her up. Er...you shut her up. And before you ask, you told her you have cameras on her and if she makes a noise, you'll start breaking her toes."

"What?!? What in the actual fuck, Peri? Why would you tell her that? I'm not going to break her toes!"

"You won't have to. She was picking up what you were puttin' down. She'll be quiet."

Leaning her elbow on the chair, Mawg laid her face in her hand and pinched the bridge of her nose. This was getting wildly out of control. She finished writing the "do not enter" sign and headed back down to the utility closet.

As they entered the bay area and neared the door to the utility closet, she heard crashing and banging from inside. Looking down at Peri, she raised her eyebrow and let out an exasperated sigh. "Did you happen to tie her to anything? Or did you leave her free to flop around like a fish?" Peri's sheepish expression was all the answer she needed.

"I mean, technically YOU left he—"

Mawg bent down and looked like she was tying her shoe.

"You know you're wearing heels, right?"

He could envision the steam coming from Mawg's ears like a cartoon character. Her voice was low and deadly calm. "If I end up in prison, I will let the scariest woman on the block suck you off every day. You think Jake's very clean mouth was full of bacteria? Wait until Methanie with the rotting teeth gets a hold of you, toe boy." Silence.

Getting back up, she unlocked the utility door and stepped inside. Mrs. Whitney was on her arms and knees with her hands and feet still tied. In an attempt to get loose, she had managed to knock some plastic bottles of cleaner off the bottom shelf. A broom and mop had fallen on top of her.

"We need to present a strong front and you need to be the hammer. Show her who's boss. Kick her ass if necessary."

Rolling the tension out of her neck, Mawg thought, "If I have to kick a grown woman's ass because YOU left me no other choice, I'm kicking yours next."

Sighing in annoyance, she picked up the broom and mop and moved them out of the way. Mawg placed the bottles of cleaner back on the shelf and came to stand behind Mrs. Whitney, whose ass was in the air as she scrambled.

"Turn over and sit down. NOW." Mawg's voice may have been commanding, but Mrs. Whitney was panicking like a defensive, feral animal. Straddling the woman on all fours, Mawg leaned down and grabbed her by the back of her hair.

Bending so her mouth was near Mrs. Whitney's ear, she whispered calmly, "Do you want to live?" Mrs. Whitney continued trying to scream, her angry cries muffled.

Mawg slapped her, but because she was standing behind Mrs. Whitney, it didn't land with the force she'd hoped. It did, however, quiet her cries momentarily.

"Do you want to see your husband again?" She nodded. "Then I need you to sit here, quietly, for the next 24 hours. Do that, and this will all be over. Are we understood?" Mawg could see the war waging within the proud woman. Oh, she wanted to rip Mawg's eyes out, but she was unable to do anything but nod.

The human sympathy from earlier was gone, and Mawg's face morphed into a cold, ruthless expression.

"Do you know what happens if you lie to me? Or if you try to escape?"

Mrs. Whitney may have still felt defiant, as witnessed by her raised chin, but she wasn't stupid. She sat quietly and waited.

"I'll take a hammer and smash your toes. And if that doesn't convince you to cooperate, your fingers will be next."

"Oh my demon, Mawg the Enforcer has finally arrived!"

She watched Mrs. Whitney's shoulders drop as she nodded in acknowledgement.

"Good. Now, flip over and sit on your ass."

Mrs. Whitney complied, and Mawg used some nearby bungee cords to tie her to a support pole by her waist. She wasn't going anywhere, and there was nothing close enough within reach she could grasp.

Turning to leave, Mawg called over her shoulder, "I'll be back later with food. But don't forget...I'm always watching."

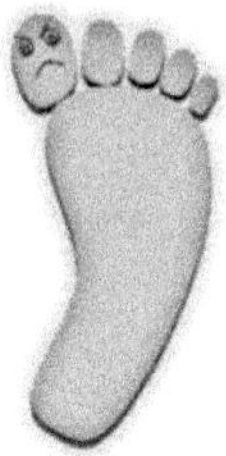

CHAPTER THIRTY-SEVEN

Remembering she didn't have her car since they'd come in the rental van, Mawg called ride share to pick her up in the front of The Church. She avoided walking through the building, and instead walked around the outside to the front street.

"Who the fuck was that in there?!"

Mawg was visibly shaking, her body starting to process all the recent events since Declan disappeared. "You were right. I realized she wasn't going to take me seriously unless I went there."

The ride share arrived and they headed back to the house. She needed to get out of the Evelyn costume and eat before her blood sugar dipped too low. She was already feeling light-headed.

As they got to the house, she was putting the key in the lock of the front door when a 'ding' with a text message came through. She got in the house, peeled off Evelyn's outfit and hung the wig.

Grabbing a granola bar and eating naked on the bed, Mawg picked up the phone and saw the text from Gina.

Whitney's number is 555-3948.

Are you okay? Is she okay? Update me please.

She fired off a quick update.

Everyone fine. Thanks. Tired. Fill you in later, I promise.

She set an alarm to grab a quick nap before getting ready to hatch step two of this plan. Exhaustion took over, and the next thing she knew, she was waking to the alarm blaring an hour later. She hurried through a cold shower and got dressed.

Hopping in her car, they stopped to pick up a cheap burner phone and hit a drive-thru to pick up food for both her and Mrs. Whitney when a realization hit Peri.

"What do we do when she needs to take a dump?"

Fuuuuuck. She hadn't thought about that.

"You know, there's a lot more to kidnapping than what they show you on TV."

Mawg sighed, her arm leaning on the ledge of the car window with her head in her hand. She called Gina. "Hey…yeah, it's fine but I'm going to need your help. There are a few things we didn't think through. Yeah. Meet me at The Church and wait for me in the office. I'll head up to meet you after I feed her. Yeah….yeah, I forgot about that, too. Ok see you in a bit."

"You really shouldn't be on your phone when you drive. It's dangerous."

Mawg lost it, maniacally laughing at the absurdity of Peri's statement with tears streaming down her face. "Yes Peri, you're absolutely right. Driving and talking is the most heinous thing I've done in the past twenty-four hours." The crazed laughter continued.

"Ok number one- the sarcasm isn't necessary. Number two- It's gonna work. By this time tomorrow night, you'll have Declan back."

She was having serious doubts about the viability of their plan, but fuck it. They'd come this far. Might as well see it through and cross her fingers. They made it to The Church and she parked in the back bay area. Using her keycard to enter, she hauled the bag of fast food into the utility room and unlocked the door. Mrs. Whitney was in the same position as when she left, so that gave Mawg a little bit of hope for their plan. Hearing the door open, Mrs. Whitney tried to speak through the tape.

Mawg set the fast food bag down and kneeled next to her. "I brought you something to eat. Now, I'm going to remove the tape from your mouth. You're not going to yell, and you're not going to freak out. You're going to stay quiet, or else I'll put the tape back on and you can starve. Understood?"

Mrs. Whitney nodded, and Mawg removed the tape. She waited to see if Mrs. Whitney was going to freak out. She did not. Mawg grabbed the bag of food and asked, "Do you prefer a burger or a chicken sandwich?"

"What is this, the fucking Club Med?! Just give her whatever you don't want!"

Mrs. Whitney turned her nose up. "Chicken will suffice, I suppose." She spoke like Mawg was her employee and she was disappointed in her.

Muttering under her breath while she unwrapped the chicken sandwich, Mawg held it to Mrs. Whitney's mouth so she could eat. While she was chewing, Mawg said, "We're working out some…uh…facilities for you as well."

Mrs. Whitney swallowed her bite and replied, "You don't have facilities in this…place?"

"Don't you dare fuckin' let her out of this room."

Mawg chortled. "Yes, we have facilities. And no, you aren't leaving this room to use them. I'll bring you a bucket."

The appalled woman's mouth dropped wide open, a tiny piece of lettuce from the chicken sandwich balancing precariously on the corner of her lower lip. "How dare you treat me like this! I demand to know what this is about."

The unabashed audacity of this woman continued to baffle Mawg. "Oh, you're not in a place to make demands.

You and your husband stole something from me, and I want it back."

It didn't matter that she was in a very vulnerable position. Mrs. Whitney was still Mrs. Whitney. She lifted her chin and tried to give what Mawg assumed was a haughty look behind the eye mask. "My husband and I are upstanding members of the community. We would never sink to something as low as thievery."

"Maaaaaaaan, I really want you to punch her in the mouth."

That got a maniacal laugh out of Mawg as she shoved another bite of chicken into Mrs. Whitney's mouth. "You two are the worst kind of villains. You hide behind a facade of money and connections, but you're nothing more than upscale grifters. Your business is built on manipulation and lies."

She started to protest as Mawg leaned down near her ear and whispered, "I know about the succubus." Mrs. Whitney froze. Mawg got some satisfaction knowing she just hit her where it hurt. "And I know about you and your little demon. You're a grifter and a sham, Miranda. And your piece of shit husband is holding someone priceless to me. If he doesn't

471

bring him back to me tomorrow night, you're going home in a body bag."

Mrs. Whitney sat in shock, realizing they'd been caught. She whispered, "Declan."

"Yes. Declan."

The chicken sandwich was finished, and Mawg grabbed the tape again. Mrs. Whitney, whose voice was now icy as a glacier, replied, "Since you seem to know so much about the succubus and the power I have over it, you might do well to release me before I call harm down upon you."

Peri began to smile as he felt the years of rage buried deep within Mawg boil up to the surface. Mawg swung around to face her, hands clenched in fists at her side.

"You know what, bitch? I've spent my entire life surrounded by bullies; berating me, making fun of me, humiliating me…your threats mean nothing to me. You may underestimate me, and you might try to harm me." She leaned back down, her face an inch from Mrs. Whitney's as she poked her finger into her chest. "But if I go down, I promise I'll sink my nails into your back and drag you to the depths of hell with me. I will do EVERYTHING in my power to bring you down. Trust." She stood up and took a photo of Mrs. Whitney.

Mawg put the tape back over her mouth, turned on her heel and walked out, locking the door behind her. She heard Peri start to sniffle as she made her way to the office, then felt a tear sneak down her cheek. "Are you crying?"

"I....I'm just...I'm so proud of you. You went from 'bump on a log Mawg' to ruthless femme dom."

Mawg chuckled at that. "I don't think that's necessarily accurate, but thanks. I feel bad about threatening a human, but my guilt is taking a backseat to the fucking audacity of that bitch."

"Do you think you could do it? I mean, if it actually came down to it. Could you hurt another human?"

Mawg thought about that as they got to the office door. "I hope it never comes to that, but let me think on it and I'll get back to you." She entered the room and found Gina pacing. Seeing Mawg, she let out a sigh of relief and came over to hug her. "Jesus, I was worried something went wrong. She's still alive?"

"She's fine, but we've got some things to work out. Give me one sec and let me text Whitney so we can get that rolling." She pulled out the burner phone and typed Whitney's number in. She attached the picture of Mrs. Whitney tied up in the utility room, then text:

Bring the Irish package back to the holy place where it belongs tomorrow night at 10PM and we'll have a gift exchange.

She waited. Three minutes went by before the phone dinged:

Make sure that package arrives in one piece.

Mawg smiled. "Got him." She replied:

Same.

She turned to Gina and said, "Ok, we've got a lot of things to do. I need to call Jake and see if he found any loopholes in Declan's contract. Gina, can you find a bucket we can bring to Mrs. Whitney so she can…er, relieve herself? Just set it back in the storage area and I'll deal with that." Gina nodded and took off.

"You need to get rid of that burner phone ASAP. Break it, smash it, whatever you need to do and get it away from here. Oh, and wipe your fingerprints off it."

Mawg hadn't thought about that. "Good call, one sec." She put the phone in her pocket and walked down to the storage room. There was a little bucket of tools that had a small hammer. Gina was walking toward her with the bucket. "Perfect timing." Mawg took the bucket from her and unlocked the utility room. Mrs. Whitney started at the noise.

"Stand up." Mrs. Whitney shimmied her way up the pole she was tied to. Mawg ripped the tape off her mouth and said, "I brought something so you can relieve yourself."

Mrs. Whitney, using her full cunt voice, shook her head and said, "Absolutely not. I am not a filthy animal."

Mawg's eyebrow raised in a mix of appreciation and surprise. One thing about Mrs. Whitney…she was who she was, no matter how dire the situation. Mawg managed to tamper down her thoughts and stay stoic. "Your other option is to shit your pants and stay here in them. Even animals aren't that filthy, Miranda."

Mrs. Whitney was clearly fuming, but her Mawg's words must have landed because she raised her bound hands up and said, "And how exactly do you see the physics of this happening when my hands are tied?"

Fuck.

"The next kidnapping will go so much smoother now that we've ironed out all the wrinkles."

Mawg glared down at her sarcastic toe. Then she looked at Mrs. Whitney and made a decision.

"Oh demon, no….please don't do what I think you're gonna do."

But Mawg did. She unbuttoned Mrs. Whitney's pants and pulled them down from her hips. Mrs. Whitney gasped. "The bucket is below you. I'll step out while you do your business." On her way out of the utility room, she grabbed a pair of nitrile gloves and a couple of disinfectant wipes.

"I didn't need to see that. No one needed to see that. It's so furry!"

Mawg chuckled and stopped to peer down at her toe. "Of all the things we've seen the past few weeks, a hairy bush is what bothers you?"

"I don't need to justify my preferences to you. I don't like 1970's bush."

She was still laughing as she put on the gloves. She pulled out the disinfectant wipes and began to wipe all remnants of her fingerprints off the phone. Finished, she grabbed the hammer and smashed it multiple times until it was in pieces. Gathering the pieces, she spotted a grocery bag in a small trash can in the corner. She added the phone to the trash that had already accumulated and tied the bag up.

Standing off to the side, Gina waited for direction. Mawg handed her the bag and said, "Take this two or three miles away and dump it in a gas station trash can. Then head back here." Gina nodded, taking the bag and leaving.

Mawg walked back to the utility room that now smelled like shit. Luckily, the giant rolls of toilet paper for the restrooms were sitting on the shelf.

"Oh demon dammit! This is not in my job description."

Mawg grabbed another pair of gloves and a massive wad of the paper.

"Next kidnapping, make sure we grab adult diapers."

Plugging her nose with one hand and reaching out with the paper wadded up in her other, she wiped Mrs. Whitney's ass.

"EWWWWWWWWWWW!!!!"

Mawg tossed the paper into the bucket, along with her gloves. Then she grabbed the underwear and pants that were around Mrs. Whitney's ankles and pulled them up. Mrs. Whitney remained frozen like a statue with her head held high while Mawg buttoned the pants, removed the bucket, and said, "You can sit now." She leaned against the pole and shimmied down as gracefully as one could while bound. Mawg ripped off another piece of tape and placed it back over Mrs. Whitney's pursed mouth.

Holding the bucket a full arm length away, Mawg made her way out of the utility room.

"Oh my demon, get rid of that right this second. I cannot believe the filth you're puttin' me through today."

She hauled the bucket out through the bay and set it on the ground around the corner. "We'll figure that out later."

Hauling ass away from the smell, she got back in the building and headed up to the office. Back at the desk, she pulled out her cell and called Jake as Peri made a "hrmph" noise. She wasn't sure Jake could ever get back in his good graces after the chocolate sauce incident.

"This is Jake."

"Hey Jake, it's Mawg from The Church."

"Marvelous Mawg! Just the person I wanted to talk to. I've been digging through that contract you sent over."

"Oh man, I really appreciate you doing that. Is there any loophole to get out of it?"

"There is, but it would require getting proof this Mr. Whitney guy's been scamming people. The contract has a back-out clause if either party is caught doing something illegal. Lucky for you, I love digging for info almost as much as I love feet. I can drop it off to you tomorrow."

"Jake, you are a miracle worker. That's amazing news! Hey, I've got one more question for you."

"Shoot it at me, whatcha got?"

"What are you doing tomorrow night?"

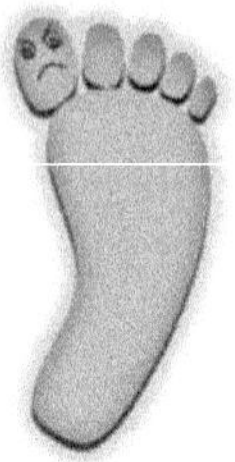

CHAPTER THIRTY-EIGHT

Sunday arrived and Mawg woke with a pit in the bottom of her stomach. So many things could go wrong.

"Ugh, here we go again. You know who you sound like? The Mawg that I met our first day together. Quit being such a fuckin' Debbie Downer!"

She got up from the couch. The entire night had been spent in the office at The Church, with a trip every few hours to check on Mrs. Whitney. Pulling her unkempt hair into a bun, she started to run down the mental checklist of everything that needed to happen to pull this off.

"Listen, it's gonna be fine. Everyone knows their part and they're all invested in this going off without a hitch. They won't let you down."

She put on her running shoes, ready to go help Mrs. Whitney relieve herself. "It's not them I'm worried about, Peri. This entire scheme is my plan, and if it fails, people I care very much about could get hurt." She laughed halfheartedly. "No pressure."

"Mawg...Mawg, look at me."

She sighed and looked down at her toe.

"Do you have any grasp of how strong you truly are? When we first met, I told you that I chose you for a reason. Beneath that beige-colored monstrosity of a wardrobe and the depressing attitude, I saw it. And over the past few weeks, I've watched it begin to blossom. It's not about the clothes, or your meatsuit, or your career. You have the heart of a fighter, Mawg. That's so rare. Many humans puff their chests in false bravado, but you...even though you might be scared shitless, you do what needs to be done."

Tears were welling up in Mawg's eyes.

"You were nervous to take that first tour of The Church. You did it anyway. You were scared to start a new career. You did it anyway. You were scared to be vulnerable with Declan. You did it anyway. And now you've got a massive

task in front of you and you're scared again. But you know what? You're gonna do it anyway. Because that's just who you are."

She was sniffling and wiping tears from her face.

"That's true strength and courage, Mawg. And that's why this is gonna work out. Because you're gonna will it into existence, and the universe is gonna pay attention. When a middle-age woman recognizes her strength and begins to wield it, she is virtually unstoppable."

She said nothing, still sniffling and wiping tears from her eyes. Kneeling down, she wrapped her hand around her left big toe.

"Hey! Hey, what the hell are you doing?"

"I don't know how to hug you, but I want to hug you. So just shut up and let me hug you." She sat there for a few moments with her hand wrapped around her toe. "I love you, Peri."

She began to cry, the tears coming from both of them.

"Ok, ok.....that's enough sappy shit for us, kiddo. I got a reputation to uphold. Come on, let's go help Mrs. Hairy Bush take her morning poo so we can be done with that."

Mawg chuckled at "Mrs. Hairy Bush". That would be Mrs. Whitney's code name from now on. She headed down the stairs and out to the bay to grab the bucket sitting outside the back door. Her phone rang as she stepped outside. It was Gina.

"Morning, were you able to get in touch with Jessica and Tori?"

Gina sounded as exhausted as Mawg felt. "Yeah, they're in. And just FYI, you're going to be in debt to Jessica for at least a year."

Chuckling, Mawg turned on her heel and stopped dead in her tracks. Mr. Whitney walking down the alley toward her. She was seized with panic, but thankfully Peri wasn't.

"Play dumb immediately or I'll take over."

Still holding the phone to her ear, Mawg called on all the actress skills she'd learned the past few weeks and smiled. "Hi, can I help you?"

His dead eyes never changed. Not one flick of emotion. "Where is the manager?"

Mawg attempted to look slightly confused. "Are you talking about the Irish guy or the redhead lady? Sorry, it's my first day here."

He looked annoyed at having to speak with one of the poors. "The redhead."

"Oh the cleaning guys told me she won't be in until tonight. I need to see her too, I've got paperwork to fill out. You want me to leave her a message?"

"Yes, tell her she needs to check in immediately."

"Okaaaaaay…with who?"

He looked disgusted with the entire conversation. "She'll know." He turned around and walked off. Mawg waited until he was around the corner of the building, then freaked out. She looked at the phone. "Gina…you still there?"

"I'm here. And yes, I heard all that."

"You need to hide out. He can't find you before the performance! Do you have somewhere to go that he doesn't know about?"

Gina's voice cracked, frightened. "I'll figure something out."

"You can go to my house. He doesn't know about me and wouldn't look there. I'll text you the address. Use the ride share app and don't drive. He'll be on the lookout for your car. I'll meet you there in like 30 minutes."

Gina was quiet. "Thank you, Mawg. I don't know why you're being nice to me with everything I've done."

Mawg exhaled. "I'm done being mad at you. It wasn't your fault. You do everything possible to pull this off tonight and we'll call it even. Understood?"

"Understood. Ok, I'll see you soon."

"Gina…." Mawg warned, "Be cautious and be careful. He's hunting for you."

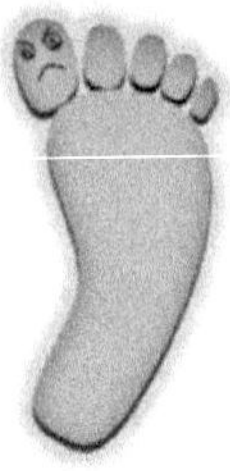

CHAPTER THIRTY-NINE

Gina showed up to Mawg's house thirty minutes later. She was on edge knowing that Whitney was after her.

"Do you really think we can pull this off?"

Hands on her hips and trying to convey her most positive outlook, Mawg said, "Gina, a wise being once told me that when middle-age women put their minds to something, they're virtually unstoppable." Peri's little face lit up in a smile. "We're going to succeed. I'm willing it into existence."

Mawg sent one last batch of texts to ensure everyone involved was ready. All confirmed.

"I need to catch a quick nap so I'm not running on fumes tonight. Do you want to lay down as well, or do you just want to hang out?"

Gina sat back in the chair. I think I'll throw on a show and try to take my mind off everything, if that's okay with you."

Mawg handed her the remote and headed back to the bedroom. Setting an alarm, she crashed.

The alarm went off 90 minutes later, shaking her out of a foggy dream. She walked into the bathroom and splashed cold water on her face to wake up. It was nearing showtime, and she needed to be alert. She showered, then woke Gina who had fallen asleep on the couch. They gathered up the bags of supplies and headed back to The Church.

They made it inside undetected and headed up to the office. Once inside, they locked the door and closed the blinds. She needed to keep Gina hidden.

"I'm going to talk to the security guys really quick. When I come back, I'm going to knock three times, wait, and then knock three times again. If you don't hear that pattern, don't open the door."

Gina nodded, and Mawg walked out to find security. She gathered them all for a quick meeting to give instructions and a heads up on what to look out for that evening. Once they confirmed they understood, she headed back to the office.

Knock, knock, knock……….Knock, knock, knock.

Gina opened the door and let her in.

"Ok security has their instructions so we should be good there. Now, do you remember where you need to hide out until the performance?"

"I do. But before I do that, I need to prep the stage and the A/V guy."

"Ok, I had security close the front stage curtains, so that should be no problem. Just stay hidden after you're finished. All of this falls apart if Whitney finds you before the performance."

"Understood. Mawg…thanks again."

Mawg waved her off. "If I was in your position, I'd want someone to help me. Now, go prep the stage and hide."

Gina took off out the door.

The afternoon preparations passed quickly, and Mawg found herself pacing in the office, running through the plan over and over. She'd used the small, attached bathroom to get ready and was in full Evelyn gear.

"If you recite that one more time, I'm gonna give you a chin hair."

Hands on her hips, she stared down at her toe. "I thought you could only do that if I was trying to harm you?"

"You're harming my mental peace. That's close enough."

Shooting Peri her standard glare of displeasure Mawg made her way out of the office to double check everything was in place. The stage was curtained off, and she walked up its stairs. The A/V guy was on his laptop, making last minute tweaks to the rack of cameras that were set up for the performance. Mawg walked up to him. "You received the instructions from Gina earlier, didn't you?" He gave her a thumbs up. "Yep, the extras are all in position and I just checked them. We're good to go." Mawg clapped him on the back and said, "Excellent, thank you."

She went backstage and found Gina hunched up on the floor behind a stack of mattresses that were leaning against the wall. Hearing the footsteps coming, her head shot up in fear. "It's just me," Mawg said. "How are you feeling? Are you okay?" Gina stared at the brick wall to her left.

"I've been sitting here having an existential crisis, but otherwise I'm fine."

Mawg sat on the floor next to her and criss-crossed her legs. "I guess I've never really asked. How old are you?" Gina chuckled. "I tell everyone I'm forty-seven, but I'm actually three hundred and twenty-nine human years old." Mawg's eyebrows shot up in surprise. "And in three hundred and twenty-nine years, you only took the life of one human…accidentally?" Gina nodded. "I've always known when to stop. When we suck a life source, it's similar to how a vampire sucks blood. If they're mature and strong enough, they can stop before killing the person. BUT, it takes a lot of strength and willpower."

"Are vampires real?"

"Yes." Gina and Peri answered simultaneously.

"Huh…I guess I shouldn't be surprised. Do you want to know a secret of mine, Gina?"

Gina's eyes raised in surprise. "Sure, if you'd like to share."

Mawg leaned in conspiratorially and whispered, "I have a demon inhabiting my toe."

Gina's eyes perked up and she chuckled. "No shit? I've heard about the little toe guys. Is he with you all the time?"

"For the eight thousandth time, we are NOT doing little toe guys."

"Yep, he's always here with me. At least, for the next ten years or so."

Gina smiled at her. "You didn't have to share that with me…but I appreciate that you trust me with that information."

Mawg reached out her hand and squeezed Gina's. They looked at each other, the weight of what they were about to do landing in between them. Looking Gina in the eye, Mawg said, "We're gonna pull this off. And you're going to be free." She squeezed her hand one more time and got up, brushing herself off. She started to walk off then turned back over her shoulder. "Oh, and Gina?"

"Yeah?"

"May your release be….thoroughly enjoyable."

She heard Gina laughing as she walked away.

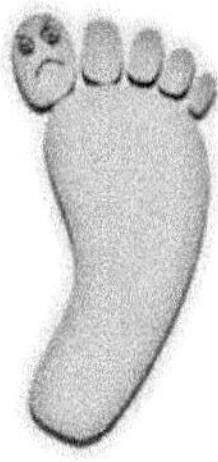

CHAPTER FORTY

"Oh goody, I see Meat Suit Mania is back with a vengeance."

That was no joke. The orgy of bodies and limbs seemed to pick up right where they left off the last Sunday she was here. Except this time, there were about twenty people involved. She saw a hand pop up from the middle of the pile to stroke a free dick nearby. One woman on the edge of the pile had another woman straddling her face while a man was thrusting his hand inside her. No one knew who was touching them, and they didn't care, so long as they were being pleasured.

The rooms were bustling with activity as well, save two that had been reserved for the exchange. Mistress Nikki was peeing on a man when she saw Mawg walking by. She paused to give her a large smile and a wave, then turned back and peed on him some more.

"Two things. One, I love her. Two, now do you see why the dog pee pads make sense?"

Mawg chuckled nervously, trying to stay focused. Standing off to the side of the stage and drinking a gin and tonic to calm her nerves, she surveyed the room. So many people from so many different walks of life. No one being hateful, mean, or judgmental. In The Church, it didn't matter what your political, religious, or general life beliefs were. It only mattered that you were honest and vulnerable enough to ask for what you wanted. There was something for everyone, and Mawg realized she'd come to love this place. It was becoming a second home, and she would do everything possible to protect it.

"They're here."

Mawg's eyes flashed to the entrance. In walked Mr. Whitney. In his hand was a leash, and attached to the leash was a man with a beautiful swimmer's body. Covered head to toe in a rubber bondage suit with a ball gag in his mouth, his hands were tied behind his back. Bondage suit be damned, he was standing with his chin lifted and his shoulders back. Declan was not a man to cower. Steve the security guard stopped them, as was the protocol they set up. He leaned down to say something in Whitney's ear.

When one thinks of rage, it's easy to picture something explosive. A loud eruption that overwhelms everything and everyone in the nearby vicinity. But what Mawg experienced watching Whitney attempt to demean her man was icy and quiet.

"Keep calm."

She thought, "Oh, I'm calm. I'm quite calm, in fact. Remember when you asked me if I could actually do it? Take another human's life?"

"I do."

"Well, I could. In this instance, I could do it. And I would have no remorse. I wouldn't be sad and I wouldn't feel one ounce of guilt."

"You know I'm here with you no matter what. But we need to stick to the plan. Whitney will get what's coming to him in the end."

If Whitney could sense the death stare from Mawg, he didn't show it. Listening to what Security Steve was whispering in his ear, his face displayed agitation. Whitney was a man who wasn't used to taking direction. But Security Steve didn't back down, and Mawg gave a sigh of relief. He then walked Mr. Whitney into the room Mawg had designated.

"Showtime, kiddo."

Mawg walked backstage. Gina and the muscle men were gearing up to begin the performance. Mawg had always thought Gina was stunning, but tonight she was especially so. Naked as a jaybird, she glowed. It was like her body recognized what was about to happen and it was reverberating with anticipation. Mawg caught her eye and gave her the go-ahead nod. With a wink of acknowledgement, Gina turned to the muscle men and said, "Let's do this, boys." Mawg cued the A/V guy who was watching her for the signal, and she heard the pounding drumbeats begin.

Walking off the stage, she ran directly into Jake's chest He had the snake mask in hand and was ready to fill in for Declan's role. Mawg asked, "How are you feeling? Ready for this?"

"Uuuuuuugh, make him go away."

Jake gave her a cheeky grin. "You know me, I love an audience." He winked and put the mask on, patting her on the shoulder as she walked off. She knew he would do a phenomenal job, and walked away with no worries about the performance.

Heading to the utility closet, she grabbed Mrs. Whitney who was still tied up and wearing the eye mask with tape across her mouth. In the back room, Mawg found a tub of wrapped toys and pulled out a ball gag. Two could play at this game. She tore the tape off Mrs. Whitney's mouth and she released a yell. Mawg's cold, dead voice cut in. "You're five minutes from freedom. Say one more word and that all goes away." Mrs. Whitney shut up and let Mawg put the ball gag on her.

"You know, maybe you should think about becoming a Dom. You're kinda good at bein' the Enforcer."

Mawg took a deep breath. The time was finally here. With her head held high, she marched Mrs. Whitney to the room next door to where Declan was being held. Security Steve was standing between the rooms, per her request. His eyebrow raised at the sight of Mrs. Whitney, but he said nothing. Mawg could hear the performance kicking off, and the muscle men were all on stage. It was almost time for Gina's entrance as Eve.

Mawg put her hand on the doorknob and opened the door, dragging Mrs. Whitney in with her. She shut the door and turned on the overhead light. In the middle of the room, they'd recreated the circle that Mawg had seen on the floor during Gina's last ritual. In the middle of the circle was a chair with Tori and Jessica standing by it. Beneath the chair was a tub full of gelatin.

"I knew it! I fuckin' knew they kept some here!"

Mawg brought Mrs. Whitney into the circle, careful not to drag her feet through it, and sat her on the chair. Jessica used a rope to tie Mrs. Whitney's waist to the chair, and Tori picked up her bound feet and began to remove her shoes.

Jessica noted, "Her little toe guy is screaming bloody murder. Don't let her loose or she'll rage and tear you apart."

Mawg didn't say anything, but she could feel the fear from Peri course through her as she looked up at the TV screen they'd had brought in. On screen was the room next door.

Mr. Whitney was sitting in the spectator chair in the corner, looking like he didn't have a care in the world. Still in the bondage suit and ball gag with his hands tied behind his back, Declan stood in the middle of the room attached to the leash in Whitney's hand.

Peri could feel the rage simmering within Mawg.

"Easy, now isn't the time."

She stepped out of the circle and walked over to the shelf on the wall where the A/V guy had left a lapel microphone. She turned as she attempted to put it on her shirt and looked at the scene unfolding. Jessica had tied Mrs. Whitney to the chair, her hands roped together in her lap. She'd taken the ball gag out of her mouth and Tori had removed her shoes, holding her bound feet above the container of gelatin.

Mawg heard the crowd begin to cheer, and she knew time was of the essence. She grabbed Mrs. Whitney by the back of the hair, causing her to yelp. "You're going to release the succubus now, or things are going to get really ugly."

Jessica, who had been standing behind Mrs. Whitney in the circle, piped up. "Mac said to tell you 'fuck you'. He's not as well-spoken as she is, apparently."

Mawg could feel Peri making her heart rate rise with his anxiety. Hand still in Mrs. Whitney's hair, she leaned her face over to growl at Mrs. Whitney's foot.

"Hey asshole…do you like snackies?"

Jessica piped up behind her after a moment. "He's not saying anything, but I'll go ahead and say that answer is yes. All the little toe guys are suckers for food."

Mawg took a moment to nod slowly, taking that information in. "Well then…why don't you be quiet and have a snack?" She turned to Tori, who was holding Mrs. Whitney's feet and gave her the nod.

Down into the gelatin went Mrs. Whitney's feet.

"Ohhh, if I didn't hate him so much I'd feel sorry for him. That's just foul."

Mawg leaned back up to address Mrs. Whitney, who was now squirming in the chair, presumably because Mac was raging. "Now…Either you release the succubus, or we'll do it for you. One way is much less painful for you."

Mrs. Whitney's normal icy exterior broke, and her cheeks reddened as she spat, "Go to hell!"

Mawg could hear the drums beating in the main room and knew she was running out of time. She grabbed the lapel mic and turned it on, holding it near her mouth. "Whitney! Do you hear me?"

She saw Mr. Whitney on the screen, jumping up from the spectator chair and looking around like he saw a ghost.

Mawg knew she had his attention. "I'm curious, how does a grifter worm his way into high society?"

"I've always loved the word grifter. It's almost as fun as charlatan."

"Because I'd truly love to know," Mawg continued. She leaned down next to Mrs. Whitney's head and whispered into the microphone. "You see, I did a little research on the two of you." Mrs. Whitney stiffened at that statement. "Well…I didn't, but a very good lawyer friend did. And prior to your marriage in 1998, neither one of you existed. Poof! Not a lick of information about either one of you. No birth certificates, no driver's licenses…nothing. Why is that?"

Mrs. Whitney chimed in. "Honey, can you hear me? Don't say a word. Not a single word." Mawg tightened the grip on the back of her hair and made her yelp.

Mawg watched his eyes searching the room at her cry, and when he found nothing, he panicked and walked over toward Declan.

"Touch him and she dies."

Peri had seen Mawg explore a tremendous amount of emotions in their time together, but this was the first time he'd seen her turn icy and terrifying. That wasn't an idle threat. She meant every word.

Mr. Whitney must have believed her too, and he took a step back as Mawg continued. "I had a feeling you might not be interested in a sharing session, so I had some of my friends do some digging. You know how pesky friends can be when you give them a mystery to unravel."

She caught a slight twitch in Mr. Whitney's expression. That statement got his attention.

"Would you like to know what they found?"

Whitney stood staring off at the wall, waiting.

"We both know that your wife has been meeting with Gina at the nail salon to discuss your next marks. But…" Mawg bent down to look directly into Mrs. Whitney's face, her knees creaking at the effort. "Did you know she's also meeting someone else there once a month?" She looked to the screen at Mr. Whitney, whose facial expression showed that he did not, in fact, know that was occurring.

Mawg waved a hand nonchalantly. "Oh, she's not cheating on you. It's nothing like that. Your Miranda is the pillar of what a high society wife should be in your world, even though she's a royal bitch."

"What's that old expression? The higher the class, the bigger the ass?"

Mawg ignored Peri and continued. "However, she has been meeting with a woman named Mary as well."

She watched on screen as his normally emotionless stare turned incredulous. "Mr. Whitney. I'm going to allow you the floor to tell us. Who is Mary?"

He looked around the room, panicked, but refused to answer.

Mawg shrugged like she didn't have a care in the world. "Have it your way, I guess. Mary, our dear sweet Mary, is Miranda's sister." She stood silent, letting that hammer drop.

Mrs. Whitney cut in with a dry, annoyed tone. "So I meet with my sister. Is family time a crime, now?"

"You're right," Mawg said as she slapped her hand on Mrs. Whitney's shoulder. "You meeting your sister to get your nails done is not a big deal. But do you know what is?"

Mr. Whitney, listening to the exchange, continued to keep a stoic expression on his face, but Mawg noticed a little tic as his fingers were drumming on his leg.

She smiled, knowing she was getting to him. "My lawyer friend discovered that Mary and Miranda's maiden name is Borden. So, while we couldn't find any information about you or Mrs. Whitney prior to your wedding, we WERE able to learn more about Miranda Borden…and her high school sweetheart, Jimmy-Lou Phillips."

Now she had Whitney's attention. His eyes were wide, and she watched him mentally calculating how to get out of this.

Mawg continued. "Jimmy-Lou Phillips apparently got himself into a teensy bit of trouble. See, he got caught scamming old people out of their social security checks." She turned to look at Mrs. Whitney. "That seems like a pretty scummy thing to do, doesn't it?"

As Mr. Whitney began to unconsciously pace, Mawg said, "So Jimmy-Lou did a little time in the pokey for that. But when he got out, he disappeared. There was no trace of Jimmy-Lou or Miranda after he was released. Poof! They vanished."

Whitney was pissed, and she watched his fists clench at his side. "A year later, there was a record for a marriage license for the Whitneys on file. Which is interesting, because there is no legal name change on file for either of you."

There was no arguing he'd been caught. "So what exactly do you want?"

Mawg chuckled. "Oh, it's not about what I want. It's about what is legally binding. Remember those pesky friends I mentioned earlier?"

Mr. Whitney began pacing again.

"One of them is a lawyer. And he reviewed your contract with Declan for The Church's lease. It seems there's a clause that states the contract is null and void if either party is found doing something illegal. Operating a business under a name that's not legally yours…well, that seems illegal to me. Don't you think?"

She expected Whitney to come unglued. His real estate empire was about to be dismantled. What she didn't expect was for him to pull a gun out from behind his jacket and point it at Declan.

"Whoa! Ok,ok… he's panicking like a cornered animal. Stay calm."

There was no time for Mawg to process the sheer terror she felt seeing the gun aimed at Declan.

"Fuck you, you nosey bitch! You should have stayed out of my business!"

Mawg, who still had Mrs. Whitney's hair wrapped in her hand, kept her voice calm and said, "Put the gun down Whitney, or your bitch wife dies too." She leaned her head down by Mrs. Whitney's face, getting ready to give her a command when the old bat raised her bound hands from her lap and smashed them into Mawg's forehead.

Stars exploded in her eyes as Mawg stumbled back, releasing her hair. That was all Mrs. Whitney and Mac needed. She kicked her feet that were still tied out of the gelatin right into Tori's knees, causing her to fall back.

Jessica, who had been standing behind Mrs. Whitney with an annoyed look on her face, jumped into action. She leaned over the back of the chair and wrapped her arms around Mrs. Whitney's neck, attempting to choke her out again.

But Mrs. Whitney and Mac weren't having it. "Not this time, bitch." Mrs. Whitney threw her body forward with the chair still tied to her waist. As she bent forward, the chair lifted into the air with Jessica on the back of it. The surprise move caught Jessica off-guard, and she flew forward, letting go of the chokehold.

Mrs. Whitney was standing hunched over, the rope that had been keeping her tied to the chair now loosened. She shook off the chair, raised her bound hands to rip the mask off her eyes and turned her body to look for Mawg.

As Mrs. Whitney's eyes locked on Mawg, she felt terror rip through her body. But it wasn't hers. It was Peri's. He was so frightened, he was causing Mawg's body to tremble.

But Mawg was void of fear. What she experienced instead was an icy cold storm brewing within her soul, like the rage of the past forty-five years had solidified into a massive glacier. It was not Mrs. Whitney that stood in front of her. It was Julie. It was her ex. It was the kids from school. It was everyone who had overlooked her, mistreated her, and used her.

There was no thought to her action. Mawg sprang at Mrs. Whitney and threw the full force of her body into the woman. They tumbled to the ground, with Mawg landing on top of her. And while Mrs. Whitney and Mac were scrappy, Mawg had a secret weapon. She had her hips. Using every bit of her body weight, Mawg slammed her ass and hips into Mrs. Whitney's stomach. She heard the "ooph" as the wind was knocked out of her.

Jessica and Tori were finally coming back to their feet and Mawg yelled, "Help me hold her down!" Tori scrambled and sat on her legs while Jessica ran over and grabbed ahold of her wrists. Mac may have made Mrs. Whitney strong, but he was no match for the three women.

With Mrs. Whitney subdued, Mawg peered to the screen to see Mr. Whitney still holding the gun pointed at Declan.

Mawg held the lapel microphone, which was miraculously still attached to her shirt, and said, "Whitney…take a look up in the corner above the door."

His eyes rolled up to the corner. There was a tiny camera, focused directly on his chair.

Outside the door, the crowd began to boo and hiss. Whitney looked around like a cornered animal, the color draining from his face. They never had cameras in the rooms, and he took that for granted when he walked in.

"The crowd and security outside are watching a livestream of you right now. Your face is displayed on every TV screen in this building. And the cops should be here soon-"

She heard a commotion outside Whitney's door. It swung in and there stood Gina, naked and glorious.

Seeing her, Whitney said, "Oh good, it's about time. Take care of this," and pointed to Declan.

Gina sauntered over to Mr. Whitney, standing directly in front of where the gun was pointing. She held out her clenched fist, opening it to let the ring drop to the floor. "Go fuck yourself," she said as her fist clocked Mr. Whitney across the jaw. His arm flew back and the gun went off, firing into the ceiling.

All hell broke loose. Gina jumped on Mr. Whitney and began to beat him senseless until he was knocked out cold. The gun had fallen from his hand and Gina kicked it to the opposite corner. She turned to Declan and said, "You're safe, but I'll be right back."

She ran over to the room where Mawg had Mrs. Whitney in a compromising position and grabbed the ball gag that was laying on the floor. "Mawg, go to the other room and get Declan." She snapped the leather of the gag between her hands menacingly. "This bitch has tormented me for years, and I want to be the one to watch her go down." She took the ball gag and looked down at the wide-eyed Mrs. Whitney. "Ohhhhh, I have been dreaming of this."

Mawg nodded and sprinted to the other room. Security Steve, seeing the women running back and forth followed Mawg through the door. She turned and put a hand on his chest. "Go help Gina. She's going to need it with Mrs. Whitney." As Security Steve nodded and left, Mawg's eyes fell on Declan.

For the past three days, she'd stuffed down the fear of losing him in order to complete the mission, but now that it was over, she fell apart. Sobbing, she ran to him and began to untie and unhook the bondage suit. The moment his arms were free, they enveloped her so tight it almost took her breath away.

"Mawg," he whispered into her ear. It was only one word, but it had the power to drop her to her knees. She would have fallen, if his arms hadn't been holding her up.

The cops arrived and began trying to sort out the mess between the two rooms. Once Mawg and Declan explained what happened with Mr. Whitney and confirmed they had video proof of him pulling the gun, the cop gave them freedom to go. They stepped over to the next room, where Security Steve was holding Gina while another batch of cops put her in handcuffs.

Mawg's eyes went wide. "Wait, what's going on?"

The cop nodded his head to Gina and said, "Red here confessed to kidnapping this woman. We're taking her in."

Mawg's incredulous eyes looked over to Gina. "Can I have a minute to speak with her, please? She's a long-time employee here."

The cop nodded and turned to Declan. "I'd like to get a full statement from you."

As they turned to chat, Mawg whispered to Gina, "Why did you do that? You just got your freedom back."

Gina stared into her soul. "A wise woman once told me I've been the victim and I've been the villain. This time, I wanted to be the hero." Mawg began to tear up again, the weight of Gina's sacrifice bearing down on her.

"Mawg," Gina whispered, "I'm still free. I'll just be…relocating for a bit. A jail cell full of women who are in desperate need of being touched is like a candy store to a succubus. Plus, you know I can coerce the guards to let me out whenever I want." She winked. "Don't be sad. You can come visit me anytime."

"She's gonna get another charge for breaking and entering incarcerated vaginas."

Mawg wiped her eyes and gave a small laugh, as to not attract the attention of the cop. Security Steve had procured a long jacket for Gina. She put it on and placed her hands behind her back when the cop came over to cuff her. As they were on their way out the door, Gina stopped and asked, "Do you remember how you felt during your first tour?"

Mawg smiled at the memory. "I do."

As they ushered her away, Gina looked over her shoulder and said, "Don't ever forget that. That's the key to being an amazing concierge…always remember your first time."

Mawg whispered, "Thank you, Gina. For everything," as they hauled her out the door.

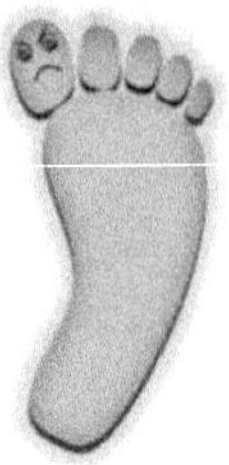

CHAPTER FORTY-ONE

"Breaking news tonight, as real estate mogul Edgar Whitney was arrested on multiple charges including attempted kidnapping, false impersonation, false identification, and 142 counts of fraudulent misrepresentation. Whitney, best known for being one of the largest commercial property owners in the country, is actually Jimmy-Lou Phillips, a convicted con artist who spent a three-year stint in federal prison for social security fraud in the 90's. Sources say the police are also questioning his wife, Miranda Whitney, who was his alleged accomplice. In a bizarre turn of events, another unidentified woman was also arrested for the attempted kidnapping of Miranda Whitney. Tune in for the 10:00 news as we learn more about this shock to the real estate world."

Mawg clicked the remote and turned off the TV, hearing Declan get out of the shower. She began to straighten up the bed, setting it up so he would be able to rest easily. He had little fat on his body to begin with, and days of being held captive made him look gaunt with dark circles under his eyes. She walked out to the kitchen to grab the charcuterie plate and bottle of water she'd thrown together when they got back to his house.

"The man's been tormented for a week and you give him a fruit and cheese tray? He needs a steak, or a casserole or something."

She frowned at her sarcastic toe. "I fully plan to feed him, but I don't want to shock his system either. We don't know what they put him through. Shut it."

She rounded the corner to the hallway with the plate and water in hand, and saw him leaning on the door frame, watching her. The chocolate brown eyes that she'd dreamed about for so long burned a hole into her heart. He was wearing only grey sweatpants and his hair was still wet. Water droplets still clung to his chest, and the hip bones she loved so much were even sharper due to the recent weight loss.

"I can hear your vagina screaming. This is so not the appropriate time, you hussy."

Mawg agreed, and walked toward him with the plate extended in her hand. "Peri thinks you need more sustenance, but I wasn't sure how your body was feeling so we'll start with this."

He looked down at the plate, then back into her eyes as she stood in front of him. He took the plate with one hand and reached out with the other, wrapping it around the nape of her neck. She was always greedy for his touch, but this kiss was different. Deep and slow, it held a promise. He released her lips and brought his forehead to rest against hers. "Mawg," he whispered, "Sweet, strong, beautiful, savage, fierce, protective Mawg." He placed soft kisses along her forehead. "Please do not EVER put yourself in danger like that again. You have no idea the panic I felt at the possibility of losing you…"

She stayed locked in his arms but pulled her head back to look him in the eye. "I understand. I mean it, Declan, I really do. I was terrified, too. But you know what? I'd do it again, no matter the outcome. And do you know why?"

His face was pained, envisioning how poorly that situation could have played out.

She continued, "I spent forty-four years of my life hiding. I hid from judgement, I hid from pain…and hell, I even hid from myself. Do you know what that got me? Declan, I wasn't living, I was…just existing. Existing is not living. But this?" she gestured between them, "This is worth defending. The Church is worth defending. You are worth defending. And I'll be damned if I sit back and let anyone take it from us."

Declan stared in awe at her, then set the plate and the water on the nearby dresser. He reached for her hand and walked them over to the bed. She began to protest, "You really need to rest, I don't think this is a goo—"

His lips crashed down on hers, his hands in her hair. She moaned against his mouth, having missed his taste and touch for the past week. Their clothes came off in a flurry, and moments later they were nothing more than entangled, grasping limbs on the bed. There was no planning, no forethought, just an aching need as they rolled around groping and panting. She needed to feel him inside her and reached down to wrap her hand around the very hard length of him. "Declan….now…please…"

He groaned as her hand stroked him, then guided him inside her. They both gasped at the sensation, staring into each other's eyes. She watched as his eyes grew dark and the devilish grin she'd missed returned. He held eye contact and he thrust himself into her, watching her mouth open and her eyes roll back. Over and over, their skin slapped together as the pressure built. Then he grabbed her left leg and lifted it into the air to take her deeper.

"Demon dammit, not again....."

Peri flailed in the air as the two humans continued to merge their meatsuits. He sighed and gave in, knowing this was a losing battle.

"Wheeeeeeeeeeeeeeeeeeeee!!"

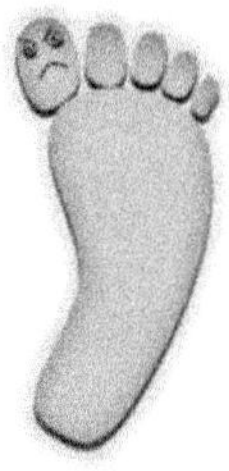

EPILOGUE

Mawg chuckled through the glass as Gina relayed a story about her latest prison conquest. She'd spoken the truth that fateful night three months prior at The Church. She was having the time of her life in prison. She had the entire cell block under her thrall, bringing her commissary gifts and begging to make a meal of her pussy. If anyone could handle three years in prison, it would be Gina. They said their goodbyes and Mawg promised to come back in two weeks, as was their usual routine.

She headed back to The Church to prepare for the Grand Reopening. Once word got out about Mr. Whitney being the building owner for The Church, the business turned into a bit of a circus. News vans and reporters would show up, wanting to grab soundbites and conduct interviews. The anonymity that was promised to members was becoming harder and harder to deliver.

Declan and Mawg made the tough decision to close down the main area of The Church for a few weeks to let the din die down. They continued to have the front entry bar open for business, but reached out to all the members individually to explain the plan. They would not announce the reopening to the public, but instead, communicate directly with members. They added extra security measures so the members would know how seriously their need for anonymity was being taken.

Since the Whitney Group had dissolved, their assets had been relinquished, including the building they were in. The plans for expansion had been put on hold indefinitely. Two months after the incident, a potential buyer emerged.

Mawg, determined not to allow The Church to be blindsided by shady business dealings this time, went into research mode. The Cathedral Corporation had an interesting portfolio of properties under its belt. Thirty-two of their buildings housed Sinsuality, a regional chain store that sold adult toys and videos. Their other tenants included a couple of topless dance clubs, a few restaurants, two veterinarian offices, and a plasma center. Mawg called and spoke to the owners of a few of the businesses to see how they felt about their landlord. All had glowing reviews. The deal moved forward and

Cathedral Corporation became the new landlord for The Church.

She and Declan were busy giving instructions and organizing for tonight's reopening. As she was counting liquor bottles at the bar, she looked up to see him across the room. He'd gained back the weight he lost during the abduction, and if it was possible, he looked even stronger than before. His hair had grown out and was now almost touching his shoulder. He had it pulled back and looked like a Celtic warrior, and it made her mouth water.

"For the love of demon, can you please think of somethin' other than that man's meatsuit? You're killin' me."

Mawg looked down at her toe and grinned. "No, no I can't. You'll just have to deal with it. It's kind of your fault anyway."

"How do you figure that?"

"You're the one that brought me here. I never would have met him without coming here, sooooo….. your fault."

Peri grumbled, annoyed that she was right.

"By the way, can you finish making your payments to Jessica so we can get another pedicure? Things are getting pretty janky down here."

All of the help from Jessica to kidnap Mrs. Whitney had cost Mawg dearly. Jessica told her no more pedicures until she coughed up $1,000. She paid off $750 of it, and needed to make one more payment to get even. Her toes were paying the price.

The bottle count was finished and Mawg checked it off the long list. That was her last task besides getting ready for the evening. She found Declan and let him know she'd be back within a couple of hours, and headed to her house to shower and clean up.

Peri got chatty when they got home and she hopped in the shower.

"Sooooo....this whole "Dicklan is my ooey gooey love boy" thing...have you been thinking about what's next?"

Mawg thought about it. "Honestly, I haven't been looking that far into the future. Things are going really well. We're both happy and I like that we both have our own space. Our relationship is right where it needs to be."

"You truly surprise me sometimes. If I was a human woman and I risked my life to save a man, I'd expect an engagement ring in return."

Mawg laughed at that. "Peri, you know me. I enjoy having my own space and my freedom. I love where our relationship is right now. If he asked me to marry him, would I? I mean…probably? But I'd definitely want to have a thorough conversation about what the expectation would be. I don't want to give up my house, and I don't want him to give up his either. There are a lot of things to consider." Peri smiled.

"Mawg the Practical."

She finished showering and got dressed. Tori had created her a custom-designed dress, and it made her feel like a siren. It was a long, black silk wraparound dress with 3/4 length sleeves and a deep v-neck. It had a slit that went up to mid-thigh. She was sex in silk, and it felt glorious.

They got back to The Church and she made her way to the office. Declan was shirtless in cargo pants and boots, getting ready for the Eve performance. He'd just showered and his wet hair was hanging. He looked up, hearing her enter the office and he froze. She knew the fire in his eyes well. It burned right before he would ravage her.

She got a cheeky grin and held up her hands in front of her. "No…I see exactly what you're thinking, and you are not going to rearrange the hair and makeup it took me forever to put together."

He sauntered over, his cologne melting her defenses. Damn the man, he knew her weaknesses. He didn't touch her, but leaned in and whispered into her ear, "I'll be a gentleman…for now. But when that performance is over, I'm pulling that dress above your hips and I WILL have my feast."

She shivered, knowing he meant every word. He kissed her forehead, grabbed her ass, and turned to grab the snake mask. "I've got to get backstage, but I'll be back as soon as it's finished."

She leaned back against the desk and bit her lip, the anticipation making her panties damp. He groaned at the vision of her, then headed out the door.

The next hour passed and the lights came down and the music pumped up. Members were starting to file through the curtain and the energy on the main floor was intense. The mats had been set up in front of the stage for the Meat Suit Mania crew. She grabbed a gin and tonic from the bar and surveyed the room. She was happy. She was at peace. And she finally had everything she wanted.

The first two members hit the mats for MeatSuit Mania. Meanwhile, bodies were bumping and grinding all around her. It seemed the club being closed the past few weeks had created a desire for a night of wild fuckery.

"Do you feel that?"

Mawg looked down at her toe and thought, "What?"

"It feels like someone's watching you."

She took a look around the room. Nothing stood out to her. "It's probably just the vibe everyone's giving off tonight that's heightening your senses."

Members continued filing in. It was going to be a packed house. MeatSuit Mania was up to eight people now but was quickly growing. She heard the rhythmic Viking music begin and knew the Eve performance would start in about five minutes. She'd been through enough of these to know the routine now.

"There it is, I feel it again. Somebody's watching you, I swear on my demon existence."

She turned to do a full 360 of the room. Nothing seemed out of sorts, until she turned toward the bar. Sitting in a darkened corner was a pair of eyes, fixated on her. It was difficult to see the person due to the lighting and angles, but Peri was right. That Dick was definitely staring at her.

"Do you recognize him?"

She thought, "I can't see much of anything except for his eyes." Mawg didn't like the feeling of being watched. It left her on edge.

The room was in full swing and the lighting changed as the drum's beat began. It was time for the show. She gave one last look toward the bar, but the eyes had disappeared. Whatever, she was probably just being silly.

She stood in the crowd that was now gathering to watch the show. People were shoulder to shoulder, and the heat radiating off the bodies made it palpable. To her right, a man was casually stroking his partner. On her left, a stunning woman with smooth, dark skin was topless and dancing by herself, completely content.

The masked muscle men walked out onstage and the crowd roared. They moved into position and lined up for the reveal of this month's Eve. When it was time, she emerged from the back curtains of the stage.

Mawg was sipping her gin and tonic when she felt a tingle up the back of her spine. She sensed as he walked up behind her and leaned down to whisper in her ear. In a voice that was smooth enough to spread cold butter, he said, "I hear you've been checking up on me."

She turned, ready to scream for security when her voice caught in her throat. He was beautiful. Mawg normally wasn't attracted to blonde men, but something about him had her speechless. His high cheekbones were sharp and his gaze was like a drug.

"Hey! What the fuck are you doing? Snap out of it!"

Mawg shook her head, clearing out the fuzziness and gathering herself. "It seems you have an advantage on me. I don't know who you are." She turned back around to the stage to see Declan come out in the snake mask.

He was at least 6'5, and she felt him lean down to her hair and inhale deeply. She swung around, ready to throw hands. "What the fu—"

His eyes were now gold, and she saw raw desire there as he grabbed her wrist that swung at him.

"Mawg...I think we got a problem, Mawg."

She felt a thrill run through her body as the chilled hand lightly squeezed at the pulse of her wrist. He smiled a cat-like grin and said, "I would prefer not to have a fist fight with my new tenant on our first meeting."

She was stuck with him holding her wrist, unable to move even if she wanted to. But that was the problem. She wanted to…but she didn't.

"Mawg...MAWG! That is not a human."

Her eyes widened as she stared at the man.

"That is a vampire. The new landlord is a fucking vampire."

About the Author

Jen Xant's inspiration for The Adventures of Peri and Mawg was born through her involvement in the Booktok and Indie Authortok communities. Her goal is to write fun, spicy books that highlight the strength and sexiness of middle-age FMCs. When she's not writing, you can find Jen on TikTok talking about her hatred of yard work, her love of pineapple on pizza, and books written by her indie author friends!